The Secret Life of Albert Entwistle

'Wonderful . . . Will have every reader cheering on Albert from the sidelines. An utter treat'
KATE MOSSE

'Albert is such an endearing character – flawed, funny and awkward, but completely relatable. I wanted to give him a good shake and then a huge hug. This is a wonderfully warm story that completely drew me in'
RUTH HOGAN

'A great big hug of a book! . . . Will put a smile on everyone's face'
MICHAEL BALL, RADIO 2

'A heart-warming, joyous love story – original, hopeful and totally charming'
ADELE PARKS, *PLATINUM*

'Really heartwarming, joyful but also so poignant. Really can not recommend this book highly enough . . . A beautifully, authentically-told story with vivid characters and you will miss them when you reach the end'
LORRAINE KELLY

'A brilliant book! [I] recommend to all'
MATT LUCAS

'This rollicking love story entrapped me, chapter by chapter. True in its detail and its scope'
IAN MCKELLEN

'Prepare to fall in love with Albert Entwistle! . . . Wonderfully heart-wrenching . . . Touching and tender'
S. J. WATSON

'A total triumph. Romantic and heartbreaking and uplifting all at once'
LAURA KAY

'Wonderful. Written with such a good heart, filled with joy and strength and optimism . . . It's inventive and fun but most importantly, true'
RUSSELL T DAVIES

The Secret Life of Albert Entwistle

Matt Cain is a writer, broadcaster, and a leading commentator on LGBT+ issues. He was Channel 4's Culture Editor, Editor-In-Chief of *Attitude* magazine, has written for all the major national newspapers, and presented the flagship discussion show on Virgin Radio Pride. He's also an ambassador for Manchester Pride and the Albert Kennedy Trust, plus a patron of LGBT+ History Month. Born in Bury and brought up in Bolton, Matt now lives in London with his partner, Harry, and their cat, Nelly.

By Matt Cain

Shot Through the Heart
Nothing But Trouble
The Madonna of Bolton

The
Secret Life
of Albert
Entwistle

Matt Cain

REVIEW

First published in Great Britain in 2021 by
HEADLINE REVIEW
An imprint of HEADLINE PUBLISHING GROUP

First published in paperback in Great Britain in 2022 by
HEADLINE REVIEW

5

Cataloguing in Publication Data is available from the British Library

ISBN 978 1 4722 7508 0 (B format)

Bluebell graphic © Digital Bazaar/Shutterstock

Typeset in Dante MT by CC Book Production
Printed and bound in Great Britain by Clays Ltd, Elcograf S.p.A.

MIX
Paper from
responsible sources
FSC® C104740

Headline's policy is to use papers that are natural, renewable and
recyclable products and made from wood grown in well-managed forests
and other controlled sources. The logging and manufacturing processes are
expected to conform to the environmental regulations of the country of origin.

HEADLINE PUBLISHING GROUP
An Hachette UK Company
Carmelite House
50 Victoria Embankment
London EC4Y 0DZ

www.headline.co.uk
www.hachette.co.uk

For Harry, my very own Albert

Chapter One

Albert Entwistle was a postman. It was one of the few things everyone knew about him. And it was one of the few things he was comfortable with people knowing.

One dark and frosty December morning he arrived at work, safe in the knowledge that the day ahead would be the same as any other – and exactly the same as it had been for years and years.

It was a few minutes before six o'clock when he cycled into the yard at the back of the Royal Mail delivery office on the industrial estate at the edge of Toddington town centre. A cold, hard light leaked out of the windows of the one-storey, grey-brick, corrugated-iron-roofed building, a building cheered only slightly by the woodwork and doors, painted the distinctive red of the company's branding. Albert let out a yawn as he dismounted and chained up his bike. He checked his watch. The minute hand was approaching the hour. By the time he walked through the door it would be 6 a.m. *Exactly as it should be.*

He unfastened his duffel coat and tugged his ID card out from around his neck, leaning forward to touch it to the magnetic sensor. The familiar buzz told him the lock had been released. He walked inside.

'Alright, Albert?' said the security guard, barely looking up. Ste Stockton was a handsome man in his twenties with muscles that looked like body armour. He was so obsessed with sharing images of his physique online that he rarely took any interest in whoever entered the building – a quality Albert acknowledged wasn't ideal in a security guard but, all the same, he appreciated in Ste.

'How do,' Albert said with a nod. It was his standard greeting and delivered in a way that made it clear no response was necessary or desired. Over the years he'd become adept at deflecting opportunities to interact and, as he'd entered his sixties, noticed that people paid him less and less attention anyway. This suited Albert perfectly; if he had his way he'd be invisible.

As he fringed a line of trolleys and headed down the corridor to the main sorting office, he braced himself for the hardest part of his day. Albert always tried to dodge his way through the waves of chatter that peaked and crashed between his colleagues, particularly on Monday mornings; so many of them wanted to exchange summaries of what they'd done over the weekend. These days, most people left him alone, though some of his newer colleagues made the mistake of assuming that, because they had a life away from work, he must do too. When they realised he didn't, they'd feel sorry for him.

'Have you ever thought about taking up a hobby?' they'd ask.

'What about bowls?'

'My Auntie Mabel used to *love* doing jigsaws.'

Hoping he wouldn't be subjected to any such attention today, he buzzed open the door and stepped into the hall.

Albert's first hurdle was making it past the office of the Delivery Centre Manager. Marjorie Bennett was a loud and chatty fifty-something who seemed to have no filter when it came to asking people about their personal lives – or talking at length about her own. If she wasn't being indiscreet about her husband's piles, she was keeping her colleagues abreast of every symptom of her menopause. Today, her office door was wide open as she regaled the cleaner with a detailed description of her hot flushes.

'Honestly,' she said, 'they're so bad I swear you could fry an egg on my stomach.'

Albert kept his head down and scurried past. He didn't understand why so many people appeared so comfortable talking about their most intimate experiences. It was clearly something that had been encouraged by celebrity interviews, not to mention the social media that seemed to obsess everyone. Depression, addiction, abuse – nothing seemed off-limits any more. But Albert didn't go in for any of that. He'd survived by keeping the experiences that had most affected him to himself.

Come on, he told himself, *time to get on.*

He weaved his way through a jumble of steel carts stuffed with sacks of mail. Some of the younger staff were sifting

3

through the letters and parcels, dropping them into grey sacks held open on stands. Albert headed towards the centre of the vast, strip-lit hall, where each of the postmen and women had their own sorting frame. Semi-circular desks were surrounded by rows and rows of shelves divided into thin slots, one for each address on their round. It would take them the next three and a half hours to sort their mail into the correct sequence of their daily walk, which in Albert's case was made up of 667 addresses.

He hung up his coat and high-vis cycling vest, trying not to catch the eye of his colleagues.

At the desk to his left, Jack Brew was sipping from a mug of tea and dissecting the latest performance of the town's football team. Jack was bald-headed, in his fifties, and had so much body hair sprouting from every opening of his clothes that Albert sometimes wondered if he might be part wolf. Jack regularly moaned about his wife, calling her a 'nag' when, as far as Albert could make out, all she was trying to do was nice things, such as buying a present for his mother's birthday or booking their next family holiday. Although, Jack's treatment of his wife was nothing compared to the roasting he reserved for the manager of Toddington FC.

'At the end of the day,' he pronounced, 'that joker couldn't run a bath, never mind a football team.'

The men nearby grumbled in agreement, which prompted Jack to run with his theme. At times like this he reminded Albert of his dad. *I wonder if that's why I've never really liked him.*

Jack was so engrossed in his discussion that he simply

raised a hand in greeting. Albert felt his shoulders slacken with relief.

It looked like he was safe from the threat of conversation from the frame behind him too. This was occupied by one of the office's few postwomen, a young mother called Sue Frinton. Sue was addicted to competitions and, over the years, had won all kinds of prizes, from holidays and a car to a trolley dash around the local branch of Asda and something called a 'vampire facial', her explanation of which had made Albert feel queasy. She'd earned her nickname, Tsunami, because she was so disorganised – her sorting frame was always a mess, and she arrived late every morning. She still wasn't in today, and by the time she did arrive, Albert knew she'd be too flustered to chat. *At least I know I can always rely on Tsunami.*

Unfortunately, the same couldn't be said of the postman working to his right. Smiler was a cheerful, wiry man in his forties who had so much energy he struggled to stand still and on the rare occasions he sat down would be unable to stop his leg from jiggling. His sorting frame was decorated with pictures of the ten-pin bowling team of which he was captain and all five members of his family pulling silly faces as they undertook various madcap activities. Smiler regularly customised his work uniform and today he was wearing a string of tinsel around his neck and a Santa hat with a sprig of mistletoe tied to the end.

'Hiya, mate,' he said brightly. 'Good weekend?'

Albert let out a little breath, as if he'd suffered a light blow to the stomach.

'Yes!' he squeaked, a note of panic in his voice. Keen to

shut the conversation down, he added, 'Do you want a cup of tea?'

'No, thanks,' said Smiler, 'I'm all sorted.' He grinned as he held up a mug painted with an image of a reindeer whose nose turned red whenever the mug was filled with hot liquid.

Albert nodded and excused himself. It was ten past six and by now he felt sure all his colleagues would have made their hot drinks and the kitchen area would be empty. But he was surprised to see someone hovering over the kettle in the common room. The young man – mixed-race and as tall as a lamp post – had hair shaved down to his skull at the back and sides, and jeans that were so tight Albert wondered how on earth he managed to sit down. *More to the point, it wouldn't surprise me if the underpants I'm wearing are older than he is.*

Albert stepped back, pretending to be busy looking at his phone. Although he had no messages to read, he did at least take comfort from a picture of Gracie he'd saved in his photo album.

The staff common room was barely more comfortable than the working areas, with tatty office tables and plastic chairs. An old TV was mounted on one of the whitewashed walls that were stained nicotine yellow – even though no one had been able to smoke in there for years. Albert caught sight of his reflection in a mirror that had been half-heartedly decorated with an almost threadbare garland of tinsel. He might well be the oldest member of staff on the team but at least he didn't look sixty-four. In fact, he could probably pass for a man in his late fifties. All right, so his skin was more lined than it used to be, but the walking he did every day kept his body fit. And he had a full head of hair that was still, mostly, the colour of a Digestive biscuit or a nice cup of tea.

'Alright, dude?' said the boy suddenly. 'I didn't see you there.'

Albert's spirit sank like a broken lift. 'Oh, yes, how do,' he managed, looking at the floor.

'I'm Ty,' the boy said, approaching him and holding out his hand, 'Ty with a "y". Short for Tyger.'

Albert had no idea what he was talking about but shook his hand anyway.

'It's my name?' the boy said, as if it were a question.

'Oh, yeah, r-r-right,' stammered Albert, allowing his eyes to flicker in the boy's direction, and nodding. 'Nice to meet you, Ty.'

'And how about you?' Ty asked.

'I'm Albert,' he forced himself to say. 'Albert Entwistle.'

'Sweet, man. And how long have you been a postie?'

'Ever since I was sixteen.'

'Is it?' Ty paused, as if deciding how to respond. 'Man, that is sick!'

Albert didn't know if he'd just been insulted. He reminded himself that it would be polite to reciprocate and ask Ty about himself. 'Are you in to help with the Christmas rush?'

'Yeah, I'm an agency worker?' Ty said, his intonation rising again at the end of the sentence.

Albert noticed Ty had made his drink in Albert's own blue-and-green striped mug. He felt too shy to tell him.

'Oh, yes, terrific,' he said. And then, because he thought he should, he added, 'Welcome.'

Ty thanked him and left the room.

When the door was closed, Albert felt the anxiety leak out of him.

He made his usual cup of strong tea – with a splash of milk and two sugars – in the only mug that was left, one emblazoned with the image of a woman looking as if she were being electrocuted and the slogan 'Danger: PMS'. He picked it up and slunk back into the main sorting office.

As he was creeping over to his frame, Marjorie stepped out of her office and announced she was selling home-made mince pies to raise money to send her ill grandson on a special trip to Disney World. Ever since Bradley had been diagnosed with a rare form of cancer she'd been promoting various initiatives to help reach her fundraising target, convinced that boosting the boy's morale would give him the best possible chance of beating the disease. More than once Albert had wanted to contribute – on one occasion he'd even held the money in his hand and approached her office. But then he'd seen her break down in tears as she was telling Sue about the impact chemotherapy was having on the boy – and just picturing walking into the midst of such an outpouring of emotion had made him turn around and retreat.

'Come on, gang,' Marjorie called as several of the staff gathered around, 'get a load of these bad boys – the best mince pies in the whole of Lancashire!'

Once again, Albert put his head down and scurried past. He'd already exhausted his capacity for conversation. He just wanted to lose himself in his job.

*

Albert finished his sorting and arranged all his mail into sacks. He then grabbed a trolley and loaded it all into a van. As he pulled out of the gates, a smile traced its way across his face. He was about to start his favourite part of the day.

The sun had come up to reveal a cloudless sky and one of those bright but chilly winter mornings that always made Albert feel energetic. He spotted a snowman decoration one of his colleagues had hung from the rear-view mirror, checked no one was watching, and gave it a twirl.

He drove north down Toddington high street, passing the grand Victorian town hall, and rows of shops and businesses that had once been the flourishing soul of the community but were now almost deserted. Every other unit seemed to be boarded up, giving the impression of bad teeth spoiling a smile. There was still a tanning shop, two hairdressers, and – inexplicably, to Albert – three nail salons. These were complemented by a handful of vaping shops, pound stores, a Cash Converters, and a whopping five branches of Greggs the baker's. But the family-run department store that used to attract shoppers from all over Lancashire had closed down five years ago – as had the independent bookstore, the jeweller's, and the old toy shop where he used to buy his tin soldiers. Not that Albert felt nostalgic for the past, far from it. Even so, he felt saddened – the council had tried to cheer it up for Christmas with some newly commissioned festive lights and an extravagantly decorated tree, but the high street still looked forgotten and forlorn.

Albert came to a stop at the traffic lights and tapped out a beat on the steering wheel while a raisin-faced woman crossed the road, tugging away on a cigarette. His mam always used to say smoking while walking down the street was 'common' and, even though she'd been dead for eighteen years, he could still hear her voice as clearly as if she were sitting in the van next to him. He shook the thought of his mam out of his head; it would only spoil his day.

The lights turned green and Albert drove past the library, which was supposed to have been saved from closure but never seemed to have its doors open, the old parish church, which now attracted more visitors to its themed craft fairs than to its religious services, and a statue in the market square of a nobleman who'd been born in the town. For the last few weeks, the statue had worn a traffic cone on its head, which the local police hadn't yet got round to taking down. Albert thought it looked rather jolly and liked to imagine whoever had put it up laughing to themselves mischievously each time they passed.

After a brief stretch of dual carriageway, busy with stragglers late for work or returning from the school run, he came to a main road lined with rows of stone terraces, where the traffic thinned. As he accelerated, glimpses of the Lancashire moors winked at him through the gaps made by the occasional side street, a sight that never failed to cheer him. He passed the doctor's surgery, the school and the garden centre, the forecourt of which still had a pile of Christmas trees for sale, not that he felt any temptation to buy one; there didn't seem any point when neither he nor Gracie would appreciate it. At the top of the road he parked his van outside Cod Almighty, the chip shop he liked to visit for his weekly treat. He unloaded the trolley, checked his sturdy walking shoes were fastened tightly, and did up his coat against the bracing cold. He was ready to begin his walk.

He delivered mail to almost every house along the odd-numbered side of the road, breaking away at intervals to cover the cul-de-sacs and side streets. He posted letters through every model, size and fit of letter box: ones that were fixed to the bottom of the door and forced him to bend down, setting off a twinge in his lower back that he tried to ignore, others that were too narrow to fit all but the thinnest letters through them, yet more that were blocked by a hard brush that scratched his fingers, and, finally, those that were just as he liked them – wide, easy to open, and positioned at waist height.

Here and there, mail was snatched out of Albert's hands by overenthusiastic dogs. He had, on occasion, been chased out of gardens by terriers intent on defending their territory, but he'd got to know every potential attacker on his walk and now came armed with biscuits and balls to distract them. At one rather grand property, guarded by a particularly aggressive Border collie, Albert kept a stick hidden in a nearby bush, knowing a few waves of it would warn off the dog and send it retreating back to its kennel.

The extra Christmas parcels and cards on today's walk meant there was more toing and froing between the van and the trolley than usual. But Albert didn't mind – it gave him more opportunity to observe the world as it went about its business. And in observing, he allowed himself to feel part of this community.

On today's walk alone he glimpsed window sills and mantelpieces filled with evidence of births, deaths, marriages and divorces. He encountered signs of new jobs or offers of places at university, as well as indications that people were struggling with debt or suffering ill health. Through bills, legal notices and personal cards or letters, the mail he delivered offered insights into all of their lives – and sometimes he'd let his mind wander and imagine the stories behind the correspondence, stories he knew could never happen to him. Yet Albert was careful to limit his face-to-face contact with people to the strictly superficial. He'd wave through the window to people who weren't at work, or say a polite hello if he had to knock to give them a parcel or if he required a signature. But the brisk pace he kept encouraged them to think he was too busy to stop and chat. When he delivered mail over the counter of shops or to the secretary in the high school, he always appreciated the warm greeting but was careful never to engage in conversation.

'I mustn't dawdle,' was how he ended each exchange – and, if there was ever the slightest danger of being drawn into a chat, he'd nod at his bag and add a cheery, 'These letters aren't going to deliver themselves!'

No one ever argued.

He had to be careful when he delivered mail to a handful of people he could tell were desperate for human interaction. About a third of the way through his walk, he'd come to a little crescent of bungalows overlooking the moors. One of the residents was an elderly woman he knew was called Edith Graham, although she rarely received any mail. Nor had he seen her hosting a single visitor in the five years she'd lived there. But he had once witnessed the sad sight of her trying to strike up a conversation with some uninterested binmen, and on another occasion he'd caught her engaged in what looked like a very involved discussion with a pair of Jehovah's Witnesses. Other than that, as far as Albert could tell, Edith spent every morning snuggled into a heavily cushioned armchair in the corner of her living room, angled so that she could watch the TV but also look out of the window. Every morning she'd spot Albert and wave. And every morning, she'd sit forward and smile hopefully.

But Albert always kept his head down, as he did today. *I can't stop, I've got work to do*, he told himself, a little guiltily. *And anyway, what would I say?*

He strode on and, as he reached the upmarket detached houses that bordered the park, he started to need the loo. He spotted a little brick public toilet block on the other side of the railings. But he looked away. When he was growing up, his dad – a police constable – had been scathing about the things he said went on in there. He'd told Albert stories that had repulsed and frightened him.

'Filthy', 'disgusting', 'animals' . . .

All these years later, Albert couldn't forget the words his dad had used to describe the men who met up in the toilet block. And all these years later, he still didn't dare venture in there. Telling himself that he'd just have to hang on for the loo, he gripped the handle of his trolley and pushed on.

When he passed the stone lion that guarded the entrance to the park, he knew he was halfway through his walk. He checked the time on his watch and saw that it was three minutes past twelve.

Not bad for a busy day.

He looked around to check no one was watching and patted the lion on the head. 'All right, lad?'

Back on the main road, Albert delivered mail to a final few addresses, including the doctor's surgery, where he used the toilet, and the betting shop, where a ruddy-faced manager dressed as an elf was huffing and puffing as he pinned up Christmas decorations. Then Albert returned to his van, turned on the engine, and powered up the heating so he wouldn't have to sit shivering as he ate his dinner. He switched on the local radio station to listen to the news, lifted a cheese and pickle sandwich out of his lunchbox, and unscrewed the lid of his flask of tea.

There wasn't much going on in Lancashire today; he sat through features on a member of the Lancashire Pork Pie Society who for the first time had been invited to be a judge at the British Pie Awards in Melton Mowbray, and a man who'd been fined because his parrot had been shouting swearwords at passing schoolchildren. But it was a perfectly pleasant way to pass the time and once Albert had finished his sandwich, he unwrapped his regular treat: a Crunchie bar. The honeycomb centre reminded him of the cinder toffee he used to love as a child, a big block of which he'd been given as a good-luck present on the day he'd started work as a postman. But shops didn't sell it on its own any more; at least that was his excuse for allowing himself to eat chocolate every day. That and wanting to keep the memory alive – the memory of how happy he'd felt when he'd been given the present.

After dinner, it was time for Albert to tackle the even-numbered side of the road. This was the shorter section of his walk, although it did include a large council estate. The Flowers Estate was so called because each of its streets was named after a well-known bloom; Crocus Lane, for example, led on to Tulip Drive, and Buttercup Avenue gave way to Iris Street. When Albert was a child, many of the other boys from his school used to live on the estate; in those days, it was home to people in low-paid jobs such as manual labourers and factory and mill workers. And it may have been a little rough around the edges but it was a friendly place where people would chat over garden fences and kids would play rounders or football in the street. He had no idea what had gone wrong but it had deteriorated from being rough-around-the-edges to what his mam would have called 'dog rough'. He shook the memory of his mam out of his head.

As he walked through the estate, Albert had to pick his way over broken glass and piles of little metal cylinders that, according to the local newspaper, were evidence of the use of a drug called laughing gas. He stepped around a rusty, twisted old bike and a cluster of supermarket trolleys that had been abandoned in the middle of the pavement. Every garden he passed seemed to have become a dumping ground for old furniture. On one patch of dead grass there was a three-piece bathroom suite that had been there for so long weeds were starting to sprout from the plughole of the sink. On top of the toilet seat someone had plonked a blow-up Father Christmas that was slowly deflating.

Each day, Albert hurried through this section of his walk and avoided making eye contact with the gangs of track-suited youths who, more often than not, were lounging around on the dilapidated garden walls – and sometimes shot him distinctly threatening glares. He put his head down and said nothing to the drunk who was swaying from side to side and mumbling to himself at the bus stop. And he didn't stop to look when he passed two women hurling insults at each other.

Although there was one resident of the estate to whom Albert found himself curiously drawn. Nicole Ashton was a young and apparently single mother who lived in the last house he called at, just a few metres away from a cobbled alleyway that led to his own house at the end of a red-brick terrace. He was pretty sure she was reaching the tail end of her teens, and she lived with a toddler. He had no idea who the child's father was or what Nicole did for a living, although he had worked out she was doing some kind of training course because he'd delivered letters to her from the local adult education centre. He assumed she must attend classes in the evening because each day, at roughly the same time, there she'd be, standing at the door, smoking and flicking through her phone. Despite the December chill, today was no exception. Nicole was wearing big fluffy slippers and had pulled a dressing gown over her leggings and hoodie. She didn't even look up as Albert walked down the path to give her some kind of final demand from the electricity company. Behind her, Albert could make out a chubby little girl in the hallway, amusing herself on a play mat, singing a nursery rhyme to a battered old cuddly toy.

'How do,' he said, handing over the bill to Nicole.

She looked up and in her eyes he recognised a flicker of unease, but she quickly covered this up with a scowl and snatched the letter out of his hand. He couldn't help wondering what had happened to make her so unfriendly. For a brief second he imagined himself chatting to her and finding out. But the idea made him prickle with fear. *No, no good could come of that.*

There was an awkward silence. Nicole stubbed out her cigarette and turned to go back inside.

'Well, I mustn't dawdle,' Albert blurted out.

Nicole shut the door behind her.

He nodded at his bag and announced to no one in particular, 'These letters won't deliver themselves!'

Albert drove back to the delivery office, stopping to collect the mail that had been left in a couple of post boxes en route. He dropped off the packages he hadn't been able to deliver then looked at the clock on the wall: it showed 2.13. *Bloomin' 'eck, that's not bad at all.*

He returned to his sorting frame to do his paperwork. But just as he sat down, he heard the distinctive sound of Tsunami coming back from her walk. He looked up as she flung her coat across her desk. Sue was in her early thirties and had red hair and a face and arms that were sprinkled with freckles. Today, she was wearing reindeer horns on her head and Christmas baubles in her ears – and she looked flushed.

'You'll never guess what,' she said, as her coat slid to the floor.

Seeing that Jack and Smiler weren't yet back in the office, Albert had no option but to respond. 'What?'

'I've only gone and won another competition – I just had an email!'

'Congratulations,' said Albert. And then, because he knew it was expected, he added, 'What have you won this time?'

A grin swept over Sue's face. 'A year's supply of salad cream. I'n't it great?'

How on earth do they measure a year's supply of salad cream? Albert wanted to ask.

Thankfully, the conversation was interrupted.

'Albert, love,' Marjorie said, standing over him and holding out an envelope, 'you've got a letter from HR.'

Albert corrugated his brow. He received a letter from Human Resources once a year, when he was sent advance notice of his annual 'performance and development review'. He'd have to fill in endless forms about his hopes and aspirations for his career progression, something he always thought was pointless when it was perfectly obvious he wanted his career to carry on exactly as it had for the last forty-nine years. But this was different. And it didn't look like anyone else was receiving a letter.

He took the envelope off Marjorie and turned it over in his hands.

'Well . . . aren't you going to open it?' she asked. As her eyes bore into him, the vein on her neck bulged like a snake swallowing a rat.

In an instant, he understood this was going to be the most important letter he handled all day. There was no way he could open it now; he'd wait till he got home and was with Gracie.

'Erm . . . no, it's OK thanks,' he said. 'I'll read it later.'

Marjorie looked crestfallen. 'Alright, love, if you're sure. But you know I'm always here if you need me.' She smiled at him as if he were a puppy with a sore paw.

'Yeah, thanks,' Albert managed meekly.

As she walked away, he folded up the letter and tucked it into his pocket. Judging from her expression, it was going to deliver bad news.

Chapter Two

Albert took the letter from Human Resources from his pocket and put it on the mantelpiece.

I'll open it in a bit, he reassured himself. *Once I've got myself settled.*

He rested the crumpled envelope next to his paltry cluster of Christmas cards. Although he'd delivered thousands on his round, this year he'd received only three: one was from Smiler, who gave cards to everyone in the office; one was from his mam's second cousin in Blackburn, who Albert hadn't seen for years and who always called him Alfred; and one was from his dentist – and that hadn't even been signed by hand but printed with the signatures of everyone who worked in the surgery. But he could hardly complain; he hadn't sent a single Christmas card since his mam had stopped doing it from both of them when she became too ill. Since then, the number that arrived at the house had dwindled each year. But he told himself he preferred it this way, and tried not to feel a pang of sadness when confronted with the stark evidence of how few people cared about him.

Albert hadn't bothered putting up a single Christmas decoration, either. He hadn't seen the point; it wasn't as if he was expecting any visitors. Now that he thought about it, he hadn't had any visitors all year, not unless you counted the man who'd come round to fit his new smart electricity meter, or the plumber who'd come to unblock the sink and told him off for scraping bits of food down the plughole. *Oh, and that time in the summer when the kids from next door threw their ball into my back yard.*

He remembered how flustered he'd been when he'd answered the doorbell and the kids' dad had invited himself in and sauntered through the house to get to the yard. Once he'd found the ball, he'd stood in the kitchen with it tucked under his arm, asking Albert what he thought about the current form of Toddington FC. Albert hadn't known what to say, so had resorted to discussing the weather. When that topic of conversation had dried up, the ensuing awkwardness had sent his neighbour retreating to the door. No one had set foot over Albert's threshold since.

'But we like that, don't we?' he said to Gracie. 'We like it when it's just the two of us?'

Gracie was Albert's cat, an all-grey crossbreed he'd brought to live with him as a kitten, shortly after his mam had died. He'd named her after Gracie Fields, his mam's favourite singer from her youth, whose songs she'd sing around the house when he was a boy. Just as he did every day when he got in from work, he picked Gracie up to cradle her in his arms, stroking her long fur and tickling her in her favourite spot behind the ears.

'You're perfectly happy, aren't you, my little girl?'

With a purring Gracie in his arms, he took her on their usual stroll around the house, an end terrace in which he'd lived all his life. He began in the front room, which was painted a cheery yellow and stuffed with a plush three-piece suite, his mam's old display cases of crystal ornaments, and a 40" TV and sound bar – the most extravagant purchases of Albert's life but devices he found it bafflingly difficult to operate. He really didn't understand why he now needed three remote controls, a mobile phone and a consistent WiFi signal just to watch TV. *Is that supposed to be progress?*

He padded through to the back room, which contained the kitchen and washing machine, as well as the old family sideboard and dining table, although Albert only ate at the table on Christmas Day. He'd never quite been able to shake off the memory of a confrontation that had happened around that same table almost fifty years ago. It was a confrontation that had determined the course of his life – and one he wished he could forget.

In his arms the cat continued to purr. 'Have you had a busy day, Gracie?' he asked, softly. 'Have you been guarding the house?'

Gracie miaowed loudly and jumped down on to the floor. She hovered around her feeding area and nuzzled Albert's shins.

'Come on,' he said, fondly, 'let's make your tea. I bet you're hungry, aren't you?'

He went to the fridge and pulled out a packet of chicken livers, which he put on the cooker to boil. He did give her regular tinned food in the morning but in the evening he took the time to spoil her. As the smell began to fill the kitchen, Gracie became visibly excited. She'd been off her food a little lately so her enthusiasm made Albert smile.

Then he remembered sitting in the office and overhearing Jack Brew making fun of a woman on his round who lived alone with three cats.

'There must be something wrong with her,' Jack had bellowed to his colleagues, 'because you never see her with any people. She's one of them crazy cat ladies.'

Albert took the pan off the boil and tried not to think about it.

Once Gracie was happily gobbling her livers, he made his own tea. As it was Monday, he was having sausage and mash. Tuesday was egg and chips, Wednesday and Thursday were cottage pie (he always made enough for two portions), and Friday was takeaway. Usually this was fish and chips but sometimes he treated himself to pizza, and once he'd even had a curry – a chicken tikka, which he'd actually quite enjoyed. But that had been shortly after his mam died, before he'd given in to the comfort of clinging more and more tightly to his routine.

As usual, he ate his tea on a tray, sitting on the sofa watching the *BBC News at Six*. Gracie followed him through to the front room and sat licking her paws while Albert tried to concentrate on the TV and ignore the letter from HR.

At half past six he did the washing up, drew the curtains,

and went upstairs. As usual, he walked past the closed door of the back bedroom, a room he avoided entering unless he had to. He continued along the landing to the front bedroom, which was where he'd slept ever since he was a boy. There, he took off his uniform, put on the pyjamas he'd left neatly folded on the end of his bed, wrapped himself in his maroon, plaid dressing gown, and stepped into his cosy, padded slippers. Then he returned downstairs to settle in for an evening of TV.

Although Albert knew the programme schedule of his favourite channels by heart, he couldn't predict what Gracie would do. Tonight, she chose not to sit on his lap but curled up in front of a radiator – and this didn't suit him at all. He switched off the heating, knowing that as the warmth leaked out of the radiators she'd search for it elsewhere – and with any luck would find it on his lap. A cold nose would be a small price to pay in return. Sure enough, by the second episode of *Coronation Street*, she was pawing at his knees.

'Hello, my little girl. Are you coming for a cuddle?'

The cat snuggled into the groove between his legs, stretched herself out and was soon fast asleep. Albert picked up her little paw and held it in his hand.

Gracie was still asleep on his lap when *I'm A Celebrity . . . Get Me Out Of Here!* began at nine o'clock. In this episode, a comedian Albert had never found funny, a pop star he'd never heard of, and somebody who called himself a 'social media influencer', a profession he'd never understood, were sitting around the camp talking about their biggest fears.

'Mine's spiders,' said the pop star, pulling a face.

'Mine's snakes,' said the comedian, squirming. He turned to the influencer. 'What's *yours?*'

'People,' Albert said out loud, talking over the influencer. 'People.'

As the chatter on TV continued, Albert couldn't help considering his answer. He hadn't always been frightened of people; when he was at school he'd been quite sociable and had lots of friends, friends like Tom Horrocks and Colin Broadbent. When they were little, the boys had played British Bulldog, Piggy, and Finger, Thumb or Icky in the playground, later on meeting up to go to the pictures or the local temperance bar, later still sneaking into pubs, each of them doing their best to look old enough to be served at the bar, goading each other on and revelling in the shared thrill of transgression. It was a transgression they knew was only minor and might even make their fathers proud, reminding them of a similar rite of passage in their own youth.

But then everything had changed.

Albert had been given a blunt message about what his friends thought of people like him, what the world at large thought of people like him – of the real him, the him he'd been careful to keep well hidden. As a result, he'd gradually begun backing away from everyone and had first retreated into his work, later into caring for his mam. Little by little, he'd been overwhelmed by a new shyness, a shyness that was bolstered by fear, like a current he'd been powerless to swim against – until he was drowning in it.

But it doesn't do to dwell.

'Any road, we're still here, aren't we?' he said to Gracie. She didn't reply but rested her head back on his lap. 'And we're alright as we are. Just the two of us – me and my girl.'

At ten o'clock, the programme finished and Albert had to disturb Gracie to stand up and switch off the TV. It was time for bed.

But before that, he was going to allow himself a treat. It wasn't something he did every day but something he saved for special occasions or when he wanted to cheer himself up. *Or when I want to take my mind off a scary letter on the mantelpiece.*

He went over to his old stereo and took out a CD of classic songs from the musicals. He wasn't such a fan of musicals himself but the songs reminded him of happier times. They reminded him of his teenage years – and someone who'd made him happy.

He checked there were no gaps in the curtains and the door was firmly shut, and pressed Play. He didn't turn up the sound too loud as he didn't want the neighbours to hear him. But he kicked off his slippers and began dancing around the room to 'Shall We Dance?' from *The King and I*, twisting and skipping with a skill and agility that would have left his colleagues open-mouthed. Gracie was used to witnessing these private performances so didn't even raise her head, although Albert directed all his moves at her. As he did, he could feel his shyness and reserve dissolving like the two teaspoons of sugar he took in his mug of tea. And he leaped and twirled around with an energy that surprised even himself, savouring every moment of the joyful release.

Next he played 'I Could Have Danced All Night' from *My Fair Lady* and then 'Singin' in the Rain'. As he danced away every last inhibition, he could feel the happiness vibrating through him. If he spent most of his time feeling like he was drowning, now he was rising above the water like some kind of beautiful creature who was being set free. *If only all my life could be like this. If only I could always feel this free.*

And then, once again, the letter on the mantelpiece caught his eye. All of a sudden he realised what he must look like. A little out of breath, he went over to check there really were no gaps in the curtains. As he caught a glimpse of the dimly-lit street outside, he felt the heat rushing into his cheeks, staining them with shame. *Bloomin' 'eck, lad, what are you doing prancing around the front room? What's got into you when you know you've important news to deal with?*

He switched off the music and snatched up the letter. Once he'd caught his breath, he ripped open the envelope and tugged the single sheet of paper out. He began reading.

Dear Mr Entwistle,
It has come to our attention that in three months' time you will be celebrating your sixty-fifth birthday. In advance of this special occasion, Royal Mail would like to offer our congratulations, together with our heartfelt thanks for so many years' loyal service.

Well, that's not too bad.

As you are no doubt aware, the company has a policy of compulsory retirement at sixty-five.

No, no. That can't be right.
He tried to read on but the words began swirling around the page and he was starting to feel sick.

We understand that some members of staff feel they aren't ready to retire and may wish to challenge this ruling.

Too right I do.

But we're afraid there is no possibility of a postponement.

Hell fire.

If you'd like to discuss the matter with your Delivery Centre Manager, Mrs Marjorie Bennett . . .

Albert held on to the mantelpiece to steady himself. This couldn't be happening.
I can't stop working. How can I carry on being me if I'm not a postman?
He looked at the letter again but there it was, in black and white – notice of his compulsory retirement.
He remembered how reassuring he'd found his routine today, as he did every day. He remembered arriving at work

that very morning, secure in the knowledge that today would be the same as every other day.

How wrong he'd been.

Because today was a day that changed everything.

Chapter Three

Nicole Ashton sneaked a look at her phone. There were no texts but just the thought that one might arrive soon sent a jolt of excitement running through her.

'Now remember girls,' chirped her teacher, 'you're never fully dressed without a manicure!'

Nicole took a long, calming breath and tried to focus. She nodded at the teacher. Joyce Bennett was a slim woman, approaching sixty, who always had her platinum-blonde hair blow-dried so extravagantly it looked a little over the top for her surroundings. As usual, her skin had been sprayed with a fake tan the colour of butterscotch, which Nicole assumed was a perk of her job as head of the Hair and Beauty department at Toddington College.

'And what's my motto?' she added.

All around Nicole, her fellow students chorused, 'Life's too short for bad nails!'

Joyce's face lit up. 'Fabulous. Now let's spread some sparkle!'

Nicole felt a rumble of nerves. She was more than three

months into her course and tonight, for the first time, she'd be performing a manicure on a client. Most of the girls had been assigned an elderly pensioner, as these tended to be the only women with time to spare and a willingness to let an untrained youngster loose on their nails. But she'd been allocated a matronly woman called Marjorie who was in her fifties and worked in the local Post Office. More to the point, she was Joyce's sister-in-law, so Nicole knew that every little detail of her work would be reported back. She wanted to do as well as possible, to propel herself one step closer towards her ambition of one day running her own beauty salon; an ambition that might seem desperately improbable at the moment, but one she always kept in mind. *I have to smash this.*

She looked at Marjorie and smiled with a confidence she tried to force herself to feel. Her client's hands were already stretched out on two white towels, and Nicole had lined up her products and tools at the side.

'Now I'm going to start by cleaning your hands,' she explained, falteringly.

She reached for a sanitising spray and applied it to each side of the hands and then wiped over them with cotton wool.

'And now I'm going to file the nails to make them neat and tidy.'

'Don't forget, girls,' Joyce called out as she worked her way around the room, 'while you work it's important to chat to your client and make her feel special. Remember, the salon should be a safe space for her to talk about whatever she wants. What do I always say?'

All around Nicole, the girls looked up from their nails. 'What happens in the salon stays in the salon!'

Nicole felt a wave of fear lick her belly. This was the part she found difficult. But she knew that if she was to succeed as a beautician, she needed to get over her unease at chatting to strangers. 'So . . . you're Joyce's sister-in-law?' she attempted.

'Yeah,' Marjorie said, 'we've known each other for thirty-five years. She married one brother and I married the other. People used to say we were Toddington's answer to Di and Fergie.'

Marjorie smiled at the memory but Nicole wasn't sure what she meant.

'Although this was way before all the toe-sucking,' Marjorie added.

Nicole was completely lost.

Thankfully, Marjorie was happy to carry on talking. 'That all seems like a long time ago now,' she said, wistfully. 'These days, my Fred has piles the size of a bunch of grapes and I'm saddled with the change of life. Honestly, love, it's awful. I get such bad night sweats it's like sleeping in a paddling pool.'

Oh my God, this woman's full-on.

'Oh, and my sex drive's gone through the floor,' Marjorie rattled on. 'Mind you, that might not be such a bad thing; my fanny's gone so dry you could strike a match on it.'

Nicole wasn't sure how to respond. She gave what she hoped was an appropriate, if embarrassed, murmur of sympathy.

As she moved on to the second hand, she stole another quick glance at her phone. Still nothing. *Oh come on, I'm going to burst if he doesn't text soon.*

'Anyway, how about you?' asked Marjorie. 'I see you've got a little girl.'

'What?' Instantly, Nicole felt defensive. 'How do you know that?'

'I saw it on your phone, love. On your screensaver.'

Before she replied, Nicole reminded herself of Joyce's feedback the first time she'd done a blow-dry on a client. She'd said that Nicole was one of the most talented students on the course but her client had complained that she came across as a bit hard. At the time Nicole had resisted the urge to give an epic eye-roll; as a young black woman, all she had to do was be slightly standoffish and white people assumed she was angry and aggressive. If she ever said anything vaguely political this only exacerbated the problem. On her last course, she'd made one single – very polite – enquiry about why there weren't any sessions dedicated to Afro hair and her tutor had accused her of 'threatening behaviour'. But why couldn't people see that she wasn't aggressive but shy? *No one ever stops to think I might have lived through experiences that have left me wary of opening myself up.*

She rearranged her features into a smile. 'Yeah, that's Reenie,' she replied. 'She's just turned two. She's really into Peppa Pig at the moment. She goes downstairs to the crèche while I come up here to do my course.'

Nicole considered adding that the first time she'd done this she hadn't been able to stop worrying about her and had slipped off to the toilets to have a little cry. She considered adding that at the same time as wanting to keep her daughter close, she also worried Reenie would grow up to be shy like her and so wanted to make sure she mixed with other kids. But she didn't feel comfortable sharing this kind of confidence.

She finished the filing and straightened out both hands to examine her work. *Hmm, I'm actually quite pleased with that.*

She stopped and drew in a deep breath.

Now don't mess things up by being rude . . .

'I'm going to apply some cream to the cuticles,' she explained, sweetly, 'just to soften them up before I start pushing them back.'

Marjorie nodded. 'So who's the girl's dad?' she probed. 'You're very young to have settled down.'

Nicole's fingers stiffened. She didn't want to tell Marjorie she hadn't settled down. She didn't want to tell her she'd fallen in love with a boy called Dalton when she was just fifteen, overawed by his talent as a songwriter and his ambition to make it as a musician, but a year later she'd fallen pregnant and a relationship that until then had been all about fun had suddenly turned serious. At first Dalton had been supportive and had begged Nicole to keep the baby, even though she was worried about how they'd afford it, and how it would affect her career plans. He'd promised to stick around – and he had. Until a record label in London showed the slightest whiff of interest in some songs he'd written, when he promptly disappeared down south, abandoning her two months before the baby was due. Then, he stopped answering her calls. Nicole had been devastated and found herself forced to drop out of her course and put her ambitions on hold.

And now here she was, starting all over again, living on a council estate miles away from her friends, studying at this night school where she didn't really know anyone, with no one to babysit so she could go out and get to know people – and the only contact she had from Dalton was the money the Child Support Agency forced him to pay into her account every month. He regularly missed these payments, now the music career he'd left her to pursue had amounted to nothing. But he'd decided to stay on in London and hadn't even bothered to come home to meet Reenie. But she didn't want to divulge any of that information to Marjorie; she'd hate people to think of her as some stupid, naive girl who'd let a man walk all over her. *I might have been like that once but I've learned my lesson – and I'm not like that any more.*

'Oh I broke up with Reenie's dad a while back,' she said, briskly. 'But we're perfectly happy without him. The two of us manage fine on our own.'

Of course this wasn't strictly true. Nicole tried not to think about how overdrawn her bank account was – or how she was going to afford Christmas. The fear slammed into her. *Don't think about that now. Stay focused on your manicure.*

She finished massaging the cream into Marjorie's cuticles and put the left hand into a nail bowl that had been filled with warm water.

Marjorie narrowed her eyes at her. 'Well, if you're not with Reenie's dad, who's the new fella?'

My God, this woman's unreal. Has she got no boundaries?

'Come on, love, you can't fool me; I've seen you checking your phone. And I recognise that look a mile off.'

Nicole took a deep breath and swallowed the urge to tell Marjorie to back off. 'Yeah, I *have* started seeing someone,' she said reluctantly. 'But I'd rather not talk about it, if you don't mind . . . it's still early days, and I don't want to jinx anything.'

More to the point, it's none of your business!

'Come on, love,' Marjorie persisted, 'you can tell me. Do you think he's The One?'

'Please, can you just give it a rest?' Nicole snapped. 'I really don't want to talk about it—'

She saw the dejection on Marjorie's face and stopped herself. *Girl, don't mess this up now.*

'Sorry,' she managed. 'It's just all a bit new and I've not got my head around it yet.'

She did her best to smile in a way that made it clear that topic of conversation was now closed. She quickly finished Marjorie's right hand and popped it into a nail bowl.

'Now I'm going to gently push back the cuticles,' she said, 'so the nail plate looks a bit longer.'

They hit a bump of silence and before Marjorie could fill it with another personal question, Nicole jumped in with one of her own.

'Anyway, how about *your* man?' she asked. 'How did you meet him?'

She gave a quiet sigh of relief as Marjorie launched into a long story about love at first sight striking to the sound of Wham! in a Toddington nightclub that had long since been demolished. Nicole tuned out and allowed her memory to rewind to the first time she'd met her new boyfriend, Jamie. They'd matched online the previous summer, when Jamie had been back in Toddington to stay with his family during the university holidays. He was studying to be an engineer at Leeds and from the moment they'd begun messaging, Nicole had been encouraged by how different he'd seemed to Dalton. When they'd met for their first date, things had gone brilliantly. Because she had no one to look after Reenie, she'd had no choice but to bring her along; she and Jamie had gone for a walk around a local reservoir while Reenie had her afternoon nap in her buggy. Nicole had been worried this would put Jamie off but he hadn't seemed remotely discouraged. On the contrary, he seemed interested in her life and opinions – and when he insisted on pushing the buggy, the muscles stood out on his arms in a way that made her feel slightly short of breath. Not only that, but when Reenie woke up he was great with her and seemed to genuinely enjoy playing with her.

Within a few weeks, Jamie was regularly staying over at Nicole's place and she could feel her soul coming alive again. But in September he'd gone back to Leeds for the start of his final year and he'd only been back to visit her once all term, for a weekend at the start of November when they'd taken Reenie to a local bonfire and firework display and Nicole had felt her soul soaring again. But as soon as he'd left, she'd found herself missing him even more. She'd consoled herself with the thought that he'd be back in Toddington for Christmas. And tonight was the night he'd finally be coming home.

But will the connection between us still be there?

What if it's faded in all the time he hasn't seen me?

What if being around his uni friends has made him realise he wants someone cleverer than me – someone with no baggage?

As she took Marjorie's right hand out of the nail bowl and began to dry it, she snatched another look at her phone – but still he hadn't replied.

Oh come on, Jamie, you said you'd text as soon as you got home. You must be back by now . . .

She began pushing back the cuticles on the right hand while Marjorie jumped forward to her wedding day and began talking Nicole through every last detail. In between giving the occasional nod, Nicole replayed in her head the FaceTime conversation she'd had last night with her best friend, Lisa.

'Your defences are, like, bound to be up,' Lisa had said, using her phone as a mirror in which to straighten her hair. 'Dalton put you through hell.'

Lisa was a mixed-race girl who'd been in Nicole's class at school and still lived in their hometown of Huddlesden, where she worked as a sales assistant in a women's clothes shop. One of the reasons Nicole had hated moving away was because she'd known how difficult it would be for her to carry on seeing Lisa and her other friends; although Toddington was only a forty-five-minute drive away, none of them had cars, so most of their communication since then had been limited to messages in the WhatsApp group she'd set up, and the occasional conversation on FaceTime.

'Well, how do I break my defences down, Lise?' she asked. 'How do I make myself stop worrying?

Lisa dropped her straighteners. 'Girl, you just need to chill. Whatever you do, don't start being needy and texting him all the time. Don't put him under any pressure – you don't want to, like, scare him off.'

Nicole had promised to heed her advice – and had felt comforted by the conversation. But as soon as she'd put the phone down, insecurity had set in. It didn't matter how many times she reminded herself of how she felt when she was with Jamie – or how the connection between them was strong enough to weather the separation – by the time she went to bed she'd started to lose conviction.

And now my head's all over the place.

She picked up her cuticle nippers and re-set her face into a smile. 'I'll just tidy up your cuticles; it'll make your polish look better.'

As she began cutting off the excess bits of skin sticking up at the sides of Marjorie's nails, Marjorie launched into a graphic description of the injuries she'd sustained while giving birth to her youngest child.

'Honestly, love, it was like pushing out a Christmas turkey. It was like a war zone down there afterwards – I tore right through. I've never seen so much blood in my life—'

'And how are you two getting on?' interrupted Joyce, her eyebrow arched expectantly. 'Everything alright?'

Nicole could feel her spirit slump. She hoped she hadn't been too brittle earlier.

'Oh yeah,' replied a beaming Marjorie, 'don't worry about us, we're getting on like a house on fire.'

She gave Nicole a wink and Nicole smiled back at her gratefully.

'Fabulous,' said Joyce, 'keep it up. It looks like you're on course to get top marks, Nicole.'

Nicole could feel the smile splitting her face.

She dropped her cuticle nippers back into the jar of disinfecting fluid and gave each of Marjorie's nails a wipe. 'Now I'm going to start applying your base coat,' she explained. 'And then we'll do the colour.'

But Marjorie wasn't paying attention. 'Well, whoever this fella is,' she said, 'I hope he's worth it. And I hope he realises how lucky he is.' She reached out and gave Nicole's hand a little squeeze.

Out of nowhere, Nicole could feel her eyes filling with tears. She sniffed them back quickly. 'Thanks,' she managed. 'Thanks a lot.'

She dipped her brush into the polish and stole what she promised herself would be her final glance at her phone. But all that was looking back at her was a photo of Reenie dressed in her pyjamas, her hair in little Bantu knots, smiling as she held up George Pig, the cuddly toy she carried everywhere.

Still there was nothing from Jamie.

Chapter Four

'Bloomin' 'eck,' said Albert, just a few minutes after he'd arrived at work. 'You're not serious?'

Marjorie examined her newly painted nails and gave him a sympathetic smile. 'I'm afraid I am, Albert. You've got to come to the Christmas do because it's your turn to do Secret Santa.'

'Secret S-santa?' Albert stuttered. 'But what's *that*?'

'It's like a raffle. Each member of staff is given the name of someone else they have to buy a present for. You spend a maximum of £10 and no one knows who's bought what, as all the presents come from Secret Santa. Anyway, it's your turn to arrange the draw.'

Albert opened his mouth but no words came out. He couldn't believe what he was hearing. He'd hardly slept; he was too worried about the fact that he was being forced to retire in three months' time. And now here he was, being hit by this second bombshell – an order to socialise with colleagues who had as little interest in talking to him as he had in talking to them.

'I know, love, I know the Christmas do's not your thing,' Marjorie said soothingly. 'But look at it from my point of view; no one wants to organise Secret Santa because they all want to get bladdered. If I tell them *you're* allowed to opt out, they'll all want to get out of it. And then where would we be for team morale – and Christmas spirit?'

Albert thought this over and wasn't sure how he could argue against it. He certainly didn't want anyone to think he was some kind of Scrooge. *Although I'll hate every minute of it.*

'Alright,' he bleated. 'I suppose I'll just have to do it.'

He sloped towards his sorting frame.

'Oh, there's one more thing,' Marjorie called out after him.

He turned around. 'Yeah?'

'Everyone has to wear a Christmas jumper.'

The expression on Albert's face caused Marjorie to visibly wince.

'I'm sorry, love,' she said. 'I'm really sorry.'

Albert shook his head in disbelief. He spotted a stray bauble in his path and kicked it out of the way.

A few hours later, Albert was still struggling to get to grips with this latest burst of bad news. It had been all he could think about on his walk; however hard he'd tried, for once he hadn't been able to lose himself in the job. He'd thought about the Christmas party as he'd waved his stick at the Border collie, who for some reason was particularly snappy today. He'd thought about it as he'd delivered parcel after parcel of Christmas presents to stay-at-home mums eager to stash them away before their children returned from school. And he'd thought about it as he'd passed Edith Graham, who'd been decorating her little Christmas tree and had given him a look and a wave that were particularly pleading. But then, just as he was coming to the detached houses by the park, something happened to distract him from the news.

On Pear Tree Street there was a big van parked outside one of the smart stone houses. 'Get a Move On!' read a logo emblazoned on the side, with a London address and phone number. There'd been a SOLD sign outside the house for at least a month now and the previous occupants had moved out a week earlier; the new owners must be moving in today. Albert could see removal men lugging in hefty gym equipment, a slanted desk that looked like it belonged to an artist of some kind, plus boxes and boxes of books. He was intrigued.

Across the road, two women were pretending to have bumped into each other and struck up a casual conversation. Albert recognised them as Jean Carter and Beverley Liptrot, two housewives who organised the annual summer street party and were renowned as gossips. He couldn't resist stopping his trolley and perusing the contents so he could listen to what they were saying.

'Get a load of that!' said Beverley, nudging her friend.

Albert looked up to see a young man stepping out of the van carrying a framed black and white drawing of two semi-naked men with handlebar moustaches and muscles so big they looked like they'd been pumped up like an inflatable. When he peered closer, he could see the two men had thick bulges straining at the crotches of their jeans. He could feel himself blushing a deep shade of burgundy.

Jean, on the other hand, looked at the picture with the same expression Gracie adopted when she was eyeing up a bird. 'Hey,' she said to Bev, 'it reminds me of that stripper we got for your hen night.'

The two women gave a loud cackle and Bev's gradually gave way to a smoker's cough. As the removal man passed by, Albert read the inscription: 'Tom of Finland'.

'Can you believe it?' Jean said. 'Gays *on our street*?'

'I know, i'n't it fabulous?' said Bev. 'I love gays, me.'

As he listened to the women's enthusiasm, Albert couldn't help remembering the words his dad had used to describe the gay men he'd arrested in the public toilets.

'Filthy', *'disgusting'*, *'animals'* . . .

Of course, he knew it was no longer acceptable to call gay people things like that and these days you couldn't arrest someone for being gay. Even so, he'd never actually met any gay men in Toddington, or at least none who admitted to it in public. But these new arrivals were generating fierce excitement; as well as the neighbours across the road, another two women were standing at the doorway to the house chatting to a pair of shadowy figures he could only assume were the new residents. The sound of the women's theatrical laughter came drifting down the drive.

'Gaybours?' the woman on the left said. 'Honestly, you two are *hilarious!*'

Albert pretended to consult something in his bag so he could continue listening. As he heard the women say goodbye, he looked up and recognised them as Margaret Bainbridge and Sheryl Crowther, both of whom came striding down the driveway with all the confidence of a pair of supermodels strutting along the catwalk.

'Well, it were obvious they liked us,' crowed Margaret.

Sheryl nodded. 'Let's invite them round for a dinner party. Gays love a party.'

As they swished past, Albert noticed Beverley grinding out her cigarette and checking her make-up in a mirror. He couldn't pretend to be busy any longer; he needed to get in quickly. In his hand was a parcel addressed to the previous owners of the house, who'd failed to set up a forwarding address. It was his job to deliver it.

Come on, lad. Just get it over with.

As he walked up the path, he could feel his heart rate quicken and a trickle of sweat running down his back. He took a gulp of air.

The door had been left open so the removal men could pass in and out. He rang the bell and stepped to one side to make way for the young man who'd carried in the explicit picture. And then a fresh-faced man, who was of Chinese heritage and looked to be in his thirties, came bouncing down the hallway.

'Be careful with our Tom of Finlands,' he instructed the removal men in a camp voice and an accent Albert thought might be from Essex. 'I know they look like porn but they're legit works of art!'

As he came closer, Albert saw that the man had short hair, shaved at the sides, and he was wearing eye make-up and some kind of gloss on his lips.

'Hi, darling,' the man said with a smile.

'I'm not your darling,' Albert barked before he could stop himself. He had no idea where the words came from; it was as if they'd said themselves.

There was an awkward silence. Rather than taking offence, the man looked at him curiously. 'OK, well, what can I do for you?'

'S-s-sorry,' Albert stammered, 'I'm sorry. It's just, I've got this parcel – it's for the people who lived here before.'

'Who is it, Danny?' shouted a voice from the back of the house. Another man appeared; he was a few years older than the man at the door, with a brown beard and thin, wire-framed glasses. In his hand he was carrying a selection of screwdrivers. 'Oh, good morning,' he said when he saw Albert.

Unlike the other man, he sounded like he was from a well-to-do family. He walked down the hallway and gestured to his tools. 'Honestly, I'm hopeless with DIY. I can never work out which of these I need.'

'How do,' said Albert, feeling his shoulders stiffen. 'I was just telling your . . . erm . . . friend—'

'Actually,' the younger man interrupted, 'I'm his *boy*friend.' But there was no malice in his voice, and he smiled at Albert kindly.

Albert broke his gaze and looked down at his feet. 'Sorry . . . erm . . . yes. I was just saying I've got a parcel for the people who lived here before you.'

'Righto,' said the older man, putting down his screwdrivers and taking the package off him. 'They said they'd call in next week, so we'll be sure to pass it on.'

'Ta,' said Albert. 'Anyway, I mustn't dawdle.'

'Just a minute,' said the older man, 'now we're moving in, I guess we'll be seeing a lot of you.'

Oh, please just let me go.

'I'm Daniel,' the man carried on, 'and this is Danny.'

Both men held out their hands and Albert shook them. He hoped they didn't notice his hands were clammy. There was a clumsy pause.

'Most people find that funny,' said Danny. 'That we're a couple and we basically have the same name.'

'Oh, right, fair do's,' said Albert. 'Sorry, I'm not very good with jokes.'

'We've just relocated from London,' Daniel explained. 'We're hoping to have a more relaxed life here. I'm a writer and Danny's a designer, so we can both pretty much work from home. Although I'll be doing some lecturing at Manchester University too.'

Albert wasn't sure how to reply. 'I'm Albert,' he managed. 'I'm a postman.' *Oh, what did you say that for? They know perfectly well what you do!*

Danny smiled at him again and a wicked glint entered his eye. 'Hey, I bet you can tell a few stories. You must have come across all sorts of shenanigans on your round . . .'

'Yes, well . . . I'd better be off,' Albert boomed. 'These letters won't deliver themselves!'

He turned and scarpered down the driveway.

'Goodbye then,' Daniel called out after him.

But Albert kept his head down and didn't reply.

*

Once Albert was back at the delivery centre, he tried to pull off his usual trick of slipping into the office unnoticed. But he was no match for Marjorie. She called him over and thrust a list of the staff who were coming to the Christmas party into his hand, together with a stocking, and told him to get on with organising Secret Santa.

He slunk over to his desk, where he found a spare piece of paper. He wrote down all the names, then cut them up and placed them in the stocking. He started the draw at the far side of the office and worked his way around as quickly as possible, hating every minute.

When he returned to the central area surrounding his own frame, he found Jack Brew eating a barm cake stuffed with chips and flicking through a Toddington FC fan forum on his phone.

'Alright, Jack,' he began, cautiously, 'I'm doing Secret Santa this year. Do you want to find out who you're buying for?'

Jack furrowed his brow and swallowed a mouthful of chips. 'Not really, like, but go on then.'

He had brown sauce oozing out of the side of his mouth and a few drops of it had fallen on to his shirt. Albert tried not to look at it as he held out the stocking. Jack thrust his hand to the bottom and rummaged around for a minute before pulling out a name.

'Barbara?' he said. 'Who the 'ell's Barbara?'

As Jack spoke, a chunk of chip flew out of his mouth and landed on the back of Albert's hand. Albert wanted to let out a groan of disgust but instead found himself quietly wiping it off before Jack could see what he'd done.

48

'She's one of the cleaners,' he answered.

'Not to worry,' said Jack. 'I'll get our Doreen to do it; she knows what women like.'

And with that he went back to his chip barm and his phone.

As Albert backed away, he felt a wave of annoyance. Sometimes the nasty things Jack said affected him deeply. An image of his dad flickered to life in his mind but he shut it down. He didn't want to think about that today.

He trundled over to Sue's frame and she drew the name of the security guard, Ste. 'Oh, I was hoping I'd get him,' she said. 'I saw some Christmas-pudding-flavoured protein shake in Aldi the other day – I bet he'd love that.'

Next was the turn of Smiler, who drew Marjorie. 'Easy,' he said, as he bounced around on the spot. 'I'm going to get her a fan like those old Spanish women use so she can cool herself down when she's having a hot flush.'

Albert sat at his frame, feeling a huge sense of relief that the draw was over. *Well, almost over.* He still had to pull out the name of the person he'd be buying for – and he'd lost track of which names had already been taken.

As he put his hand in the stocking, he tried to feel enthusiastic, telling himself that he should at least make an effort to get into the festive spirit.

He pulled out the final name. It was Jack.

Suddenly, the Christmas party felt like it was going to be even more of an ordeal than he'd originally imagined.

As he walked down the high street, Albert could feel the dread seeping through him. He wasn't sure he could think of anything he wanted to do less than go to the office Christmas party. He wondered if it ever occurred to all those people who socialised without any unease at all just how torturous it was for someone like him to be thrust into that kind of situation.

Come on, lad, stop feeling sorry for yourself.

As he passed the statue of the nobleman, the traffic cone now removed from its head, he told himself to focus on the positive. Buying the Secret Santa gift for Jack had turned out to be surprisingly easy. He'd gone straight to the merchandise store in the football stadium and had been greeted by several options that cost under the all-important price limit of £10: there was a Toddington FC-themed flask, water bottle, bobble hat, scarf, slippers and calendar. But when he'd spotted a baby's bib with the team's logo printed on it, a sense of mischievousness had stirred inside him. He remembered the brown sauce that had oozed out of Jack's mouth and the lump of chip that had landed on his hand. Jack would have no idea who'd bought the gift so he'd taken it to the till and paid for it before he had chance to change his mind. As he continued down the high street, he tried to feel buoyed up by this little success.

He was heading towards Klobber, the only fashionable men's clothes shop left in Toddington – and a place he'd always avoided. But he'd overheard some colleagues talking about buying their Christmas jumpers, and this was the only place they said they'd been able to find them. When he came to a stop outside the shop, blasting out of the entrance was music dominated by a drumbeat and the sound of a man rapping about the various sexual activities he wanted to perform on his 'ho'. Albert scrunched up his hands into fists and went inside.

From every direction he was confronted by walls festooned with bright tracksuits, see-through tops that looked like they'd been made out of the material used for fishing nets, and trousers that seemed for reasons unfathomable to him to have been slashed with scissors. Just when he was about to turn around in despair, he spotted what he was looking for; piled up on a table was a big stack of Christmas jumpers.

Bingo!

Albert went over and began rifling through the pile with the desperation of a newly released prisoner hitting an all-you-can-eat buffet. His fingers ran over reindeers, Santas, elves and snowflakes – and there was even a design featuring a stocking with the word 'HUNG' knitted underneath. He gulped.

'Are you OK, babe?' came a girlish voice from behind him.

He turned around to see a young woman with a blow-dry so perfect she looked like a blonde Kate Middleton.

'How do,' he said. 'I'm just looking for something to wear to our work Christmas do.'

He read the woman's name badge; she was called Scorpia.

'No problem,' she said. 'How about this?'

She held up a bright red jumper featuring three Christmas bells and the slogan 'Jingle My Bells'.

'It'll look incred,' she assured him.

Albert gave another gulp and, this time, he was sure it was audible. 'Oh, I'm not sure about that. Maybe something a bit more understated?'

He picked out some of the less sexually forthright designs and handed them over. Scorpia led him to the back of the store, and into the changing rooms. *The sooner I get this over with, the sooner I can get out of here.*

But then he caught sight of himself in the mirror and stopped. There was no denying that, with his personality-free clothes and short-back-and-sides haircut, anyone who saw him would think he was dull and boring. He looked like the kind of man people would call a 'drink of water'. But he didn't feel like that inside; inside he felt like he was a whole bundle of fun. *Or at least I would be, if I could only work out a way of getting the fun out of me.*

He tucked in his vest and slipped on the first jumper. But the colour made his face look pallid and washed-out. He tried on the second. But the collar was too high and it itched his neck.

'How are you getting on, babe?' shouted Scorpia from the other side of the door.

Babe? Why does she keep calling me 'babe'?

'Yeah, nearly there,' he shouted over the music. The third jumper, which was navy blue and scattered with snowflakes, was the least boisterous of all three designs and fitted him well. He stepped out to show Scorpia.

'That's gorge,' she said. 'You look really cuddly.'

Albert tried not to flinch. Cuddly was the *last* thing he was aiming for. *What if somebody actually wants to cuddle me?*

He decided he'd just have to hope they didn't as this was the only jumper that was remotely suitable. 'OK, I'll take it.'

'And what are you going to wear on the bottom?'

Albert glanced down at his jeans and Scorpia followed his eyes.

'Don't tell me you're planning on wearing those granddad jeans?'

"Granddad jeans"? 'Erm . . . I *was* going to,' he attempted, 'yeah.'

'Babe,' Scorpia said, 'we need to get you some new jeans.' She looked at him with all the urgency of someone negotiating a hostage situation. 'Don't panic, I know just the thing.'

She asked Albert's measurements and pulled out a pair of blue Levi 501s. 'And I'm going to pick up a pair of boots too,' she added chirpily. 'You can't possibly go to the party in those brogues.'

Albert was about to protest but Scorpia silenced him with the details of a multi-buy discount the shop was offering for one day only. 'So basically the boots are free!' she trilled.

'Terrific,' was all Albert could reply.

He disappeared back into the changing rooms. Both the jeans and shoes fitted perfectly, and he had to admit she'd done a good job. As he contemplated his reflection in the mirror, he told himself that he'd gone from looking like a drink of water to a glass of Vimto.

He opened the cubicle door to show her.

Her face lit up. 'Babe,' she said, 'you look *phenom!*'

To his surprise, Albert could feel a smile creeping across his face.

He told himself to get a grip.

Chapter Five

Albert smiled tightly at some colleagues he barely knew and held open his sack so they could drop their Secret Santa presents inside. 'Ta very much,' he said, trying his best to sound jolly.

He and the staff of the Royal Mail's Toddington delivery centre were in the upstairs function room of The Boot and Slipper, a pub on the street where the majority of the town's nightlife was concentrated. Albert had been relieved to discover that, unlike most of the venues, this one didn't have windows plastered with advertisements for shots of brightly coloured spirits for the price of £1, something the local newspaper claimed was responsible for regular fights on the street and puddles of luminous vomit decorating the pavement every Sunday morning. The Boot and Slipper was a cosy old pub, with wooden beams running along the ceiling and an old wrought-iron fireplace with a tiled hearth on which currently stood a Christmas tree that dominated the room. Albert wasn't into pubs, but if he had been, this was just the kind of place he might call into for a quiet pint. *Maybe tonight isn't going to be so bad after all.*

As he scanned the room for people from whom he still needed to collect presents, he noticed that what he was wearing was pretty much in keeping with the rest of the team's outfits. He suddenly felt a wave of affection for Scorpia.

As he continued bundling the presents into one of the Royal Mail sacks he'd borrowed from the office, he was subjected to the occasional line of banter. 'A busman's holiday, is it, Albert?' was the favourite. But he could handle this and, so far, he was managing to carry out his duty without as much awkwardness as he'd feared.

Just when he was daring to think that he might actually start enjoying himself, Marjorie announced that it was time for them to sit down for the meal – and she'd done a seating plan to 'encourage team bonding'. Albert quickly stashed his sack of presents and began scouring the tables for his name.

He spotted it.

He blinked in disbelief; of all the staff in the office, Marjorie had decided to sit him in between Jack and the agency worker, Tyger. *So much for this not being as bad as I thought.*

He slumped into his seat.

''Ere, cop hold of that,' said Jack, thrusting the end of a Christmas cracker into his face.

Albert limply took hold of it and let Jack tug away the majority of the cracker. As he proceeded to read out some lame joke, Albert zoned out and looked around him. Not only was he sitting in between Jack and Tyger, but he was also sitting opposite the security guard, Ste. Albert couldn't think of a single thing he had in common with any of them. He felt like maybe he belonged to a different species to everyone else, or there was just something wrong with him, like a crucial nut or bolt had come unstuck in his brain. He took a pull on his pint of cider. *This is going to be a long night.*

Albert knew that he could down a few more pints and allow drunkenness to conquer his inhibitions. But he hadn't enjoyed drinking since his teens and didn't like the sensation of losing control; he couldn't bear the idea of letting down his guard and giving away too much.

No, I'll just have to muddle through.

Once all the crackers had been pulled, he turned to listen to what Ste was saying to Tyger.

'You want to get down the gym and get jacked, mate. You know what they say? Do curls, get girls.'

Albert scoured his brains for any kind of contribution he could make to the conversation. He failed. And his failure only made him feel even more disappointed in himself.

Jack was telling his friends about a woman on his walk who he was convinced had been 'giving him the come-on'.

'You know they call her Annabella Anyfella?' said one of his mates.

'Yeah, yeah, I'm not daft,' said Jack. 'She's had more pricks in her than a second-hand dartboard.'

The three men growled with laughter.

Albert hated it when Jack and his friends denigrated women like this. He wished he had the confidence to say something but, once again, felt trapped by his shyness.

He wondered how long it would take for the food to arrive.

This really is going to be a long night.

*

As the dessert plates were being cleared, Albert spotted his chance to escape from the table; he retrieved his Secret Santa sack and began distributing the gifts.

As he worked his way around, he discovered that most of his colleagues were feeling emboldened by drink. The harmless banter of earlier had evolved into ribald comments about 'big packages'. When he approached the women from the finance department, they looked at him like a pack of hyenas ogling a plump wildebeest.

'Does Santa want to empty his sack?' one of them said, before they all collapsed in a riot of giggles.

Thankfully, people soon started opening their presents. Somebody had bought Smiler a baseball cap with the smiley face emoji on it, Tyger received his own mug, which seemed to disappoint him but pleased Albert, and Tsunami opened a multipack of salad cream, which everyone found hilarious.

'Well, you did say you liked it!' shouted Jack.

There was an intriguing gift for Barbara the cleaner, who unwrapped an apron printed with the words 'Behind every great man is a woman rolling her eyes', something that made Albert wonder if Jack's wife Doreen might not be such a doormat after all.

And Jack himself received his baby's bib with good nature and was happy to model it for his workmates.

'It's a shame you didn't get it a few hours ago,' said Sue, pointing out a trail of gravy running down his jumper.

As the entire party rumbled with laughter, Albert kept his head down, although in his own little way he was pleased he'd been able to ignite some banter. It made him feel like the fun inside him had managed to surface, albeit briefly.

Finally he pulled out his own present and took it over to a stool at the quiet end of the bar. He couldn't remember the last time he'd been given a present.

As his colleagues began pushing back the tables to create a dance floor, he opened the package.

His heart sank.

It was a jigsaw.

He turned the box around and saw that the image to be pieced together was a photo of the Lancashire moors. As he examined it, Albert remembered one of his younger colleagues telling him that their Auntie Mabel did jigsaws to pass the time and realised that whoever had chosen the present must feel sorry for him. In that moment he realised just how desperately he wanted to go home.

A DJ with custard-blond hair had set up his equipment and was playing 'Merry Christmas Everyone' by Shakin' Stevens. For a brief second he imagined leaping up from his stool, bursting on to the dance floor and letting loose some of his most impressive moves. He pictured his colleagues' faces, and he couldn't help letting out a little smile. But there was no chance he could bring himself to go through with it and the fantasy faded away.

He spotted Tsunami tottering along the edge of the dance floor with a sprig of plastic mistletoe, kissing everyone she could. Over in the far corner, Ste had removed his jumper and was showing off his abs to the women from finance, one of whom ran her fingers over his stomach and squealed. And Smiler was standing at the opposite end of the bar, hugging colleague after colleague and telling them how brilliant they were, even those he'd never met before. 'You know what,' he said to Barbara, 'I really, *really* love you.'

I don't think anyone will notice if I slip away.

Albert drained his pint but just as he was stepping off the stool, he was interrupted by Marjorie.

''Ere, where do you think you're going?'

She was groping her way over to him, her Christmas jumper removed and her too-tight camisole now riding up to expose folds of flab at the sides of her waist.

'Sit back down, love!' she slurred. 'I want a little chat!'

Albert felt a knot of fear tightening in his stomach. But there was no escape. He sat back on his stool and rested his jigsaw on his lap.

Marjorie perched on the stool next to him, narrowing her eyes at him. 'You know, you *are* a funny one, Albert Entwistle. You don't give much away, do you?'

'I just like keeping myself to myself,' he attempted.

She didn't take the hint. 'Yeah, but I bet you've got a few skeletons in your closet. Come on, I can tell you're hiding something.'

Albert could tell that the alcohol had sent Marjorie's intimacy threshold plunging way lower than its usual rock-bottom setting. He realised he was clinging on to his jigsaw like a shield.

'Give that 'ere!' Marjorie said, snatching it off him and plonking it on the bar. As she leaned in, she enveloped Albert in a fug of white wine. 'So what are you doing for Christmas?' she asked.

'I'm just having a quiet one,' he said, wriggling on his stool.

There was a pause and Marjorie peered at him. 'What's

your story, Albert? I know you've no family and you live on your own . . .'

Oh, do we really have to do this?

'Yeah,' he managed. 'My dad died when I was twenty-five and my mam died eighteen years ago. I've lived on my own ever since.'

Marjorie nodded. 'And is it true you had to look after your mam when she was ill?'

'She was ill, yeah. For a long time.' With a prickle of guilt, Albert remembered how part of him had been relieved that his mam's illness had diverted people's attention away from his personal life; for years, people had assumed he was too busy looking after her to have one. How he wished Marjorie would make the same assumption.

'So there's no one special in your life?' she asked.

'No,' he said, as emphatically as he could.

There was another pause. It was as if Marjorie were waiting for him to say something.

She took a sip of her wine. 'What's this someone told me about you having a sweetheart when you were a lad? Some lass from Chorley?'

Albert could feel himself stiffen. He hadn't thought about Susan for a long time and hadn't seen her for what must be forty years. She'd been a bookish girl, a few years younger than him, and they'd met through a friend of his mam's. The two of them had gone out for walks on the moors a few times, and on a handful of occasions they'd spent the evening having a few drinks in pubs like this one. But they'd only been courting for a couple of months when Susan broke it off

60

and started seeing a schoolteacher she'd ended up marrying. The last Albert had heard, they'd moved up to Cumbria and had a few children. But now Marjorie was dragging up the memory – and it made him feel unsettled.

'Erm . . . yeah, I did have a girlfriend once,' he ventured. 'But that was a long time ago.'

Marjorie leaned forward, too drunk to pick up on Albert's discomfort. 'And what happened . . . how come it didn't work out? Did you just not fall in love with her?' she asked.

No, I was never in love with Susan, Albert wanted to say. And then he considered what he really wanted to say. *I was in love once but it wasn't with a girl.*

Even though he hadn't said the words out loud he could almost hear them echoing around the room.

The love of my life was a man, not a woman.

Albert wondered what Marjorie would say if he came out with it. If he told her that not only had he been in love with a boy but it had ended so unhappily – so painfully – that he'd decided he was never going to put himself through anything like that again.

He drew in a ragged breath. 'Sorry,' he said, 'all that happened so long ago now. I don't like to think about it.'

'You know, it always helps to talk,' Marjorie persisted. 'It isn't good to bottle up your emotions.'

But what good could it possibly do to go over it all now? And how could you possibly understand?

He murmured, 'I'm alright, Marjorie, honestly.'

She put her hand on Albert's shoulder and gave it a rub. He tried not to baulk. There was a pause filled by the sound of drunken laughter coming from the dance floor.

''Ere, let's have a dance,' said Marjorie.

Albert was aware of a look of horror appearing on his face. In his head he replayed his earlier fantasy and couldn't help thinking how ridiculous it seemed. 'No, ta,' he said. 'I'm perfectly happy here.'

But Marjorie wouldn't be deterred. 'Rubbish!' she protested, as she tumbled off her stool and began tugging at his arm. 'Come on, it's the Christmas do! You've got to have a dance!'

'If you don't mind,' he said, 'I'd rather not.'

'Get out of it! I won't take no for an answer.'

She began pulling harder and Albert struggled to keep his balance on the stool. 'Please, Marjorie. Don't.'

As she tugged and tugged, he was left with no alternative but to shake her off.

'Will you just leave me alone?' he found himself shouting. 'Just go away and leave me alone!'

Marjorie's hand fell to her side and she looked shocked – and more than a little hurt. Albert quickly scanned the room to make sure no one was watching. Thankfully, Ty was vomiting violently all over one of the tables, and this was monopolising everyone's attention.

I need to get out of here now.

As Cliff Richard launched into 'Mistletoe and Wine', Albert reached for his jigsaw and deftly made his escape.

What a fool he'd been to think the night might not be as bad as he'd feared; it had ended up being far worse. Because it had stirred up all kinds of feelings he'd thought were buried deep in the past but which he could now feel bursting into his present.

Chapter Six

Just carry on as normal. That's what Albert told himself as he set off on his favourite walk. *Just carry on as normal and it will all be fine.*

It was an overcast morning but he checked the sky and it didn't look like it would rain. He stamped his feet in the heavy walking boots, pulled on his gloves and tugged the hood of his duffel coat over his head. He locked his front door and caught sight of Gracie, who was sitting on the window sill watching him leave. He looked around to check no one was watching and gave her a wave.

'See you later, my little girl.'

It was Christmas Eve, which this year fell on a regular working day, but Albert had been told to take a day off as he was owed so much annual leave. He'd decided to pass the time by following his usual Sunday routine. At nine o'clock he'd popped to the corner shop to buy a newspaper and had then returned home, where he'd made his regular Sunday morning breakfast of two fried eggs with the yolk still running, two rashers of streaky bacon with the rind still on, two pork sausages, a small tin of beans and three slices of his favourite black pudding – all mopped up with a few rounds of toast taken from his Warburton's loaf. He knew it was a lot, but it was his weekly indulgence – and besides, it meant he wouldn't have to bother making dinner and could go without eating again until it was time for his tea.

As the minute hand of his watch hit midday, he strode away from his house and headed towards the end of his street. There, he turned right on to the main road, walking away from the town centre. After fifteen minutes, he crossed over and came to the entrance to Toddington Hall, a big Tudor manor house – although he was embarrassed to say he'd never been inside. It was to the area behind the hall that he was heading.

He crossed a railway bridge and accessed a footpath that led past some ramshackle farm buildings and up on to the hilltops, a route that was known locally as going 'over the tops'. When it was summer, if he could be absolutely sure he was on his own, he'd sometimes hum the tune to 'The Hills Are Alive' from *The Sound of Music* and whirl around with his arms outstretched, allowing himself a few moments of release. But that was the last thing he wanted to do today. Besides, it was December – it was muddy underfoot and so exposed to the winter wind that the cold almost took Albert's breath away.

As he climbed up the hill, he allowed himself a brief memory of how much he used to enjoy Christmas Eve as a boy. All day he'd be consumed by excitement, wondering if Father Christmas would call at his house to give him the presents he'd asked for in his letter. Before he went to bed, he and his mam would leave a pint of beer and a mince pie on the little table at the bottom of the stairs – not forgetting a big, fat, knobbly carrot for Rudolph. Albert's dad would come upstairs to tuck him in, and the two of them would look out of the window and up at the sky to see if they could spot Father Christmas's sleigh. But happy memories like this were only vague, subsumed under the unhappiness of what had come later. *And that's what I want to block out. That's what I'm trying to stop rushing back.*

Before long, Albert came to a boundary stone, although the engraving had long since worn away, so he had no idea which boundary it was supposed to mark. Here, he stopped and looked around him. The sky was the colour of steel – or a particularly painful bruise. And the moors stretching out before him had lost the luscious green colour of the long, coarse grass that had flourished over the summer before turning a shade of sepia or deep gold. Here and there, large patches of the foliage had been burnt away, scorched by the wildfires that were a common feature of the summer, and the heavy rain of the autumn had formed deep bogs Albert had to take care to step around. He understood why many people found the landscape austere and unwelcoming but the moors were his favourite place in the world.

Looking ahead of him, he could make out the tips of the buildings in the neighbouring towns and villages, nestled in the gaps between the undulating Pennines. Rotating around to look back, he contemplated all of Toddington, anchored firmly into the landscape at the foot of the hill. The skyline of the town was dominated by the parish church and the clock tower of the town hall. It had changed remarkably little since his childhood – although the football stadium and a few high-rise blocks of flats were new additions, and most of the factory and mill chimneys that had served as landmarks fifty years ago had now been demolished. It was a familiar sight, and one he found reassuring. But even though he stood in this same spot at this same time every Sunday, unless it was hailing or snowing, today he felt different – as if something inside him were shifting.

He sucked in his breath and moved on.

When he came to the next stile, he turned right to take the path down the hill. But rather than following it all the way to the lane where it eventually came out, he found himself taking a detour to a small cluster of trees. His heart began hammering in his chest as he entered the woodland. As if drawn by some magnetic force, he picked his way through the undergrowth, over the uneven ground, pushing out of his path any bare twigs and branches that blocked his passage. When he emerged on the other side, he found what was pulling him towards it.

A few metres in front of him stood a Second World War bunker or pillbox. The sight of it knocked the breath out of Albert's body. It looked exactly as it had the last time he'd seen it – on that disastrous night, when he was a teenager.

Oh, what am I doing?

He really didn't want to be here but at the same time he couldn't make himself leave.

The bunker was a hexagonal structure with a flat roof. It

looked like it had been made out of some kind of mould into which concrete had been poured. Now that he thought about it, Albert wondered how the whole thing had been transported to this hillside and manoeuvred into position, before being cemented into the ground. He was sure that if he were able to use the internet on his phone, he could find out by accessing the website of one of the societies that documented local war history. But for him the bunker was the setting for a very different history. He'd resisted its pull for many years but today it had finally got the better of him.

Once he'd composed himself, he scrambled up the slope at the side of the structure to reach the entrance, which was in the wall that stood on the highest point of the hill. He ducked down to pass through the low archway.

As soon as he entered, he felt an ache take hold in the core of his gut. But still it wasn't enough to make him leave.

A weak light spilled through the small openings, halfway up the walls, at which Albert assumed soldiers would have been stationed if the country had been invaded. The structure had never been removed from the hillside, and, twenty-five years after the Second World War had ended, the teenage Albert had become a regular visitor.

This was where, one long spring and summer, he'd come – in secret – to meet the boy he loved. This was where the tight grip of desire had taken hold of him and made it impossible to defend himself from impulses he'd spent years trying to suppress. This was where he'd felt dizzy, almost high on love – and had experienced a happiness greater than any he'd ever imagined was possible.

But this was also where something terrible had happened that would destroy his happiness – and replace it with a gutting sadness he hadn't been able to escape, ever since.

He hadn't been back to this place for nearly fifty years, but now that he was here, the ache in his belly was growing. He ran his fingers along the walls and they felt just as rough and gnarly as they had all those years ago. He kicked at the ground and dislodged a few matches and cigarette butts. In his day, he'd created a mattress out of a pile of old blankets he'd smuggled out of the house and brought up here to spread out on the ground. It was here, on these blankets, that he'd held a young man in his arms and softly kissed his forehead as he'd whispered in his ear how happy he made him, where he'd run his fingers through a young man's hair and pulled him nearer so he could breathe him in, where he'd felt so close to a young man and so fused with his spirit that he couldn't imagine them ever being apart. But memories like these were too much to bear.

Worried he might be about to throw up, Albert felt his way to the exit and yanked in a breath of air. In an instant he was hit by another fragment of memory: two young men dancing on the hillside, dancing with their arms locked around each other as one of them sang out loud, safe in the knowledge that they were too far away from the town for anyone to see or hear them. Albert's ache grew so strong he began to fold in on himself.

It was a mistake to come here. What good can it possibly do to delve back into all this now?

He stumbled down the slope and rested his back against

the wall of the bunker. He stayed there for a few minutes, trying to regulate his breathing, trying to forget.

Then he banged his fist on the wall and pushed himself away. Without turning to look back, he re-entered the woodland. It was only when he rejoined his regular path on the other side that his heart rate began to slow.

As he made his way down the hillside, he tried reminding himself that if he just carried on as normal – as he had done for years – then everything would be fine.

But somewhere deep inside, he knew that carrying on as normal was no longer an option.

On his way home, Albert felt shaken and unmoored. He found himself calling into the corner shop.

'Alright, Albert?' said the shopkeeper. Ted Hardacre was a solid, dependable man who'd owned the shop for so many years that Albert couldn't remember who'd had it before him. 'I didn't expect to see you here again today. Is everything OK?'

'Yeah, yeah,' Albert insisted. He grabbed a Crunchie and thrust the coins over the counter. 'I'm terrific, thanks.'

Once Ted had dropped the coins into the till, Albert snatched the chocolate bar out of his hand and made a dash for the door.

'I know I've said it already,' Ted shouted after him, 'but Merry—!' Albert shut the door before Ted could reach the end of his sentence.

Walk, he told himself, *just walk*.

He tucked the Crunchie into his pocket and accelerated down the road, taking the shortcut through the Flowers Estate.

Although it was starting to grow dark, and even colder with it, there were several children still playing out in the street. On the corner of Tulip Drive, a mum was keeping watch while her partner smuggled several Argos bags out of the boot of his car and around the back of the house. In that moment, Albert was struck by the realisation that he'd be spending Christmas alone. He remembered what it had felt like to be loved. And, all of a sudden, it was as if he were losing that love all over again.

His legs felt weak, but he recovered himself and pushed on. *Keep walking. Just keep walking.*

Just before he reached the cobbled alleyway that led to the back of his house, he passed the home of Nicole Ashton. He wasn't surprised to see her standing in the doorway. Except, this time, she wasn't smoking or flicking through her phone but engaged in a passionate embrace with a young man. He didn't recognise the man – although he couldn't actually see much of his face, as Nicole had a hand on each of his cheeks and was kissing him vigorously. He couldn't hear what she was whispering to him between kisses but the look on her face brought back that hollow feeling in the pit of Albert's stomach. However much he wanted to stop staring, he couldn't. And, even though he knew he shouldn't be listening to their conversation, he couldn't stop himself.

'Enjoy Christmas Day,' Nicole said, aloud.

'Oh, I don't know about that,' the young man said. 'How am I supposed to enjoy it when I won't be with you?'

Nicole suddenly spotted Albert over the man's shoulder. 'Oh hello postie!' she called out.

Albert was shocked that she'd spoken to him and it took him a few seconds to react. He managed to give her a little wave and she shot him a bright smile.

The happiness visible on Nicole's face was so intense it caused the hollow feeling inside Albert to swell. He realised just how many years had passed since he'd felt happy – since he'd been wanted, since he'd been touched. It was so long ago, it might as well have happened to a different person. He pulled his hood up and directed his eyes back at the ground.

'Merry Christmas!' Nicole shouted, and the boy with her raised his hand in a wave.

Albert nodded his head but it felt like a dead weight. He could feel his entire body sagging and he almost had to drag himself home.

As soon as he was inside, he was going to pull up the draw-bridge and shut out the world – shut out everyone's excitement about Christmas, shut out the happiness on everyone's faces.

If only he could shut out his memories.

George Atkinson. That's the new boy's name.

He's tall and slim, with delicate features and hair that when it catches the light looks like burnt gold and reminds Albert of the grass on the moors in winter. But it's his eyes that are most striking; eyes that are such an intense shade of blue they border on violet. Albert finds it difficult to take his own eyes off them.

George has recently started as a pupil at Albert's school. It's September 1969 – the beginning of Albert's final year – and word has spread around that there's a new boy whose family has moved to Toddington from Yorkshire. From what Albert has heard from the other boys, George Atkinson likes musical theatre, Hollywood cinema and dressmaking – and has joined the local theatre group. It hasn't taken long for his new classmates to seize on this and start calling him 'queer'.

One morning, Albert is waiting to go into assembly with the boys from his form, who are lined up on either side of the corridor. George comes rushing in late and attempts to dart down the passageway and join his form without attracting attention. But some of the rowdier boys spot him.

''Ere comes Georgina,' one of them shouts.

'Backs to the wall, lads!' says another.

The boys stretch out their legs and block his way. George has to stop but he refuses to look at them.

''Ere, Georgina, we're talking to you!' one of them practically spits at him.

'Yeah,' says another, 'di'n't your mam tell you it's rude to ignore people?'

But still George says nothing; he simply steps back and lowers his head.

Although Albert wants to intervene to protect him, he doesn't dare. He doesn't dare do anything that would make the other boys suspect he shares the same secret as George – the secret that he's attracted to boys rather than girls. Because, unlike George, Albert is able to hide his secret.

''Ey, don't you go to some kind of *theatre* group?' asks one of the boys, pronouncing the word 'theatre' as if it's some kind of contagious disease.

'Yeah,' says another, 'ain't you some kind of *showgirl?*'

They begin waggling their bottoms and making their wrists go limp, performing an outrageous parody of femininity.

Again, George doesn't react.

'Why're you so shy all of a sudden?' taunts one of the boys.

'Go on,' jeers another, 'do us a dance.'

'Can you do t' can-can?'

'Go on, Georgina, get them legs up!'

They begin kicking his feet. They kick his feet so he'll dance. They kick his feet so they can carry on sneering at him.

George has no choice but to do as they say.

As the laughter spreads around the boys lined up along the corridor, Albert notices that his friends Tom and Colin are joining in. He wants to tell them to pack it in but it becomes clear that every single boy is laughing – every single boy except him.

The injustice of it cuts through him. He doesn't understand how they can all be so horrible to George, how it doesn't occur to a single one of them that he's a human being who must be feeling broken and humiliated. He can feel his pulse accelerating and the anger roiling inside him.

I can't stand by and watch this. I can't stay silent and watch everyone laughing at him.

But something blocks him from acting.

''Ere, I saw that,' says one of the boys, 'I saw you looking at my dick.'

It's as if he's just drawn blood.

'You dirty bastard!' shouts one of his friends, a crazed glint in his eye. 'You dirty, filthy queer!'

Thankfully, just as Albert's thinking he can't stand by in silence any more, a teacher rounds the corner. 'What's going on 'ere, lads?'

The boys snap back and fold themselves against the wall. 'Nothing, sir,' they chorus.

The teacher looks at George. 'Atkinson?'

'Nothing, sir,' echoes George.

The teacher frowns and whips out his keys. As he unlocks the hall, George slopes away, though not before receiving a rough shove from one of the boys. But he refuses to hang his head and holds it high.

When he passes Albert, his eyes very briefly flicker in his direction. And he must be able to read the mixture of empathy, guilt and longing on his face – because in that moment it's as if a secret understanding flashes between them. And Albert knows that he may be able to hide his secret from the other boys but he can't hide it from this one.

Chapter Seven

By Christmas morning, Albert was desperate to shut out his memories. He decided to throw himself into as many festive traditions as he could.

He knew that most people would be starting Christmas Day by giving each other presents, so he began his by giving Gracie hers. He'd been to the big pet store on the retail park on the edge of town to buy her a stocking full of cat treats and a fluffy Santa toy on the end of a string.

'There you go, my girl,' he said as he placed them in front of her. 'Happy Christmas.'

He unwrapped the stocking and, for a while, Gracie amused herself by pawing around the discarded paper, but for some reason she turned up her nose at the treats. She did like the Santa toy, though, and for a good half an hour Albert whipped it to and fro in front of her, yanking it out of reach just as she pounced. It always surprised him that Gracie never tired of playing the same games she'd played as a kitten, even though she must now have racked up enough cat years to be an old lady.

Just when he was telling himself that he wasn't bothered about the fact that he hadn't received any presents himself, he remembered that he *had* been given a present – the jigsaw from Secret Santa at the Christmas party. It might have disappointed him at the time but he should probably get over himself and have a go at it now. *It's not like I've anything else to do.*

He opened the box and made some space on the coffee table so he could turn all the pieces the right way up and spread them out. As he began slotting them together to recreate the picture of the Lancashire moors, his mind pieced together memories of some of the best Christmas presents he'd been given as a child.

There was the green tractor he'd loved riding when he was four. He'd used his little feet to power it along the pavement, struggling to keep up with his dad as he walked to the corner shop to buy his cigarettes. He'd even been allowed to ride it in the house, rumbling around on the kitchen lino and bashing into furniture. But in those days, his mam hadn't minded. In those days, she'd had a great sense of fun and a loud, rolling laugh that always made Albert smile. He couldn't know just how much this would change, just how much the atmosphere in the house would change.

Then there was the bright red bicycle he'd received at the age of seven. On Christmas Day, his dad had taken him out in the street on it, running along at the side of him as he'd somehow managed his first, very wobbly, ride. His mam had watched from the doorway, clapping and cheering him on. She was heavily pregnant and there was lots of talk of Albert having a brother or sister to play with by next Christmas. But this wasn't the first time he'd heard this – and already he was starting to doubt that it would ever happen. Already he could pick up on a nervousness in his mam's voice. Already he could sense that the atmosphere in the house was changing.

But, without doubt, his favourite Christmas present of all time had been the one he'd received when he was nine. He'd raced down the stairs on Christmas morning to find that Father Christmas had left him a wooden fort for his tin soldiers, a fort that came complete with a little drawbridge that wound up and down. But rather than enjoying his happiness, his mam had spent much of that Christmas Day with a sad, faraway look in her eyes. Albert remembered his dad saying that another little brother or sister had gone to join the others in Heaven. He didn't know why this kept happening but he did know that when they went it was as if each of the babies took part of his mam's spirit with them. She'd gradually stopped singing songs by Gracie Fields, then she'd gradually stopped laughing – until all the joy had disappeared from the house completely. Albert had tried to cheer her up and had even tried to sing her some of her favourite songs, but nothing he did worked – in fact, it seemed to turn her sadness into annoyance. On Christmas Day, he'd taken his fort and enacted endless battles around it, escaping into a world of play.

Today, as he completed the borders of his jigsaw and began filling in the pieces towards the centre, he remembered feeling grateful for every present he used to receive at Christmas. For weeks before the big day his dad would remind him that if he wasn't a good boy, Father Christmas wouldn't call at his house and instead he'd be given a sack of coal. But as Albert grew older, even though he always was a good boy, he started to worry that he'd come downstairs to a sack of coal waiting for him under the tree. When he stopped believing in Father Christmas and realised the presents were coming from his mam and dad, this only made him worry more. Because deep down he was starting to think that he was bad – he was starting to think that the secret he was hiding made him bad. And he lived in fear that, one day, his mam and dad would discover his badness.

He paused to wipe the memory from his mind.

When he snapped into position the final piece of the jigsaw, he stepped back to admire his work. But the finished picture ignited more memories of being on the moors with George. He left the jigsaw on the coffee table and went through to the kitchen.

Every Christmas since his mam had died, Albert roasted a small turkey crown, which he finished eating on Boxing Day. He knew that he could probably save himself the trouble and buy a smaller breast that would be enough for one, but he liked going through all the steps of preparing a roast and working out the timings for the vegetables, stuffing and mashed potato he made to go on the side. Besides, Gracie loved eating the turkey giblets and he wouldn't dream of depriving her of her Christmas dinner. As the aromas began to waft around the kitchen, she nuzzled his shins and started purring loudly.

'Hang on a minute, my little girl,' he told her gently, 'it's not ready yet.'

Albert served Gracie at the same time as he sat down at

the dining table. While she gobbled up the giblets from her bowl on the floor, he ate his roast turkey to a soundtrack of Christmas carols playing on the radio.

He and his mam had listened to carols on the radio while they'd eaten Christmas dinner together. In the years following his dad's death from a heart attack, she'd become increasingly fragile, had ventured out of the house less and less, and had begun to depend on Albert more and more. Gradually, he'd learned to clean, shop and cook. Towards the end of her life, he'd had to serve her meals in bed. But even then, she'd always insisted on being helped downstairs to eat at the dinner table on Christmas Day. Albert remembered her final Christmas, when she'd moaned at him for undercooking the turkey and overcooking the sprouts, even though he'd been quite pleased with how they'd turned out. By that stage she was unrecognisable as the woman he'd known when he was a young boy. As the years had passed, she'd become an increasingly sour, judgemental old woman – and she always reserved her most savage insults for Albert.

'Albert, you're a dead loss.'

'Albert, you're a waste of space.'

'Albert, you can't do owt right.'

Even when she was diagnosed with cancer, she seemed to enjoy using this as another stick with which to beat him: he didn't understand what she was going through; he wasn't being gentle enough with her; he wasn't giving her enough drugs to relieve the pain.

It was as if she wanted to punish me for something. To make me feel worse about myself than I already did.

Today, as he finished his dinner and began clearing the pots from the table, he told himself that he much preferred his home life now it was just him and Gracie. It was a terrible thing to admit but he didn't miss his mam at all.

He washed up, scraped the leftovers into Tupperware containers, and returned to the front room to watch TV. Gracie trotted after him and jumped on to his lap. He held her paw in his hand and stroked his thumb over the soft, warm pads. But whatever he watched, he just couldn't concentrate. His mind only had the capacity for one thought. *Now that I'm coming to the end of Christmas, what happens next?*

He couldn't escape the thought that this was going to be his last Christmas as a postman. He stared at the letter from HR lodged between his little cluster of Christmas cards. He couldn't resist picking it up to reread it.

As he allowed the significance of the words to register, Albert gave in to imagining what his life would be without work. How would he fill his days? Would all his time be like this? Would he end up spending days and days without speaking to another human being?

A hook of emotion ripped into him. He knew what it was; it was loneliness.

'There it is,' he said out loud. 'I've admitted it; I'm lonely.'

As if repulsed by his admission, Gracie shook her paw out of his hand.

I'm lonely and I can't deny it any more.

He knew what he had to do.

He switched on the stereo. But this time, he didn't pick out a CD of cheery songs from musicals. He picked out the soundtrack to *West Side Story*. He checked that the curtains and door were shut and no one could see or hear him. He skipped forwards until he came to the song 'Somewhere'. And he pressed Play.

As he picked up Gracie and swayed her around in time to the music, he was transported back to a springtime when he hadn't been lonely, when he'd shared his life with George, when George had sung him this very song as they danced together on the hillside.

The thought comforted him for a moment, but beneath it he felt troubled. One idea kept preying on him.

If I'm lonely now, it's about to get a whole lot worse.

Chapter Eight

'Higher!' Reenie shouted, a grin splitting her face. 'Higher!'

Nicole wished that every day could be like this. She stood in the doorway to her living room watching Reenie bounce on her little trampoline as Jamie held her hand. She didn't think she could possibly be any happier.

Two weeks ago, Jamie had sent her a text to say he'd arrived home late because his train had been delayed, and he'd apologised for not texting but his phone had run out of battery. Since then, he'd been to visit her at home four times – coming for this, a fifth time, on Boxing Day. These visits had been so wonderful that Nicole had told herself she'd been silly to doubt Jamie's commitment to the relationship. Although she reassured herself that it was perfectly natural for her to feel insecure after the experience she'd had with Dalton. *But girl, you just need to chill now and stop letting that get in the way of your feelings for Jamie.*

She leaned on the doorway and gazed at the two of them playing.

'Let's do it again,' Jamie said, 'but this time let's twirl you around!'

As he smiled at her daughter, she felt a tickle in her heart.

Jamie had a cute, boyish face and a sturdy frame that was padded with a thick layer of muscle, courtesy of the effort he put in as a member of the university swimming and rowing teams. He had pale white skin and fair hair that usually flopped down over his forehead but stuck up whenever he ran his hand through it. And he had eyes that were between blue and green, neither one colour nor the other but an unusual mix of the two – and one Nicole found utterly arresting, especially when he used them to smile at her. She'd heard descriptions of people smiling with their eyes but had never come across this in real life. That was until she met Jamie.

Reenie came to the end of her first twirl. 'Again!' she squealed at Jamie. 'Again!'

Scattered all around the trampoline were the presents Nicole had given her on Christmas morning. In keeping with Reenie's latest obsession, most of these were Peppa Pig-themed; there was a Peppa Pig tea set, playhouse, cash register, art set, hair-dryer and ice cream van. Nicole had scoured the local charity shops to buy the majority of them second-hand, picking up a few others with the coupons and discount codes she'd spent months hunting down on money-saving websites and an app she'd downloaded on to her phone. Even so, she'd spent more money than she could afford but she'd worked out that she could just about get by if she tightened her belt and spent less on herself for the next few months. In any case, she'd already decided she was giving up smoking. She'd managed perfectly well when she'd been pregnant and had only started again because of the stress of being a single mother. Although right now that stress seemed like a distant memory. Earlier that afternoon, Jamie had turned up clutching a present for Reenie that had turned out to be a Peppa Pig indoor trampoline and had swiftly eclipsed all others as her favourite gift that Christmas. Even better than seeing how happy it made Reenie was seeing Jamie smile at Reenie with his eyes. It made Nicole's heart sing.

All this happiness was almost enough to make her forget how much she hated the house in which she and Reenie lived. It was a rain-stained, red-brick, semi-detached council house surrounded by a shabby privet hedge, with an uninspiring interior of whitewashed walls and cattle-brown carpets. She'd had so little money when she moved in that she'd only been able to afford basic furniture, including a functional table and chairs, and a futon that was so uncomfortable she could feel the wooden slats through its cushioning. Every time she sat on it, she thought she'd positioned herself on top of a stray book or the hard edge of one of Reenie's toys. The place simply wasn't cosy – and it still didn't feel like home, after nearly six months. A few weeks ago, she'd covered the bare light bulbs with some cheap lampshades when her money came through from the CSA, and this had made a little difference. But it would take a lot more to blind her to the house's worst feature – its location on the Flowers Estate.

Nicole didn't feel safe when she walked through the estate as many of the young men who sat on the walls drinking out of cans of lager would whistle at her, suck their teeth, or call out sexual innuendos, even if she was pushing Reenie in her buggy, which she invariably was. On one occasion, one man had followed her for a few streets, detailing the various sexual activities he wanted to perform on her – until she'd barked at him to back off and threatened to call the police, her hands shaking as she reached for her phone. Since then, she usually made her way home the long way round, cutting down the ginnel behind the row of terraced houses to the north to avoid the estate.

When she'd first been offered the house, she'd had her reservations. But at the time she'd been desperate. When Dalton had walked out on her, her mum had promised to help look after the baby so Nicole could finish her course, albeit switching down to part-time hours. From the start she'd been wary, as her mum had never been dependable. Then, true to form, she'd met some man who owned a bar in Lanzarote and within a few months of Reenie being born had moved to the Canary Islands, abandoning her daughter and putting the family home on the market. She'd told Nicole that, at forty, she didn't feel ready to be a grandma and wasn't sure she was cut out for the role. Her mum's attitude hardly came as a surprise to Nicole; she hadn't been cut out for the role of mother either, and still wasn't playing it very well. In any case, Nicole had been forced to join the waiting list for a council house and had been left with no option but to take up the first one the borough had offered, which was here on the notorious Flowers Estate. And however much she hated it, she knew she'd just have to put up with it. *At least for now. At least until I've got my career up and running.*

'Baby,' she called out to Jamie, 'do you want a glass of wine?'

He swung Reenie to a stop and gently placed her back down on the trampoline. 'Yes, please, Nic. I'd love one.'

She went back into the kitchen and pulled a bottle of white wine out of the fridge. She wasn't very knowledgeable about wine and had only been able to afford the cheapest bottle of white on offer in Lidl. Part of her worried that, as Jamie had enjoyed a much more financially privileged upbringing, he'd be able to spot a cheap wine. But there was nothing she could do about it. She poured two glasses and carried them through to the living room.

'I hope this is alright,' she said, handing his over. 'I'm sorry I can't afford anything fancy.'

Jamie gave her a kiss on the lips. 'Nic, don't worry about it. It's not as if you need to impress me; you've done more than enough of that already.'

She smiled and felt her embarrassment fading.

'Oh, and just so you know,' Jamie added, 'I couldn't care less what I'm drinking as long as I'm here with you.'

His words tugged at Nicole's heart. Before she felt over-whelmed by her emotions, she went back to the kitchen to check on the food.

Although it was Boxing Day, she was cooking a full turkey dinner. as Jamie had been obliged to spend Christmas Day with his parents, brother and grandparents. Even though she had to concentrate on the timings, she felt confident in her abilities as a cook; her mum had always been hopeless, so she'd had to start learning in her early teens. Now it was time to show off what she knew.

'Right, guys,' Nicole announced, 'tea's ready.'

She gestured to the table and Jamie jumped up.

Nicole held out her arms to Reenie. 'Come on, big girl,' she said, 'let me help you into your high chair.'

Reenie stuck out her bottom lip. 'No,' she said, 'Jamie do it!'

Nicole looked at Jamie and rolled her eyes affectionately. 'See what you've done?' she said. 'I think you're just going to have to do as she says.'

As Jamie lifted Reenie up and fastened her into her Peppa Pig high chair, Nicole carried in the food. She couldn't wait for Jamie to taste it. She had considered asking him to carve the turkey but hadn't wanted him to think she was the kind of woman who needed a 'man of the house'. *Anyway, if he wants that role it won't do him any harm to work for it.*

'Wow!' said Jamie as she put his plate down in front of him. 'This looks amazing!'

Nicole smiled. Before she sat down, she leaned over Reenie's plate and began to cut up her food.

'No!' shouted Reenie. 'Jamie do it!'

Nicole gave a little chuckle. 'Alright, alright!' She looked at Jamie. 'Would you mind?'

Although she was pretending to be exasperated, she was glad Reenie kept asking for Jamie. And judging from the expression on Jamie's face, he was enjoying it.

'Mmm, not only does this look amazing,' he said, tucking into his food, 'but it *tastes* amazing too.'

Nicole felt a glow of satisfaction. 'So I take it this is very different from a night down the Students' Union?' she asked.

Jamie's eyes glittered. 'Yeah, you should see the state of my mates after a few drinks – I think Reenie probably has a better line in conversation.'

They both turned to look at the little girl as she banged her fork and spoon on the table. 'Yum, yum!'

She had drool all over her chin and Nicole wiped it up with a piece of kitchen roll.

'She doesn't drool as much as my mates either,' said Jamie.

Nicole laughed. Then she stopped herself. 'Oh no! I forgot the gravy!'

She dashed back into the kitchen and slid the gravy boat off the worktop. Just as she was carrying it through to the living room, she caught sight of Jamie and Reenie laughing together. She stopped to savour the moment. And to her surprise she realised for the first time that she was glad she'd moved to Toddington – even if it meant living on the Flowers Estate and had involved leaving her friends behind. Because if she hadn't, then she wouldn't have met Jamie. And the three of them wouldn't be together now.

Eating together like a family.

A few hours later, Nicole was lying in bed cuddling up to Jamie.

After they'd finished eating, he'd done the washing up while she'd tidied away Reenie's toys. When she'd announced it was bedtime, Reenie had insisted Jamie be the one to read her a story. Once again, Nicole had gladly given in to her wishes. She'd sneaked outside to smoke a cigarette, which she'd told herself would be her last, then had freshened up and reapplied her make-up. When Jamie had come through to her bedroom, he'd surprised her by producing a gorgeous pair of crystal solitaire earrings. She had no idea how he'd been able to afford such an expensive Christmas present if his only income was his student loan, but she'd held them up to her ears and they looked so beautiful she decided not to ruin the moment by asking. Instead, she kissed him, he kissed her, and suddenly they were kissing each other with greater and greater urgency, and before she knew it they were falling back on to the bed and pulling off each other's clothes.

She looked at their clothes now, strewn all over the floor, and realised that if anyone saw them they'd probably think the sex they'd had was fast and frenzied, whereas in truth it had been the complete opposite. She always felt safe and respected with Jamie in a way she never had with Dalton. The first few times they'd taken their clothes off together, she'd been nervous; his body was so hard and solid that it had made her feel anxious about hers. She knew she'd lost the baby weight but she'd been left with more of a tummy than she used to have. And she'd always had small boobs but her breasts seemed to have shrunk a little since she'd given birth, something no one had warned her about. But Jamie didn't seem to mind. What she saw as her imperfections only seemed to turn him on more. And the sex they had was affectionate, tender and – a word she was only just allowing herself to use – loving.

But dare I say that word out loud yet?

After today she had no doubt that she *was* falling in love with Jamie, but dare she express it?

She reassured herself that now was the perfect moment to open up to him. *I can always say, 'I think I might be falling in love with you,' just to take the edge off a bit.*

She decided to wait for Jamie's heartbeat to slow down and his breathing to settle – then she'd start a conversation.

'Nic?' He beat her to it.

'Yeah, baby?'

'I'm really sorry but I've got to go.'

She tried not to freeze in his arms. *'What?'* Her voice sounded high-pitched and she tried to lower it. 'What do you mean you've got to go?'

He kissed her forehead softly. 'I'm sorry, but I can't stay tonight.'

So much for telling him I'm falling in love with him.

She pulled herself up and looked him in the eye. 'Why not?'

'I've just got to get back home, that's all.'

She watched a thought flash across his face but it didn't make it to his lips. 'How come? Sorry, I don't get it.'

He frowned tightly. 'It's my mum and dad, Nic. I didn't want to say anything, but they don't like me seeing you.'

Nicole suddenly became aware of her nakedness and reached down to the floor for her bra. 'But where's this suddenly come from? Why are you only mentioning it now?'

'Sorry,' he said, 'but I didn't want to spoil the day. And I didn't want to say anything in front of Reenie. Then as soon as she went to bed I came in here . . . and we got a bit carried away.'

Nicole pulled on her bra and fastened it behind her, then gathered the duvet around her bottom half. She told herself not to lash out or be confrontational.

'Alright, so what have they said?' she asked in a matter-of-fact tone. 'If they're being shady about me, surely I'm entitled to know why?'

He gave another frown. 'It all blew up yesterday. I suppose they can see we're spending more time together. So they started asking questions, and basically didn't like my answers.'

Nicole arched an eyebrow at him. 'What, they think I'm not good enough for you?'

Jamie looked down and avoided her gaze. 'Something like that, yeah.'

'But why, Jamie? What do they think's wrong with me?' She knew perfectly well what they thought was wrong with her but she wanted him to say it. She wanted him to say it out loud so he could hear how bad it sounded – and then, hopefully, he'd be as outraged as she was.

'Oh, I don't know,' was all he replied. 'I don't know.'

'You *do* know. You *do* know.'

He tugged his hand through his hair and as usual it was left sticking up on his head. Ordinarily this would make her smile but this time it didn't.

'OK, well, if you won't say it, I will,' she stated. 'Your parents don't think I'm good enough because I'm a single mum and I live on a council estate and I survive on benefits. Your parents are snobs, Jamie.' *They might be racist too*, she wanted to say, but she held back; she'd learned from experience that white people were particularly sensitive to this accusation and once she brought it up, they tended to shut the conversation down.

Jamie surprised her by nodding. 'I know, Nic. You're right; they are. But honestly, I'm not listening to them.'

She reminded herself to stay calm. 'Well, why are you going home then?'

He gave a shaky sigh. 'Because I need to win them over gradually. I don't want to piss them off, Nic. I need them to keep paying my allowance till I've got through uni.'

She had to stop herself from snapping at him. *Forgive me for not sympathising, but an allowance isn't something I've ever had. It didn't even cross my mind you were getting one.*

He ran his thumb along her shoulder. 'Just bear with me for a bit while I try to keep them happy. It'll all come good in the end, I promise.'

She shook him off and drew back. '*What?* And in the meantime, I'm supposed to hide away like some dirty little secret? Like some bad girl you're ashamed of?' She realised she was shrieking. *Bang goes staying calm.*

Jamie moved towards her and held out his arm. 'No, Nic, not at all. You know that's not what I think of you ... And it's not as if I'm going to see you any less. I just need to try not to piss them off, that's all.'

They lapsed into a loaded silence and Nicole could feel the tension rising like a wall between them.

'Honestly,' Jamie went on, 'I know how to handle my parents. Trust me, please.'

Trust me, please.

When he said those words, he reminded her of all the men who'd let her down in her life. Not just Dalton, who'd asked her to trust him before he went to London and had promised to come back – but never did. But also her dad, who'd left her mum when Nicole was just a few years old and had initially come home for half-hearted visits that became less and less frequent until they stopped altogether. And then all the other men her mum had brought into her life for a few years at a time, insisting Nicole force herself to call them dad and then, just as she was feeling she might want to, they disappeared. And it wasn't just the men who'd let her down but her mum too. The way she'd walked out on her when she'd needed her most had made Nicole vow never to do anything like that to her own daughter. That's when she'd decided she was a lioness who'd do anything to protect her cub. And that meant only entertaining the idea of starting relationships with men she knew she could depend on – and Reenie could depend on too. But Jamie had spent the day making Reenie adore him and now, a few hours later, here he was telling Nicole that his parents wanted him to break up with her and he had to keep them happy.

Am I just being stupid? Is he actually mugging me off?

She pushed his arm away and stood up to get dressed. 'Look, if you're going,' she said, 'I'd rather you just go.'

He looked at her and nodded.

She couldn't believe this was how the day was ending.

All those promises I made to myself about not taking any more shit. About not letting another man walk all over me!

As she watched Jamie get out of bed and pull on his clothes, she blinked back the tears. Once he'd left, she was going outside to smoke a cigarette. She'd have to give up another day.

Chapter Nine

Albert's alarm sounded at 5 a.m. and immediately he knew something was wrong.

Don't be daft, he tried telling himself. *It just feels strange because you've had a few days outside your normal routine.* He tried not to think that pretty soon he wouldn't have a routine. He wouldn't have anything resembling a life.

It was the 27th of December and the first working day after the Christmas break. He'd been looking forward to resuming his regular work schedule, if only for the next three months. But, as he silenced his alarm, he couldn't escape an unsettling feeling.

He switched on the light and slowly hauled himself up into a sitting position.

Where's Gracie?

The cat always slept at the end of his bed. She didn't go to sleep at the same time as he did, as she liked to slip out of the cat flap for one last prowl around her territory before turning in. But she was always lying curled up by his feet when he woke up. Except that today she wasn't.

'Gracie?' he called. 'Where are you, my little girl?'

There was no miaow or sound of any movement. He stood up and pulled on his dressing gown, slid his feet into his slippers and went to the toilet. Ordinarily, Gracie would follow him into the bathroom and sit on the side of the bath until he turned on the cold water tap for her to have a drink; she always refused to drink water unless it was fresh from the tap. But still there was no sign of her.

He padded downstairs and into the kitchen. Normally, by this time, she'd be ready for her breakfast, but he noticed that she hadn't touched the chunks of meat he'd left out for her last night. He felt a sudden chill.

He rushed through to the front room, and there she was – stretched out in front of a radiator.

'Gracie,' he said with relief. 'What are you doing there?'

She didn't move.

He held on to the radiator and lowered himself to his knees. When he gave her a stroke, she barely opened her eyes, just mewled at him plaintively. He noticed she was panting.

'Bloomin' 'eck, Gracie, what's the matter?'

He slowly lifted her up, but when his hand gripped her under the stomach she let out a cry. He ran his fingers over her belly. A little lump he'd noticed a month or so ago had grown bigger. *Hell fire.*

He had to take her to the vet straight away. He rang the surgery and the recorded message told him it opened at 8 a.m.

He had to let Marjorie know that he wouldn't be going into the office. He hadn't spoken to her since their altercation at the Christmas party but he couldn't dwell on that now.

And he knew it wouldn't be a problem for her to call in an agency worker like Ty to cover for him. But what should he tell her? He didn't want to return to work to be met by pitying glances – and whispers about him being a sad old man who lived alone with his cat. He'd just have to lie.

'Hello, Marjorie,' he typed into his phone, 'Albert Entwistle here. I'm really sorry but I'm poorly and won't make it in today. I hope to be back tomorrow. Ta very much, Albert.'

Putting a kiss at the end was out of the question and he wouldn't even know how to add one of those emojis everyone used. He hit Send and turned back to his little girl.

She looked seriously ill – and he was starting to really worry about her. It didn't occur to him yet to worry about himself.

Albert arrived at the vet's surgery as soon as it opened, and a haughty-looking receptionist took his details. He struggled to tell her his name and address as he hadn't spoken more than a few words for days and it took a while for his lips and tongue to warm up. When he eventually managed it, the receptionist instructed him to take a seat in the waiting area. 'Mr Hoggett's running a bit late but he'll be with you shortly.'

Albert sat down and lifted Gracie's basket on to the seat next to him. 'It's OK, my little girl,' he whispered to her, 'the nice vet will be here soon and he'll look after you.'

As he folded his arms and waited, he wondered if he should have brought Gracie here sooner; as soon as he'd noticed the lump on her stomach. He leaned down to look in her basket but she was lying still, with her eyes closed. He felt the guilt settling in the pit of his stomach like a stone.

After an increasingly anxious half an hour, Mr Hoggett finally barrelled in. He was a chubby man in his thirties, with thinning hair and greying sideburns.

'Sorry I'm late,' he said. 'You know what it's like at this time of year.'

The whiff of booze on his breath reminded Albert that most people had spent Christmas and Boxing Day celebrating with family and friends, while he'd been hiding away with his cat. *My lovely little girl who can barely lift her head. My lovely little girl who's all I have in the world.*

Mr Hoggett excused himself to set up his consulting room and ten long minutes later called Albert in. Without any hesitation, Albert handed over the basket containing Gracie.

'Here she is, Mr Hoggett,' he said, opening the lid carefully.

'Please,' the vet said, 'call me Duncan.'

Albert nodded. 'This is Gracie,' he said, as he lifted her out and she opened her eyes. 'Please be gentle with her – she's very special.'

Duncan lowered her on to the table. Whenever she'd been to the vet's before, she'd always been curious to explore her surroundings. But this time, she lay down and curled herself up as if she wanted to go to sleep. Albert felt a bolt of panic shoot through him.

'And what seems to be the matter?' Duncan asked.

Albert explained what had happened this morning.

The vet put his hand under Gracie's stomach and felt the lump. She gave a weak cry.

'When did you first notice the growth?' Duncan asked.

'About a month ago,' Albert said meekly. 'But it didn't seem to bother her, so I didn't think anything of it.'

'And has she been off her food?'

'No. Actually, yes. But I just assumed it was the change of weather.' Although, now that Albert thought about it, the cold had never put Gracie off her food before. The stone of guilt sitting inside him bulged to the size of a boulder.

'OK,' said Duncan, 'I think we'd better run some tests.'

Albert went putty-faced but he nodded and stepped to one side.

Duncan performed an ultrasound scan on Gracie and then pushed, poked and prodded her until he'd managed to extract a tiny sample from her lump. Albert looked away and trained his eyes on a vase of fake flowers standing on the side.

'OK,' said Duncan, 'I'll just go and have a look at this. I'll be back in a few minutes.'

Once he'd left the room, Albert went over to Gracie and began to stroke her in her favourite spot behind the ears. She gave very little response.

The receptionist poked her head around the door and asked if he'd like a cup of tea.

'I'm fine, thanks,' Albert replied. 'I just want to get this out of the way, and then we can go home.'

She gave him a warm smile and suddenly she didn't look quite so mean. For a fleeting moment, Albert was surprised to find that he wanted her to hug him. He had no idea where this had come from. He couldn't remember the last time someone had hugged him. *Come on, lad, pull yourself together.*

When Duncan came back into the room he was wearing a grave expression.

'OK, Mr Entwistle,' he said, 'I'm not going to mess you about – I'm afraid Gracie has cancer.'

Cancer. Albert's heart took a dive to his stomach.

He looked at Gracie and saw how peaceful she seemed. *But how can she have cancer?* Outside in the waiting room, a dog barked. Gracie didn't even look up. Albert put his arms around her protectively.

'But presumably you can operate?' he asked. 'You can cut it out, can't you?' He was aware of the note of desperation in his voice.

Duncan picked up his mug and drained the coffee dry. 'I'm afraid not. How old is she now, eighteen?'

Albert nodded.

'Well, that's a very advanced age for a cat. I'm afraid her body wouldn't take it.'

Albert's heart plummeted further. Duncan looked at him with an expression of concern that for the first time made him seem kind.

'If it's any consolation,' he said, 'it wouldn't have made any difference if you'd come here sooner.'

Albert could feel his guilt lifting but was too upset to feel any relief.

'So what happens now?' he asked, drawing himself up. 'What are the options?'

Duncan frowned. 'I'm very sorry but I think the best option is to put her to sleep.'

As Duncan explained how much pain Gracie was in and

how this was only going to get worse, Albert zoned out. He allowed the vet's words to become muffled, as if he were hearing them underwater. He looked again at the fake flowers and rubbed a few of the petals between his fingers. He noticed that they were covered in a light film of dust. For some reason he found himself wondering what his mam would say.

'Mr Entwistle?'

Albert snapped himself back to the present. 'Sorry, yes?'

'I was just saying you can stay with her while I give her the injection. But before that, would you like a few minutes on your own? To say goodbye?'

Albert could only nod.

Duncan backed out of the room.

Once the door was shut, Albert bent down and rested his head against Gracie's. Despite the pain she was in, he could hear her start to purr.

'Bye bye, my little girl,' he said. 'My beautiful, special little girl.'

As he felt the softness of her fur and breathed in her familiar nutty scent, he couldn't quite believe this was the last time he'd be able to do this. If only he could keep stroking and smelling her for ever.

He tried not to choke on his sadness. *Come on, lad, don't fall to pieces.*

'You know you're the best friend I've ever had,' he went on. 'And I'll never stop loving you.'

He checked there was no one at the door and nuzzled her the way she liked to nuzzle him. Her purring grew louder. He could feel the tears welling in his eyes and sniffed them back.

He held her paw in his hand and stroked her soft, warm pads the way he did when they were sitting together on the sofa. 'I'll never stop loving you, Gracie, and I'll never forget you.'

He could hear the sound of Duncan's footsteps in the corridor.

'Bye bye, my little girl,' he said. He let go of her paw and pulled away.

As the door opened, he managed to fix his face into something approaching a smile.

Duncan stepped inside. 'Alright,' he said softly, 'I won't prolong the agony any more. But before we do this, you need to know that losing a pet can be a traumatic experience, especially when you go home afterwards. When a pet dies it's like the soul is gone from a house – and most people find it hard to be on their own. Is there anyone you'd like to call?'

Albert drew in a wobbly breath. There was no one he could call, even if he wanted to. After Gracie was gone, he'd be completely on his own. But he was too ashamed to say so.

He picked up Gracie one last time and cradled her in his arms. 'No, no,' he insisted, fighting back the wave of sadness that threatened to engulf him, 'it's OK. I'll be alright.'

But even as he said the words, he wasn't sure that he would.

Chapter Ten

The moment Albert arrived home, he knew he wouldn't be alright.

He went into the kitchen and made himself a cup of tea. He sank down on to a chair to drink it but instead just sat staring at Gracie's bowl of food that lay untouched from last night. After he had no idea how long, he stood up and tipped the tea down the sink.

He sloped through to the living room, where he flopped down on to the sofa. He could feel the sadness burning a hole within him. He was going to switch on the TV but didn't have the energy to concentrate on anything. Instead, his eyes were drawn to the Christmas treats Gracie had refused to eat and the little Santa toy that was lying on the carpet. He tried to remember her playing with it on Christmas morning, but he could only see her little face as the vet had given her the injection and the sparkle left her eyes as the life had leaked out of her.

As the morning gave way to afternoon, Albert felt wrung out and exhausted. There was no way he could go into work like this. He texted Marjorie to say he'd been diagnosed with flu and wouldn't make it in until after New Year. He didn't feel guilty; he might not be physically ill but he was in more pain than he'd suffered with any illness.

He plodded upstairs and lay on his bed for a few hours. From next door he could hear the sound of the children playing with their toys. But their giggles only made him feel more dismal. They made him realise that he had no connection to any other human being on the entire planet.

There are billions of people in this world and not a single one of them cares about me.

The loneliness bore through him. Slowly he sank into a heavy sleep.

'Hello, Albert, are you alright?'

These are the words that start everything.

It's the Easter holidays, six months after Albert first set eyes on George. A travelling funfair arrives in town and Albert goes along with some of his friends. In between trying out the rides, they sink pint after pint of cheap beer and, as this is the first time Albert has really tried alcohol, he's soon drunk. Somehow he becomes separated from his friends and, realising that he's losing control and starting to feel vulnerable, he begins to stagger home. But he struggles to walk properly and has to sit down on the edge of the pavement and put his head between his knees to stop it from spinning. He's sitting like this when George appears, on his way home from one of his theatre rehearsals, and asks if he's alright.

''Ere, let me give you a hand,' he says.

He hauls Albert up and puts his arm around him. He asks where he lives and slowly begins leading him off in that direction. Albert's so drunk he's only partially aware of what's happening, but one thing that strikes him clearly is how good it feels as he nuzzles into George's neck and shoulders.

He's so lovely. He's so lovely I want to kiss him . . .

Much to his surprise, when they reach the ginnel behind his house, Albert finds that he does. He kisses him. He has no idea what's possessed him, other than assuming he's fired up by the alcohol. He only gives George a quick peck on the lips but it's a reckless act and one that will later terrify him enough to avoid ever getting drunk again. It terrifies him the second he does it. And yet it gives him an intense thrill. It sets his heart cannoning in his chest and his stomach flips over as if he's riding a rollercoaster. But his pleasure is soon overwhelmed by a rush of shame, a rush of disgust at what he's done. He steps back and looks away.

'Sorry,' he says, folding his arms, 'I don't know what came over me.'

There's a beat.

'There's no need to apologise,' chirps George, 'I actually enjoyed it.'

With the alcohol surging through him, this is all the encouragement Albert needs. It's all he needs to stamp out his shame.

Something stirs within him and compels him to initiate a second kiss. Now he knows it'll be welcomed, he allows himself to be much freer. He opens his mouth wider and when George does the same, he even slips in his tongue. But he has no idea how he's supposed to kiss someone, let alone another boy. *Once you've slipped your tongue in, are you supposed to move it around?*

'Sorry,' he says, breaking away, 'I don't know what I'm doing. I hope I'm not slobbering on you.'

'Of course you're not, you daft bat.'

George smiles at him. It's a beautiful smile, one that illuminates his entire face and creeps into his eyes. He reaches for Albert and pulls him back in. 'Now shut up and kiss me again.'

This time, when Albert opens his mouth, he feels the tip of George's tongue lightly tickling his. He's so overcome with excitement that his vision starts to blur. When he senses George beginning to pant, he knows he must be feeling the same thing that's stirring within him. It's as if the air is crackling around them and they're somehow being lifted up and away from their ordinary surroundings.

But after less than a minute, they hear the sound of voices in the distance. They snap themselves apart and Albert blinks himself back to his surroundings.

'Who the 'ell's that?' whispers George.

'I don't know,' says Albert. 'But we shouldn't be doing this.'

His throat tightens and he steps further away. *I've got to get inside and sober up.*

But George doesn't look regretful. 'We shouldn't be doing this *here*,' he corrects Albert.

Albert wrinkles his brow. 'What do you mean?'

'That doesn't mean we shouldn't be doing it at all,' George

says, 'just somewhere we wouldn't have to worry about getting caught.'

He looks around and spots the gap between the bricks in the wall. He tells Albert that he'll leave a note for him there the next day – with details of how they can meet in secret.

'But I don't want to force you into owt,' he adds. 'Only come if you want to.'

Then he smiles at him again, this time with a wolfish glint in his eye.

And with that, he saunters off.

Albert woke up alone in his bed, the room around him dark, and for a few seconds felt gripped by the excitement he'd experienced when he'd gone back to the ginnel and found the first note from George. It was an excitement laced with fear, fear of what he was giving in to, fear of what this said about him, fear of what would happen if anyone found out about it. But ultimately his excitement was so strong that it overpowered the fear.

Then he remembered.

He hadn't seen George for nearly fifty years. His life was empty. Gracie had died.

The heavy load of sadness pressed down on him again.

There was no longer any sound coming from the house next door, just a weighty silence all around him. He hadn't known it was possible for a human being to feel so lonely.

He had to do something.

He tried thinking back to a time when he felt connected to other people. The best he could come up with was the time just before his mam died. At least then he was still needed, even if he wasn't sure he was wanted. At least, back then, he still could feel a link to the life he'd led as a young man.

He suddenly felt compelled to do something he hadn't done in a long time. Before he knew it, he was hauling himself out of bed and plodding across the landing.

He stood in front of the door he'd hardly opened for eighteen years. And for the first time in a long while, he contemplated what was behind it.

Chapter Eleven

Albert pushed open the door to his mam's bedroom. He took in the sight of the heavy wooden bed, wardrobe and chest of drawers that matched the dining table and sideboard in the kitchen. He sat on the edge of the bed and heard the once-familiar creak of the mattress. The sound reminded him of his past, of all those years he'd spent caring for his mam . . . This is where he'd sat when he'd come in to check she was comfortable, when he'd laid out her tablets with a glass of water every morning, when he'd brought her meals, drinks and books to read. *This is where I sat when I got home from work and came to keep her company – and had to listen to her criticise me and make me feel like a waste of space.*

Albert rarely came in here since his mam had died, only forcing himself to give the room the occasional once-over with a Hoover and duster. Other than that, he'd left it exactly as it had been when his mam was alive. He knew other people might think that was morbid but it wasn't out of any lingering sense of sentimental attachment; he just hadn't seen the point in clearing it out – and he still didn't. *It's not as if I ever have any guests to stay over. And her old clothes and jewellery are hardly going to be worth anything.*

He looked at the bedside table and picked up a photo that stood in a silver frame. It showed a young Albert, aged three or four, with both his mam and dad standing behind him. He felt a sad smile crawling up his face but pursed his lips to force it away. The photo had been taken outside the front of the house, he had no idea who by; in those days, friends and neighbours popped in and out all the time. His parents must only have been in their twenties and both looked so young, his mam with her thick brunette hair and full figure, his dad with the big, bushy moustache of which he was so proud. They looked happy, too; his dad had his arm around his mam and her face was animated by a huge grin. But less than a decade after the photo had been taken, she'd stopped smiling altogether, after losing all the babies she'd conceived after Albert. Years later, he'd learned what he thought had caused his mam's despair; he'd seen a documentary about mothers and babies with blood groups that were 'rhesus incompatible', which meant that, although the first baby survived, subsequent pregnancies were affected by the antibodies that had built up since then. He hadn't, of course, understood any of this at the time; all he knew was that with each death his mam became more and more withdrawn, more desperate and more angry at the world. It was enough to repel their old friends and neighbours. That was when she started to take it out on Albert.

As if I didn't deserve to survive.

As if one of her other children would have turned out better than me.

As if my living could never outweigh so much disappointment.

He set the photo back on the table and took a long, slow breath.

He picked up the photo next to it, which was a professionally taken one of his dad in his police uniform and helmet, aged about thirty. Albert remembered his dad letting him try on his helmet, even though it came down well below his ears. He remembered watching him polish his silver badge and clean his shoes on an old newspaper he'd spread out on the kitchen table. He used to be so proud of his dad and would tell the other boys at school stories of him catching criminals and solving crimes, just like the characters in *Dixon of Dock Green* and *Z-Cars*. But, as he'd grown older, Albert's pride had morphed into shame – not a shame in his dad but in himself. Because it became clear that he could never be the son his dad wanted him to be.

Albert could remember so clearly his dad's expression of disgust as he'd sat at the breakfast table telling them about the late-night raids he'd carried out on the public toilets and the 'animals' he'd arrested for engaging in what he saw as the depraved act of having sex with other men, an act that at first he wouldn't name but, as Albert grew older, he'd describe in more detail – until his mam would protest and make him stop. But Albert was beginning to understand that he, too, was attracted to other men. He was beginning to understand that, however hard he tried, he just couldn't feel the same way about girls as his friends Tom and Colin did, that he just didn't want to do the kind of things they always talked about doing with girls. And no matter how guilty he felt about this, no matter how much he pretended it weren't true, he knew that if his dad ever found out, he wouldn't understand – and he'd find him every bit as depraved as the men he arrested in the public toilets.

He put the photo down and massaged his temples. Coming in here had certainly made him reconnect with his past. But that had only made him feel worse.

And yet, he felt compelled to carry on.

He unlocked the wardrobe door and reached up to the top shelf, where his mam had kept her albums of old photos: photos of the holidays they'd taken him on as a boy, and the times all three of them had dressed up for weddings and christenings. Resting on top of these he spotted an old tin box he'd been forbidden to touch and that his mam used to call her 'box of treasures'. When he was little she'd told him she'd put her old jewellery in there, and so, even after she'd gone, he'd never opened it. But now, for some reason, he wanted to. He lifted the tin down and placed it on the bed.

Albert removed the lid and lifted out several pieces of jewellery that looked like they could do with a good clean. Underneath, he found a battered old family Bible, at the front of which had been written the names and birth dates of everyone on his dad's side of the family. There was a lock of hair his mam had once shown him and said belonged to her own mother. And there was a pair of knitted baby booties with a matching bonnet and six of the wristbands given to patients admitted to hospital, each of them marked with his mam's name and date of birth. As he took them all out and spread them on the bed around him, Albert felt the sadness plucking at his heart.

But then he came to something else he hadn't expected to find, and it made him gasp out loud.

It was another old photo.

But this one was of him and another boy.

What? It can't be . . .

He felt as if every scrap of air had been knocked out of his lungs.

George. My George.

Albert hadn't seen the photo for nearly fifty years; he'd always assumed it had been destroyed. But now here it was, in front of him, and here was George bursting back to life, just as he was bursting back to life in his memories, with an intense, almost hyper-real, clarity. Albert was breathless with shock. He couldn't take his eyes off it.

The photo showed the two boys, aged sixteen, when they'd sneaked off to Blackpool for a day trip together. It showed them in a photographer's studio, dressed up as cowboys, with George's arm draped around Albert's shoulders. Although it was in black and white, so it didn't capture the intense blue of George's eyes, it did capture his fair hair and soft features. It also perfectly captured the boy Albert used to be. And one thing struck him about it more than any other.

I was happy then.

For one spring and summer I was completely happy . . .

He paused to catch his breath.

But what's the photo doing in Mam's box of treasures? How come it wasn't destroyed?

He put it to one side and delved back in to see what else was in there, hoping this might answer his questions. Underneath a small tin of old coins, he found a few tatty ration books, a scuffed silver locket with nothing inside, and a handful of faded postcards. Then Albert was shocked to find something else that belonged to him – something else he thought had been destroyed – a bundle of notes, each of which was labelled with the initial 'A'. Even though he hadn't seen these for nearly fifty years, he recognised them immediately. The sight of them jerked him back in time and set his heart rate soaring.

Surely not . . .? I don't understand . . .

These were the notes, the notes George had left for Albert, the notes he'd hidden in between two loose bricks in the outside wall of his yard. Several times a day, Albert had walked down the ginnel and slipped his fingers into the gap to see if there was anything there. This was how they'd been able to conduct their relationship, and how they'd been able to keep it secret. But now here the notes were, in his hands, bringing his secret life bursting into the present and reminding him of how happy he'd been each time he'd unfolded one of them. It was this happiness that had first inspired him to become a postman; in quite a simple way he'd thought that by delivering mail he'd get to spend his life making other people happy. If he hadn't been so shocked at finding the notes, he'd have allowed himself a smile at his youthful idealism.

As he unfolded the one on top, his heart began to thump in his chest.

Meet me on the railway bridge at the back of Toddington Hall at 7 o'clock. I know somewhere we can go.

Straight away the memories of that first meeting came crowding back into his head. But he held them at bay.

He picked up the next note.

If you fancy coming back for a second helping, I'll be free tonight. You know where to go.

Albert's heart slammed into his throat.

I don't believe it, they're all here. And they're actually in the order George sent them.

His fingers raced to the bottom of the pile. He unfolded the last note, the note George had sent him on that terrible night, that terrible night that had brought about the end of their relationship. And this note, far from making Albert happy, had thrust him into a deep unhappiness that had lasted the rest of his life.

He couldn't read it. He threw it back into the tin as if it were burning his hands.

But he couldn't tear himself away. Once again, he was mystified as to how it had found its way into his mam's room.

But this doesn't make any sense.

It changes so much of what I've believed for so long.

It changes so much of how I thought my secret life ended . . .

He wasn't sure he could bring himself to consider all the questions it raised. He began gathering up the jewellery and trinkets that were spread around him and placed them back into the tin with the photo of him and George. He pressed the bundle of notes carefully on top.

He snapped the lid shut and slid the tin back into the wardrobe. Then he closed his eyes and tried to calm his breathing.

As Albert walks towards the railway bridge, he feels the outline of George's first note in his pocket.

When he catches sight of George waiting for him, his heart leaps into his throat.

I'm doing this. I'm actually doing it.

As he draws closer, he's so nervous his hands begin to tingle.

When he comes to a stop before George, he isn't sure whether to shake his hand or hug him. In the end, he does neither but gives an awkward shuffle on the spot.

'So you came,' says George.

'Yeah, of course I came.'

Albert doesn't like to say he very nearly didn't. He doesn't like to say he's been fighting the urge to come ever since he found George's note. He certainly isn't going to say he's made a deal with himself that he's only going to come once. *Just this once to get it out of my system. Just this once, then I'll get back to being normal.*

As if picking up on his unease, George gives him a gentle smile and touches him, once, lightly, on the arm. 'Come on. Come with me.'

He begins striding off towards the hillside that leads up to the moors and Albert follows, quickening his pace to keep up. He can see that the path ahead is muddy and is glad he's worn his boots.

'Where are we going?' he asks.

'I'll tell you when we get there,' replies George. 'It's a secret place nobody knows about. But it's a good way off. I hope you don't mind a walk.'

Albert says that he doesn't, and there's a short silence. They stumble to fill it with a stilted conversation about school and which teachers and lessons they like. George asks Albert what his mam and dad do for work and if they've always lived in Toddington. And Albert asks George about his impressions of the town and if his family have settled in yet.

'I think my mam and dad quite like it here now,' he replies. 'We moved because my dad got a job in the bedding factory and it's a step up from what he were doing before. My mam works from home as a seamstress; she takes in repairs and does alterations for the posh department store in town.'

Albert nods but is so nervous – and excited – that he finds it difficult to concentrate. As they continue walking, his heart beats twice for every step he takes. He knows that once they're at this secret place they'll start kissing again, kissing like they did the other day. After that, he doesn't know what will happen. Although he's terrified of finding out, at the same time he's gripped by such desperation that he can feel it twitching in every muscle of his body.

After a while, they come to a cluster of woodland and George holds up the branches of a tree so Albert can pass underneath.

'Bloomin' 'eck,' says Albert, his anxiety intensifying for a moment. 'Where are you taking me?'

George laughs. 'Don't panic, we're nearly there now.'

When they emerge on the other side, George points to a bunker that looks like it was put there during the Second World War.

'That's it,' he says. 'What do you think?'

'Yeah, it's terrific, that is,' says Albert. He strides around the perimeter, pretending to peruse it. But all he can think about is what they're going to do when they go inside.

Hell fire, am I really going to go through with this?

Just get in there and get on with it, lad.

'Nobody ever comes here,' George reassures him, 'especially not in the evenings. It's miles away from anywhere.'

He steps through the entrance and Albert follows him.

'It's a bit low,' George warns, 'so you have to crouch—'

But before he can take another step, Albert lunges towards him and kisses him hungrily.

George gives a gasp that morphs into a chuckle. 'By 'eck, someone's feeling lusty. And here's me thinking we've come up here to admire the view.'

Albert doesn't say anything but kisses him again. He kisses him with more confidence than he did that first time in the ginnel. And he reaches up with his hands and buries them in George's beautiful, fair hair. But he's so eager and agitated that he's worried he's kissing him too forcefully.

After a while, George pulls away. 'Steady on!' he teases. 'You're like a bull at a gate.'

Albert frowns. 'Sorry, I'm a bit het up. I haven't done this before.'

'Well, we ain't in a race,' George says, 'there's no rush. Just try and relax.'

He kisses Albert more softly. And, to Albert's surprise, each of his soft, gentle kisses has more impact than all of his more forceful kisses put together. He follows George's lead and lets him set the pace. As he does, a warm, hazy feeling spreads through him and all of his fear fades away. It's as if the edges of his world are softening.

'That's better, isn't it?' asks George.

'Yeah,' says Albert, 'that's lovely, that is.'

It's so lovely how could anyone say it's wrong?

George lifts his collar and begins stroking Albert's neck. When he touches his skin, Albert feels it burn. He had no idea that the simple act of touching could be so erotic. He had no idea that his skin could be so sensitive.

Before he knows it, he's pulling off his jumper and George is doing the same. They toss them on to the ground and, as skin touches skin, Albert feels that warmth transforming into a raging fire inside him.

In that moment, he knows there's no way he can stick to the deal he's made with himself.

There's no way I can come here just once.

Chapter Twelve

For three days after Albert shut the door on his mam's room, he stayed in the house and festered in his own sadness.

He remembered once hearing a comedian on a TV panel show describing the period in between Christmas and New Year as the 'perineum' of the year. At first he hadn't known what she'd meant but when he'd looked up the word he'd realised it was a perfectly accurate description and had laughed out loud. Now he didn't find it funny at all.

He didn't feel like doing anything so he dragged his duvet downstairs and lay under it on the sofa. He couldn't be bothered cooking so mainly ate his food raw or just had bowls of porridge. He thought about doing his laundry and put a load of his work uniforms in the washing machine but forgot to take them out and, when he did eventually remember, decided to just leave them. He felt no inclination to water the pot plants or clear away Gracie's uneaten food, which had stiffened so it looked like scraps of cardboard scattered in the bowl. In the morning, he couldn't even face pulling back the curtains so left them closed.

After days without speaking to anyone, he began to feel desperate to use his own voice. When he saw an advertisement on TV for a 'virtual assistant' called Alexa, he considered buying one just so he could talk to it – but he was so bad with technology there was no way he'd be able to set it up. Eventually, he settled for speaking to Gracie, even though she wasn't there any more.

'Hello, my little girl,' he said, 'wouldn't it be nice if we could have a cuddle?'

But the lack of response only made him even more aware of his loneliness.

When it came round to Sunday, he'd run out of milk and had nothing left to eat. However much he wanted to stay at home, he had to get out of his pyjamas, take a shower and get dressed. He had to go to the shop.

As he stepped into the cold air and closed his front door behind him, he felt vulnerable and a little frightened. *Get out of it, lad. You've walked down these streets thousands of times.*

He pulled his coat around him and set off. When he hit the main road, he spotted the gay couple who'd moved into Pear Tree Street on the other side of the road, walking in the direction of Toddington Hall. The men caught sight of him and gave an enthusiastic wave. Albert trained his eyes on the pavement and pretended he hadn't seen them.

When he reached the shop, Ted Hardacre was speaking to someone on the phone. Albert's response to this was disappointment, rather than his usual relief. He picked up a pint of milk, some porridge oats, a Warburton's loaf and a tin of beans, and handed them over with a £10 note. But Ted gave him his change without breaking away from the phone. Albert slipped out of the shop in silence.

He decided to walk home the short way. The Flowers Estate was quieter than he'd ever seen it, although Nicole Ashton was standing outside her front door in her big fluffy slippers with a dressing gown wrapped around her. She was sending messages on her phone and smoking a cigarette. As he drew nearer, he noticed she was crying.

Before he could think about it, he found himself calling out to her. 'What's the matter? Are you alright?' It was as if the words had escaped from a long-forgotten compartment, buried somewhere deep inside him, a compartment that had recently been rediscovered.

Nicole looked up and seemed surprised that he'd spoken to her. She dropped her phone into a pocket and knuckled the tears out of her eyes. 'Oh, hello, postie.'

Albert came to a halt at the bottom of her path and rested the bread and milk on her gate. 'How do,' he said. 'I was just wondering if you're OK.'

With every word he spoke he surprised himself more. *Albert, what's got into you?*

Nicole took a drag on her cigarette and slowly blew out the smoke. 'To be honest,' she said, 'I've been better. My boyfriend's parents don't want us to be together, and I think he might be mugging me off.'

Albert wasn't sure what that meant but he got the general gist. 'I'm sorry about that,' he said, then he paused.

If I carry on speaking to her, she's going to start a conversation every time I see her. She's going to think I want to be her friend. For a moment – so brief, he wasn't even sure it happened – part of him wondered if that was what he was hoping, if that was why he'd stopped and called out to her in the first place.

'You know, I'm worried he can't be proud of me,' she went on. 'I'm worried he wants to hide me away like some dirty secret. Do you have any idea how that makes me feel?'

Albert looked down and kicked a stone off the path. 'I do, yeah,' he said, gravely. 'I know just how that makes you feel.'

Nicole stubbed out her cigarette on the wall. 'I'm supposed to have stopped smoking,' she said, 'but I can't face it at the moment.'

Albert nodded. He wanted to leave. But at the same time, it was as if he were rooted to the spot.

'You know, I really want us to be together,' Nicole continued, 'and I really think he's worth fighting for. But I don't know whether I'm deluding myself now. Oh, maybe I should just give up on it.'

Albert felt another pain in his chest and the image in the photo of him and George flashed through his mind.

'Don't give up,' he found himself saying.

Nicole looked at him expectantly.

'A long time ago . . . well . . . a *very* long time ago, I was in love with someone I was told I shouldn't be. We had to keep it a secret.'

There was a short silence.

'But it ended. And I've regretted that ever since.'

Albert stood still as he considered what he'd said. He couldn't believe he'd just given someone who was almost a complete stranger a glimpse into his big secret, the secret that had determined the course of his life. The full impact of what he'd done suddenly hit him.

He had to leave.

But Nicole was walking down the path towards him. 'So what happened to her? Why did it end?'

Albert knew that there was no way he could answer the question. At least, no way he could answer it that would make him feel comfortable. 'Sorry, I've got to go.'

He picked up his bread and milk and walked away.

Albert only went out of the house on one other occasion. That was to pick up Gracie's ashes from the vet's. He was given them in a little wooden casket with a nameplate attached and when he got home he put it on the mantelpiece so he could see her from the sofa.

'There, that's nice,' he said to her. 'Just the two of us, together again.'

It was New Year's Eve and he made himself beans on toast for tea then settled down on the sofa. He switched on a chat show in which a Hollywood actor was telling the presenter how he'd fallen in love with his latest leading lady, despite the fact there was a twenty-year age difference and both of them were married.

'Oh, we knew people wouldn't approve,' he told the host, 'but we just couldn't stop ourselves.'

All of a sudden, Albert saw himself on screen. The actor's

words reminded him of how hard he'd tried to resist developing feelings for George.

He found himself rising to his feet and going back to his mam's room. Once there, he opened the wardrobe and pulled out the tin box. This time, rather than sitting on his mam's bed to lift out the contents, he took it downstairs.

He switched off the TV and lowered himself on to the sofa. He pulled out the bundle of notes and slid out the one from the top of the pile. Once again, there was George's handwriting looking up at him, in exactly the same way as it had before, nearly fifty years ago. Every line, bar and curl reconnected him with the boy he'd been when he'd first set eyes on it. He remembered thinking that George's handwriting was much freer and more flamboyant than his own. His was neat and boxy, and each of his letters could probably have still fit into the squares of the graph paper he'd learned on. But George's hinted at a much more riotous, undisciplined personality.

Like all of George's subsequent notes, this first one was signed simply with the initial 'G'; it would have been far too risky for him to write out his name in full. Albert put it down and began reading the others. At the beginning they were brief, as neither of the boys wanted to commit to paper emotions which, if discovered, could have landed them in jail; just three years earlier, Albert's dad had railed about homosexuality being made legal, but, when an intrigued Albert had looked the story up in the newspaper, he'd discovered the age of consent was twenty-one, an age the boys were still several years from reaching. So George's early notes bore simple messages, suggesting nights to meet up or telling Albert he was thinking of him.

The sun is shining and I'm smiling because I know it's shining on you too.

But then one note made him sit up and let out a little gasp.

The bluebells you gave me are beautiful. Every time I look at them I think of you.

Albert sighed.

On the fifth evening he goes to the moors to meet George, Albert's walking through the woodland and notices that a thick carpet of bluebells is springing up around him. He's never paid much attention to bluebells; they're just a wild flower that appears in the Lancashire countryside every spring. But it suddenly strikes him that the flowers aren't just blue; they're such an intense shade of blue that it borders on violet – and reminds him of George's eyes. He picks a bunch and takes it to the bunker.

When he sees George, he holds up the flowers so they catch the last rays of sunlight. And he notices that their shade of blue does indeed match the exact shade of George's eyes.

'How do, George,' he says. 'I picked these for you.'

George gives a smile so wide it almost reaches his ears. 'Oh Albert, they're lovely!'

'I thought they'd match your eyes,' Albert explains.

George lets out a loud sigh. 'Albert Entwistle, I never knew you were so *romantic*!'

Albert wrinkles his nose as George lightly kisses him on the cheek. 'Yeah, well, let's not get carried away. That's probably about as romantic as I get.'

But he's so gratified by how happy the flowers make George that for the rest of the spring, Albert takes him a bunch of bluebells every time they meet.

Albert set the note down on the sofa and felt his Adam's apple swelling in his throat. Before he knew it, he was crying deep, guttural tears. It was the first time he'd allowed himself to cry for decades and, once he started, he couldn't stop.

When he was little, if he ever cried, his dad would say he looked like a 'melted welly'. Now not only must his face look like it was melting, but he could also feel snot leaking out of his nose and a low wailing sound escaping from his mouth. The heat prickled his face and his body began convulsing, as if in shock at expelling such an intense emotion after such a long time. But even though Albert was feeling acute pain, he was dimly aware that part of him was pleased to feel it. Because it transported him back to a time when he'd lived with the intensity of his feelings for George. Slowly, the gulf between who he was then and the man he'd become since was beginning to close.

Have I really changed that much after all?

As the tears finally began to slow and he dried his eyes with a handkerchief, Albert wondered where George might be now. If he, too, might not be so very different from the boy he'd been all those years ago. He pictured what he might look like today and allowed himself to wonder what he might be doing.

Might there even be a chance our story isn't over?

Then he checked himself. He remembered the last time he'd seen George; when the person he loved more than anyone else in the world had looked him in the eye with a very different emotion to the one that had lit up both of their lives since the night of the funfair.

George had looked at him with an emotion Albert had recognised as hatred. And he'd said quite clearly that he never wanted to see him again.

Albert remembered why he'd be wrong to allow himself any hope. He remembered why he'd had to bury his emotions, leave them in the past, and move on. And as he did, he could feel George slipping away from him again.

Oh, I've made such a mess of everything. I had everything I wanted and I let it go.

He put the notes back in the tin and replaced the lid. He realised that when he himself died, whoever was clearing out the house would probably stumble on the notes and have no idea of the passion that inspired them. In which case, it would be as if Albert had never felt such emotions, as if he'd never loved George. *And it will be just like Mam always said; I really will have been a waste of space.*

He went through to the kitchen and pulled a bottle of cider out of the fridge. On his way back from the vet's he'd called into an off-licence on the other side of town; he'd wanted to pick up several bottles without Ted Hardacre asking questions. He poured out a pint glass and sank half of it in one swig. He may have spent most of his life avoiding alcohol but, now that he thought about it, the only good thing that had ever happened to him had come about as a direct result of alcohol obliterating his inhibitions.

And now I want it to obliterate me.

I want to stop feeling like this.

I just want it to be over.

He picked up the glass and drained it dry.

Chapter Thirteen

'I love you, Albert.'

George says the words softly as the two boys are lying on the blankets they've dragged out of the bunker and on to the hillside. It's the beginning of May and they've been sneaking off to meet up in their secret place for just over a month. In that time, the weather's changed and the days have started to become warmer, although the evenings are still cold, especially if the sky's clear, as it is on this particular evening. Neither of the boys wants to light a fire in case anyone down in the town spots the smoke and wonders who's up there. But if they spread their coats over themselves and cuddle each other tightly, it's just about warm enough for them to lie under the stars.

They've spent most of the evening trying to spot the constellations – but the only one they've been able to find is the Plough. Instead, they've made up their own formations, pointing out to each other the shape of a seesaw, a sheep, a dog, and even a wheelbarrow. Then George tries to convince

Albert that he can see stars arranged in the shape of a love heart. That's when he comes out with his declaration.

'I love you, Albert Entwistle,' he says again.

Albert pulls George closer to him and runs his fingers through his fine, fair hair. 'What do you mean, you love me? Can two lads say that?'

'I don't see why not,' George replies. 'Just because we ain't heard two lads say it before don't mean they can't.'

Albert pauses to think this over. No one has ever told him they love him – he's never even heard anyone say the words to someone else. The only time he's heard people talking about love is when he's watching a film at the pictures, and that's always a man loving a woman or a woman loving a man. His parents don't talk about love at home; families like his just don't use that kind of language. And for years Albert has lived in fear that if his parents ever find out about the way he is then they'll *stop* loving him. Not only that, but he's had so many reminders of what everyone around him thinks of people like him – and not just the boys at school but all the adults he knows who spit out the word 'queer' as if they're disgusted even to let it hover on their lips – that he's gradually come to believe he's so rotten and wrong, deep in his core, that no one could ever possibly love him. That he's actually unlovable. That he'll never get to feel or share in the emotion that all the films and pop songs tell him is the most amazing thing in the world. That he's destined for a life of loneliness and misery. And now here's George telling him not only that he loves him, but that he loves him exactly as he is, almost *because* of the way he is. *Finally, it makes me feel I'm not rotten or wrong.*

It's a lot to take in, and Albert isn't sure how to react. At the same time, hearing those words does something wonderful to him. It's as if they've set his heart free – and he can feel it taking flight.

George sits up and looks at him with those vividly blue, almost violet, eyes. 'Come on then,' he says, a nervous smile playing at his lips.

'Come on what?'

'You're supposed to say it back to me now.'

Albert hesitates once more. There's no question of his feelings, there's no question that he feels the same way about George. George does something to him that no one and nothing else in his life has ever come close to doing. Just thinking about George makes him well up with an intense, beautiful joy. Just picturing his face makes him frightened of the lengths he'd go to, the sacrifices he'd be prepared to make, in order to make him happy. For a while Albert has been carrying around this feeling without quite knowing what it is – and now he has a word to describe it. But he isn't sure he can say that word out loud, especially not with George looking directly at him. He feels too self-conscious.

'But don't you think it sounds a bit daft?' he argues.

'Oh, so what if it is?' says George. 'There are worse things in life than sounding a bit daft.'

Go on, lad, say it. Say that little word.

Albert looks up at the stars. 'In that case,' he says, 'I love you too.'

He hasn't realised that, as well as feeling wonderful when the words are said to him, saying them himself will make him feel just as good. As he does, it's as if his heart soars up into the sky.

'There,' says George, 'I bet you can see that heart now, can't you? I bet you can see that heart in the stars.'

Albert laughs and kisses George gently on the forehead.

'Yeah, I can see it,' he says. And he turns to face him. 'And I do love you, George.'

Albert woke up on the sofa, his head resting on the side of a cushion, the zip digging into his cheek. He was fully clothed and had a tongue that was desperately dry. Lying next to him was his mam's tin, the lid askew and the notes lying open inside.

He felt a powerful urge to be sick.

Albert had no idea how long he'd been out for the count, but daylight was streaming through the curtains and he had to blink until his eyes adjusted. When he stood up, his head throbbed violently. He staggered over to the mirror and saw that his skin was the colour of mushy peas.

Hell fire, is this a hangover? He'd only had one before, and it had been so long ago he could barely remember. Although he was pretty sure this one was worse.

He was desperate for a drink and lurched through to the kitchen, where he drew himself up in front of the sink and glugged down as much water as he could, straight from the tap. He grabbed some strong painkillers from his first-aid box and tossed them into his mouth, washing them down with one more gulp of water. He turned off the tap and took several deep breaths.

Bloomin' 'eck, I feel awful. What have I done to myself?

But somehow, the physical pain he was experiencing began to unchain something within him; it ignited some kind of survival instinct. Without him making any conscious decision, something told him he couldn't stay like this; he needed to do everything he could to make himself feel better.

He dragged himself up to the bathroom, where he took off his clothes, ran a shower and stood under the jets of hot water for much longer than it took to get himself clean. After he'd dried himself, he brushed his teeth and went through to his bedroom to get dressed.

Once the painkillers had kicked in and his headache was receding, he found that he wanted to improve the state of his surroundings too. When he came back downstairs he noticed that the house was starting to smell like a blocked drain. He cleared away his empty bottles and put them in the recycling bin. Then, without even thinking about it, he took out the Hoover and duster and threw himself into a blast of housework. He rescued his work uniforms from the washing machine and, when he sniffed them and realised they'd started to rot, put them back in again with a double dose of detergent. He watered the plants and emptied the bins of all the rubbish that had built up over the last few days. He threw away his Christmas cards and, without any sentimentality, scraped the dried-up food out of Gracie's bowl and washed it. He gathered up her Christmas presents plus a few other old toys, took the casket down from the mantelpiece, and put all her belongings in an old shoebox, all of which he took upstairs and pushed under his bed. He didn't need any of it lying around; if he wanted to remember Gracie, he had plenty of photos.

'Don't worry, my little girl,' he said out loud, 'I won't forget you.'

Now there's another memory I need to deal with.

Without stopping to think about it, he went back downstairs and picked up his mam's tin. He took out the notes George had sent him and the photo of the two of them together and propped them up on the mantelpiece in the space left by Gracie's casket. Then he took the tin back up to his mam's room. As he slid it back into her wardrobe, he remembered clutching it last night and thinking about what would happen when he died. Suddenly this seemed like a ridiculous thought; today was the start of a new year and he should be thinking about life, not death. *I should be coming up with resolutions to make my life better, not thinking about giving up on it.*

Before he knew it, this is what he found himself doing. And the funny thing was, even though everything in his head felt foggy, at the same time he could see things much more clearly than he had for a very long time.

One thought stood out from all the others.

I can't go on living like this. I might have thirty years left.

I want them to be happy.

Albert could see now that for decades he'd been loosely holding on to an empty, grey life. But today was a new day. As of today, he wanted to take his life in both hands and squeeze it tightly, to get everything he could out of it while he still could. And he was ready to make whatever changes were necessary for this to happen, however difficult they might be.

As he continued to blast through his chores, Albert felt a new spirit stirring within him. He recognised it as the same spirit that inspired him to dance around to music when no one was looking. Now that he thought about it, it was the same spirit that had flickered to life when he'd given Jack Brew a baby's bib at the Christmas party. It might even have been the same spirit that had led him to drink last night – not, as he'd thought, because he'd been looking to obliterate himself, but because he'd wanted to recreate the state he'd been in when he'd been brave enough to kiss George. The state he'd been in when he'd allowed love to enter his life.

He looked at the photo of George standing with his arm around him and felt a new determination growing. It was a determination to bring love back into his life.

Because, without Gracie, without his job as a postman, he'd convinced himself that there was no hope – but now he could feel his hope reawakening. And, however he looked at it, there was no escaping the fact that there was only one way for Albert to improve his life. There was only one way for him to feel happy again.

He picked up the photo.

'George, I'm coming to find you.'

Chapter Fourteen

Nicole leaned on the buggy and pushed Reenie down the high street. Overhead, the sky formed a sheet of unbroken grey that looked like it would soon give way to rain. The Christmas lights still swung from the lamp posts and merrily skipped across the road, but they were joined by a horde of signs promising spectacular reductions in the January sales. As it was a Friday morning, only a few elderly shoppers had come to take advantage. And now the rush to look good for Christmas and New Year had passed, very few people were visiting the town's three beauty salons. But it was to look at these that Nicole had caught the bus to the high street. She wanted to focus her mind on her long-term career goals. *And my New Year's resolution of moving one step closer to achieving them.*

She stopped outside the first salon and pretended to browse a list of treatments in the window. But her gaze drifted to the other side of the glass, to a beautician with a spray tan that made her look like an amber traffic light. She was busy painting a customer's nails glittery pink.

'Look at that, big girl,' Nicole said to Reenie. 'That's what Mummy's going to do when she's finished college. That's why Mummy has to leave you to go and study, so that one day she can do the same thing as that nice lady in the white coat.'

At that moment, the nice lady in the white coat glanced up and spotted Nicole – and shot her a look that could strip the enamel off teeth.

Nicole returned the woman's look with a scowl. 'As it happens, I've always thought that place is a bit tacky.'

She pushed the buggy on, with her spine straight and her chin up, determined not to be discouraged.

She wheeled Reenie to a stop in front of the next salon, a much more upmarket establishment, and gave her a drink from her bottle of juice as she glanced through the window.

'Now this salon is fancy,' she told Reenie. 'This is where the posh ladies come.'

She watched a couple of skinny white women chatting to a taut-faced receptionist. When the customers disappeared into the treatment rooms, the receptionist sat on a stool and began tapping away at her computer, her back ramrod straight.

'Posh!' shouted Reenie. And she waved at the woman excitedly.

Although Nicole spotted the receptionist's eyes flick upwards, the woman pretended not to notice them.

'Never mind her,' she told Reenie. 'Mummy's salon won't be anything like that either. That place is much too stuck-up for people like us.'

She lifted the brake and moved on.

This year she was late making her New Year's resolutions as she'd been to a party on New Year's Eve. She'd been invited to Lisa's place along with the rest of their school friends and this suited her as it meant Reenie could go to sleep in the spare bedroom and she didn't have to find – or pay for – a babysitter. So Nicole had packed their things in an overnight bag and caught the bus to Huddlesden, excited to enjoy her first night out since moving away. Her friends had been keen to find out how things were going with Jamie, especially after the big argument they'd had on Boxing Day. She'd told them that, despite her concerns, she'd decided to keep faith in the relationship.

'Well, that's great,' Lisa had said, 'I hope he comes good. But don't push him; wait till he's ready to commit. Relax and let him come to you.'

Instinctively, this kind of advice made Nicole bridle. But Lisa was so insistent that she'd found herself overruling her misgivings and following her suggestion. So when Jamie had texted her the following day to ask if they could meet up, she'd agreed. When he'd come to visit her at home, she'd made sure they'd enjoyed themselves, without initiating any kind of confrontation – and had done the same the following night. She hadn't even complained when he'd left at the end of the night to go and sleep at his parents' house. But she was finding it hard to take such a passive role in the relationship. To make up for it, she'd decided to focus on another area of her life over which she *could* exert some control. And that's what had brought her to the high street; she was looking for something to stoke her ambition, looking to visualise exactly what it was she was working towards.

She parked Reenie's buggy outside the third salon, directly in front of the window, and crouched down next to Reenie.

'Now this place is called Top to Toe,' she told her, 'and it's my favourite salon in all of Toddington.'

The two of them fell into silence as they watched a pair of cheery girls in branded uniforms chatting happily to their customers. When one of the girls spotted them, she said something to her colleague and they both turned and waved.

'Look at that, big girl!' said Nicole. 'They're waving at you! One day, I want to work there. And one day, I want to run my own salon just like it. One that does treatments for girls with hair like me and you!'

Reenie clapped her hands.

'Mummy promises she's going to work really hard to make it happen. Mummy's going to work really hard, so me and you can stop worrying about money, so me and you can have whatever we want.'

As she kissed Reenie on the head, she could feel her inner lioness stirring. She reminded herself that, after the instability of the last few years, what she wanted more than anything was to create a stable environment in which to bring up her cub. *And I'm ready to do whatever it takes.*

She felt the first drops of rain on her forehead. 'Come on, let's go.'

She set off down the street. Although it was raining, she refused to bow her head, and made sure she was walking tall. She took a long, fortifying breath.

She was ready to see Jamie.

*

'Have a good trip, baby,' said Nicole. 'Try not to miss me too much.'

She flashed him a playful grin.

'Oh, I can't promise that,' he replied. 'Anyway, I'm not sure I'd *want* to stop missing you.'

He smiled at her with his eyes and Nicole felt her heart give a little wobble.

The two of them were standing on the main concourse of Toddington's train station. Jamie was about to catch the train back to Leeds for the start of the new term and Nicole had made sure Reenie was asleep in her buggy before coming to see him off. She looked up to check the digital clock next to the departures board; there were still fifteen minutes to go until his train set off for Leeds. Surrounding him on the floor were a big suitcase full of clothes, toiletries and books, plus a rucksack and a Waitrose bag for life, both of which were stuffed full of the Christmas presents he'd received. Nicole couldn't help noticing the box for some kind of posh coffee machine peeping out of the big carrier bag. It prompted her to wonder just how wealthy his family was. His mum was a doctor and his dad a lawyer but she didn't really have any idea what kind of money people doing jobs like that earned. Although, if his parents didn't want him to see her, that suggested he lived in a world very different to hers – and one they thought far superior. *But I'm not going to let that make me feel inadequate.*

She did her best to look nonchalant. 'Thanks again for the earrings,' she said, angling her ears towards him so he could see. 'They're gorgeous.'

'It was my pleasure,' he said. 'And they look beautiful on you.'

As she smiled, Nicole realised how strange it felt to be out with Jamie in a public place; so much of their relationship until now had been spent in her house, because she struggled to find childcare when the college was closed. As soon as this thought occurred to her, she found herself wanting to gauge how he'd react to being seen in public with her and Reenie and make sure his parents' disapproval wasn't having any effect. *I want to make sure he isn't trying to keep us secret.*

She took Jamie's hand and kissed it, then held it up to her cheek. When he smiled and began to stroke the side of her face, she felt a flurry of relief. Not for a second did he look around to check if anyone had seen them; his eyes stayed trained on her.

'You know, I'm sorry things have been a bit tense lately,' he said. 'I know it can't have been easy for you. And I really appreciate you being so patient.'

Nicole felt delighted that he'd brought up the subject but forced herself to suppress a smile. 'That's OK, baby,' she said, 'I'm perfectly chill about it.'

I know that's not strictly true but at least I want it to be.

'Anyway,' she went on, 'I start back at college on Monday so I'll have my hands full before I know it.'

'Well, good luck,' he said. 'I'll think of you when I'm stuck in the library.'

He stroked her cheek one more time and leaned in to kiss her fully on the lips.

Oh, it's obvious how he feels about you. You just need to try and genuinely chill about it.

Out of nowhere, she remembered the advice she'd been given by the postman, who'd told her something very different to Lisa. He'd surprised her by stopping in the street and telling her that she should do everything she could to fight for the relationship. And one of the reasons why the advice – coming from such an unlikely source – had made such an impression on her was because she'd known it was just what her grandma would have said.

Nicole had always enjoyed a close relationship with her grandma. It was her grandma who'd taught her how to cook and braid her hair. It was her grandma who'd looked after her while her mum had gone out on countless dates. It was her grandma who'd stepped in every time her mum's latest boyfriend had left her. But it wasn't just that Nicole depended on her; despite the huge difference in age, she'd always felt that her grandma was a kindred spirit and someone who loved and would never judge her. And that's why she'd named her daughter after her – although as soon as her personality had begun to come through, she'd shortened Irene to Reenie. But her grandma had never met her namesake; she'd died when she was only in her mid-sixties, shortly before Nicole had found out she was pregnant. With all the drama that had been going on at the time, she wasn't sure she'd grieved for her properly – it was only since moving to Toddington that she'd allowed herself to give in to the full force of her sadness. And then, just when she was wishing she could speak to her grandma about Jamie, the postie had appeared and for a brief moment it was almost like he was taking her place, as if her grandma were speaking to her through him.

But now here she was in the station with Jamie, and that kind old postie and her grandma seemed so far away.

'Actually, Nic,' Jamie said suddenly, 'before I go, I just want to tell you that I think you're amazing.'

She gave a little scoff. 'You what? What are you on about?'

'Just the way you juggle everything – being a mum and going to college and running a home. You're amazing. And I'm really proud of you. I'm really proud you're my girlfriend.'

Nicole could feel the happiness lighting her up from within. She reminded herself to keep cool. 'Oh, yeah, well, sometimes I'm not quite sure how I do it myself. But thanks, baby, thanks a lot.'

They said their goodbyes and Jamie leaned down to kiss a sleeping Reenie on the forehead. Then he picked up his bags and kissed Nicole one last time. She watched him walk away, show his ticket to the staff at the barriers, then turn to give her one final wave.

'Let him go off and do his thing and he'll come back to you,' Lisa had advised.

But no matter how many times she repeated this to herself, it still didn't feel right.

And she missed her grandma.

Chapter Fifteen

Albert cycled down the main road into town. He was nervous about starting what was going to be a new phase in his life. But – for the first time since that spring and summer in his teens – he was brimming with hope about the future.

It was a frosty morning so he'd wrapped himself up with a thick scarf, woollen gloves and two pairs of socks. It was his first day back at work since Christmas; on New Year's Day he'd texted Marjorie to ask if he could take the rest of the week off work as annual leave. He'd apologised for the short notice but knew she wouldn't complain as he still had so much holiday to take. Once she'd agreed, he'd set about using the time off to prepare himself for his search for George.

Although he had no idea what this would involve, he did know that George had left Toddington, so at the very least it was likely Albert would have to travel, probably to somewhere he'd never been before. People on TV often talked about stepping outside their comfort zone, and Albert was well aware that his was much smaller than most. If he was going to be straying outside its limits, he wanted to make sure he was ready.

He'd started by going into a mobile phone shop to upgrade his smartphone to a more advanced model. The man who'd served him had sold him a handset with more memory and capacity and had also showed him how to perform basic searches on the internet and use the app store so he could set up a personal email account. Although Albert knew most people could perform these tasks without giving them a second thought, he allowed himself a feeling of satisfaction at conquering his first hurdle.

Next, he'd logged on to Amazon and ordered a book about building up your confidence and had read it through twice. Then he'd accessed YouTube and watched several motivational videos that were packed with useful advice.

'Fight your demons.'

'Feel the fear and do it anyway.'

'Do one thing that scares you every day.'

Feeling emboldened, he'd sat down one morning and typed 'George Atkinson' into Google. But all he'd found had been articles about a famous American football player. If it hadn't been immediately obvious that this wasn't the George he knew, discovering that the footballer's nickname was 'Butch' had extinguished any last glimmers of hope. Albert had gone on to trawl through page after page of search results. But still there was no sign of his George. He'd tried every possible spelling of his name, including adding his middle name and initials, but nothing had worked. He'd even tried searching for George's parents and sister. That, too, had proved unsuccessful.

But he wouldn't let it get to him. He wouldn't feel daunted or bewildered. He hadn't seen George for nearly fifty years; tracking him down was never going to be easy.

The next step was to look on social media – but so far this was proving much more difficult. He'd downloaded the apps for Facebook, Twitter and Instagram and had set up accounts using his name, email address and the password GeorgeAtkinson1953. But very soon his excitement had given way to dismay when he'd been asked to choose privacy settings, find friends he didn't have, upload photos, and add a location. It was starting to feel like too much.

He'd come to the conclusion that he was going to have to ask someone for help. He knew this would involve interacting with whoever he asked on a much deeper level than he was used to. He wasn't sure he could do it. But then he'd remembered: you should do something that scares you every day.

As he cycled through the dark, empty streets, he thought about which of his colleagues he could ask. He decided against Jack, Smiler and Sue; they sat next to him, so knowing he was indebted to them ran the risk of making him feel uncomfortable. There was Ste, who was always on social media, but Albert couldn't face being drawn into yet another conversation about his gym routine.

Then, all of a sudden, another, more surprising, idea popped into his head. It was a little radical, but at the same time something told him it might just be right.

It was a person he'd probably be seeing on his walk later that day. It was a person he'd initially found a little hard but had recently discovered was actually quite soft. And it was a person who'd recently told him she was in some kind of relationship that provoked disapproval and had to remain secret – just like his with George had.

Nicole Ashton.

On the surface, Nicole was so different to Albert and such an unlikely person to ask that he wondered if he was actually losing his mind. But he dismissed his reservations and followed his instinct. *After all, I've decided that I need to shake up my life and break out of this rut.*

He assured himself that he was ready to do it.

As he walked into the main sorting office, Albert was met by an atmosphere of weariness. All activity seemed to be unfolding much more slowly than it had before Christmas; the chatter of his colleagues was reduced to a desultory hum, and the staff sifting through the sacks of mail were doing so as if in a trance.

Albert went over to his sorting frame and hung up his coat and high-vis vest. But rather than pursuing his usual strategy of avoiding his colleagues, he decided that he was going to be brave and speak to them.

'How do,' he said to no one in particular. And then he added, 'Happy New Year.'

'Alright, Albert,' came the mumbled, communal response, with a couple of heads raised in mild curiosity. 'Happy New Year.'

He glanced around and saw that Tsunami was engrossed in entering a competition to win a holiday, presumably looking to brighten up her new year. Jack was moaning to a friend about his wife Doreen putting him on a healthy eating plan. And even Smiler wasn't smiling but telling one of the other postmen about some kind of stand-off he was having with his teenage daughter.

'I never thought it would happen,' he said with a sigh, 'but she told me I'm embarrassing.'

Even though Albert had taken an extra week off, nobody seemed remotely curious to discover what he'd been up to. *Can't they tell I've had a momentous two weeks? Can't they read it on my face?*

He supposed he'd become rather good at pushing them away. But he reminded himself that he'd come into work determined to engage in conversation – if only to warm himself up for the conversation he was hoping to have with Nicole. He decided to go and speak to Marjorie; he hadn't seen her since their altercation at the Christmas party and needed to face her at some point. Besides, of all his colleagues, she was usually the one who was most up for a chat.

Come on, lad, she won't bite. She's just got a big gob on her, that's all. It might be awkward but you can do it.

He approached Marjorie's office and, as ever, the door was standing wide open. As he drew nearer, he saw that the windows had been flung open too, letting in gusts of wintry air. Marjorie was sitting at her desk, trying to cool herself down with the fan she'd been given by Secret Santa.

'How do, Marjorie.'

She looked up from her computer. 'Oh, hiya, Albert. Just give me a minute, I'm burning up.'

As she closed her eyes and accelerated her fanning motion, Albert rocked backwards and forwards on the balls of his feet. He didn't want his nervousness to get a grip so tried to distract himself. He looked around and saw a framed photo of Marjorie's family, a knitted kitten that looked like it had been made by a child, and one of those squeezy stress relievers in the shape of a penis. He could feel himself starting to blush so looked away.

After a minute or so, Marjorie opened her eyes and slowed down the fanning. 'That's it, it's easing off now.'

She dabbed at her forehead with a tissue. 'Alright, love, what can I do for you?'

Albert took a step inside and drew in a long, steadying breath. 'I just wanted to say I'm sorry for what happened at the Christmas do. I shouldn't have snapped at you.'

There, that wasn't so bad, was it?

Marjorie threw her fan shut with a click. 'Don't be daft, love, it was me who overstepped the mark. Honestly, I was bladdered. I'm terrible on the white wine.'

'You weren't that drunk,' Albert insisted, hoping he sounded sincere.

Marjorie squeezed her fan between her hands. 'Anyway, I won't be getting bladdered again for a while now – I'm doing Dry January.'

Albert paused while he cast around for something to say. *Come on, if you're going to find George, you're going to have to get on with people.*

'And how's it going?' he asked. 'Are you enjoying it?'

Marjorie let out a loud chuckle. 'Am I 'eckers like. It's torture. It's just given me another reason to hate this miserable month.'

Albert nodded but this time couldn't think of any response. So far, he was enjoying January more than he had any month for a long time.

'In case you haven't noticed,' Marjorie went on, 'practically the entire office has come down with a severe case of the January blues.'

But before Albert could reply, she'd clicked her fan open again.

'Sorry,' she said, 'it's starting up again. Honestly, I feel like a bloody furnace.'

Albert frowned and began retreating to the doorway. 'Well, I'll leave you in peace.'

'Ta, love. And we might all be miserable but it's good to have you back.'

Albert was surprised at how much he enjoyed hearing her say that. 'It's good to *be* back,' he said with a smile. And he surprised himself by how much he meant it.

Albert drove up the high street and, now that it was daylight, discovered that the atmosphere of lethargy wasn't just confined to the office but seemed to be shrouding the whole town. The sky was the colour of slate and, although there were hardly any cars on the road, the traffic crept along. The Christmas lights and decorations had been taken down but the advertisements promoting the January sales were still up –

and promised even further, life-changing reductions. But there were only a handful of shoppers trudging up and down the pavement and they seemed entirely unexcited by the prospect.

After driving down the dual carriageway, Albert reached the road that divided his walk into two halves. On either side was a trail of dead or dying Christmas trees that had been tossed out of the stone terraces and on to the pavement, where they were waiting to be collected by the council. It was a sad, sorry sight, but one Albert resolved not to let dampen his spirits.

He parked up and set off on his walk, determined to try out a friendly smile on everyone he saw. But the streets were deserted and the only people he passed were two surly teenagers in school uniform playing truant and smoking down a backstreet. Even the Border collie that usually terrorised him stayed slumped in its kennel, barely lifting its head as Albert delivered the mail.

The only person who looked like she was pleased to see him was Edith Graham. As Albert approached her bungalow, he could see that she wasn't sitting snuggled up in her usual armchair but standing at the window looking out at the street. When she caught sight of him, she gave him a wave that was more enthusiastic than usual. Albert found himself doing the same.

She pointed towards the door and beckoned him over.

Oh no, can I do this?

But Albert remembered how lonely he'd been over Christmas – and it suddenly occurred to him that she might have felt as bad. If she was still feeling that way, he might be able to help her.

Besides, speaking to her will be good practice for when I see Nicole.

He walked up the path and stood waiting at her front door. As her silhouette filled the frame, he tugged in a deep breath.

Edith opened the door, her distinctive white hair and delicate, lined skin looking even more striking in close-up. She was wearing a pale green skirt and jumper, and her perfume smelled of a flower, but one Albert didn't recognise.

'Hello,' she said, 'I was hoping I'd see you.'

She smiled at him and Albert couldn't help but feel a little uplifted. 'Thanks,' he said. 'It's Edith, isn't it?'

'Yes, Edith Graham.'

'I'm Albert. Albert Entwistle.' He held out his hand and she shook it. Then he remembered he had nothing to deliver. 'I'm sorry, I haven't got any mail for you today.'

She shook her head. 'Oh I'm not bothered about that – I was wondering what had happened to you. I was starting to get worried. You usually come every day during the week, and the other chap does Saturdays. Have you been alright?'

It was only a simple enquiry but Albert was so touched he was lost for words. 'Oh, sorry, yeah,' he managed. 'I just had some things to sort out over Christmas so I took an extra week off.'

She looked relieved. 'That's alright then. And did you get everything done?'

As he thought of his search for George, Albert could feel his unease stirring. He did his best to suppress it. 'Well, I've made a start. But it'll take a while yet.'

He remembered that he needed to speak to Nicole and told himself he'd better get going.

Hang on a bit, said a voice in his head. *Edith might not have spoken to anyone for days. Surely you can spare her a few minutes?*

'And how about you? Did you have a good Christmas?'

She let out a sigh. 'Oh, you know, it was the same as ever. There isn't much to celebrate when you're on your own.'

Albert wanted to tell her that he'd been on his own too. But for some reason the words wouldn't come out. Instead, he settled on, 'I'm sorry about that. So you don't have any family?'

At this slightest prompt, Edith launched into a detailed account of the story of her life. She told him that she'd been born in Toddington eighty years ago and was from a close family, but they were all dead now. For years, she'd worked as a dressmaker – and in her spare time had designed the costumes for a local theatre group. She'd also been known as something of a local beauty, with many admirers who'd taken her out in the evenings. But, although she'd received several proposals of marriage, she'd never accepted any of them. 'I suppose I made a bit of a mess of it really,' she said, with a hint of sorrow. 'I was always holding out for something better and ended up missing the boat.'

'Well,' offered Albert, 'we all have regrets.' He hoped that didn't sound trite.

'Yes, we do, don't we . . .?' Edith paused and her forehead creased into a frown. 'I suppose in my case I got so much attention I never imagined it would stop. And then the next thing I knew, I was an old spinster. I bet most of the men who took me out don't even remember me any more.'

'Don't say that,' said Albert.

'Why not?' said Edith. 'It's true.'

As he listened, Albert realised how much he wanted it not to be true. And then, deep inside him, a memory sputtered back to life. He remembered what it was that had made him want to become a postman; he'd been so happy when he'd received letters from George, he'd wanted to spread some of that happiness to other people. He knew that people didn't really send letters like they used to, but the recollection gave him an idea.

But I couldn't . . .

Could I—?

'A penny for your thoughts?' interrupted Edith.

Albert knew that for his idea to work, he'd have to keep it a secret. 'Oh, I was just thinking about something I've got to deliver,' he said, 'that's all.'

He remembered he wanted to catch Nicole and looked at his watch.

'Well, I'm sorry if I've kept you,' said Edith.

'No, it's OK,' insisted Albert. 'I've enjoyed talking to you.'

Did I really just say that?

But, as he said goodbye and began walking down the path, he realised that he *had* enjoyed talking to her.

As he was reaching the end of the path, he stopped and turned to ask one last question. 'Actually,' he said, 'that perfume you're wearing is really nice. But I can't quite place it – what does it smell of?'

Edith stroked her cheek and smiled. 'Oh, it's orchids, my favourite flower.'

As he nodded and gave her a wave, he realised he was looking forward to putting his idea into action.

*

Albert nibbled his Crunchie as he worked through the second half of his walk, all the time feeling nervous about the conversation he was hoping to have with Nicole. But when he arrived at her house on the Flowers Estate, for once she wasn't standing outside. He looked at his watch and realised he must have missed her having her regular post-lunch cigarette.

His eyes settled on the bell at the side of the door and he dared himself to ring it.

As he strode up the path, in his head he repeated the advice of the YouTube video. *It's OK to be frightened. But don't let this stop you doing what you want to do.*

He pressed the bell and heard it ring.

At first there was no answer but, just as he was reaching out to press it a second time, the door was flung open. An angry-looking Nicole hissed at him to be quiet.

'Don't ring the bell again!' she whispered.

In that moment, the confidence Albert had built up burst like a pricked balloon.

'S-s-sorry,' he stammered. 'I didn't mean to . . .'

Much to his surprise, Nicole looked at him for a moment and then smiled. 'It's fine, I'm not annoyed at you. It's just my daughter has got a cold so I've put her down for a nap. I really don't want anything to wake her up.'

Albert stood in silence as Nicole listened out for any sound of movement. 'Actually,' she said, 'I think we've got away with it.'

Albert could feel the relief spread through him. But he'd been left feeling unsure of himself, and a silence set in between them. He thrust out an envelope that was clearly thin enough to fit through her letter box. 'I wanted to give you this,' he said.

Nicole took it. 'Oh. But why did you ring?'

Her directness made Albert feel disconcerted. 'Erm . . . nothing . . . it's OK. I'm sorry I disturbed you.'

He turned and walked away.

'I'm sorry for snapping!' Nicole called after him.

But it was too late. Albert had already given in to his fear.

Chapter Sixteen

It's a warm evening in June and Albert is with George in their secret place on the moors. They're discussing their favourite films and George tells him his is *West Side Story*. He explains it's a modern version of Shakespeare's *Romeo and Juliet* that's set in 1950s New York and tells the story of the forbidden love that springs up between Tony and Maria, two young people from rival gangs and communities. George says he saw the film at the pictures and he and his mum loved it so much they bought the soundtrack on record.

'I listen to it all the time,' he says. 'It's so romantic!'

Albert pulls a face. 'Sorry, but I've never seen the film.'

'What? You *have* to see it, Albert! It's practically our story!'

George feels so strongly that Albert should experience something of *West Side Story* that he announces he's going to perform some of his favourite songs from the soundtrack. He invites him to take a seat on a nearby rock and leaps on to the flat roof of the bunker.

'Now I'm going to start with "Tonight",' he says. 'Tony

and Maria sing it to each other on the fire escape outside her apartment. Do you get it?'

'Get what?' says Albert.

'It's like the balcony scene in *Romeo and Juliet*! You know, the famous balcony scene? Never mind, watch this.'

With that, he launches into the song. He has a powerful voice, with a range that allows him to sing both the male and female parts, and he even adopts a Puerto Rican accent when he's pretending to be Maria. Although he's playing both genders and the action is supposed to take place in the 1950s, he's still wearing his men's clothes from 1970; a wide-collared shirt with a psychedelic print and a new pair of on-trend bell-bottom jeans. But he throws himself into the performance with such conviction that it hardly matters – and Albert is soon lost in the show.

Next, George performs 'I Feel Pretty', which he explains is a comic number sung by Maria, as she tells her friends that her love for Tony makes her feel like the most beautiful girl in the world. As he sings, George skips around the stage, adopting exaggerated feminine gestures that remind Albert of a pantomime dame and have him gurgling with laughter.

Then George says he's going to round off his show with one more number – 'Somewhere'.

'This is my favourite,' he says. 'It's when Tony and Maria sing about how unfair it is that they're not allowed to be in love. They hope that somewhere in the world there's a place for them, a place their love can survive and be free.'

As he sings the opening lines, the mood changes and becomes much more serious. Soon, Albert can feel the emotion lodging in his throat.

Oh, this song's lovely. And George is right – the words sound like they were written for us.

George slides down from the bunker and moves over to Albert. As he draws nearer, Albert finds himself rising up and taking George into his arms. Slowly, the two of them begin to dance. On the side of the moors high above Toddington, they dance to the sound of 'Somewhere'. And they dream that – one day – they, too, will find a place where their love can be accepted, a place where their love can be free.

The day after trying to call on Nicole, Albert sat in his van listening to 'Somewhere'. And he could feel a new courage seeping into him.

He felt annoyed at himself for backing out of the conversation with her and decided to make another attempt at it. This time, he wouldn't let fear get the better of him. When the song came to an end, he stopped the CD and set off.

Once again, there was no sign of Nicole. But this time, Albert decided not to ring her bell but to tap on her door instead. Within seconds, she answered.

'Oh, hello,' she said, 'I'm glad you're back.' Once again, she was whispering and explained that her daughter was having another nap as she still hadn't recovered from her cold.

'I'm sorry about that.' Albert shifted his weight from one foot to the other. 'Are you not smoking today?'

'No,' she said, proudly, 'I've given up.'

'Oh, well, congratulations.'

'Thanks.'

She explained that she'd just finished braiding her hair and Albert complimented her on the result but wasn't sure what else to say on the subject.

'And how's it going with your boyfriend?'

Nicole smiled again. 'Much better, thanks. I mean, his parents still don't approve but I'm trying not to think about that. Anyway, he's gone back to uni now so I'm just going to have to relax about it.' She was still speaking in hushed tones and in between sentences her eyes flitted upstairs. Her nervousness was putting Albert on edge.

'You know, when you walked past the other day,' she went on, 'I was ready to give up on it. It was you who made me stick at it.'

Albert could feel a smile creep up his face. 'Well, that's nice to hear. And I'm glad you did.' He felt a surge of confidence and paused to steel himself for what he was going to say next. 'Actually, there was something I was hoping you could help me with.'

As he said the words, Albert couldn't help thinking they sounded ridiculous. *Why would someone like Nicole want to help me?*

Thankfully, she didn't seem to think so. 'Sure,' she said. 'But let's not do it here. Why don't you come in?'

Albert hadn't expected this and a stab of panic pierced his

chest. *Are there rules about going inside a customer's house? Will I get into trouble?*

He dismissed the concern. *Oh, what does it matter if you break the odd rule? Your life isn't run by Royal Mail. Well, it won't be soon, anyway.*

Nicole crept down the hall and Albert stepped inside.

Once they were safely in the living room, she closed the door and adjusted her voice to its regular volume. 'That's better,' she said, 'I can relax now.'

Albert found himself relaxing too.

'I'm Albert,' he said, holding out his hand. Nicole shook it.

'I'm Nicole. It's good to meet you properly.'

There you are, lad, you're doing well!

Albert looked around and saw that scattered all over the carpet were several toys in the shape of a pink pig.

'Sorry,' said Nicole, 'it's a tip in here. But I didn't expect any visitors. It's usually just me and Reenie on our own.'

He was going to tell her that nobody ever visited him either, but the words wouldn't come out.

'Do you want a cup of tea?' Nicole asked.

'No, ta, I won't stop long.'

'Well, at least sit down.' She gestured to some kind of low-seated sofa.

Albert put his bag at the side and perched on the edge. 'Sorry,' he said, 'I think I've just sat on something.' He lifted himself up and swept his hand underneath.

'Oh, you won't find anything,' piped Nicole, 'it's just my cheap futon. Honestly, it's like sitting on a sack of spuds.'

They both gave a tentative chuckle.

'So, how can I help you?' she asked.

Albert drew in a shaky breath.

'I'm looking for someone,' he said. 'I'm trying to find them online.'

Nicole nodded. 'OK . . .' There was a short pause. 'Is this the same someone you told me about the other day?'

Albert could feel himself stiffen. 'It is, yeah.' He didn't want to give her the chance to ask any more questions so followed this up quickly with, 'I've been trying to join social media but I'm struggling. I'm rubbish with technology.'

Nicole smiled. 'Well, I'm sure I can help you there. Let's have a look at your phone.'

Albert handed it over and Nicole inched closer to him. Within seconds she was darting through his skeleton accounts and asking him questions about his preferred security, privacy and location settings. She advised that if he was looking for someone, he should keep all his accounts as public as possible. Then she leaned back and pointed the phone at him.

'We need to take a photo.'

Albert could feel himself tensing again. 'Do we have to?'

'Absolutely!' said Nicole. 'You can't do anything unless you've got a profile pic.'

She stood up and led him over to the window, where she promised him the light was better. Then she held up her phone slightly so that it was pointing down at him, which she assured him gave the most flattering angle.

'There you go,' she said, studying the result, 'that's mint. Whoever this girl is, I'm sure when she sees it she'll be sliding into your DMs.'

Albert didn't understand what she was talking about but it hardly mattered; his attention had stuck on 'girl'. All of a sudden it dawned on him how difficult finding George was going to be without revealing way more about himself than he actually wanted to.

Fortunately, Nicole didn't seem to have noticed his unease. She sat back down to upload the photo to his various accounts, busying herself with a process she called 'filtering the shit out of it'.

'Now,' she said, 'I need to show you how to search for someone. It's really simple and all the socials work in pretty much the same way.'

She accessed Facebook and showed him the search bar at the top of the screen. 'If I search for my name on Facebook, for example, several options come up.' She explained that some kind of algorithm worked out which of the people suggested by the search lived closest to your location and moved them to the top of the list. 'Also, once you've added all your friends, people who are friends with your friends come up first.'

Albert didn't like to tell her that he didn't have any friends. Suddenly the futon felt even harder than it had before.

'Here I am,' Nicole went on, and she showed him her profile. She explained that she was sending a 'friend request' from his account to hers. Then she picked up her phone and accepted it.

'Look,' she said, 'me and you are friends now.'

Albert looked at his profile page. 'One friend,' read the notification under his name. He felt such a rush of gratitude he almost started crying.

Just as he was trying to compose himself, Nicole asked, 'Now what's her name?'

'Whose name?'

'The woman you're looking for.'

Albert's stomach fell away. He jumped up and grabbed his bag. 'Oh, it's OK, I'll do that when I'm home.'

Nicole looked worried. 'Sorry, did I say something wrong?'

'No, no,' he blurted, 'I've just remembered how much mail I've got to deliver, that's all.'

She looked down and saw that his bag was hanging open and there were only three letters left in it.

'Albert,' Nicole said softly, 'is it a man you're looking for?'

All of a sudden, Albert felt like he was drowning again but this time he was subsumed by a wave of shame.

'What makes you say that?' he asked, looking at the floor.

Nicole shrugged, as if it were only of minor interest. 'I don't know, I suppose it's the way you reacted when I called her a woman.'

Go on, tell her she's right.

Go on, now's your chance.

Go on, let down that drawbridge.

'Yes, it is a man,' Albert found himself saying.

He could feel the silence curdle between them. All he could hear was the sound of his heart beating in his ears.

Nicole looked in his eyes and smiled. It wasn't a sympathetic smile. It wasn't a dismissive smile. It was the smile of a friend.

But Albert wasn't sure he deserved it.

'Just so you know,' Nicole said, 'that doesn't matter to me

in the slightest. And I think you'll find it doesn't matter to most people any more.'

Albert picked up his bag and made for the door. 'Yeah, well, if you don't mind, I don't want anyone else to know. I haven't really told anyone before.'

'That's OK,' Nicole reassured him, 'that's totally cool.'

Albert opened the door and made his way down the hall.

'Oh, and Albert,' Nicole said, whispering again, 'let me know if there's anything else I can do.'

'Thanks,' he replied, as he opened the front door. 'Thanks for everything.'

As he made his way down the path and back on to the street, all kinds of thoughts began pinballing around his head.

On the one hand, he was overcome with relief; he'd revealed his secret to someone for the first time in nearly fifty years – and that person hadn't minded at all. In fact, if he wasn't mistaken, once he'd opened up to her, she'd warmed to him even more.

On the other hand, now that he *had* opened up, he felt horribly exposed.

I've only been looking for George for a few days and already it's making me do all kinds of things I didn't expect.

He was terrified about what was going to happen next.

Chapter Seventeen

That evening, Albert spent hours scouring social media for George. Again, he tried every possible spelling of his name and searched for every possible family member. But again he failed to come up with any leads.

I don't understand it . . . he can't have just vanished into thin air.

Then another voice in his head told him that George *could* have vanished – if he'd emigrated, if he'd started a new life somewhere no one would find him . . . *or if he's dead.*

His heart flinched as he remembered all the people from his childhood who'd died of all kinds of causes: cancer, heart attacks, road accidents . . . And then his mind began swirling with images of falling tombstones and news reports about gay men dying of AIDS in the 1980s and 90s. But that thought was too terrifying to contemplate – he had to shut it down.

In order to keep his hopes alive, he dug out the notes George had sent him. He spread them out on the sofa and, one by one, picked them up to read. Pretty soon he came across a recurring theme.

One week till Blackpool.

I hope the sun's shining in Blackpool.

I'm so excited about our first ever day out!

He picked up the photo that had been taken on that day. And he allowed the memories to come rushing back . . .

As he strolls along the promenade, Albert can't believe he's getting to spend a whole day with George.

'Who'd have thought it?' he says. 'Who'd have thought me and you would have a whole day to ourselves?'

'I know,' says George, 'ain't it brilliant? I feel so free!'

Even though they're surrounded by people, he stretches out his arms and gives a twirl.

Albert's about to check no one's watching but stops himself. *We're in Blackpool – it doesn't matter here.*

So that no one saw them together in Toddington, they caught separate trains and met on the platform in Blackpool North station. Now they're here, they're sure they won't be spotted by anyone they know. It's July, and Toddington Wakes week – when all the mills and factories shut down and most of the town's population travels to Blackpool for their annual holiday – has already taken place at the end of June. Of course, they're mindful that while in public they must behave as if they're only friends, but even so, they feel free of the worries that surround meeting up at home.

'I feel like a carefree, beautiful butterfly!' gushes George.

Albert rolls his eyes. 'There ain't many butterflies in Blackpool, George. You might have to settle for a seagull.'

'Alright,' says George, 'I feel like a seagull. A big handsome seagull, flapping its wings and sailing off into the air!'

As if on cue, a flock of seagulls hovering overhead barks loudly. Albert and George burst into laughter.

It's a bright, sunny day and they continue strolling up the Golden Mile in the direction of Fleetwood, until they come to the old war memorial. There, they jump on one of the vintage beige and green open-top trams and sit upstairs so they can enjoy the view as they ride back down the seafront. They shade their eyes as they look at the grand old Metropole Hotel, the stylishly modern Lewis's department store, the fleets of charabancs lined up in the coach parks just off the front, the rows and rows of shops selling kiss-me-quick hats and cheeky postcards, and the countless kiosks serving burgers and fried onions. And Albert comments that he's never seen the beach so busy; there are so many people crammed together, he can hardly see a square foot of the golden sand that gives the promenade its name.

But I couldn't care less about that. I couldn't care less because I'm here with George.

When they reach the Pleasure Beach theme park, the boys jump off the tram, race across the road and go on ride after ride. George squeals at the top of his voice but his expressions of terror are lost amidst the sound of everyone else yelling around them. Just as their carriage is roaring down the biggest dip on the Grand National, he yells, 'I love you, Albert,' and Albert feels brave enough to yell back, 'I love you, George!' When the ride's over and Albert steps off, his legs wobbling and the adrenaline rushing through him, he isn't sure whether this is from the thrill of the ride or the thrill of shouting out in public that he loves George.

After a quick game on the Arabian Derby that Albert tells George he used to play as a child – but which George's camel wins – they grab fish and chips and head back to the seafront to explore the piers. On the South Pier they go into the amusement arcade and play pinball and various games on the slot machines. They treat themselves to a stick of rock, which they snap in half and crunch their way through as they lean against the railings and look out over the beach. They watch couples sunbathing on wooden deckchairs, families playing cricket or building sandcastles, and children riding donkeys, the sound of their laughter bouncing along the air.

When they come to Central Pier, one of the first attractions they see is a photographer's studio that gives customers the chance to pose wearing fancy dress.

George breaks into a smile. 'Come on, Albert, I love fancy dress.'

But Albert is held back by an instinct not to draw attention to himself. 'Really? Are you sure?'

'Yeah! Come on, it'll be a laugh.'

Without waiting, George skips inside and begins rummaging through the racks of costumes. When he comes to the Western section, he picks out the bright pink dress of a saucy saloon girl and holds it up to Albert.

'Oh, I like this. What do you think?'

Albert's face falls. 'Are you serious?'

'Am I 'eck serious! As if I'd do that here!'

In the end, George finds them each a cowboy costume.

'Bingo!' says Albert. 'That's more like it!'

They change into the costumes and, when it comes to having their picture taken, Albert's surprised at how relaxed he feels. Just as the photographer is directing them into position, George puts his arm around him. But Albert remains perfectly relaxed, safe in the knowledge that to any bystander George is only embracing him in the way one friend might embrace another. The thrill this gives him is as strong as the one he got on the rollercoasters.

'Smile, lads!' calls out the photographer.

And Albert does.

He stands proudly, with George's arm draped around him, and beams at the camera.

Albert looked at the photo and knew he'd found the inspiration he needed. He was more determined than ever to find George.

He held the black and white photo up and looked into George's eyes. He wished he could see the colour of them; the intense shade of blue that matched the bluebells he used to pick for him.

He pictured George's gentle, sensitive smile each time he

gave him a bunch of bluebells. And he felt the same happiness surging inside him.

He made a promise to himself.

Not only am I going to find him but I'm going to find him by the spring – by the time I see my first bluebells.

As he strode along the streets of his postal round the next day, Albert decided that if his search had hit a dead end online, he'd just have to take it offline – and into the real world. He'd start by rewinding to the last place he knew where to find George; his old house.

Rather than driving back to the delivery centre at the end of his walk, he took a detour to the west of the town, to a street of two-up, two-down terraces very similar to his own. There, he parked outside the house where George had lived. It had been decades since he'd seen it and it took him a few minutes to steady himself.

That's where George slept. That's where he ate and watched telly and did his homework. That's where he lay in bed dreaming about us.

He seized a breath. Once he felt ready, he stepped outside.

Albert didn't want to draw attention to himself so didn't linger and stare at George's old house. In any case, Albert had never visited him at home. The only times he'd come to the street had been when he'd wanted to deliver a note, which he did around the back of the house. He'd casually stroll down the cobbled street, leaning down as he passed the unused coal shed at the bottom of George's yard. And he'd slip a note inside, picturing the excitement on George's face as he found it.

He walked around to the backstreet again. As it was just about wide enough for cars to pass down, the walls and coal sheds had been demolished and the yards tarmacked over to create more space for parking. Albert ambled down the street, trying to reconnect with his younger self, coming here to deliver letters to the boy he'd loved. But everything looked so different he couldn't even remember which house had belonged to George. He might as well have been walking down a different street.

I'm not even sure what I'm doing here. It's not as if I'm going to find any clues after so long.

He plodded back to the front of the houses and over to his van. Then, just as he was pressing the button to unlock the door, something caught his eye. It was a TO LET sign nailed to the front of one of the houses. And it gave him an idea.

'Marjorie, can I have a word?'

Albert could feel a swarm of butterflies flapping away in his stomach.

'Yeah, of course you can, love,' she said, looking up from her computer. 'What's up?'

Albert stepped into her office and closed the door. Once he'd blocked out the noise from the main sorting hall, he became acutely aware of the silence.

'Erm . . . I was wondering if you could let me into the archive room,' he said.

'The archive room? What do you want to go in there for?'

'There's someone I'm looking for. Someone who moved away from Toddington years ago. It all happened in a bit of a hurry and I want to know if they left any record of a forwarding address.' He was careful not to specify the person's gender.

Marjorie drew in her mouth tightly. 'Well, you know I'm not supposed to let anyone in there.'

'Yes, sorry, I realise that.'

'And I'm not a jobsworth or anything . . .'

He needed to be a little more persuasive. 'I'd really appreciate it, Marjorie. If there's any way you could bend the rules just this once . . .'

She moved out from behind her desk and came round to perch on the front. 'Who is it you're looking for?'

Albert had known she'd ask questions.

Marjorie narrowed her eyes at him in the same way as she had at the Christmas party. 'Is it that lass from Chorley? Susan or whatever her name was?'

Come on, Albert, you've got to see this through.

'No,' he managed, 'it's not Susan.'

Marjorie was leaning closer.

'So who is it then?' she asked.

He cleared his throat. Then it was as if his lips started moving of their own accord.

'It's a man. The person I'm looking for is a man.'

In the distance Albert could hear the sound of a steel cart rattling over the floor of the sorting office.

'And is this a man you were . . . in love with?' Marjorie asked.

Albert drew in a long breath. *Can I do this?*

'Yes,' he said. 'Yes, it is.'

There, I've said it.

I've actually said it.

And there's no way I can un-say it now.

A grin swept over Marjorie's face. 'By 'eck, Albert, you took your time!'

He was so shocked he almost forgot his fear. 'What do you mean? You *knew*?'

Marjorie reached for her fan and clicked it open to begin cooling herself. 'Well, I had my suspicions, if that's the right word. I knew you were hiding *something*.'

Albert realised that his fingers were tightly gripping the ID card hanging from his neck. He let it fall and rested his hands by his side. 'Yeah, well, you were right.'

'You know, it all makes sense now.' Marjorie was becoming more and more animated. 'Why you were so private for so long, why you were so desperate to keep yourself to yourself.'

'I suppose I was a bit . . . but it's alright, isn't it? You don't mind?'

'Mind? Why should I *mind*?' She put her fan down and stepped closer to him. 'Albert, it's brilliant. It's bloody brilliant!'

The adrenaline began live-wiring through his body. 'Oh, great, thanks,' he enthused. 'Thanks for being so understanding.'

'Albert, don't be silly! Come here!' She held out her arms and threw them around him. 'Oh, I know we're not supposed to give hugs at work, but bollocks to that! This is a special occasion – and I'm so happy for you, saying it out loud!'

Albert could feel himself tensing under her embrace. It was the first time he'd been hugged for decades – the first time he'd been hugged since George.

Marjorie soon became aware of his discomfort. 'Sorry, you're not a hugger, are you?'

'No, not really.'

She stood back and ran her hands down her thighs. 'Well, I hope you find him, love. And before you say anything, I totally understand you won't want this broadcasting around the office. I know I've got a gob on me but I can actually keep a secret. The ones that need keeping, anyway.'

She gave him a wink and Albert knew he could trust her. He felt a pang of guilt for misjudging her in the past. Once again, he was struck by how positively people responded to him the more he opened up. For a brief moment it gave him a vision of what his life could be like in the future, And he saw that it could have other people in it – and be a little less lonely.

Albert approached the door to the archive room, gripping the key in his hand. He put it in the lock and turned it.

He'd never been inside before and had no idea how the room was organised. But judging from the sight before him, very little organisation had gone into it at all. His eyes flitted over tables straining under the weight of mounds of box files. There were parts from old computers and microfiche machines piled up on the floor, and row after row of grey steel cabinets, all of them unlabelled.

Hell fire, where do I start?

He began fingering a few of the files on the table closest to him; he discovered that they contained information to do with the delivery centre's accounts. Next to them was a box overflowing with the receipts signed by customers every time they came in to pick up a package. Behind that was a shelving unit stuffed full of the time sheets filled in by all the postmen or women, and the stacks of paperwork they had to complete every day.

He wondered how far the records stretched back, then remembered that the team had only moved into this building at some point in the 1980s. But George had left town in September 1970. *So what did they do with the records before then?*

He rummaged around the room, opening folders, pulling out drawers and lifting up bundles. But none of them transported him any further back than 1986. Then he saw one shelving unit that did at least have a label on it. It was scribbled with the address of what used to be called the GPO, or General Post Office, the old building in the town centre in which Albert had started work that same summer of 1970. He felt a jolt of electricity run up his spine.

Bingo!

He picked his way through the contents of the shelves until he came to a row of old notepads. He inched one out and recognised it instantly; it was one of the pads in which the postmen used to enter the information for the forwarding addresses set up by customers on their walk. Each pad had been affixed with stickers bearing the name of the postman it belonged to on the spine. The one he was holding belonged to a member of staff whose name he didn't recognise. He slotted it back into the row and did his best to picture all the postmen who'd made up the team when he'd started work. *And which of them delivered to George's address?*

He had a vague recollection of it being a cantankerous

older man who'd snapped at him on his first day at work. *But what was his name?*

Albert scrutinised the spines of several pads until he came to the one that answered his question. *Gerald Flitcroft, that's him!*

He lifted down all the pads with the same label and slid them on to the nearest table. He began combing through them, allowing them to take him further and further back in time.

1985 . . .

1978 . . .

1970.

He opened up the pad and scanned through the pages until he came to the month of September. And there, springing out at him, was George's old address. His eyes tracked over to the column next to it and there was his surname.

Atkinson.

The sight of it made Albert's head spin and he had to make a real effort to stay focused.

His eyes tracked further to the right and in the next column was an address.

It was in Bradford.

He finally had his lead.

Chapter Eighteen

Albert bounded into the office the next morning feeling happy and hopeful. It had rained heavily during his cycle into work but this had done nothing to dampen his spirits.

'How do,' he said to Ste as he took off his raincoat. 'It's a lovely day for it.'

For once, Ste looked up from his phone. 'What are you on about?' he said. 'It's pissing it down.'

But Albert didn't reply. As he entered the sorting hall, he caught sight of Marjorie sitting behind her desk and gave her a wave. He said hello to Barbara, who was coming to the end of her shift. And he shot a beam at the younger staff, who were sifting through their sacks of mail.

'Morning, gang,' he chirped, 'are we all excited about the new day?'

They looked at him in stunned silence. As he trotted on, he could hear them whispering behind him. 'What's got into Albert?'

Happiness, he answered in his head. *I'm happy because I'm going to find George.*

He passed the staff notice board and, for once, paused to read the announcements. There were the usual advertisements for training courses and union meetings but alongside these was something new that drew his attention; it was a poster inviting all the staff to join the Royal Mail team at a pub quiz the following week. The event was being organised by Marjorie to raise money to send her grandson on the once-in-a-lifetime trip to Disney World. Before he could talk himself out of it, Albert picked up the pen dangling from the poster and added his name to the list.

When he arrived at his frame he was greeted by Smiler, who was already sorting through his mail, his leg jigging away under the desk. 'Alright, mate,' he said.

Albert paused. *Go on, talk to him.*

'How are things with your daughter?' he asked. 'Is she coming round yet?'

Smiler winched an eyebrow, clearly surprised that Albert was showing an interest. He explained that his daughter had recently told him she wanted to stop going on the family days out he organised every Saturday to spend more time with her new boyfriend.

'The whole thing's been really upsetting,' he said. 'You know, I live for my kids and she used to say I was her hero.'

Albert wondered what he could say to make him feel better. He trawled through the memory of his own teens to come up with something that might provide comfort.

'Yeah, but don't forget how tough it is to be a teenager,'

he attempted. 'There's so much you're still finding out about yourself. And they may be difficult to love at that age but sometimes it's the age when they need loving the most.'

Albert could see Smiler blinking in shock. It was a reaction he shared himself. *Did those words really just come out of my mouth?*

'You could try inviting her boyfriend along on your family days,' Albert found himself suggesting. 'You never know, you two might get on.'

Before Smiler could reply, Sue burst in, dripping wet because she'd forgotten her raincoat *and* broken her umbrella. 'God, it's tipping it down out there,' she said, dabbing at her hair with a towel, 'I'm absolutely wet through.'

Albert spotted the opening for a conversation but wasn't sure whether he dared take it. To his disbelief, he found himself wanting to.

'But just think of all that sunshine you'll be getting when you win that holiday,' he said.

Sue scrunched up the damp towel and tossed it into a corner. 'Yeah, that'd be nice. It's our only chance of a holiday this year. We can't afford to pay for one; our John's still out of work.'

'Oh, I'm sorry to hear that,' Albert said. 'But I bet it's nice for John to know you're on his side. At least he knows he isn't going through it on his own.'

Sue looked at him like he had something stuck on his face. A similar reaction unfolded inside Albert's head. Then Sue's shock morphed into a smile.

'Albert,' she said, 'that's a lovely thing to say.'

He could only imagine that somewhere deep inside him this was what he'd always wanted someone to say to him.

As he sat back down, he felt a warm, comforting glow. He didn't want to start sorting through his mail just yet. Before he did, he was going to speak to Jack.

He looked over and saw that he was mid-anecdote, telling two of his friends about breaking his January diet to take his wife Doreen to a Chinese restaurant that had opened recently.

'So what was it like?' Albert asked, sliding in between the friends. 'Was the food good?'

'Oh, hello, Albert,' said Jack, non-plussed. 'Yeah, it were cracking. And they do massive portions, like – their plates are the size of a dustbin lid.'

'Sounds like my kind of place,' said one of the friends.

'Oh, and you'll never guess who else were in there,' said Jack. 'Them gays who've just moved into Pear Tree Street.'

Jack's friends inched closer but Albert tried not to show any particular interest.

'Now you know I've nowt against gays,' Jack said, 'I love that Paul O'Grady programme where he rescues dogs. But those two don't half ram it down your throat. At one point they were actually holding hands at the table – in the middle of the restaurant!'

His friends began tutting loudly.

'Now that's not on, is it?' said one of them.

'Why can't they do that kind of thing at home?' said the other.

Albert could feel his happiness being sucked away.

'I wouldn't care but our Doreen insisted on going over and chatting to them,' Jack went on.

'Oh yeah? And what were they like?'

'All I'll say is, you can tell which of them is the man and which is the woman.'

Surely the point of a gay couple is that neither of them is the woman? Albert wanted to say. But he stayed silent.

'The older one's obviously the man,' Jack clarified. 'In fact, he doesn't seem gay at all. But the younger one's much more of a proper gay. You know, he speaks like Julian Clary and walks like a girl.'

His friends nodded.

'But what I was thinking was,' Jack continued, 'if you're going to go out with someone like that, why not just go out with a woman?'

'Yeah,' the one friend agreed, 'it doesn't make any sense.'

'Anyway, on the way home Doreen said she wanted to invite them round for drinks. But I had to put my foot down. I mean, what if one of them made a play for me?'

Oh, I don't think there's much chance of that.

'And what did your Doreen say?' asked the other friend.

'She accused me of being homophobic! Homophobic, me! Honestly, you can't say owt these days. It's all gay rights this, Gay Pride that. But what about us straight people, that's what I want to know? I mean, why isn't there a Straight Pride?'

Maybe because straight people have never been made to feel ashamed of who they are. Maybe because it's never been illegal to be straight.

Albert was surprised at the force of his anger. But instead of voicing his objections, he slunk away to his sorting frame.

Listening to Jack talk about the gay couple had not only wiped out his happiness, it had also reminded him of why he'd hidden away for so long. It had reminded him why he'd retreated into himself.

He let out a long sigh.

He'd been kidding himself when he'd dared to imagine a future in which he became friends with his colleagues.

He picked up a letter and began sorting his mail.

The rain continued for the rest of the day and became even heavier when Albert strapped on his bag to set off on his walk. But he tried to stay positive. Today was the day he'd be putting into action his plan to cheer up Edith.

As he fought his way through the rain towards her bungalow, he took out of his bag a plastic box that contained a single potted orchid.

'Oh, hello, Albert,' said Edith as she opened the door. 'This is a nice surprise.'

She gave him a smile that, rather than accentuating her wrinkles, seemed to smooth out her face.

'But isn't it a foul day?' she said, gesturing at the sky.

'It's certainly wet,' he said, handing over the package, 'but I've got something for you that might just brighten things up a bit.'

She pulled the box apart and lifted out the purple flower. As she turned it around in her hands, the joy on her face was evident. Albert could feel a similar emotion springing up inside him.

'Oh, Albert, it's gorgeous,' she cooed. 'But who's it from?'

'Search me,' he said. 'Is there a note?'

She dipped her hand into the empty box. 'To the unforgettable Edith,' she read, 'who will always be in my heart.'

Albert felt satisfied as he heard the words. He'd been worried about what to write but had remembered Edith saying she thought all the men from her life had forgotten her so had seized on this.

'And it's signed by "an anonymous admirer",' she said.

They looked at each other and widened their eyes.

'I think you'd better come in.'

Albert stepped inside, took off his coat and wiped his shoes. Edith made him a cup of tea in the kitchen, then invited him into the front room.

As Albert took a seat on the sofa opposite her armchair, he looked around, expecting to see the typical living room of an elderly spinster. But there was nothing typical about it at all. The walls were covered with framed posters from old theatre productions, the lamps were draped with lengths of vintage patterned chiffon, and dotted around were cushions, rugs and throws that looked like they'd come from North Africa. Standing next to the TV was an antique dress mannequin on a wooden stand, around which hung a measuring tape and various strips of ribbon. And in the centre of the room was a coffee table, on which stood a beautiful hand-blown glass vase and piles of books about art and fashion. Into the space between them, Edith slotted her orchid.

'There,' she said, 'isn't that lovely?'

'It's terrific,' Albert agreed. 'Do you have any idea who might have sent it?'

She shot him a mischievous look and blew on her tea. 'To be honest, it could be one of many. You wouldn't think so now, but in my day I was a bit of a femme fatale.'

Albert protested that this didn't surprise him at all, whilst at the same time trying to hide his surprise.

'It could be Harold,' she said. 'He was my first love. He was a mechanic and looked like Paul Newman. But he had awfully rough hands and they always smelled of Swarfega.'

Albert smiled. 'And what happened to him?'

'I was only a teenager when we were courting, and I didn't want to settle down – even though that's what was expected of women in the 1950s. The Swinging Sixties were still a long way off. Mind you, I think that whole sexual revolution was mainly a London thing. I don't think the sixties reached places like this till the seventies.'

'No,' said Albert, trying to keep the sadness out of his voice, 'I'm not sure they did.'

Edith took a sip of her tea. 'Or actually,' she said, 'it could be from Dennis.'

She told him that Dennis was a singer she'd met when she was in her twenties and worked in Manchester. 'He treated me like a real lady,' she said. 'And he looked just like Sidney Poitier.'

'Oh, so was he black?' Albert blurted out before he could stop himself. 'Sorry, it's just . . . I don't remember seeing those kind of relationships back then.'

'He was black, yes,' said Edith. 'Although we didn't use that word then; it was considered rude. If we wanted to be polite we said 'coloured', which nobody says any more. Although I'm glad about that; Dennis always thought it was disrespectful.'

As she continued sipping her tea, she explained that Dennis was from the West Indies and used to take her to the all-night Caribbean clubs in Moss Side and Hulme. 'But you're right,' she said, 'mixed-race relationships weren't common in those days. And we caused quite a scandal.'

'I'm sorry,' offered Albert. 'Is that why the relationship ended?'

Edith frowned. 'Not at all. I left him for another man. I'm sorry to say I broke his heart. I suppose I still wasn't ready to settle down.'

Albert grinned. *Now she's blowing my expectations out of the window.*

'So what makes you think Dennis might be the one who sent you the orchid?'

'Well, it was just the kind of thing he'd do . . .but the most likely candidate is William.'

She told him that William was a solicitor from Preston who used to call her his 'duchess' and take her out for drives in his Triumph Herald. 'He was always sucking on an Uncle Joe's Mint Ball,' she said, 'which was a little off-putting. And he was probably the least handsome man I ever went out with. But he was the kindest – and my mam and dad loved him.'

Albert asked how the relationship had ended and she told him that she just hadn't thought William was exciting enough and had let him go. 'But I can see now that he was the one that got away.'

She looked out of the window. Albert followed her gaze and for a few seconds watched the rain stream down the pane of glass. It struck him that, just as he had a past strewn with experiences that had shaped him, so did Edith. Just as he had an inner drama that was motivating his actions and emotions, so did she.

'Anyway,' she said, placing her empty cup on the coffee table, 'that's enough about me. How about you? I can see you're not married. So do *you* have a one that got away?'

Albert finished his tea and put his cup next to Edith's. 'Funnily enough, I do, yeah. And I've just started looking for him.'

He froze in his seat. He'd had no intention of saying the word 'him'; it had just slipped out.

He paused as his revelation hovered in the air between them. No response registered on Edith's face. Albert tried not to let the fear take hold of him.

'That doesn't bother you, does it?' he asked, cautiously. 'That it's a man?'

She wrinkled her nose. 'Why should it bother me? You know, I used to spend a lot of time in the theatre, I was often around gay men. Although that was another word we didn't use at the time.'

'No,' said Albert. In his head he heard echoes of all the words people used – and they were all insults.

'Queer', 'poof', 'pervert' . . .

'I suppose if we wanted to be polite about that kind of thing we didn't use any word at all,' said Edith.

Albert swallowed. 'I guess that's why I've never really thought of myself as gay,' he said.

'What do you mean?' asked Edith.

'Well, when I was a teenager I fell in love with another boy. But that was something I did, it wasn't who I *was*. And when I got older, I knew I was attracted to men rather than women, but I didn't ever meet anyone else who felt the same as me. The only ones I knew about around here were the men who met in public toilets. But they did that in secret; it wasn't something they were proud of. And it wasn't the kind of thing I wanted anything to do with—'

He stopped and let out a sigh. 'Sorry,' he said, 'I'm not really used to this. I'm not sure I'm explaining myself very well.'

'I understand,' said Edith. 'But you know things aren't like that any more. They haven't been for years.'

'No,' said Albert, 'and that's terrific, it really is. But by the time things started changing, I'd shut that side of me down.'

A new silence set in between them.

'I don't know,' said Edith, after a while, 'look at us two. We both had the chance to be happy and we both let it go.'

Albert could feel sadness filling the atmosphere between them. He remembered that he'd come here to cheer Edith up.

'We might have let happiness go,' he said, 'but we might still be able to get it back. Whoever sent you that orchid obviously still cares about you.'

She tilted her head, as if thinking it over. 'Yes, maybe you're right. Anyway, it's certainly brightened up my day.'

As she looked at the orchid and smiled, Albert decided he was going to repeat his plan every week.

Every week he was going to deliver something that would give Edith a little hope.

It was another quiet day and Albert had far less mail to deliver than before Christmas. But a few streets after Edith's, he came

189

to another package that he needed to deliver face-to-face. It was addressed to Daniel and Danny.

As he walked up their driveway, Albert felt nervous, but nothing like as tense as he'd been the first time he'd met them. He stood under the canopy and stamped his feet to shake off the rain. He rang the doorbell.

When Daniel answered, Albert explained he needed a signature for the package. As he obliged, Danny appeared behind him.

Come on, now's your chance to apologise.

'How did you enjoy your first Christmas in Toddington?' he began.

The men looked surprised he was making conversation.

'Oh yes, it was wonderful, thank you,' said Daniel. 'We were invited to *several* parties.'

The two of them gave each other a knowing look and giggled.

'It's been pretty mental,' said Danny. 'But everyone's been legit welcoming.'

Albert noticed again that Danny was wearing make-up and tried not to stare.

'I'm pleased to hear it,' he said. 'Although I'm sorry *I* haven't been too welcoming.'

There was an awkward pause.

'That's OK,' said Daniel. 'Not everyone wants to stop and chat. Not everyone likes parties.'

'No, but I was rude,' said Albert. 'It's no excuse but I had a lot on my mind over Christmas.'

Daniel stroked his beard. 'Well, whatever it was, I hope it's all been resolved now.'

'Let's just say it's moving in the right direction,' said Albert.

Danny joked that it looked like it would never stop raining and said they'd been looking forward to going on a long walk that morning but had been forced to postpone it.

'Oh, I didn't realise you two were walkers,' Albert piped.

'Yes,' said Daniel, 'I grew up in the Lake District, so I'm from a big walking family. It's one of the things we were hoping to do more of around here.'

Albert told them he'd always been a keen walker and they asked if he could recommend some routes. He talked them through his regular Sunday walk at the back of Toddington Hall and threw in a few other options too.

'Let me know how you get on,' he said. 'And if you want any more ideas, just give me a shout.'

Danny gave him a smile. 'Thanks, darling—' Then he froze.

Albert remembered his reaction the last time Danny had called him 'darling'.

'That's OK,' he said. And, out of nowhere, he found himself saying, 'You can call me "darling" whenever you like.'

The two men stared at him, astonished.

If only George could see me now.

Chapter Nineteen

It was Friday afternoon and Nicole and Reenie were at a children's soft play centre called Pandemonium. It was a place she often brought Reenie when she wanted to get out of the house; on weekday afternoons there was no maximum play time, there was free WiFi, and she didn't need to spend much – the entrance fee was cheap and she could make a cup of tea last for a few hours.

Nicole took the little girl on her favourite curvy slides, cushioned roundabouts and climbing ropes. But when Reenie scarpered off into the toddlers' area and dived headfirst into the ball pit, she decided to leave her to it. She went to buy herself a cup of tea and found herself an empty table.

'Mummy's going to be sitting here,' she called out to Reenie.

If only I wasn't here on my own.

She looked around the hall to see if there was anyone she knew. The first thing she noticed was that she was the only black woman, but that was nothing new. There were two or three grandparents she'd seen before and a few tables of mums chatting. She caught the eye of one of the mothers and tried to shoot her a smile. But in return the woman looked her up and down and pulled a face like she'd just swallowed a mouthful of orange juice after brushing her teeth.

For the first time since she'd given up smoking, Nicole was suddenly desperate for a cigarette. It was at times like this that she most missed Lisa and her friends back in Huddlesden. She did get on with the girls on her course and they'd met for the occasional coffee but she'd never been able to take their friendship to the next level as they were always going out for drinks and she still had nobody she could ask to babysit. After months of inviting her along, they'd stopped asking.

Oh, I wish I had just one person to talk to.

Actually, I could always call Mum . . .

She took out her phone and scrolled through her contacts. Even though her mum was in Lanzarote, if she called her on WhatsApp audio using the venue's WiFi, it wouldn't cost her anything. She dialled the number and within seconds, her mum picked up.

'Nicky!' she warbled. 'Great to hear from you!'

Nicole felt broadsided by how happy this made her. 'Hi, yeah . . . erm . . . thanks, Mum.'

She explained that she was in a children's play area, and her mum told her she was at work in the bar. Nicole pictured her dressed in her favourite leopard-print top with a plunging neckline to show off her boob job.

'So how's it going?' Nicole asked. 'Are you still enjoying it?'

Her mum switched her on to speakerphone. 'Yeah, yeah, work's fine. Although Dave's been at it again. Last night he went out with the boys from the darts club and he didn't get in till ten this morning. God knows what he got up to.'

Nicole tried not to sound exasperated. 'Mum, I don't know how you can put up with that kind of thing.'

She heard what sounded like doors opening and glasses being stacked one on top of the other. 'It's fine, Nicky,' her mum replied, with a note of irritation, 'he's not that bad. He just needs a blow-out every now and then.'

'I know but—'

'Anyway,' her mum snapped, 'I'm busy so I can't speak for long. I need to get the bar ready for the five o'clock rush.'

But Mum, we haven't spoken in weeks.

'Did you want something?'

Nicole opened her mouth to tell her mum how lonely she was feeling, how much she was missing Jamie since he'd gone back to uni. But it suddenly seemed pointless.

'No, nothing in particular,' she replied, cheerily. 'Everything's fine.'

She heard the sound of running water, as if a tap had been switched on. She felt like a nuisance.

'Alright, Mum, I'll leave you to it.'

As she said goodbye, she realised her mum hadn't even asked about Reenie.

She saw from her home screen that she'd received a message on Facebook Messenger. She clicked on the icon. It was from Albert.

'Where are you?' it read, rather bluntly. It was obvious he

wasn't used to communicating like this. 'I want to chat to you about something.'

Nicole smiled.

'Am in Pandemonium,' she typed. 'It's a children's play area.' On to the end of her sentence she tacked the emoji for an eye-roll.

Then she had an idea.

No, I can't.

Oh, why not?

'Come and join me,' she typed.

The three dots came up to show Albert was typing a reply. 'I'm working,' it said.

'What about after your round?'

'I've got to get back to the office.'

'Come after that,' she insisted. 'I'll be here all afternoon.' She remembered how touched he'd seemed when she'd become his friend on Facebook. 'It'd be mint to see you,' she added.

The three dots flashed up again.

'OK,' came the reply, 'see you later.'

Nicole smiled and finished her tea, watching Reenie writhing around the ball pit. She started to take off her shoes so she could go in and join her daughter. Once Albert arrived, she'd come out again to enjoy some adult company. Finally, she'd have someone to talk to.

An hour later, Reenie had made friends with a chubby boy who had a snotty nose and glasses with lenses so dirty it was a wonder he could see anything. Nicole left the two of them playing so she could go back to the table and wait for Albert.

He arrived a few minutes later and stood by the entrance looking around the room. He seemed nervous and bewildered. She waved at him and he looked relieved to see her.

'My God,' she said as he approached the table, 'talk about a rabbit in the headlights.'

'Sorry,' he said, 'I've never been anywhere like this before.'

'Well, in that case, you've missed out.'

She gave him a hug that was much more enthusiastic than she'd intended and, although it was clear this wasn't how he usually greeted people, was pleased when he reciprocated.

'I don't have to take my shoes off, do I?' he asked.

'Not if you're sitting here,' she answered. 'But you do if you want to go into the ball pit.'

She gave him a mischievous look and he seemed to loosen up.

Out of the corner of her eye, Nicole could see some of the other mothers looking at the two of them curiously. She imagined they must make an odd couple – she a nineteen-year-old single mother and he a sixtysomething postman still in his uniform. Not that she cared.

What are you staring at? she wanted to shout. Instead, she unleashed a wintry smile.

Albert went to the counter to buy them each a cup of tea. When he returned, he sat down opposite Nicole.

'So is everything still alright with your boyfriend?' he asked.

She realised she still hadn't told him Jamie's name or which university he was at. She filled him in on the details and then brought him up to date. 'So it's alright, I suppose. I mean, I knew when I met him he still had to do his final year at uni. I just didn't realise how much I'd miss him.'

Albert gazed into his cup of tea. 'Yeah, I can imagine that's hard. But surely you don't just have to sit around pining for him? Surely there's something you can do?'

Nicole tucked her legs under her chair. 'At the moment I'm just trying to give him some space. He's promised he wants to make it work so I just need to let him deal with this thing with his parents. In the meantime I'm trying not to get worked up or insecure about it. You know, my grandma used to say that going out with a man who doesn't want to be with you is like trying to hold on to a cat that doesn't want to be held.'

'I had a cat,' said Albert. 'She died at Christmas.'

Shit!

'Oh, I'm sorry,' said Nicole. 'I didn't mean to upset you.'

'No, it's fine,' Albert insisted. 'I do miss her but you didn't upset me. In fact, that's the first time I've thought about her without being sad. It just feels nice to remember her now.'

Thank God for that.

'And what was she like?' she asked.

'Gracie? Oh she was lovely.' A smile inched up his face. 'And that's a great piece of advice; if a cat doesn't want to be held, there's nothing you can do to stop them wriggling away.'

'Yeah, my grandma used to say it to my mum every time a man left her, which was basically every year or so. Not that she ever listened.'

To be honest, she was a crap mum, she wanted to say. Then, to her shock, she realised she had said it.

'Oh, sorry,' she added quickly. 'You're not supposed to say things like that about your mum, are you?'

Albert smiled. 'Don't worry about it. Now we're on the subject, mine wasn't much cop, either.'

The two of them burst out laughing.

'Anyway, it toughened me up, I suppose,' Nicole said. 'Besides, it didn't matter that she was crap, because my grandma was unreal. That's why I named Reenie after her – her name was Irene.'

At the mention of Reenie, Nicole stood up to check she was still happy playing with her new friend. When the little girl spotted her, she came running over.

'Drink!' she shouted.

Nicole produced her water bottle and she sucked at it greedily.

'Reenie,' she said, 'this is Albert. Are you going to say hello?'

Reenie drained the bottle and thrust it back at her. 'Hello, Albert,' she said. She flashed him a toothy grin then rushed back to join her friend.

'Anyway, how's it going with *your* man?' Nicole asked. 'Any sign of him on your socials?'

Albert looked a little uneasy and she couldn't help noticing that he glanced around to check nobody was listening.

He cradled his tea in his hands as he explained that he hadn't had any success on social media, something that worried him. But he had found the address the family moved to nearly fifty years ago.

Nicole's heart heaved. *Fifty years? So does this mean he's lived without love for all that time?*

'Funnily enough, that's what I wanted to talk to you about,' Albert said. 'I don't want to mither or anything but the address I've got is in Bradford. I was wondering if you could show me how to use the map on my phone. I mean, I can obviously get to the train station and I can jump in a taxi once I get to the other end. But I want to know where I'm going – I want to get it straight in my head first.'

Nicole nodded. 'Albert, of course I'll show you. And honestly, you're not mithering at all.'

She took hold of his phone and connected him to Pandemonium's WiFi. Then she talked him through how to use the map app and also how to check train times and book his ticket in advance.

Just as they were finishing, their attention was distracted by a group of older children who came storming in dressed in their school uniform. They slung off their shoes and darted towards the play area like a set of greyhounds released from a trap. Within minutes, some of the older boys had invaded the toddler area and Reenie abandoned her friend and came retreating back to their table. Nicole tried to settle her on her lap but she began wriggling and shouting.

'Albert! Albert!'

'What's the matter?' Albert asked. 'What does she want?'

'What do you think she wants? She wants you.'

He looked like he'd just been told to fling off his clothes and run naked down the high street. 'Oh, I don't know—'

But before he had time to argue, Nicole lowered Reenie on to his lap. He froze rigid, but within seconds Reenie was looking up at him and smiling.

'She loves men,' Nicole said, rolling her eyes. 'I'm going to have to watch her when she's older.'

As Reenie snuggled up to him, Nicole could see Albert relaxing.

'Yeah, she definitely likes you,' she confirmed. 'She likes you a lot.'

Am I imagining this or is that a tear in his eye?

'George!' Reenie suddenly shouted. 'George!'

Albert looked at her, puzzled. 'George? Why's she saying that?'

Nicole rummaged around in her bag and pulled out Reenie's battered old cuddly toy. 'She wants this. It's Peppa Pig's brother, George.'

Albert wrinkled his forehead. 'You know the man I'm looking for is called George?'

'Really? Well, that's obviously a sign. My grandma must be up there sending us a message.'

Albert gave her a withering look. 'You don't seriously believe that, do you?'

'Yes! I totally believe it!'

He looked like he was smiling despite himself. Albert rested his chin on Reenie's head and drew her closer to him. 'In that case, what's the message?'

Nicole sighed theatrically. 'Isn't it obvious? She's telling you to go get him!'

Chapter Twenty

The next morning, Albert was sitting on a train to Bradford. It was his first time leaving Toddington since he'd been on a staff training course in Preston seven years ago. And the further the train took him, the more his confidence leaked away.

He looked at his watch. It was 10.28. *Only three minutes since the last time I checked.*

He couldn't believe that after nearly fifty years, he might be about to see George. It was too much to take in. Every time he thought about it, his pulse tripped and the blood sang loudly in his ears.

He looked out of the window but the sight of the countryside whizzing by made him feel sick.

Sitting across the aisle from him, a young boy and girl were kissing passionately. Albert tried not to stare; they must be pretty much the same age as he and George had been when they met. But their experience of love struck him as totally different. They were delightfully unaware of whoever was watching, and their carefree behaviour contrasted sharply with the fear he'd felt that his secret life would be discovered. Watching them, Albert felt a pang of bitterness.

He prised his gaze away.

All of a sudden, he felt a twist of panic. It struck him that he might be holding on to something from which George had moved on a long time ago. *Was what happened between us just some youthful flirtation? Have I kept it alive in my heart all this time while George let it fade and die years ago?*

George could have fallen in love with someone else just a few years after leaving Toddington. Gay men could get married now, so he might even have a husband.

Hell fire, what am I doing?

He remembered the last time he'd seen George, the hatred in his eyes as he'd said he never wanted to see Albert again. This was why he hadn't dared to search for him before. Why he'd always thought there was no hope they could ever revive the love that had existed between them. This was what had given rise to a guilt that had gnawed away at him ever since, corroding him from the inside.

And what's changed? Do I really think George will be pleased to see me now?

He swallowed and told himself that he needed to hold his nerve. In any case, it would be extremely unusual for the same family to live in the same house for nearly fifty years, especially when they could only afford to rent. He knew the best he could hope for was to find the next clue in the trail.

He rummaged around in the little rucksack he'd brought for his flask of tea. *And where are those bacon butties I made?* Even though it was only 10.37 and he'd intended to eat them for dinner, he unwrapped the tin foil and began cramming them into his mouth in huge chunks, washing the lumps of food down with the occasional gulp of tea. As he did, he patted the pocket of his coat and felt the outline of a letter. It was one of the later notes George had sent him, when he was starting to make his feelings more explicit. And of all the notes, this was Albert's favourite. He didn't need to take it out and read it to know what it said.

'How much do you love me, Albert?' George asks, as they lie back on the mattress on a cloudy but warm July evening. 'Go on, tell me again.'

Albert rolls his eyes and grins. 'Loads,' he says. 'I love you loads and loads for ever and ever.'

George tuts loudly. 'Is that the best you can do?'

'OK,' says Albert, suddenly hit by an idea, 'how's this? I love you so much, I'd still love you even if you turned into a zombie.'

George splutters with laughter. 'You what? That ain't very romantic!'

Albert pulls himself up on to his elbows. 'Get out of it! Haven't you seen *Night of the Living Dead*?'

'No, I have not! You know me, I like glamorous, *romantic* films!'

'Yeah, but zombies attack people and turn them into zombies too. So if you were a zombie and I let you come near me then that would really show how much I loved you. *I think that's romantic.'*

'Albert Entwistle, you do make me laugh.'

George leans in and kisses him. Albert notices that he tastes of the dandelion and burdock he brought up to the moors and has been swigging out of the bottle all evening. He doesn't usually like the taste but he does like it on George's lips.

'Alright,' he says, 'now it's your turn. Tell me how much *you* love me.'

George waves away his suggestion airily. 'Oh, I couldn't possibly measure it.'

'That's a cop-out!' Albert protests. 'That's just dodging the question.'

'OK, let me think about it,' says George. And he narrows his eyes and peers at Albert, as if examining his face for clues.

'I love you a little bit more than yesterday,' he says, seriously, 'and a little bit less than tomorrow. How's that?'

Albert feels on fire with happiness and wants to give George the biggest grin possible. But he forces himself to keep a straight face and shrugs. 'I suppose it'll do.'

George nudges him. *'It'll do?* I think you'll find it's perfect. And *very* romantic.'

'I'm only joking,' Albert admits, 'it is perfect.' And he leans in to kiss George again.

As he does, he replays the words in his head.

I love you a little bit more than yesterday and a little bit less than tomorrow.

And he knows that from now on, whenever he misses

George, whenever they aren't able to be together, it will be with these words that he'll remember him.

Outside the station, Albert opened the door of a taxi and plonked himself on to the back seat. The driver was a raw-skinned man with urine-blond hair. Without even greeting him, Albert barked out the address. As the vehicle pulled away and the streets began to trundle by, he worked himself up into such a state of anxiety he couldn't take any of it in. He opened up the map app on his phone and focused on the blue dot moving towards the south-west of the city centre, towards a red pin that marked his destination.

After a while, they turned off a main road and into a residential area that was made up of row after row of red-brick terraces. On to a lamp post someone had strapped a sign that said 'You are now entering Bradfordistan'.

The driver must have read his confusion. 'You do know this is an Asian area?' he asked.

Albert said nothing. He couldn't care less who lived here.

The man took his silence as encouragement. 'Yeah, it's pretty much all Pakis now – and it's getting worse. Honestly, it's like a giant oil slick spreading over the city.'

Albert's eyes bulged and he opened his mouth to protest.

'You know, I'm not racist or anything,' the man went on, before Albert could get a word out. 'But what you've got to realise is these people aren't like us. They're just different.'

The car pulled up to the kerb and Albert thrust a note at the driver.

'Thanks, mate,' the driver said.

I'm not your mate, Albert wanted to say, but he held back. By now he was desperate to get out.

The man handed him a card with his number on it and told him to call if he wanted a lift back to the station. Albert shut the door and stepped back from the vehicle.

Thank God for that.

He looked around to survey the scene and saw that the street was surprisingly similar to any terraced street in Toddington. He spotted a wicket that had been painted on to a wall so the children could play cricket when the weather was warmer. Outside one house was a skip that had been filled with bin bags, the arm of a battered old sofa poking out into the air. And in the distance a mother was coming towards him pushing a buggy, a Lidl carrier bag swinging from either side.

So far, so familiar.

Except that this woman was wearing a burqa. It was a sight Albert had seen on TV but never on the streets of Toddington. The taxi driver's words rushed back into his head.

'These people aren't like us. They're just different.'

He remembered a recent TV documentary that claimed there were higher levels of homophobia amongst British Muslims.

What are they going to say when I knock on the door?

Oh it doesn't matter – you can't believe everything you see on TV.

He tucked the driver's card into his pocket and looked for number 51.

Once he found it, he reached out his arm and knocked on the door.

Almost immediately, the door was opened by an Asian man with a beard, dressed in white trousers with a long white tunic over the top and a white hat on his head.

'H-h-hello,' Albert stammered. 'I'm sorry to disturb you. I'm looking for someone who used to live here.'

The man narrowed his eyes suspiciously. 'Yes, who is that?'

He had a strong Pakistani accent, and Albert wondered if that meant he hadn't lived here long. His heart dropped like a stone.

'George Atkinson,' he attempted. 'His family moved here in 1970.' As he said the words out loud, they sounded hopeless.

'I bought this house off a man named Sethi,' said the man.

'And how long ago was that?' Albert noticed the man was starting to look annoyed. 'If you don't mind me asking?'

'Eight years ago.'

'And you don't have any idea who lived here before that?'

'No, no idea. Why do you want to know?'

'Oh, nothing,' Albert said. 'It doesn't matter. Sorry for wasting your time.'

Before he could say goodbye, the man shut the door in his face.

Albert stepped back from the house and took a deep breath. He rested his hands on his knees, leaned over and closed his eyes.

Oh no, this is all falling apart.

Then a voice called out to him from the house next door. 'Excuse me?'

Albert looked up. Another bearded man was standing in the doorway wearing the same traditional dress.

'Did you say you were looking for the Atkinson family?' he asked.

This man spoke in a heavy Yorkshire accent. *Could that be more promising?*

He drew himself up and moved over. The man was in his thirties and standing behind him was a woman in a headscarf who looked to be in her fifties.

'Yes,' he said, 'yes, I am.'

'My mum remembers them,' the man explained. And then he stepped to one side so the woman could come forward.

'I've lived in this house since 1974,' she told him. 'And I do remember the Atkinsons, yes.'

Albert wanted to jump up and down on the pavement. The woman picked up on his excitement and gave him a smile.

'Would you like to come in?'

Hoping they couldn't tell he was nervous, Albert followed the man and his mother through to the front room. He introduced himself and they told him their names were Tariq and Mina Chaudhry. Tariq gestured to Albert to sit down.

As he lowered himself on to the sofa, he took a quick look around the room. In the centre of the ceiling hung a rather grand chandelier and on the wall above the fireplace was a clock featuring a picture of what he could only assume to be Mecca. In an alcove next to it was a frame containing a few verses of what looked like Arabic while in the opposite corner was an enormous flat-screen TV, the remote controls spread out on a footstool before him. Albert tried his best to relax.

'The Atkinsons lived here when my family first moved in,' Mina explained, 'when I was only a girl. They weren't particularly friendly, but you have to remember lots of white people didn't speak to us in those days. People used to say we were "taking over".'

The awful truth is, some poeple still do.

Albert wasn't sure what to say. 'I'm sorry about that,' he managed. 'That can't have been very nice.'

'No, it wasn't,' Mina said. 'But the Atkinsons lived next door for a long time so towards the end I did have a few conversations with Edna. By that time I was much older, with my own family. But I'm afraid they moved away about thirty years ago.'

'And do you know where they live now?'

'The last thing I heard, Mike had died and Edna was living in an old people's home. Then somebody said she'd died too.'

Hell fire.

Albert did his best to stay positive. 'I'm sorry to hear that,' he said, 'but it's actually the son I'm looking for – George.'

'Yes,' said Mina, 'I heard.'

There was a long pause. She steepled her fingers under her chin.

'I never met George,' she said eventually. 'By the time we lived here he'd moved away. He didn't get on with his parents – they were what you'd call estranged.'

Albert inched forward on the sofa. 'Yes,' he said, 'that doesn't surprise me. But did Edna ever say anything about him or what he was doing?'

Mina looked to Tariq for reassurance. He gave her a nod.

'Well, Edna and Mike didn't really like the way George was,' she said. 'He was gay, you see. I'm not sure if you know that.'

Albert felt a fluttering of fear. He chose his words carefully. 'Yes, I did know that.'

Mina frowned. 'Well, they'd had some kind of confrontation and Edna and Mike had told him he couldn't live in their house. So he moved away – and he never came back in all the years they lived next door.'

'Do you have any idea where he moved to?' Albert asked. By now he was sitting on the edge of the sofa.

'Funnily enough, I do. The last I heard he'd gone to the Gay Village in Manchester.'

The news brought Albert's heart to a canter. 'Really?'

'Yes. I remember it well, because I was only a teenager at the time and I was surprised to hear there was a whole village of gay men. I remember imagining what it must be like. At the time it seemed exciting and almost exotic but thinking about it now, it was probably full of men whose families had thrown them out. Isn't that sad?'

Albert didn't answer; his heart was thumping so strongly he could feel it in his fingertips.

'Is there anything else you can tell me?' he asked.

'Yes,' she said, 'he was working in a bar. I know that because his dad went to Manchester one night and tried to convince him to come home. I remember Edna saying he felt dirty afterwards and needed a good bath.'

Albert could feel the bile leap into his throat. 'Can you remember which bar he worked in?'

She shook her head. 'Sorry, no.'

Albert's breathing had become shallow and he reminded himself to fill his lungs and exhale. 'That's OK, you've been really helpful. Thanks ever so much.'

At that moment a clattering sound came from the stairs. Albert turned to see a boy of around seven or eight enter the room wearing an adult woman's high-heeled shoes and a Disney princess dress. His nails were splodged with glittery varnish and his face smeared in make-up.

Tariq stood up. 'Amir, what are you doing down here?'

Oh, please don't shout at him.

'I wanted to see who you're talking to,' the boy replied, calmly.

'This is Albert,' Tariq explained. 'He used to know a man who lived next door.'

Albert cleared his throat. 'Hello. It's good to meet you, Amir.'

The boy smiled and tottered off into the kitchen.

'Amir is my grandson,' said Mina. 'He wants to be a girl so we let him dress up at home.'

'He's had a lot of trouble at school,' explained Tariq, 'and with the kids in the street too. So we only let him dress up in the house. But if that's the way he is, we don't want him to be unhappy . . .'

There was a pause and Albert felt a spike of guilt. He remembered what the taxi driver had said and wished he'd had the courage to give him a piece of his mind – or to stop the taxi and get out without paying. But he could see now that he'd buckled under fear of prejudice. *Just like I've done my whole life.*

'Well,' he said, brightly, 'if only all parents could be like you.'

Mina and Tariq gave him a warm smile and Albert felt another rush of guilt.

'George was my boyfriend,' he blurted out. 'That's why I want to find him.'

Did I really just come out with that? What's happening to me?

Mina and Tariq's smiles grew wider.

'Well, in that case, I hope you do,' said Mina.

'Yeah, best of luck, mate,' said Tariq.

Albert could feel himself buoyed up with happiness. Whatever was happening to him, he liked it.

He stood up and thanked them once again. Just as he was about to leave, he called through to the kitchen. 'Bye, Amir!'

The little boy poked his head around the door frame, his lips surrounded by smudges of red lipstick. He broke into a grin and in his eyes Albert could see just how happy he was.

'Bye!' Amir said. And he gave him a little wave.

As Albert stepped back on to the street, he heard the door close behind him.

He pulled out of his pocket the card the taxi driver had given him. He screwed it up and tossed it into the skip. He took out his phone and clicked on the map icon. He was going to walk back to the station.

Albert took a seat in the end carriage, as it was the quietest and he wanted to be alone with his thoughts.

As the train pulled out of the station, he found himself wanting to share his news with someone; he took out his phone and texted Nicole. When he told her that he'd discovered George had moved to the Gay Village in Manchester, she responded with a flurry of emojis that not only included faces with their tongues hanging out but rainbows, two men holding hands, a pair of cocktail glasses, party streamers, a Spanish dancer, and even an aubergine – although Albert was sure she must have added that by mistake.

He decided to fill her in on the rest of the details in person and asked if she was free the next day. When she told him she was, he invited her round to his house.

Why not? I'm feeling brave.

He was feeling so brave that he added a kiss on to the end of his message. It was the first time he'd ever done that but this was the first time it had felt appropriate. He smiled and pressed Send.

As the wintry countryside began to chug by, he thought about the house in Bradford to which George had moved. It was sad to think of him living there with his parents, his spirit withering under the weight of their disapproval. And it reminded Albert of the life into which he'd sunk once George had moved away.

It's a regular weekday evening in 1975, when Albert is twenty-one years old. As usual, the Entwistle family is in their front room watching TV.

While his mam and dad are each sitting in their preferred

armchair, Albert's positioned between them on the matching sofa. The family's three-piece suite is upholstered in brown velour and has tassels running along the edges, tassels which Albert often twiddles as he watches TV. The room's heavy with smoke as his dad tugs away on a Capstan Full Strength, occasionally tapping the end of his cigarette into a free-standing ashtray that's positioned within reach of his right hand.

The announcer introduces a new drama called *The Naked Civil Servant*. Neither Albert nor his parents know much about it but it turns out to be about a man called Quentin Crisp, a man who wears make-up and swishes through the streets of London, a man who's attracted to other men and doesn't care who knows it, even if his determination to flaunt his sexual preference gets him into all kinds of trouble.

As the subject matter becomes clear, Albert's dad begins to rub the ends of his moustache between his fingers. 'This is revolting,' he fumes. 'What's ITV doing, showing us this filth?'

Albert can feel the goose bumps race up his arm and begins tugging at the tassels on the sofa. He wants the programme to be about something else. He wants it to be over.

But on it goes. And every second is excruciating.

In one scene, Quentin Crisp declares himself 'one of the stately homos of England'.

'I don't know,' Albert's dad splutters, 'why do they think good people like us want to watch this pervert?'

Albert's mam doesn't reply. When his dad sets off on one of his rants, she usually just leaves him to it. And around this time, she's taking some tablets that give her a glassy-eyed, half-vacant look.

'What if there's kiddies watching?' Albert's dad goes on. 'What if they decide they want to grow up and be perverts, too?'

Albert feels sick with shame. He considers leaving the room but doesn't want to draw attention to himself. Instead, he sits there and says nothing. He sits there pulling at the tassels on the sofa.

'Honestly, this programme's a disgrace,' his dad mutters. 'I've a good mind to complain.'

'Oh, turn it off,' says Albert's mam, finally. 'We don't want to watch it, so why don't you just turn it off?'

Thank God for that!

His dad hauls himself out of the armchair and switches off the TV. The room sinks into silence. Albert lets go of the tassels and runs his palms over the cushions of the sofa.

His dad lights another cigarette. 'You know, it's t' parents I feel sorry for. What must that fella's mam and dad be thinking, seeing their son parade around like that? How anyone can put their parents through that is beyond me.'

Why's he saying that? Is he trying to give me some kind of warning? Albert's mind flashes back to that terrible night in September, to that terrible night his happiness with George ended, to that terrible night it was destroyed.

'Thank God you're a proper lad, Albert,' his dad goes on, breathing out a cloud of smoke.

Albert sees no alternative other than to go along with his dad's line. 'Yeah, well, it beats me how anyone could be like that,' he says. 'You're right, Dad, it's revolting.'

As he speaks the words, he can feel the guilt rushing back into him. The guilt about the terrible thing he did to George.

'That reminds me,' says his mam, softly, 'I were speaking to June Burton in the greengrocer's the other day. Her Susan i'n't courting, you know. So if you want to take her out, I reckon she'd be keen.'

Once again, Albert feels rotten and wrong. And he just wants to be rid of it.

He clears his throat. 'That sounds terrific, Mam. Ta very much.'

His dad says nothing. He takes a drag of his Capstan Full Strength and rests his hand over the edge of the armchair.

Albert's eyes settle on the end of the cigarette and he watches it burn.

Albert shook the memory out of his head and waited for his insides to settle.

He needed to grab hold of something positive.

In Mina and Tariq, he'd encountered yet more evidence of how attitudes had changed since he was young. And it was becoming increasingly clear to him that the more he opened up to people, the more they liked and warmed to him.

As the train hurtled its way home, he wondered if everyone he knew would respond in the same way. So far, every single person he'd told he was looking for his old boyfriend had responded positively, regardless of their age, culture or religion. It was enough to make him think that, one day, he might be able to do what he'd always thought would be impossible. One day, he might be able to share his secret with everyone.

Then again, there'll always be small-minded people like that taxi driver. There'll always be small-minded people like Jack Brew.

He remembered sitting in the office in silence as Jack and his friends had made fun of Daniel and Danny.

What if they did the same to me?

Am I ready to subject myself to that, or worse?

He reminded himself that his mission was to find George – and that was all. He focused on his objective. As soon as he was back in Toddington, he was going to follow up his new lead.

And it's only mid-January. There's still time to find him before I see my first bluebell.

Chapter Twenty-One

'Come in, come in!'

Albert stood to one side so that a distinctly hyper-looking Reenie could come charging down the hall.

'You might regret inviting us over,' Nicole joked as she followed her daughter in.

As if it were the most natural thing in the world, Albert stretched out his arms and enveloped her in a hug. 'Don't be daft, kid. It's good to see you.'

She gave him a wry smile. 'Let's hope you're still saying that when we've left.'

Albert hung up their coats and ushered them into the front room, where Nicole unpacked some toys before sitting Reenie on the floor next to the sofa.

He felt slightly unnerved welcoming guests into what had for a long time been his very private refuge. But he didn't want this to show so busied himself making a pot of tea in the kitchen. Once it was ready, he carried it through to the front room on a tray, with a plate piled high with biscuits.

He'd actually enjoyed browsing the shelves of the supermarket rather than working his way up and down the aisles selecting exactly the same quantities of exactly the same foods as he always did. It made him realise how much his life had changed in the space of just a few weeks.

As he entered the front room, Nicole was looking at the photo of him and George that he'd propped up on the mantelpiece.

'Is this him?' she asked. 'Is this George?'

'Yeah, that's him.'

She nodded approvingly. 'He's cute. And you can see how happy you are too.'

'Thanks,' said Albert. 'We were.'

He set the tray down on the coffee table and invited his guests to tuck in. ''Ere, have a Bourbon.'

Nicole took the biscuit. 'Thanks, but I need to stop eating. If I pile on a load of weight, Jamie'll take one look at me and run a mile.'

'Get out of it,' said Albert. 'You're a beltin' looking lass. I'm sure Jamie couldn't care less what you eat.' And with that he manoeuvred an entire Hob Nob into his mouth.

Nicole hoisted an eyebrow. 'Look at you – you can tell you've been single for a while.'

'Really?' he said. 'Why do you say that?'

She gave him a playful look. 'Shovelling all that food in your mouth! What's George going to think if he sees you after fifty years and you've turned into Humpty Dumpty?'

They both laughed.

Reenie looked up from her toys. 'Humpty Dumpty!' she

burst out. 'Humpty Dumpty!' Nicole handed her George Pig and she began re-enacting the nursery rhyme with him on the arm of the sofa.

Albert reached across from his armchair and picked up a Malted Milk. He decided he'd stop eating after that. Even though Nicole was teasing, she had a point; he'd been single for so many years it no longer occurred to him whether or not someone found him attractive.

Not that he'd had much success following up his lead for George. He'd searched online for George Atkinson in the Gay Village in Manchester but this hadn't yielded any results, and he wasn't sure what else to do as he didn't know much about the area. He remembered people at work talking about a TV series that had been set there called *Queer as Folk* – but that was in the 1990s and at the time he hadn't felt brave enough to watch it. His only exposure to the Gay Village had been the few times it had featured on *Coronation Street* but all this had taught him was that it was filled with gay bars and night-clubs – and that everyone who went there was young, stylish and gorgeous. He was hoping Nicole could tell him more. He updated her on his visit to Bradford and everything Mina had revealed about George's move to Manchester.

She gave a jig of excitement. 'You know what that means? You'll have to go to the Village. I've been a few times – it's unreal.'

Albert pulled a face. 'But I'm a bit nervous. Won't they all laugh at me?'

'Laugh? Why do you say that?'

Albert gestured at himself. 'Look at me – I'm an old man. I'll look a right state next to all those trendy kids.'

'No, you won't! Anyway, not all the bars in the Village are for kids. Some of them attract a much more mature crowd. Which one did George work in?'

Albert frowned. 'I don't know. Mina couldn't remember.'

'Shit. You do realise the Village is big, Albert? Really big?'

Nicole picked up her phone. After running a search she began reading a description aloud. 'Manchester's Gay Village is a collection of bars and businesses all located within a hundred metres of the Rochdale Canal. Many of the most prominent venues line Canal Street, although others are spread out around the surrounding area, bringing the total number to over forty.'

'Forty?' Albert moved from his armchair to sit next to Nicole. 'Did you say forty?'

Nicole nodded and showed him the screen. 'I told you it was big.'

'Hell fire. How am I going to find George in forty bars?'

Nicole bit her lip. 'Now let's not panic. Let's see if we can narrow it down.'

She found a website listing all the bars and clubs in the area. Straight away it was clear that some of them had only been open for a few years. As she read the details out loud, Albert took out a pad and paper and began writing down a list of venues that might have been open as far back as the 1970s. They found an article about the history of the Village but it turned out that surprisingly little had been documented, something the author put down to the secrecy with which most gay men had to conduct their lives prior to the 1990s. Just as they were managing to finally whittle down their list,

Albert became aware of a bad smell. He stopped and asked Nicole if she could smell it too.

She picked up Reenie and sniffed her bum. 'Sorry, I need to change her nappy.'

She asked where the bathroom was, grabbed her bag and carried Reenie upstairs. While she was gone, Albert continued his search. With every bar he uncovered, he was bombarded by a new selection of photographs showing gay people having what looked like great fun, dancing with their shirts off, cavorting with drag queens, and hugging and kissing each other as if they didn't have a care in the world. He couldn't get his head around it. It only took half an hour to travel from Toddington to Manchester. *How could I not have realised this existed?*

'Albert?' Nicole called from the top of the stairs.

He went up and found her standing in the doorway to his mam's bedroom.

Oh no.

'Sorry,' Nicole explained, 'she started nosing around while I was washing my hands.'

Albert stepped in next to her. She was staring at the heavy wooden furniture and the old-fashioned patterned bedspread with matching curtains and lampshade.

'What is this place?' she asked, a note of fear creeping into her voice. 'It's like something out of a horror film.'

'It's my mam's room,' Albert explained, falteringly. 'Or it was until she died.'

'Oh, I'm sorry. When did she die?'

'Eighteen years ago.'

'*Eighteen years ago?* And you still haven't cleared it out?'

Albert cradled his head in his hands. 'Oh, Nicole, I know what you're thinking – that I'm some sad old man who's still clinging on to his mam's things.'

She shook her head forcefully. 'No, I'm not thinking that at all—'

'Well, you should, because it's true. It's also true that I've been stuck here my whole life and have never been to a gay bar – and it turns out there's a whole village of them a few miles away.'

He let out a sigh. Suddenly he missed Gracie. Suddenly he wanted to go back to the way it had been when it was just the two of them hiding away from the world.

'Albert, what's going on?' asked Nicole. 'Where's all this come from?'

'Oh, let's be honest, this whole thing's a joke. I mean, what's someone like me going to do in the Gay Village?'

Nicole scooped Reenie up from the bed. 'Well, I don't know but we'll soon find out.'

Albert looked up. 'What do you mean, "we"?'

'As if I'm going to let you have all that fun on your own – I'm coming with you.'

He felt his heart give a little squeeze. 'But Nicole, why would you do that?'

'Because I want to. Because I like hanging out with you. Surely you've worked that out by now?'

He gave her a raw smile. 'Seriously? Do you mean that?'

'Yes! And anyway, I love Canal Street. It'll be mint.'

'Oh, Nicole, that's terrific. It doesn't seem so scary now.'

'Good. Although you might have to help me find a babysitter. I'm not sure Reenie's old enough for Canal Street just yet.'

He gave a chuckle. 'Yeah, of course.'

'But then let's go out out. Let's hit the Village!'

A few hours later, Albert had managed to narrow down the list of bars to eight or nine. But he'd still had no success finding out where George had worked. To take his mind off things he decided to clear out his mam's room.

There's no point putting it off any longer.

He pulled the drawers out of her old chest and tipped all the underwear and tights into a series of bin bags. He took down the curtains and the lampshade and gathered up the bedding and dumped it into yet more bags he lined up at the top of the stairs. He stashed her framed photos and ornaments on the top shelf of the wardrobe and pulled out her clothes and piled them up on the bed, ready to be taken to a charity shop. The furniture could stay where it was for now but the wallpaper would have to come down. He remembered his colleague Sue telling him that her husband John was retraining as a painter and decorator and needed a few jobs to get him started. He decided he'd hire him and give him a chance.

Rather than finding the activity emotional, Albert enjoyed emptying the room. It prompted him to reflect on his relationship with his mam. And it prompted him to remember some of the conversations they'd had in that very room.

'That hash were awful,' his mam snarls at him. 'It were far too salty and there were hardly any corned beef in it.'

Albert leans over the bed and lifts the tray off her. By this time her brunette hair has faded to a dull grey and her full figure has shrunk to a gaunt frame.

'Well, I made it the same way I always do,' he says, calmly. 'I followed exactly the same recipe.'

'Yeah, well, maybe it's always awful,' she caws, the tendons on her neck standing out. 'Maybe I'm normally just too polite to tell you.'

As he makes his way to the door, Albert avoids her gaze. He knows exactly the way she'll be looking at him. By now, her vacant expression has long disappeared, as have the tablets she used to take. They've been replaced by the various multi-coloured pills she takes for her cancer, as well as her high blood pressure and water retention, tablets he lays out for her every morning before he helps her to the bathroom then props her up in bed for the day. Despite this, despite all the cooking and cleaning he does, despite the countless trips he makes with her to the hospital – and despite the fact he has never once complained – his mam only ever looks at him with bitterness and irritation.

'Oh, and before you go,' she says, 'there's a cobweb on t' ceiling.'

Albert sets the tray down on the old chest of drawers. 'Really? Where?'

She nods towards the lampshade. 'Up there. Are you blind now as well as thick?'

Albert stands on the bottom of the bed and hears the

familiar creak of the mattress. He whips out his hanky and sweeps away a thin trail of dust.

'You know, I'm not surprised you're on your own,' his mam chunters on. 'You can't cook, you can't clean, you can't do owt right.'

Albert goes back to the chest of drawers and picks up the tray.

Don't say anything. Remember she's not well. Remember she lost all those babies. Remember how badly she's suffered.

'You're a waste of space, Albert,' she carries on. 'And you've made a right mess of your life. Is it any wonder no one wants you?'

If only you knew . . .

Someone did want me once. Someone loved me once.

But he can never tell his mam about George. As he leaves the room, he reminds himself of the sacrifice he has to make. The sacrifice he agreed to make on the night his happiness with George was snatched away.

But was that sacrifice worth it? Did Mam actually deserve it?

Since opening up her box of treasures and finding the notes and the photo of him and George, thoughts like these had haunted Albert. And they'd incited a wave of resentment within him.

A resentment I don't want to feel.

A resentment I just want to clear out with the rubbish.

He folded his arms and stood looking at the room he'd now divested of all signs of his mam.

He thought about the Gay Village that for so long had existed just a short distance away. And he thought about all the pictures he'd seen of so many gay men enjoying themselves.

Finally, he felt ready to join them.

For the next few days, Albert continued to search for George – and could think of little else. But he progressed no further. As the week drew on, he tried not to give up hope or let the disappointment get to him. But he became aware of the days passing by.

On Wednesday afternoon he arrived in the office to find Jack holding court with his two friends. As he drew nearer, he heard what they were discussing; Jack was updating them on his flirtation with the woman he called Annabella Anyfella.

'I mean, she were all over me, like,' he crowed. 'But I wouldn't go near her with a bargepole. I bet she's got a fanny like an empty headlock.'

Albert could feel his anger rising.

'Yeah,' said the one friend, 'I bet it's like a ripped-out fireplace.'

'Too right,' said the other, 'like a hippo's yawn.'

The three men roared with laughter.

Albert remembered the same men trotting out similar insults at the Christmas party. He hadn't intervened then. But he was struggling to stop himself now.

'Anyway, I won't be going anywhere near her,' said Jack. 'I bet she's been rogered more times than a copper's radio.'

There was another explosion of laughter. Albert tried to block it out but all of a sudden he was back at school, waiting outside assembly and saying nothing as the other boys taunted George.

Well, this time I'm not going to stay silent.

'Oh, give it a rest, Jack,' he burst out. 'You shouldn't talk about Annabella like that!'

Jack looked as if he'd been slapped in the face. 'Albert?'

'How can you judge the woman when you don't have the slightest idea what's going on in her life?'

The three men looked at each other in bewilderment.

'She's a human being, Jack. You'd do well to remember that.'

Albert glanced around for support but Sue wasn't back from her walk and Smiler had already popped in and dashed out again to make the school run.

'Albert, what's got into you?' Jack said. 'We're only having a laugh. It's only a bit of fun.'

But Albert told himself that this was the first line of defence of every bully. 'Do you think *she'd* find it funny? Do you think *she'd* think it was just a laugh?'

Jack threw his hands up in the air. 'But she i'n't here, is she? So she'll never know.'

'Well, that doesn't make it right,' Albert hit back. 'And anyway, *I'm* here. And *I* don't find it funny.'

The three men were now eyeballing each other as if Albert were losing his mind.

'Actually, I don't care what you think,' Albert said. 'But I'd be grateful if you'd pack it in and lay off the woman.'

And with that, he turned back to his desk and began completing his paperwork.

His mind soon returned to how he was going to find George. And when it did, it began moving in a new direction. Because, unbeknownst to Jack, he'd given Albert an idea.

Chapter Twenty-Two

Albert rang Edith's doorbell.

In his hand he held a box of cupcakes he'd bought from a cute little bakery that had recently opened called The Muffin Top. Inside the box, he'd slotted a note in which he'd written 'To Edith, who's beautiful on the inside as well as the outside'.

When Edith opened the door and he handed over the gift, she looked delighted. She invited Albert in to share the cakes and they sat down in the living room with the box laid open on the coffee table, next to the orchid.

'And does the new note give you any more clues?' Albert asked. 'Do you have any idea who the gifts are from?'

Edith pondered the question for a moment. 'No, not really. But it has made me think about all the men who took me out. And I don't mind saying, it's been very pleasant to remember what it was like to feel loved.'

'Oh, that's good,' said Albert. He was just about to reach for a second cake but remembered Nicole's joke about Humpty Dumpty. He leaned back and folded his arms.

'Anyway, how are you getting on finding *your* chap?' Edith asked.

'Oh, not very well, I'm afraid. And I'm starting to get frustrated. I'm starting to feel like time's ticking away.'

He filled her in on his trip to Bradford, the conversation he'd had with Nicole, and his online search of the bars in the Gay Village. Then he paused and inched closer to her.

'Funnily enough, I was hoping you could help me.'

Edith's forehead twitched. '*Me?* How could *I* help you?'

He explained that the previous day he'd overheard some colleagues at work making fun of a woman and it had reminded him of the bullying George had suffered at school – and George telling him that the only place he'd felt safe and accepted was at his theatre group. 'And didn't you say you once worked with a theatre group?'

Edith nodded slowly. 'I did, yes. I used to design costumes for them.'

Albert could feel his heart racing. 'I know it's a long shot, but I don't suppose you knew him, did you? His name was George Atkinson.'

There was a long silence and Edith narrowed her eyes. 'I'm not sure, it's a long time ago now. Can you remember which shows he was in?'

Albert told her that George had only lived in Toddington for a year so had only been able to perform in one show – a production of Shakespeare's *Romeo and Juliet*.

Edith's hand shot to her mouth. 'That's it, George Atkinson. He was Mercutio!'

'Yeah, that's him! That's George!'

Albert could hardly believe what he was hearing. Trying not to fall over his words, he told her they'd got together while George was rehearsing for the play. By the time the production had opened a few weeks later, they'd fallen in love. He was desperate to see George perform so one night had sneaked along to watch the show from a seat on the end of the back row. Under cover of darkness he'd allowed tears to trickle down his face.

'I was so proud of him,' he managed. 'He really was terrific.'

'He was,' Edith said. 'I remember being quite struck by him. He was interested in what I was doing with the costumes. And he seemed very taken with the theme of the play.'

She told Albert that if he was lucky she might still have a poster from the production. She directed him to a big wicker basket that stood in the corner of the room and he knelt down with care and lifted the lid. The basket was stuffed full of Edith's sketches and designs for her costumes, together with faded posters and battered programmes. He began sifting through them and before long found a poster for *Romeo and Juliet*. It was only a rather crude black and white illustration that had been printed with the venue details and the dates of the performances – in April 1970. But it was also covered in signatures that Edith explained had been added by the cast and crew at the party after the final performance. Albert scoured them for George's handwriting and his eyes settled on the flamboyant curl of a G he recognised from the notes George had sent him. His stomach performed some sort of cartwheel.

'Bloomin' 'eck, this is it.'

As he held it in his hands and stared at it, Albert could feel the frustration of the last few days disappear and the full force of his determination return.

I'm going to find him.

I'm going to find him whatever it takes.

I'm going to find him if I have to trawl through every last bar in Manchester.

He turned back to Edith. 'I can't believe you've got his signature in your house. I can't believe you knew him.'

'Well, don't get carried away,' said Edith, 'I didn't know him *that* well. We only had to do a few fittings for his costume. Besides, he was a teenager and I would have been in my thirties by then.'

Albert held on to the wicker basket and pulled himself upright. 'You know, he used to love going to his theatre group.'

'Well, I suspect it was an escape for him.'

'So could you tell he was gay?'

'I did sense it, yes, but that's not something we would have talked about. And, as you say, he was only with us for a year.'

'Do you know anyone who might have stayed in touch with him?'

Edith looked up to the ceiling. 'Well, there was Victor. Now what was his surname?'

Albert looked at the poster again. He examined some of the lavishly scribbled signatures, many of them overlapping, many with extravagantly extended lines. His eyes settled on a capital 'V' that looked like it had been firmly scored into the paper. He followed it along and read the surname.

'Here it is,' he said, 'Victor Hargreaves. Does that sound right?'

'That's it! Victor Hargreaves. He played Romeo and was quite the star of our theatre group. I know he's still around, because I saw him on television recently.'

Edith explained that for a few years in the 1970s, Victor had enjoyed 'a smattering of success' as a professional actor, including a short-lived role on *Coronation Street*. She'd once bumped into him at a party to celebrate the opening night of a play in Manchester. They'd had a brief conversation but Victor had been drunk and much more interested in chasing one of the waiters. Since that night she hadn't seen anything of him – till he popped up on her TV screen in a local news report about a former actor who'd opened a fancy dress shop in Blackpool.

'Do you remember what the shop was called?' Albert asked.

Edith shook her head. 'No, but can't you look these things up on the internet?'

Albert whipped out his phone and began searching. Before long, he'd found the news report. He perched on the arm of Edith's chair so they could watch it together. It was just as she remembered; it told the story of a former actor who'd moved to Blackpool to open a shop – and the shop was called Escapade.

Albert put away his phone and returned to the sofa. 'What makes you think he might have stayed in touch with George?'

She smiled thinly. 'I don't know. They were quite close in age; Victor was probably three or four years older than George. And he was always circling around him.'

Albert could suddenly taste acid at the back of his throat. 'How did George feel about that? Was he attracted to him, too?'

She batted away the suggestion. 'No, far from it. From what I remember he was always trying to shake him off. And now I know why.'

Edith smiled and Albert let out a long breath.

'But that didn't stop Victor,' she went on. 'He could be quite predatory – and very persistent.'

'Is that why you think he might have stayed in touch with George?'

'To be honest I've no idea. But I do know that Victor worked in Manchester and by the time I saw him again he was openly chasing boys – well, at least he was at theatre parties. So it's likely he went out on the gay scene, which in those days was only a handful of bars. And if he did, I'd say it was likely he bumped into George.'

Albert nodded and let out another breath. What he'd just been told was on the one hand exciting but on the other quite troubling.

What if this Victor met up with George and they got together?

What if George fell in love with him and forgot about me?

What if the two of them are still together now?

Distractedly, he reached out for another cake but again stopped himself with a reminder of Nicole's advice.

As soon as he was back on his walk, he was going to call in on her and talk over with her what he'd just learned. It would be worth holding back their trip to the Gay Village until they'd followed up this lead. He wondered if she and

Reenie might even want to come to Blackpool with him, if they fancied a day at the seaside.

Mind you, it won't be very nice in the middle of January. And who knows how Victor will greet us?

A knot of anxiety tightened in his chest. He tried to focus on the positives. Just when he was beginning to despair, he had a new lead.

He thanked Edith profusely and told himself that, however anxious he felt about meeting Victor, he had to do it. However anxious he felt about making a second trip out of Toddington in the space of two weekends, he wouldn't let this put him off. He'd go to Blackpool on his very next day off.

He swallowed at the significance of what he was going to do. And then he decided that actually, he would have one more cake.

Chapter Twenty-Three

Albert filled his lungs with sea air and let out a loud shiver.

'Bloomin' 'eck, it's cowd.'

'Yeah, it's freezing,' said Nicole.

She leaned down and peered into the buggy to make sure Reenie's woollen hat was covering her ears. They moved on along Blackpool Promenade, quickening the pace.

They passed the entrance to Central Pier and Albert was about to suggest they look for the studio where he and George had had their photo taken. But he could see that all the units on the pier were closed. They couldn't go to the Pleasure Beach, either – it, too, was closed for the winter. Instead they continued north, towards the famous Tower.

Albert suddenly felt a stab of awkwardness. *What am I doing in Blackpool with a nineteen-year-old I've only known a few weeks and a toddler in a buggy?*

He told himself to relax; he was enjoying a day out with friends and it didn't matter if they were very different to each other.

Besides, in some ways we're not. In some ways we're actually very similar.

Overhead, the sky was full of grumpy-looking clouds. Their dirty brown matched the sludge-like shade of the Irish Sea, which Albert was dismayed to discover was at high tide, covering the glorious sandy beach that had given Blackpool's seafront its name, the Golden Mile. Angry waves slapped against the sea wall beneath them, sending icy spray shooting into the air and occasionally on to their shoes.

Albert was surprised to discover how quiet the town was. The only people they passed were the occasional grim-faced dog walker, a couple of hardened runners wrapped up against the bracing wind, and an old woman sitting on a bench and feeding what looked like chicken nuggets to a corgi in a pram. Breaking through the roar of the wind was the distant tinkling of electronic music escaping from an amusement arcade and the bark of the occasional seagull.

'So how do you feel?' asked Nicole. 'Does this bring back memories of coming here with George?'

Albert frowned. 'You know what, I thought it would. I was worried I'd get all het up. But weirdly, I don't feel anything. It's just so different to what I remember.'

Albert explained that the day trip he'd made here with George had been his last visit to the town. Most of his memories stretched back before then, to the family holidays he'd taken as a child. Every June, he and his mam and dad would stay in a bed and breakfast just off the seafront for the duration of Toddington Wakes week – and these had been happy times. But after sorrow had entered their family, they'd stopped going on holiday. Albert hadn't come back to Blackpool till he'd visited with George.

The three of them passed the red-brick base of the Tower and continued down the prom, looking to their left as a gleaming new tram sped past them. But Albert had been expecting to see the beige and green open-top trams of his childhood – the kind of tram he'd ridden with George – and this one looked nothing like those. Now that he thought about it, he could see the prom itself had also been remodelled and resurfaced. He remembered seeing a TV news report about the regeneration of Blackpool seafront and how much money the council was spending on it. But when he looked across the road, stretching out as far as the Pleasure Beach was a row of run-down hotels, shabby cafés, lap dancing bars and shops selling all manner of seaside tat. Albert couldn't help thinking that, however much money the council spent on regenerating the front, it would be like applying lipstick over a cold sore.

'So what do *you* think of Blackpool?' he asked Nicole.

'Well, it's nowhere near as fancy as it looks on *Strictly*. But that might be because it's out of season. Let's be honest, nowhere looks great in January.'

Albert was grateful to her for trying to look on the bright side. Just as he was about to suggest they turn their backs on the scruffy buildings and look out to sea, he was interrupted by Reenie.

'Donkey!' she shouted. 'Donkey!'

In order to build up her excitement, Albert had told her some of the things he remembered about Blackpool, one of which were the donkey rides on the beach.

239

'Sorry,' he said to Reenie, 'there aren't any donkeys today.'

He could see from the expression on her face that she was about to burst into tears. He needed to quickly come up with something else she might want to do. From behind him came the rumble of another tram and he suggested to Nicole that she take Reenie on a ride up and down the prom; this would allow them to see the sights while staying warm and would just about give him enough time to visit the fancy dress shop, something he'd decided he should do alone.

'Come on,' he said, desperately trying to make his idea sound exciting, 'you can't come to Blackpool without going on a tram!'

He wasn't sure Reenie understood him but Nicole joined in and tried to whip up her enthusiasm. When they reached the tram stop, Albert consulted the timetable to find out if they could catch one of the old trams but he was informed that these were now classed as 'heritage trams' and only operated during the tourist season. The Blackpool he remembered didn't really exist any more – except on special occasions, when it was wheeled out for the tourists. The rest of the time, it remained hidden away in history.

He helped Nicole load the buggy on to a sleek, modern tram and paid her fare. As he stepped back to wave them off, he prepared to set off in search of his own history.

As Albert entered Escapade, a bell tinkled to announce his arrival. Almost instinctively, he ducked behind the nearest rail.

I'm not ready to face Victor. I just need to settle into my surroundings first.

He looked around him at a shop that was crammed full of all kinds of costumes, wigs and props, including plenty of guns, broomsticks and magic wands. He began rummaging through a rack in the children's section. He thought about buying something for Reenie then reminded himself why he was here.

When he reached the end of the rail, he craned his neck into the aisle and spotted Victor. He was sitting behind the counter, in front of a computer, engrossed in whatever was on the screen. Although he was wearing reading glasses, Albert immediately recognised him from the TV news report. He was a thin-lipped man with a square jaw, a dimple in his chin, and a full head of jet-black hair. Albert could see that he must have been quite dashing in his day – and in fact, he still was.

Victor looked up and saw him. 'Are you alright there?'

Albert noticed that his voice had been stripped of its Lancashire accent. He suddenly felt so tense it hurt him to smile.

'Yes, fine, ta,' he managed.

He shuffled over to the adult section, where he discovered that there was a wide choice of costumes for women – from Wonder Woman to Cleopatra, from schoolgirl to nun, from Marie Antoinette to Elizabeth I – but he couldn't help noticing that, unlike the men's, these were all sexed-up interpretations that exposed as much flesh as possible, even when it was entirely inappropriate. At the end of the rack he spotted an Oompa Loompa outfit that looked like it belonged in a strip club.

He realised that he was allowing himself to be distracted

again. He wondered if this was because of how frightened he was of finding out that Victor had indeed kept in touch with George and they'd become a couple – maybe even still were.

He told himself not to spend any more time dithering. He grabbed a cowboy costume that looked to be roughly his size and headed over to the till.

'I'll take this, please.'

Victor removed his reading glasses and smiled. When he scanned the costume into the till in silence, Albert realised it would be down to him to make conversation.

'It's quiet in here today,' he attempted. He worried this might sound critical. 'I mean, everywhere's quiet. Town's quiet.'

'Yeah, but that's normal for January,' Victor said, 'it's always dead. Although the truth is we don't get many customers even during high season; we do most of our business online.'

Albert nodded. He couldn't help thinking that, up close, Victor didn't look as good as he had from a distance. From here he could see that his hair was crudely dyed, as if it had been coloured in with a thick marker pen. And his teeth had been capped with veneers that reminded Albert of the white tiles on the walls of his bathroom at home. But he seemed pleasant enough. Albert felt emboldened to steer the conversation in the direction he wanted to take it.

'Actually, I think we have a friend in common,' he tossed in, as casually as he could manage.

Victor put down the costume. 'Oh yeah, who's that?'

'George Atkinson.'

As he said the words, Albert spotted a wince in Victor's eyes.

'George Atkinson is no friend of mine.'

Hell fire!

'Oh . . . erm . . . I'm s-s-sorry,' Albert stammered, 'I must have got it wrong.'

There was a pause, as if Victor were deciding whether or not to divulge any more. Albert noticed that he had a liver spot on his cheek that he'd tried to conceal with make-up. He told himself not to stare at it.

'I haven't seen George for a long time,' Victor offered eventually, 'but I used to know him, yeah. When we were teenagers we went to the same theatre group. And then about ten years later I bumped into him in Manchester.'

Bingo!

'Oh yeah?' asked Albert, treading carefully. 'And how was he?'

'Fine. We knocked about for quite a bit. He was very into his activism at the time. This was the seventies so he was involved with the GLF.'

Albert looked at him, puzzled.

'The Gay Liberation Front,' Victor clarified. 'I remember the whole lot of them travelling down to London for the first Gay Pride. And George used to volunteer for the Lesbian and Gay Switchboard. You know, answering phones and giving advice to gay kids who were having a hard time.'

That's him, that's my George.

Albert tried not to think that around the same time as this, he was agreeing with his dad that *The Naked Civil Servant* was revolting.

'So what happened with you two?' he asked. 'Did you fall out?'

'Oh no, we always got on well,' Victor replied. 'That was

the problem. I quite fancied George and wanted us to see if there was anything there. But to put it bluntly, he led me on a dickdance.'

Albert furrowed his brow. 'You what?

Victor rolled his eyes. 'He gave me the come-on but then told me he wasn't interested.'

Albert had to make a big effort not to express his relief.

'Anyway,' Victor crowed, 'why've you come in here asking about George? What's that old queen been saying about me?'

'Oh, nothing . . .' Albert did his best to sound nonchalant. 'Actually, I haven't seen him for a long time. But I'm trying to track him down.'

Victor eyed him with suspicion. 'So when was the last time you saw him?'

Albert didn't want to lie so tried to sidestep the question. 'The last thing I heard, he was working in a bar in the Village in Manchester. So that must have been around the time you saw him. I don't suppose you remember which bar it was, do you?'

'I do, as it happens. But why do you want to know?'

Behind the counter, Albert's eyes alighted on a stack of plastic handcuffs. 'If you don't mind,' he mumbled, 'I'd rather not say.'

Victor gave him a hard, hollow look. 'In that case, why should I tell you?'

Albert guessed he had no choice but to open up to him. He tried to remember how well opening up to people had gone for him so far.

He looked around to check there was no one listening and lowered his voice. 'George and I used to be boyfriends. It was a long time ago but . . . I really want to find him.'

Victor nodded but his lips curled. 'And why are you looking so shifty about it?'

Without realising, Albert looked around him again. 'Am I? Sorry, I didn't mean to.'

'You know, being gay isn't a crime any more,' Victor stated flatly.

'Yes, sorry, I'm aware of that,' said Albert.

Victor leaned towards him on the counter. 'Wait a minute, you're not out, are you? Nobody knows you're gay?'

Albert could feel his whole body squirming. 'Erm . . . not really, no . . .'

Victor let out a theatrical sigh. 'OK, so let me get my head around this. I get knocked back by George like I'm nothing, and here you are wanting me to help you find him so you two can have your happy ending.'

'It's not quite like that.'

But Victor waved away Albert's objection. 'I was brave enough to come out in the seventies – a decision that ruined my acting career, by the way – and here you are, decades later, wanting to avoid all the trouble but lap up the rewards.'

'Please, I promise it's really not like that.' But even as he said the words, Albert couldn't help thinking that maybe it *was* like that.

'Well, I'm sorry, sweetheart, but that doesn't work for me.' A crease of animosity puckered Victor's face.

Albert wanted to defend himself but sensed this wouldn't be welcomed.

Victor pressed the button on the till. 'Right, that'll be £24.99, please.'

Albert fumbled around for his wallet and handed over his debit card.

Once he'd processed the transaction, Victor thrust the bag at Albert. 'Here you are.'

'Ta,' said Albert. 'Ta very much.'

There was a stony silence.

Albert had no choice but to leave. 'Well, ta-ra then.'

He sloped over to the door and slowly tugged it open, the bell tinkling above his head.

There it goes – my last link to George.

His heart plummeted to his toes and he could feel his spirit wilting.

'Just a minute,' Victor called out.

Albert swivelled around on his heel.

'It was The New Union. I don't know why I'm telling you this – I must be going soft in my old age – but that was the pub where George worked. The New Union.'

Albert felt like running down to the station and jumping on the next train to Manchester. But he told himself not to get carried away. He must stick to the original plan and wait until Nicole could come with him. He couldn't do it without her.

As Albert entered the Tower Ballroom, he spotted Nicole and Reenie sitting at one of the tables on the edge of the dance floor. They were looking around them in awe. He moved over and pulled up a seat next to them.

'I take it back,' said Nicole, 'this is way better than on *Strictly!*'

Albert smiled. 'You're right, kid. It's terrific.'

Unlike the rest of Blackpool, the ballroom was exactly as Albert remembered. The vast, palatial space was dominated by a lavishly polished wooden dance floor and around its perimeter rose thick marble columns holding up two tiers of balconies finished with magnificently ornate gold-leaf carvings. A series of enormous crystal chandeliers hung from a lofted ceiling that was decorated with intricately painted frescos of goddesses and angels. Albert didn't know exactly how old the room was but he did know it was Victorian. And its splendour was breathtaking.

Sitting on the tables and chairs were several mainly older people sipping tea. Albert ordered a pot and updated Nicole on his trip to meet Victor. Just as he was telling her that George worked in The New Union, he was interrupted by an announcement that told everyone to stand by for the appearance of the famous Wurlitzer organ.

Albert sat up in expectation. 'Get a load of this,' he said. 'You're in for a treat.'

They watched as the Wurlitzer rose up from the orchestra pit and on to the stage, the suited organist sitting with his back to the audience. As he piped the distinctive sound around the room, the couples who'd been drinking tea rose to their feet, moved to the dance floor and launched into a waltz.

Within seconds, the memory came at Albert like a blow to the head.

After having their picture taken in the photographer's studio, George tells Albert he's feeling romantic – and he suggests they visit the Tower Ballroom.

As soon as they step inside, Albert stops to admire the view. Although it's familiar to him, it never fails to take his breath away. He knows that, as it's the first time George is seeing it, he'll want to savour every detail.

'Oh, Albert,' George gushes, 'it's so glamorous!'

Underneath the ornately carved ceiling, older couples are gliding around the dance floor to the sound of the famous Wurlitzer organ, the men wearing suits and ties, the women in smart dresses.

'Can you imagine us two whirling around this dance floor?' George gasps. 'Oh, Albert, it'd be so *romantic!*'

But it would be inconceivable for two male dancers to take to the floor – so inconceivable, in fact, that Albert imagines there must be a rule against it. Instead, they're consigned to watching from the sidelines.

George lets out a huff. 'I feel like we're being shut out. I feel like that's what we're meant to be part of but a great big door has just slammed in our faces.'

Although Albert agrees with George, he'd feel self-conscious dancing in front of all those people – let alone with another boy. 'I know,' he says with a shrug, 'I suppose it is a bit unfair.'

George takes hold of Albert's arm. 'It's *really* unfair, Albert! What makes our love so different from anybody else's? Why should we have to hide it away like it's something to be ashamed of?'

Albert looks around, nervous. 'Sssh, keep your voice down. You know we're not supposed to say things like that in public.'

'But why not? If I feel something, why shouldn't I say it out loud?' George lets go of Albert's arm and gestures to the crowd of dancers. 'Why are that lot allowed to and we ain't?'

Albert watches the couples twirling around the dance floor, smiling and giggling at each other as if they don't have a single worry on their minds. 'The world's made for people like them, George. It's not made for us.'

'Yeah, well I'm sick of it, Albert. I'm sick of the world. What's so wrong about you and me? Why shouldn't two men dance together? What business is it of anyone else's?'

Albert folds his arms and sighs. He feels sad that the cheerful mood of their day together has evaporated so quickly. 'Well, you're right, George. But what can me and you possibly do about it?'

Unlike Albert, George doesn't look remotely sad. On the contrary, he's getting more and more animated. 'I don't know but I want to try, Albert. As of today, I want to change the world. And whatever it takes, I'm going to do it.'

And, as Albert looks into George's intense, violet eyes, he can see just how passionately he means it.

Almost fifty years later, Albert stood watching the couples dance in the Tower Ballroom. And he saw that he'd been mistaken earlier; the scene wasn't *exactly* as he remembered.

Amidst the sea of dancers sweeping around the floor, Albert spotted a male partnership. They were both white and around his age. While the one who was leading was a solid oak of a man, the one who was following was slim, with fine features. They were both talented dancers, rising and falling in time to the music. And it was clear from their body language that they weren't just dance partners but a couple too. Albert was transfixed. But he couldn't help noticing that nobody else was batting an eyelid.

So the world *had* changed since he last came here with George. And, from what he'd heard of George's life, he had helped to change it – just as the two men dancing in front of him had helped to change it. Because he could see now that, just by being open about their feelings, every single person had the chance to change the world.

He thought about Victor's reaction to the realisation that he was still in the closet. He'd effectively accused him of cowardice but it was an accusation Albert could now acknowledge was justified.

How could the world learn to accept people like me if we all stayed hidden away? If we all continued to hide away our love like it's something to be ashamed of?

He was distracted from his thoughts by a buzzing sound coming from Nicole's phone. When she saw who was calling, a smile spread across her face.

'It's Jamie. Do you mind looking after Reenie if I take it?'

He nodded and she placed Reenie on his lap. Without thinking about it, Albert began to gently jig the little girl up and down in time to the music. Soon, she was giggling and clapping her hands. Seeing how much she was enjoying herself, he suggested they stand up and have a dance.

He carried her over to the floor, slightly tentatively, as he hadn't danced in front of anyone since George. When he spotted an opening between the couples, he slipped in and began swinging and swaying her from side to side. He wasn't sure what they were doing quite qualified as dancing but it had the advantage of not making him feel self-conscious. In any case, Reenie loved it.

'Dance!' she shouted at the top of her voice. 'Dance!'

'Yes,' Albert said with a grin, 'we're dancing!'

Dancing like I should have been able to dance with George.

He whirled Reenie around the dance floor with more and more enthusiasm. When he passed the gay couple, he caught their eyes and gave them a nod of respect.

Just as all those years ago George had felt the passion stirring within him, Albert felt the same passion stirring.

And it gave him an idea – an idea of something he was going to do as soon as he got home.

Chapter Twenty-Four

Albert marched purposefully out of his street and towards the park. It was the day after he'd got home from Blackpool and he was on his way to the public toilets, the public toilets he'd avoided for so long.

As he turned off the main road and spotted the little brick block in the distance, suddenly a familiar fear caught in his throat.

He passed the stone lion that stood at the entrance to the park and walked towards the door. As he paused, he could feel the adrenaline spike through him. He pushed the door open and went inside.

He had no idea what the toilets had looked like when he was younger but these days they had walls that were covered with standard-issue white tiles and wooden cubicles with doors that were painted a sickly shade of green. All of these had been left open, so he could see that he was the only person in there. He looked around and saw a row of three sinks, each with a single tap that gave cold water and a soap dispenser that no longer held any soap. Along the opposite wall ran one long steel urinal that looked like some kind of communal trough. In it were a handful of yellow blocks that were presumably meant to be air fresheners. Albert breathed in and could immediately tell that they'd stopped working long ago.

Before leaving home, he'd drunk a pint of water and already it was having the desired effect. He took off his gloves, stood at the urinal and unfastened his fly. But he was too nervous to pass water and kept thinking about his dad and his colleagues bursting in here to arrest people all those years ago. The memory dislodged something within him and he felt another clutch of fear. It was no use; he couldn't relax.

He channelled all his energy into lowering his shoulders and allowing the tension to seep out of his body. And then he remembered his dad teaching him a little trick when he was a child and too frightened to wee next to all the grown men; he'd told him to count down from five to one and invariably, by the time he hit one, his bladder would have opened. He tried the trick now and was grateful to see that it worked.

Thanks for that, Dad.

The thought of his dad being in the toilets with him made Albert burst out laughing. Soon, he was laughing so forcefully that he had to concentrate on his aim and not wee down his trousers. He felt a twinge of worry that someone walking past would hear him and wonder what on earth he was laughing at, but he dismissed it and carried on.

He finished and tucked himself away, then washed his hands as well as he could with cold water and no soap. As he dried them on his coat, his laughter dwindled. He reminded himself that he was here for a serious reason.

He poked his head into one of the cubicles. The first thing he noticed was that the toilets hadn't been cleaned for a long time and the ceramic bowls were encrusted with filth. There were clumps of used toilet roll left on the floor, alongside litter, a few lager cans, and even a dirty nappy. Albert's eye was drawn to some graffiti that had been scrawled in black felt-tipped pen on the walls. He peered closer and saw that it mostly consisted of X-rated doodles and insults about people he didn't know. But then he stepped further inside to examine the back of the door and there, to his shock, were the remains of rough engravings that had been scratched into the woodwork what must have been a long time ago. He moved closer and ran his fingers over them. Although they'd been painted over, possibly a few times, he was pretty sure that at some point they'd offered up names and phone numbers. He was surprised to feel something approaching anger uncoil inside him.

These were the names and numbers of men like those his dad and his colleagues had persecuted, men his dad had told him were depraved and disgusting. But these toilets were disgusting, so anyone who'd come here must have been desperate. Albert remembered how terrified he'd been of his secret desires being discovered and how much he'd tried to repress feelings he'd been told were wrong – and he imagined the men who'd come here must have experienced a similar struggle. If he hadn't been able to resist what had been bubbling up inside him, then they wouldn't either. And the only way they'd been able to meet other men who felt the same way as them had been by coming here.

Who knows? If I hadn't met George, maybe I'd have ended up here too.

As he stepped out of the cubicle and made his way over to the mirror, his anger morphed into something he was pretty sure was defiance. He stood looking at himself and didn't just see Albert Entwistle but all the men who'd come here before him.

I'm one of them.

However much I've tried to resist it, I'm one of them.

It was clear to him now that his dad had instilled in him such a fear of these men that it had blinded him to all similarities. For decades he'd doggedly told himself that his attraction to men was incidental, not a core part of who he was. He'd convinced himself that he didn't have to define how he felt about love, that he didn't have to choose a label and announce it to the world. But he could see now that he was wrong.

There was no question that his feelings had shaped who he was; they were a huge part of his identity. And this may have been the source of shame to him in the past, but now he felt ashamed of himself for hiding it. He didn't want to hide it any longer.

Besides, how can I expect George to accept me if I'm not brave enough to accept myself?

He looked himself in the eye and clenched his jaw.

Yes, I'm a gay man. And it's about time I told the world.

Chapter Twenty-Five

Nicole crouched down and read the inscription on the head-stone.

Irene Ashton
1st April 1949 – 22nd January 2016

It was the third anniversary of her grandma's death and she'd come to the cemetery to visit her grave. Before setting off, she'd put Reenie in the crèche, then she'd jumped on board a shabby old bus that had coughed and spluttered all the way to Huddlesden.

Just before the bus had stopped at the cemetery, it had driven past the house where Nicole had grown up with her mum. It had felt strange to see it again but she hadn't felt sad, because the house didn't hold happy memories for her. Now that she was here, though, she *was* feeling sad. *Because my memories of Grandma were all happy.*

When she was little, Nicole's mum would often dump her

at her grandma's house so she could go out on a date – sometimes at short notice. But her grandma would always cancel whatever she had planned and make Nicole feel like all she'd actually wanted to do was spend the evening with her. She'd put on music by Caribbean artists – Mighty Sparrow had been a favourite – and they'd make dhalpuri roti, the stuffed flatbread her grandma said reminded her of Trinidad. Nicole loved being allowed to help her stuff the split peas into the centre of the dough then flatten it out with a rolling pin – and she loved the smell of roasted geera that would fill the kitchen as they worked. If she'd done a good job, her grandma would reward her with a generous portion of her favourite mint choc chip ice cream, a stash of which she always kept in the freezer.

When Nicole was older, she continued to visit her grandma, but now entirely of her own choice. They'd still make roti and, once her grandma had decided Nicole was old enough to handle the heat of Scotch bonnet peppers, she also taught her how to make stewed curry chicken. After they'd eaten, they'd sit in the living room and drink VAT 19 rum, and Nicole would question her grandma about her childhood in Trinidad and what it had been like to move to England as a teenager. They'd also discuss Nicole's dreams for the future – and her grandma would encourage her to believe they were all within reach.

God, I miss that.

God, I miss her.

A robin landed on the headstone and began hopping along. Nicole tried not to frighten it as she gently pulled out a few weeds. She wished she'd been able to afford to buy flowers for the grave but consoled herself that at least she could tidy it up a bit.

As it was such a cold day, she was the only visitor to the cemetery. But she was glad she'd come; she enjoyed the sensation of feeling close to her grandma again.

What I'd give to be able to speak to her about Jamie.

Now more than ever she wished she could ask her grandma's advice. When Jamie first returned to Leeds, the two of them had spent a lot of time texting, calling and FaceTiming, but Nicole couldn't help noticing that their communication was becoming less frequent. Albert had reiterated his advice that she shouldn't lose faith in the relationship but every now and again, when she was on her own at home or feeling lonely, she found herself giving in to the worry that his parents might have been putting renewed pressure on him to break up with her. No matter how much she tried to dismiss it, she couldn't escape the fear that his feelings for her might be fading.

She wished her grandma would send her another sign. She drew in a long breath and looked around for something she could interpret as a message. But there was nothing.

The robin jumped down from the headstone and hopped across the grave.

Nicole watched as he flew away, into the white sky.

Nicole and Lisa sat down and spread out a menu between them. They were in Stanley's, a café in the town centre, just around the corner from the clothes shop where Lisa worked.

It was a surprisingly unfashionable choice for Lisa but she explained that she'd chosen it because she needed to be back at work in fifty minutes.

As Lisa rubbed some hand cream into her palms, Nicole complimented her on her outfit, a navy jumpsuit Lisa told her was by Lavish Alice. Suddenly, Nicole felt conscious of what she was wearing, and the jeans and sweater she'd bought the previous winter seemed faded and out of date.

A man came over to take their order and Nicole worked out that if she had a jacket potato with tuna and a Diet Coke, she'd have just enough money to pay in cash. But Lisa ordered herself a mushroom omelette with salad and a large latte – and a portion of chips on the side.

An awful thought occurred to Nicole. *What if she wants to split the bill?* She imagined telling Lisa that she didn't have enough money to pay her half and could feel the shame burning inside her.

'So how's it going with Simon?' she asked, brightly.

'Oh, it's brilliant, thanks,' Lisa replied. She explained that it was now a fortnight since she'd moved into her boyfriend's flat. 'Living together is literally a dream. Mind you, he does have some annoying habits.'

'Oh yeah? Such as?'

'Like, he always leaves his floss on the sink. *And* he snores. Actually, he doesn't snore; he makes this really annoying whistling sound.'

'Nightmare,' said Nicole, distantly.

'Oh, and we've found out we've got completely different body temperatures. He always wants to turn the heating down so I'm literally freezing. But if I turn it up he says he's, like, boiling.'

Nicole gave a laugh but was struggling to maintain interest. *If only all I had to deal with was Jamie's snoring, or feeling a bit cold.*

She was relieved when the man came back with their food. As soon as he'd gone, she changed the subject.

'Lise, I've been thinking about this idea of running my own salon. I know it's a long-term plan but I've been researching small business loans and reading up on some other people who've done it.'

'Great,' Lisa replied. And she stuffed her mouth full of chips.

'What I can't work out,' Nicole went on, 'is what to do when I finish college. I mean, should I try and find a job in a salon and get experience of that side of things? Or should I set myself up as a mobile beautician and learn how to run my own business?'

'That sounds brilliant,' said Lisa, grabbing another handful of chips.

'Which does?'

'Both.'

Lisa clearly wasn't interested. 'The thing is,' Nicole persisted, 'I'm worried about the set-up costs if I go mobile. And at the moment I'd be too nervous to take out a loan. So do you think I should try and get a job in a salon?'

Lisa stabbed her fork into her omelette and let out a sigh. 'Nic, I don't know what you're worried about. Didn't you say Jamie was, like, minted? Well, if you play your cards right, you literally won't have to work at all.'

Suddenly, Nicole wondered what she was doing chatting to

Lisa. It struck her that her oldest friend had nothing more to contribute to her life. It was a thought that had been bobbing around the outer fringes of her mind for a while but suddenly hit her with the full force of certainty. She couldn't see any point in asking her advice about Jamie.

She asked Lisa another question about Simon and sat back and finished her lunch as she feigned interest in a weekend away they were planning for Valentine's Day. She felt an ache of sadness.

We used to be so close – how did we end up pretending to be interested in each other's lives?

Lisa spotted the time on the TV and said she had to leave. When the owner brought over the bill, Nicole worried again that Lisa would want to split it.

Thankfully, Lisa stood up and handed over her card. 'I'm paying,' she said, 'and I literally won't hear any arguments.'

'But Lise—'

'It's my treat,' she insisted. 'You've come all this way.'

Nicole thanked her repeatedly. And she meant it.

But she had the impression that she wasn't just thanking her for buying her lunch; she was also thanking her for everything she'd done in the past, for everything she'd meant to her in the past. Because she couldn't escape the idea that this was where their friendship belonged – in the past.

As she sat on the bus back to Toddington, Nicole reflected on the fact that it had been only six months since she'd moved away from Huddlesden. But already it had ceased to feel like home.

For better or worse, my life's in Toddington now.

As it was so cold, Nicole had chosen to sit in the back corner, directly above the engine. She remembered her grandma telling her this was always the warmest spot on the bus. But rather than feeling sad at the memory, she found herself smiling.

She looked out of the window as rows and rows of stone terraces toddled past. She checked her messages and sent Lisa a text to say thanks again for lunch. As she put her phone away, she noticed a slip of white paper that somebody had left on the seat opposite. She picked it up and saw it was a used train ticket to Leeds.

How did that get there?

Then she realised.

Of course, it's a sign! Grandma, I knew you'd come through!

With a jolt, Nicole understood exactly what she had to do about Jamie. All of a sudden, it was perfectly obvious.

She logged into her phone and called Albert.

'Albert,' she blurted out as soon as he answered, 'I'm thinking of going to Leeds – to surprise Jamie.'

He took a second before replying. 'Well, I think that's a terrific idea, kid.'

She gave a yelp of excitement. 'I *knew* you'd get it!'

'I mean, just think about me and George,' Albert said. 'I sat around and did nothing about it for years and now I regret that. I wish I'd gone looking for him ages ago.'

Nicole breathed in and out slowly. 'But what if I get there and it turns out Jamie *has* lost interest?'

'Don't you think I've asked myself the same question?' said

Albert. 'Don't you think I'm worried that George will have lost interest ages ago? But even if that's true, surely it's better for us both to know?'

The bus stopped and a man with a cobweb tattoo stepped off.

'You're right,' said Nicole. 'I'll do it.'

'Atta girl!'

'Oh, but there's one other thing . . . will you look after Reenie for me?'

There was a pause.

'You do know I've never done anything like that before?' Albert said. 'What if she cries? What if she doesn't *like* me looking after her?'

'Albert, Reenie *loves* you! You'll be a mint babysitter, I know it.'

Nicole promised to talk Albert through exactly what he needed to do – and to turn around and come straight home if he ran into the slightest difficulty. She could hear him drawing in an unsteady breath.

'Alright, kid. I'll do it.'

She thanked him over and over again and said goodbye. Then she put the phone down and picked up the used train ticket.

Jamie, I'm coming to get you!

Chapter Twenty-Six

'Which Middle Eastern city is also the name of a type of artichoke?'

As Marjorie read out the question, Albert wasn't listening properly. He was too worked up about what he was building up to do. But it was obvious that his teammates were taking the quiz seriously and really wanted to win. They huddled together and whispered amongst themselves.

'Is it Beirut?' asked Smiler.

'What about Baghdad?' said Jack.

'God, you two are right barmpots,' said Sue. 'Who ever heard of an artichoke from Baghdad?'

'I'd never heard of an artichoke at all until tonight,' Jack joked.

Sue rolled her eyes. 'It's Jerusalem. It's a Jerusalem arti-choke.' She wrote it down, shielding the sheet with her arm despite the fact that the next team was sitting at a distance of five metres.

They were in a pub called The Drunken Duck, where

most of the staff of Toddington's Royal Mail delivery centre had gathered to take part in the quiz to raise funds to send Marjorie's ill grandson to Disney World. It was a 1960s pub with one big low-ceilinged room that lacked character and had the distinct whiff of an old dishcloth. Everyone was sitting on uncomfortably hard wooden stools but seemed to be in good spirits. Marjorie had put Albert in a team alongside Tsunami, Smiler, Jack and his two friends, and joining them was a friend of Sue's who'd just started working on the collections counter. Delphine was a confident woman with a face that reminded Albert of a Siamese cat. Although she was doing her best to feign interest in the quiz, it was clear she was much more focused on attracting the attention of Ste Stockton, who'd recently broken up with his girlfriend. She'd turned up in a tiny dress with straps as thin as spaghetti and Albert couldn't help thinking that she broke his mam's rule that a woman should show her cleavage or legs but never both. Although her strategy seemed to be working; every few minutes Ste glanced over like a shark eyeing up a particularly fleshy salmon.

'Did you see that?' Delphine asked Sue. 'He's totally checking me out!'

'Question number seven,' interrupted Marjorie, her microphone giving a blast of feedback. 'According to mythology, Romulus and Remus were brought up by which animal?'

'Piece of piss,' boomed Jack. 'A wolf.'

'Sssh!' Sue hissed. 'Don't give away the answers!'

Albert did his best to replicate his teammates' enthusiasm but he couldn't take anything in; all he could think about was how he was going to make his announcement.

The words he was going to say were going round in his head, those two little words that had frightened him for so long.

'Question number eight,' said Marjorie, 'what do you call the art of stuffing animals?'

'Taxidermy!' Sue threw in before anyone else had the chance.

'Are you sure?' asked Smiler. 'Isn't it polygamy?'

'You daft apeth,' said Sue. 'That's when you have more than one wife.'

'God, I couldn't think of owt worse,' said Jack. 'One's more than enough for me.'

'It's taxidermy,' Sue insisted. As she wrote the answer down, she glanced over at the next table suspiciously.

'I'll keep an eye on them,' said Delphine, seizing her opportunity to have another look at Ste. 'Look at the size of him,' she said to no one in particular, 'I bet he's hung like a mule.'

Albert spat his cider back into the glass, although Delphine didn't seem to notice. In fact, he might as well have been invisible. He remembered that just a few weeks ago he used to wish for just this and realised how much he'd changed. The problem was, he'd spent so long keeping his distance from his colleagues that they weren't used to socialising with him and didn't really include him.

He picked up a damp beermat and spun it between his fingers, wondering what he should do to integrate into the group. Then the soggy beermat gave him an idea; if he wanted to endear himself to his teammates he could always buy them a round of drinks.

'I'm rubbish at general knowledge . . .' he announced. 'What are you all supping?'

266

He took their orders and headed over to the bar. He added a second pint of cider for himself, and waited as the barman poured the drinks.

The quiz continued in the background with a sports round. Albert was relieved not to be included. *I really am rubbish at that!*

When he sat back down, he tipped back half of his cider in one swig. If there was ever a time he needed alcohol to loosen him up, it was now. But he was determined not to back out of his plan.

After the interval, Marjorie introduced a quick-fire music round – and one of her questions gave Albert the opportunity he'd been waiting for.

'For which Broadway musical did Leonard Bernstein and Stephen Sondheim write the song "Somewhere"?'

I know – West Side Story.

'Isn't it *Oklahoma?*' said Jack.

'I'm pretty sure it's *Les Mis*,' said Sue.

No, it's West Side Story. *George used to sing it to me when we were on the moors. We used to say it was our song.*

'Actually,' said Smiler, 'I think it's *Phantom of the Opera.*'

'It's *West Side Story*,' Albert chipped in.

Everyone turned to look at him, except for Delphine, who was still mesmerised by Ste.

'Really?' said Sue. 'Are you sure?'

'Yeah, perfectly sure.'

'But couldn't you have got mixed up? I mean, some of those show tunes sound pretty similar.'

Go on, Albert, tell them how you know.

Go on, Albert, you can do it.

He took a ragged breath. 'No, I know it was *West Side Story* because I used to dance to it with my boyfriend.'

There was a stunned silence. Jack's mouth fell open and Delphine finally tore her eyes away from Ste.

Albert hadn't made his announcement in anything like the way he'd imagined. But the important thing was he'd made it.

'And moving on,' said Marjorie, 'who released the album *Natural* in 1996?'

Albert's team had stopped listening.

'Wait a minute,' said Sue, 'are you telling us you're gay?'

Albert nodded. 'I suppose I am. Yeah, I'm gay.'

It was the first time he'd said the words. It struck him how strange they sounded coming out of his mouth.

But before anyone could respond, Marjorie jumped in again. 'Next question: which band, formed in 1990, started out with five members, then went down to four, then back up to five, and now has three?'

'Take That!' said Smiler.

Everyone's attention switched back to the quiz.

'Come on, guys,' said Sue, 'we need to stay focused. We can piss all over these amateurs.'

But what about me? What about focusing on me?

'Oh, and by the way, it's Peter Andre,' she added, 'the answer to the previous question. I used to fancy him like mad when I was a teenager.'

As Marjorie rattled her way through the rest of the quiz, Albert's revelation wasn't mentioned. But he felt as if it had pulled up a seat and joined them at the table. And he had no idea whether or not it was welcome.

Well, I can't take it back now. And even if they don't like it, I'm still glad I did it.

But the second Marjorie declared the quiz over, everyone turned to Albert. And, as if someone had uncorked a bottle of champagne, their good wishes came frothing out.

'Albert, I'm so happy for you,' said Sue.

'I only wish you'd told us sooner,' said Smiler.

In an instant, Albert went from not feeling included to feeling like he was at the centre of the group. But, although this came as a huge relief, it was also slightly overwhelming.

'So what happened to this boyfriend?' asked Sue.

'Are you still seeing him?' probed Delphine, her interest piqued.

As he did his best to answer their questions, Albert noticed Jack sloping off in the direction of the toilets.

Oh no, I hope he's not going to spoil things . . .

Jack's friends at least seemed happy. They'd clearly had no idea he was anything other than straight. But once they'd got over their shock, they jumped up to buy a round of celebratory drinks.

'Sorry if we've ever said anything out of turn,' one of them offered.

'Yeah,' said the other, 'we know our banter can sometimes get out of hand.'

'That's OK,' said Albert, 'apology accepted.'

Although it's an apology from Jack I really want.

Marjorie took hold of the microphone and instructed

everyone to swap their answer sheets with the table to their left. Delphine shot up like a rocket and sidled over to Ste, curling her team's answer sheet into a baton she proceeded to run up and down his chest.

Albert leaned back on his stool as Marjorie began reading out the answers. There was a loud cheer from his teammates when it came to the question about 'Somewhere', and a minor rumpus broke out when one of the girls from Finance disputed one of the answers, pointing out that Dubai wasn't a country but a city.

Sue arrowed her a murderous look. 'I wish that silly cow would keep her trap shut – she's just lost us a point!'

Once the marking was over, Marjorie asked for the sheets to be handed in. Just when Albert was preparing himself for another onslaught of attention, he was approached by Jack.

'Albert,' he said, 'have you got a minute?'

Albert was surprised but stood up and followed him across the room. He had no idea what Jack was going to say. *I hope he's not going to tell me not to ram it down his throat. I hope he's not going to warn me off making a play for him.*

They settled in a quiet spot by the entrance hall.

'What's the matter?' Albert asked.

Jack rose up on to the balls of his feet then lowered himself down again. 'I just wanted to say sorry – if I've ever said owt about gays that weren't very nice, like.'

Albert was taken aback. 'Oh, right, yes, well, great.'

'It's just, I had no idea – you didn't *seem* gay.'

Albert told himself that here was his chance to make a point. 'Yeah, well, maybe you need to rethink your ideas about what gay people are like.'

Jack nodded. 'OK, yeah, I will.'

'Thanks,' said Albert. And then he wished he hadn't. *What do I have to thank him for?*

'Any road, I know I can overstep the mark sometimes,' Jack went on. 'But if it's any consolation, most of the time I don't mean it.'

'Why do you say it then?' This came out more aggressively than Albert intended.

Jack frowned and let out a long breath. 'I don't know. I suppose I just want people to keep listening . . . I suppose I just want them to like me.'

Albert was intrigued. 'But you don't have to say nasty things to make people like you.'

'No, I know. But I don't want people to see through me. I don't want them to realise there's nowt to me.'

'Jack, what are you on about?'

'Oh, come on, Albert, I'm a loser. I'm no good at owt. It's our Doreen who props me up and keeps me going.'

'Your Doreen? But you're always moaning about her.'

'Yeah, but that's only so people won't see that she's brilliant and I'm crap. She does everything, Albert. She runs the show.'

'But, Jack, that's nothing to be ashamed of.'

'No, but it's nowt to be proud of, either – not if you're the kind of bloke I am. Or the kind of bloke people think I am.'

There was a silence while Albert thought about what Jack was saying. He didn't recognise the man Jack was revealing himself to be.

Just then, the door opened and Barbara and one of the other cleaners clattered through with a whiff of cigarette smoke.

The two men smiled and waited until they were back inside the main room.

'Oh, and in case you're wondering,' Jack continued, 'I'd never cheat on Doreen. I know I talk the talk and all that, but if I ever lost her I'd be a mess.'

Albert wasn't sure how to respond; he'd only just emerged from decades of keeping his most intimate feelings to himself, and now here was the man who made him feel the most uncomfortable revealing his own emotions.

He cleared his throat. 'Thanks for that. It's good to hear there's more to you than you let on. Same with me, really. But if there's one thing I've learned, it's that trying to be anyone other than yourself will never make you happy. Any road, how do you know people won't like you if you don't ever show them the real you?'

Jack looked at his feet as he considered this. 'I never thought of it like that . . . but good point.'

Just then the door was flung open again and two of the girls from Finance barrelled in from the main room clutching a packet of cigarettes.

Albert waited for the door to clang shut behind them. 'Right, come on, let's get back in and see if we've won.'

'Alright, mate,' said Jack. But rather than moving, he rose up again on the balls of his feet. 'And congratulations on coming out, like.'

'Thanks,' said Albert. And this time he didn't regret it. 'Thanks, Jack.'

With that the two men shook hands and opened the doors to go back and join their team.

Straight away they were hit by the sight of Ste and Delphine, who were leaning against a wall, kissing so passionately that Albert wondered how they managed to breathe. He smiled, glad that all Delphine's effort had paid off.

Everyone else in the room was chattering excitedly, waiting for the results of the quiz.

'Now here are the scores in reverse order,' announced Marjorie.

Albert slipped back to his table just in time to hear that his team had finished second to last. Everyone was devastated – and outraged.

'I can't believe it,' said Smiler.

'Do you think we should ask for a re-mark?' said Jack.

'If it weren't for that silly cow from Finance we'd have scored one more,' said Sue.

Albert seemed to be the only person who wasn't upset. As far as he was concerned, he'd won anyway.

The only problem was, news of his coming out was spreading across the room. One by one, heads turned to look at him and colleagues he hardly knew came over to congratulate him. *If only their congratulations weren't followed up by a barrage of questions.*

'When did you first know you were gay?'

'Have you ever slept with a woman?'

'How can you be sure you don't like it if you've never tried it?'

It was clear that the alcohol was making his colleagues feel emboldened and, although Albert was happy to discuss the subject with them, maybe the end of a long night drinking wasn't the best time. Just then he spotted the girls from Finance staggering over.

'Go on, babe,' said one of them, 'tell him about that time you tried it up the bum.'

Albert shot to his feet – he needed to get out of here. He made an excuse about wanting to go to the toilet, remembering there was a side exit through which he could make his escape.

But when he got to the cloakroom to pick up his coat, he spotted Marjorie. She was sitting on her own counting a pile of money. And, despite her jauntiness onstage, she seemed sad and weary.

'Alright, Marjorie?' he said. 'What are you up to?

She looked up from her moneybox and sighed. 'Oh hi, love. I'm just seeing how much money we've made.'

'It's been a big success, hasn't it?'

She patted down a bundle of notes. 'Yeah, it has. And everyone's been really supportive. We've raised £320.'

'Oh, that's terrific. So what's the matter?'

'Well, I know that's brilliant and everything – and I really don't want to sound ungrateful – but I'm still two grand short of my target. Two grand, Albert!'

'Oh no, I didn't realise.'

He sat down next to her and she shunted over to make room.

'The thing is,' she went on, 'I'm running out of ideas. There's only so many quizzes I can organise and mince pies I can make. Where the hell am I going to find another two grand?'

'Don't give up,' said Albert, encouragingly, 'I'm sure we can think of something.'

Marjorie's chin gave a little wobble. 'That's sweet of you, love, but we don't have the time. We've just found out our Brad's condition's worse than we thought. The doctor says he's not going to recover. And in a few months he'll be too poorly to travel.'

Albert felt his heart contract. 'Oh, I'm so sorry, Marjorie. I had no idea.'

She shook her head and gave a sniff. 'You know, he's such a lovely lad. It's so unfair he's got all this to deal with. I keep thinking about what he was like when he was little and how much he used to enjoy being around animals. This time last year, he was saying he wanted to be a vet. Now he doesn't talk about the future any more – he knows there's no point.'

Albert bowed his head. 'The poor lad.'

'The worst thing is,' Marjorie said, her cheeks flushing, 'I just have to sit back and watch it happen – there's nothing I can do to stop it.'

Albert reached out and drew her into a warm hug.

'All I want now is to make the time he has left as enjoyable as possible,' she went on. 'But it looks like I'm going to fail there too.'

Albert felt a rumble of guilt that, until tonight, he hadn't done anything to contribute to her fundraising efforts. He wished there was some way he could make it up to her. 'But Marjorie, you shouldn't be so hard on yourself,' he attempted. 'It's really not your fault.'

She broke away from the hug and rubbed the tears from her eyes. 'Oh, I know, love. But that doesn't make it any easier.'

She picked up her bag and began rummaging around in it. After a few seconds she drew out her fan and snapped it open. 'It doesn't help that I'm going through this blasted menopause. Honestly, I know I make a joke of it but it's bloody awful. I force myself to slap a smile on my face but inside I'm as miserable as sin. Some days, all I want to do is stay at home and cry.'

Albert felt a stab of empathy. ''Ere,' he said, 'give us that fan.'

She handed it over and he began fanning her as vigorously as he could.

'Oh, that's nice,' she said, leaning back and closing her eyes, 'it's better when you do it.'

'Marjorie!' The barman poked his head around the door.

'Don't mind us,' said Marjorie, her jaunty façade re-erected. 'I'm just having one of my power surges.'

The barman looked bemused. 'I was just going to say, if you're announcing how much you've made, could you let people know it's last orders?'

'Yep,' she said, 'I'm on my way.'

She stood up and Albert handed her back the fan.

'Well, thanks for sitting with me,' she said, patting him on the arm.

'That's alright, it was my pleasure.'

'Oh, and I haven't even said congratulations on your news. I hear your announcement went down well.'

Albert felt another rumble of guilt that, just as he was

starting to enjoy his life, Marjorie must be feeling like hers was collapsing. 'Yeah, yeah, but don't you worry about that. You get back in there and tell everyone how well you've done.'

She nodded and tucked the moneybox under her arm. As he watched her walk away, Albert remembered how good he'd felt when he'd made his anonymous deliveries to Edith. It had reminded him of the reason why he'd become a postman – so he could spread around some of the happiness he felt, knowing he was loved by George.

He slipped out of the side door and, as soon as he arrived home, logged into the mobile banking app he'd started using. Although his salary was modest, he'd never really had anything to spend it on – and he'd inherited his house from his parents so had never had to pay a mortgage. Consequently, he'd built up what felt to him like a lot of savings. *And they're not doing any good just sitting there.*

He found the link to Marjorie's fundraising page and clicked on a button that allowed him to make a donation anonymously.

Then he transferred the sum of £2,000.

And he patted his pocket containing the letter from George.

Chapter Twenty-Seven

Albert woke early and lay in bed reliving the night before.

I came out. I actually came out.

For a split second he felt a flurry of fear. But he dismissed it with a reminder of how positively people had responded. Then he remembered that he'd left the pub early, to dodge people's questions – but there'd be no avoiding them today.

As he cycled into the office, he tried reassuring himself that by now no one would care. *They've probably forgotten all about it already.*

He walked into the building and saw Ste sitting in his usual spot, looking like he'd been dug up.

'How do,' Albert chirped. 'Not posting any fitness videos today?'

'Nah, mate. I'm way too hanging for that.'

See, Albert told himself, *you're perfectly safe.*

'You'd better get in there,' Ste went on, 'everyone's well excited to see you.'

Excited? To see me?

With a new trepidation, Albert pushed open the door to the main sorting office.

''Ere he is!' shouted Marjorie. 'Get that music on!'

As the introduction to 'I'm Coming Out' by Diana Ross blasted out of some speakers, the entire team gathered around to cheer Albert's arrival. He noticed that they'd decorated the office with rainbow flags and bunting, and unicorn-shaped balloons were hanging from every sorting cart and frame. Sue had tied rainbow ribbons through her hair, Barbara had tied them to her cleaning trolley, and Marjorie was wearing a T-shirt bearing the slogan 'GAY ALL DAY'.

'We're throwing you a coming out party!' she announced.

Albert was flabbergasted. 'But . . . but . . . how did you have time to organise all this?'

'Oh, I've been planning it for ages!' she said, cheekily. 'I knew it'd happen sooner or later. Anyway, what do you think?'

Albert could feel his chin trembling. 'I love it,' he managed. 'But you really shouldn't have gone to so much trouble.'

'Are you joking?' she said. 'How often do we get the chance to go gay for the day?'

Albert looked at the sea of smiles spreading out before him and felt the tears building up in his eyes. 'Just a minute . . . just let me take off my coat and I'll be right back.'

He dashed over to his frame and turned away from the party while he squeezed his eyes shut and tried to compose himself.

I can't believe they've done all this for me.

He drew in a shaky breath.

I can't believe I fought against this for such a long time ... and all along, this is how they'd react.

He sniffed back the tears.

Well, the least you can do is get back over there and enjoy it.

He flung off his coat and adjusted his face into a smile. He turned back to face everyone. 'OK, gang, let's have a party!'

'Wooo!' cheered Marjorie, and she thrust some kind of non-alcoholic cocktail into his hand. 'Now, are you ready for the entertainment?'

'Entertainment? What do you mean, entertainment?'

'Get a load of this. Hit it, Ste!'

He turned around to see that Ste had come in to join them and, despite his hangover, whipped off his jacket to reveal a white muscle vest that made him look like one of the men in an artwork by Tom of Finland. He turned a dial on a huge sound system and faded out the sound of Diana Ross. As the introduction to the next song faded up, the staff began clapping along and hollering excitedly. It was 'In the Navy' by the Village People.

As the vocal came in, the main doors swung open and in burst four men dressed as the characters from the 1970s pop group; a builder, a cowboy, an American Indian and a policeman. Albert recognised them as Jack's two friends, plus Smiler and – in the middle, wearing a full-feathered headdress – Jack himself. Much to his amusement, they began dancing their way through a routine and lip-synching along to the lyrics. Some of their moves were clumsily executed, and they clearly didn't know all the words, but this didn't affect their enthusiasm. Just as the chorus was about to begin, Jack produced a sailor's hat and came over to pop it on Albert's head.

'Come on, mate,' he said, 'are you going to dance with us?'

Albert froze.

He remembered the struggle he'd mounted when Marjorie had tried to drag him up on to the dance floor at the Christmas party. *Am I really ready to dance in front of all my colleagues?*

'Oh, come on,' persisted Jack, 'everyone knows gays are good at dancing.' And just in case Albert couldn't tell he was joking, he gave him a wink.

'Well, let's see if you're right,' Albert quipped. And he gave Jack a wink back.

Jack held out his hand and Albert took it. To more cheers from his colleagues, he allowed himself to be led into the area that had been designated as a dance floor. And he joined in the routine. Even though he felt a little self-conscious, he was able to keep up with the steps easily. Pretty soon, his reserve was dissolving and he was twisting and skipping with all the skill and agility he employed at home. Just as he'd imagined, it was leaving his colleagues open-mouthed.

'I never knew you were such a good dancer,' gasped Jack.

'No, but let's be honest,' said Albert, 'there's a lot you didn't know about me.' He gave him a wry grin.

Everyone rushed on to the dance floor to join them and it soon became so crowded Albert had to give up on the routine to move around freestyle. As he leaped and twirled from colleague to colleague, he could feel himself breaking free of every last inhibition. And the happiness vibrated through him, just as it did at home – but this felt even better because other people were sharing it.

Oh, why did I spend so long dancing in private? Why didn't I realise how much better it is to dance with other people?

'In The Navy' gave way to 'It's Raining Men', which gave way to 'I Am What I Am', which was when Albert started to feel emotional again. He'd always thought the song was a bit of fun but, as he listened to the lyrics now – now that he'd accepted who he was – it meant so much more. Thankfully, Marjorie intervened with a polite reminder that, although the team had something to celebrate, they still had work to do. The soundtrack of gay anthems continued to pump around the office as everyone jigged over to their workstations.

Albert sat at his frame and began sorting through his mail. Over the next few hours, colleague after colleague came over to congratulate him – and, just like last night, their congratulations were followed by a barrage of questions. But this time he didn't mind; he was so moved by all the effort everyone had put into the party that answering their questions was the least he could do. His happiness swelled until he felt like it was lifting him up like one of the unicorn balloons.

When the time came to go out on his walk, he decided to wear his sailor hat; he wanted to keep the celebrations going for as long as possible. But then, just as he was telling his colleagues he'd see them later, something happened to yank everyone's attention away from the party. A loud squeal came from Marjorie's office and she rushed over to her door.

'Guess what, everyone?' she shouted. 'We've just hit our target!'

As she explained that someone had made an anonymous donation of £2,000 to her fundraising page, Albert ducked his head and slipped out of the office.

As he drove through town, Albert became aware that the car behind him was beeping its horn. He checked to see that he didn't have his lights on but the car carried on beeping.

When he stopped at the traffic lights, it pulled up alongside him. He looked out of the window and saw that it was being driven by his next-door neighbour. He was waving at Albert and gesturing for him to wind down his window. Albert complied, interested to hear what he had to say.

'Congratulations!' the man shouted. 'My mate Ste texted me last night. I hear you came out as gay.'

Bloomin' 'eck, news travels fast!

'Oh, y-y-yes,' Albert stammered, 'yes, I did.'

'Well, we're all really chuffed for you. The kids have been having LGBT week at school. Do you fancy coming round one night and chatting to them?'

'Yes . . . erm . . . alright, yes, of course.'

And then the lights changed and Albert had to wave goodbye.

As he continued down the high street, he felt another brief resurgence of his old fear, a fear of how people would respond if his secret got out. But this evaporated as soon as he parked his van and checked his phone; over the course of the morning, he'd received several friend requests on social media, mainly from people in the office. Several of them had tagged him in photos they'd posted of the coming out party, photos that captured the joy of the event. As he scrolled down the list of friend requests, accepting them all, he felt the warm glow inside him burning a little brighter. He looked in the mirror and remembered that he was still wearing his sailor hat. He decided to keep it on, adjusting it so it was sitting at a jaunty angle.

Just as he was stepping out of the van, Ted Hardacre came out of his shop, said he'd heard the news, and offered his congratulations. 'My wife's cousin's gay,' he added, '*and* he's single. Would you like me to fix you up?'

'Oh, I'm not sure what's happening on that front at the moment,' said Albert. 'But thanks, anyway.'

He began striding down the street. Within seconds, he was almost accosted by Jean Carter and Beverley Liptrot.

'Albert!' Jean gushed. 'It's *so* nice to see you!'

'We heard your news,' Beverley trilled. 'It's dead exciting – congratulations!'

Albert couldn't help smirking; although he'd been delivering their post for years, neither Jean nor Bev had even so much as said hello to him before. 'Thanks,' he said, 'that's really kind.'

'You know, we're very close friends with Daniel and Danny,' Bev added.

'We should all go out sometime,' said Jean.

'We could drink cocktails!' said Bev. 'We *love* cocktails!'

Albert didn't have the heart to tell them he didn't.

'You know, my husband once tried changing lanes without indicating,' jumped in Jean, lowering her voice.

As Albert understood the euphemism, he gave a little gasp.

'Between us,' she added, 'I actually quite liked it.'

He gave a cough and reverted to the excuse he used to rely on when he wanted to move on. 'Well, I mustn't dawdle – these letters won't deliver themselves!'

When he came to Edith's house, she was standing on the doorstep.

'Where've you been?' she called out. 'I've been waiting for you for ages!'

'Sorry,' he said, 'it's been quite a morning.'

'Yes, well, I wanted to give you this – to say congratulations.'

Edith held out a beautiful rainbow sash with glittery edges. 'I dug out my old sewing machine for the first time in years. I wanted to make you something special to mark the occasion.'

'Oh, Edith, thanks so much. That's very thoughtful of you.'

She lifted it up to hang it around his neck but Albert found himself hesitating.

'You don't have to hide away any more,' Edith reassured him. 'Finally, you can be proud of who you are.'

Albert took the sash and hung it around his neck.

He said goodbye and sprung on. When he passed the public toilets he gave a little salute, and when he drew up in front of the stone lion he reached up to kiss it on the cheek.

'You little belter!'

Shortly afterwards, he came to Pear Tree Street and the home of Daniel and Danny.

'Congratulations!' they said as they threw open the door and drew him into a hug.

Although he was happy to reciprocate, Albert felt a little

bashful. 'Oh, I'm not sure I deserve that from you two. Come on, it took me long enough.'

Danny shook his head. 'Yeah but the longer you leave it, I reckon the harder it is. So from now on I'm totally stanning you.'

Albert had no idea what he meant but smiled politely.

'The important thing is you got there in the end,' added Daniel. 'We always knew you would.'

Albert's eyebrows shot up to his hairline. 'Bloomin' 'eck . . . Could you tell, too?'

'Of course we could,' said Daniel. 'That's why we didn't mind when you were awkward around us.'

I don't know, all that time I was frightened of what people would think. And half of them knew, anyway!

'Welcome to the club, darling!' warbled Danny.

'Yes, welcome to the family,' said Daniel.

Albert shuffled from one foot to the other and smiled coyly. 'Ta. Ta very much.'

He felt another rumble of guilt as he remembered Victor accusing him of being too cowardly to take any risks but wanting to lap up the rewards of other men's courage. When Daniel and Danny invited him round for dinner, he insisted they come round to his house.

'We'd be delighted,' said Daniel. 'And thank you very much.'

They leaned forward to give him another hug, and Danny kissed Albert on the cheek.

As he made his way back to the main road, he could feel the warm glow inside him burning brighter than ever. He raced through his lunch and worked through the addresses on the Flowers Estate as quickly as he could. He was excited to see Nicole.

When he reached her house, he saw that Reenie had been posted at the window as a lookout. As he skipped up the path, she waved at him and his heart soared.

Once he'd been congratulated, he discovered that the two of them had made him a coming out card, on the front of which Reenie had drawn a picture of what he thought was a unicorn jumping over a rainbow.

'Happy Coming Out Day, Albert!' Nicole had written inside. 'With lots of love from your friends, Nicole and Reenie xxxxx'

'Oh, and we've got you a present, too,' said Nicole. 'The only thing is, you can't have it till tomorrow.'

Albert's eyebrow twitched. 'Oh yeah? What is it?'

'I'm not telling – you'll just have to wait and see. All I'll say is, it's something we need to do before we go to Manchester.'

Albert gave her a warm smile. Although he'd already been inundated with good wishes, Nicole and Reenie's reaction was without doubt the most moving. Because this felt like it was coming from the people who mattered most. Not only that, but it was coming from the people who knew him best.

And at last I've worked out that these two things are one and the same.

Chapter Twenty-Eight

Nicole sat Albert down and swept a cloak around him. 'OK,' she announced, 'it's time for your makeover!'

Albert mimed an expression of fear. For a brief moment he considered putting up genuine resistance, then remembered that George had always been proud of his appearance and had done things people would now class as 'male grooming'. Ever since Nicole's Humpty Dumpty comment, he'd been thinking about his appearance and whether George would still find him attractive. *Let's be honest, the last time he saw me I was a teenager – and now I'm an old man.*

'Now, I'm going to start with your hair,' Nicole explained, spraying water on to his head. 'I'm not going to do anything radical but the cut's a bit basic. I want to give it a bit of an edge.'

Albert felt a prickle of fear. 'What do you mean, "a bit of an edge"?'

She combed the water through his hair. 'I'm just going to give you a fade at the back and sides. Trust me, it'll look unreal.'

Albert did trust her, so he decided to abandon himself to

the process. He was sitting at her dining table. Spread out on a towel around him were all types of professional hair and beauty equipment she'd borrowed from college.

She picked up some clippers and began trimming the hair around his ears. By his feet, Reenie was playing with her George Pig toy and what looked like a Peppa Pig ice cream van. As he watched clumps of his hair fall on to the carpet, Albert chatted to Nicole about her course, what she was about to learn next, and her plans for when the course finished. Once she'd finished trimming the back and sides of his head, she picked up some scissors and began cutting the hair on top, adding what she called 'movement'.

'Nicole,' he asked, 'do you think George will still fancy me?'

'I should hope so – after all this,' she joked.

'No, but seriously. The last time I saw him was fifty years ago. What if he thinks I've gone to seed?'

Nicole stepped back and looked him in the eye. 'Albert, you haven't gone to seed. And anyway, George might like a more mature look. He might be into a silver fox.'

Albert mimed outrage. 'Excuse me, I've hardly got any grey!'

She chuckled. 'Alright, alright, forget about the silver fox then. But maybe he likes a DILF.'

'A DILF? What's a DILF?'

Nicole explained that DILF was a derivative of MILF. 'It stands for "Dad I'd Like To Fuck".'

Albert gave a little gasp. Then he couldn't help breaking into a grin. 'DILF? I should be so lucky. I'm old enough to be a granddad – the best I could hope for is to be a GrILF.'

Nicole threw her head back and laughed. Seeing her so

amused made Albert follow suit – and soon the two of them were laughing so much they were shaking.

Nicole gave him a little slap on the shoulder. 'Now sit still or else I'll chop your ear off!'

Once he'd composed himself, she finished cutting his hair then trimmed his nasal hair, tidied up the strands sprouting from his ears, and threaded his eyebrows – which he found surprisingly painful, and made him give out a little howl.

'Right, we're done,' she said, once he'd recovered. She whipped away the cloak and handed him a mirror. 'Ta-dah!'

Albert examined himself and saw that she'd given him a much sharper, fresher look.

'Well, what do you think?' she asked. 'I think it's mint.'

'Yeah, it's terrific. Ta very much, kid.'

Nicole nodded. 'Oh, and there's one other thing I need to talk to you about.'

Her tone of voice made Albert suspicious. 'Uh-oh. I don't like the sound of this.'

'Don't worry, it's nothing to be frightened of. But there's something else that's changed in the last fifty years. And it's something you need to be aware of before you see George.'

She moved closer and lowered her voice. 'Albert, have you ever heard of manscaping?'

'*Manscaping*?'

'Yeah.' She began picking at her teeth. 'I suppose you'd say it's tidying things up down below – like we've just done up top.'

Albert's eyes swelled in their sockets.

'Chill,' Nicole said, 'everyone does it now. I'm sure George is all over it.'

Albert looked in the mirror and could see that the colour was draining from his cheeks.

'There's no need to panic,' Nicole reassured him, 'it's easy to do. But it's one thing I'm *not* going to help you with. Go away and google it – and see what you think.'

'OK,' Albert managed. 'I will.'

Nicole clapped her hands and rubbed them together. 'Now, come on, it's time for Stage Two.'

'Stage Two?'

'Get your coat on – we're going into town.'

With Nicole beside him pushing Reenie in her buggy, Albert strode into Klobber. He was greeted by a row of mannequins with pronounced arm and leg muscles straining at the seams of the latest fashions. Once again, the music was playing so loudly he could feel the bass reverberating through him. But this time he didn't feel intimidated.

Because this time I'm with friends.

'Hi, babe!'

Coming towards him was Scorpia, with the same perfect blow-dry she'd had when Albert had come in to buy his outfit for the Christmas party. 'You off on another work do?' she asked.

Without any hesitation, Nicole stepped in. 'Actually, he's just come out as gay and is going to Manchester to look for a boyfriend he hasn't seen for fifty years.'

Scorpia shook her head in shock. 'Seriously?'

She leaned on a pile of jeans and showered Albert with

questions. He answered them all then told her that Nicole was giving him a makeover.

'I *thought* you looked different,' she said. 'That haircut is beaut!'

'Now all we need is to find him something to wear,' Nicole interjected. 'Something that'll make him look on point on Canal Street.'

With an instant camaraderie, Nicole and Scorpia began darting around the store picking up trousers and tops they held up against Albert to approve or dismiss. Once they judged that he had a big enough selection, they swept him into the changing rooms, where he disappeared into a cubicle and began trying everything on. Every few minutes, he stepped out to show the girls what he was wearing. Before long, he was heaving a huge stack of clothes out of the fitting room and over to the till.

As Scorpia scanned the price tags, she gave him a warm smile. 'Well, I hope this guy appreciates all your effort.'

'Ta,' said Albert. 'So do I.'

Into his head flashed a scene in which he found George but George told him he didn't want anything to do with him. He breathed in and cleared it from his mind. He felt a pang of frustration that, now he was ready, he was going to have to wait another week before going to Manchester. Marjorie had offered to babysit for Nicole – after working out that she was the same girl who'd done her nails at college – but she wasn't free until the following Saturday.

Be patient, lad. You've waited nearly fifty years – one more week isn't going to make a difference.

*

292

That evening, Albert looked after Reenie so that Nicole could go to Leeds.

He filled a bottle with milk, as Nicole had directed, and sat on the futon to read Reenie a story. As she snuggled into his chest, he softened his voice and began reading about Peppa Pig, pausing at the end of each page to let her turn it. It was a story Reenie had heard so many times she occasionally broke away from her bottle to point at the pictures and read the odd word along with him. But very slowly her head began to droop and, before he'd reached the end, the bottle had fallen out of her hand.

'Come on,' he whispered, 'it's time for bobo.'

He carried her upstairs and laid her down in her cot. Once he was satisfied he hadn't disturbed her, he texted Nicole to let her know Reenie was asleep. Then he lingered by the door, watching her. She seemed so peaceful, it was inconceivable that the life stretching ahead of her would be marked by all kinds of dramas and challenges. Whatever happened to her, he hoped she didn't ever feel there were parts of herself she had to keep secret from the world. He hoped she was happy.

And I hope she always feels as loved as she is now.

He tiptoed downstairs and began gathering up all the pictures he and Reenie had spent most of the evening colouring in. He straightened them out and slotted them back into the folds of the activity book.

In some ways I'm like a picture that hasn't been coloured in yet. Or one that I'm still in the process of colouring in . . .

'Well, it's certainly very colourful,' says Albert.

George twirls around to show him his new outfit. He's wearing brown paisley flared slacks and a bright orange body-hugging shirt with chest pockets, a large pointed collar, and wide, blousey sleeves. Setting off the look is a mustard-yellow floral-patterned silk scarf that's tied around his neck in a bow.

'Do you like it?' he asks.

Albert looks George up and down and nods approvingly. 'I think you look very snazzy.'

It's a warm evening in early August and the sun is hanging low in a cloudless sky. The boys have just met outside the bunker and, once they've given each other a kiss, Albert clears some twigs from a patch of grass and they sit down.

'You know, I think this orange would look great on you,' George says, gesturing to his shirt.

Albert looks at him with horror. 'Get out of it! I couldn't wear owt like that. I couldn't stand everyone gawping at me.'

George shrugs. 'Oh I'm not fussed about that.'

'Fair do's,' says Albert. 'But aren't you frightened that wearing that kind of thing will only get you into trouble? That it'll only make the other lads pick on you more?'

Now it's George's turn to look at Albert in horror. 'I hope you're not suggesting I tone myself down, Albert. I hope you're not suggesting I go from being my vibrant, multi-coloured self to being a dull, boring, miserable grey.'

Albert pulls the seeds off some long grass and rolls them between his palms. 'No, I just think that sometimes it doesn't do any harm to keep your head down, that's all. Any road, we come up here, don't we? We wouldn't kiss or owt like that down on t' market square.'

'But that's only because if we did we'd get chucked in prison.'

A weight suddenly presses in on Albert. 'Oh let's not talk about that. I don't even like thinking about that.'

George sits forward. 'But doesn't it make you angry, Albert? Doesn't it make you angry that the only place we can kiss is up here?'

Albert scatters the seeds on to the ground. *But I like it here,* he wants to say. *I like it when it's just me and you.*

'I suppose it might if I gave it more thought,' he says.

'Well, you *should* give it more thought,' George hits back, 'because it's unfair. It's like I said to you in Blackpool, what's so wrong about you and me?'

'Nowt. Absolutely nowt.' Albert pauses and pulls at some more grass seeds. 'But I do sometimes wonder . . . Why do you think we turned out like we did?'

'How do you mean?'

'Well, how come we fancy each other and not girls?' He tosses the seeds as far as he can.

George lets out a sigh. 'I don't know. All I know is I never did.'

'Me neither. All that lipstick and perfume and hairspray.'

George chuckles. 'Never mind that, what about the knockers? I wouldn't know what to do with 'em!'

They erupt in loud laughter. As George throws his head back, Albert notices that the hair at his temples has been bleached by the sun. It no longer looks like its usual burnt gold but the kind of bright, sparkling gold of treasure or precious jewellery.

'Seriously, though,' Albert says, his laughter trailing off. 'How many other lads do you think there are like us?'

'I ain't got a clue,' answers George. 'But wouldn't it be great if we could get them all together for one big party?'

Albert gives him a playful shove. 'George Atkinson, you daft beggar! You only have a party when you've got something to celebrate!'

'Yeah, I know but . . .'

Albert stands up and dusts off his hands. 'Come on, let's me and you go and celebrate. Let's have our own little party.'

George smiles at him, knowingly.

And, as Albert walks into the bunker, he stands up and skips after him.

Chapter Twenty-Nine

As Nicole's train trundled towards Leeds, she wondered if she was travelling on the same line Albert had taken when he'd gone to Bradford. Not for the first time it crossed her mind that, while she and Albert were such different people, in many ways they found themselves in similar situations.

She picked up her phone and scrolled through social media. She was nervous about seeing Jamie again but resolved to find out for herself if he'd been pulling back lately – or if he was fully committed to their relationship.

She opened her WhatsApp to see if she had a text from Albert. She hadn't left Reenie with anyone since her mum had moved to Lanzarote and was worried about how she'd adapt. But she was pleased to find a text from him letting her know that Reenie was asleep – and wishing her good luck.

She accessed Spotify to listen to a playlist of her favourite music – by J Hus, Dave and WSTRN – and looked at her reflection in the window. She'd chosen to wear a pair of skinny jeans and a black wrap blouse with flared sleeves. She couldn't afford to buy anything new and was already worried about how much her train ticket had cost. She looked up Jamie's address and discovered that it was quite a distance from the station so she'd have to catch a taxi.

Oh, try not to think about the money. You're doing the right thing.

She felt a jolt of panic.

But what if he's mugging me off?

She suddenly regretted her decision not to tell Jamie she was coming. It had seemed like a great idea when she'd had it, and even more so when she'd sent a casual message asking what his plans were and he'd said he wasn't going out because he had to work on an assignment. She'd pictured him opening his front door and throwing his arms around her – and seen herself bouncing out of the house the next morning, reassured of his commitment. But now a barrage of fears began beating at the walls of her skull.

What if he isn't pleased to see me?

What if he's actually gone out?

What if he's gone out with some other girl?

She looked again at her reflection in the mirror and tried to compose herself. If Jamie had met someone else, then she needed to know. But, as the train rattled forwards, she concentrated all her energy on willing this not to be true.

The taxi pulled up outside Jamie's address and Nicole handed over the money. She wished she could give the driver a tip but she just couldn't afford it. She jumped out quickly to escape her embarrassment.

The area she was in was called Headingley but it was dark so she could hardly see what it was like. There was a street light directly outside Jamie's house so she could at least see that he lived in a tall terrace with big bay windows, a basement floor and an attic bedroom, which she already knew was his. She looked up to see if the light was on but she couldn't tell as the thick curtains were drawn. Behind her, she heard the taxi pull away.

She walked up the few steps and rang the bell. As she waited for an answer, she wriggled her shoulders and tried to relax. But when the door opened, it wasn't Jamie who answered.

'Hello? Can I help you?'

Standing in front of her was a plummy-voiced white man with his hair in a topknot and a beard like a bird's nest.

'Oh, yes, hello,' she managed, 'I'm here to see Jamie.'

The man looked at her suspiciously.

I'm not going to rob you, she wanted to say.

'Who should I say is asking?' the man said. He was giving off a funny smell; if she wasn't mistaken it was a mixture of Twiglets and weed.

'Nicole,' she answered, 'it's Nicole.'

The man looked shocked. 'Oh, you're *Nicole*! Yes, of course. I'm so sorry, I thought . . .' But he stopped himself.

Yeah, what did you think?

'Actually, it doesn't matter,' he said. 'It's really good to meet you.'

He held out his hand and she shook it. 'It's good to meet you too.'

'I'm Toby,' he said, 'one of Jamie's housemates.'

Ah, so you're the stoner who leaves his crap everywhere.

She smiled as sweetly as she could. 'I've heard a lot about you.'

'And I've heard a lot about *you*,' he said, his jaw swinging. 'Anyway, come in.'

He stepped to one side and she walked into a hallway that was full of muddy bikes, umbrellas with spokes sticking out of them, and a bin bag full of rubbish that nobody had bothered to take out. He gestured to a doorway and Nicole walked into what she imagined was supposed to be the living room. The curtains were hanging off the rail, the stuffing was spilling out of the sofa, and a throw that was presumably meant to cover the holes was lying scrunched up on the floor. All the surfaces were strewn with dirty mugs and crushed lager cans, while the bin was overflowing with instant noodle wrappers, empty bags of Twiglets, and takeaway cartons from a fried chicken shop called Lord of the Wings.

'Sorry,' Toby said, trying to conceal the joint resting in the ashtray, 'it's a bit of a mess in here.'

Nicole smiled. 'Oh, don't worry about it. I live with a two-year-old, I'm used to mess.'

There was a clumsy silence. In the street outside a car alarm started going off.

Oh my God, is that Grandma sending me another sign?

'So where's Jamie?' she asked. 'Is he in?'

'Yes, yes, he's upstairs,' Toby said.

Thank God for that.

'If you wait here, I'll go and get him.'

'It's OK,' she insisted, 'I thought I'd surprise him. If you show me where to go, I'll make my own way up.'

Toby nodded and led her through to a staircase at the back of the house. She thanked him and picked her way up quietly, past doors that opened on to scruffy bedrooms and others that were closed and had underpants hanging on the handles. She wondered if that was some kind of code.

Actually, I don't want to think about it.

When she reached the attic, Jamie's door was closed. Thankfully, there wasn't any underwear dangling from his handle. She stopped to compose herself and then knocked.

There was no answer.

Uh-oh, what's he doing?

Outside, the car alarm finally stopped blaring.

She knocked again but still there was no answer.

She gently pushed open the door and poked her head around. And there was Jamie, sitting with his back to her, tapping away on his laptop, his noise-cancelling headphones clamped over his ears.

Nicole felt as if she too were listening to the music and the song had just gone through a key change.

She slunk over to his desk and tapped him on the shoulder. He jumped to his feet, startled. When he saw who it was, a smile washed over his face – and crept into his eyes.

'Nic!' he said, tugging off his headphones. 'What are you doing here?'

But before she could answer, he pulled her towards him and began kissing her forehead. As his lips moved down her cheeks, she closed her eyes and allowed herself to breathe in his familiar clean smell of mint-scented shower gel and citrus-infused shampoo. His kisses made their way to her mouth and, just as his lips met hers, she stretched her arms around his neck.

But Jamie broke away. 'Wait a minute, is everything alright? Who's looking after Reenie?'

As he fumbled around on his phone to switch off the music, Nicole explained that everything was fine; Albert was babysitting. She'd just wanted to see him and had thought it would be fun to keep her visit a surprise.

'Well, I'm really glad you're here,' he said. 'It's great to see you.'

'You too, baby. But I don't want to disturb your work.'

He batted away her concern. 'Don't worry about it, it can wait till tomorrow.' As if to underline the point, he clicked his laptop shut.

He took hold of Nicole's hands and pressed down on them. 'Anyway, welcome. Welcome to my humble room.'

She cast her eyes over it and saw that it was much tidier than the rest of the house, with a single bed that had been made, a neatly stacked shelving unit holding folders and books, and walls lined with framed photographs of his swimming and rowing teams alongside posters advertising albums by Ed Sheeran and Stormzy. 'I like it. And it's a lot nicer than downstairs.'

He nodded and frowned. 'So I take it you saw the living room?'

'Yeah, Toby showed me. Baby, it's gross.'

'I know! How do you think I feel having to live like that?' Suddenly, his eyes lit up. 'You know what, let's not hang around here. Let's go out.'

He said they should probably avoid the Students' Union as all his friends would be there. 'They'll want to check you out and I want you all to myself.'

Nicole fluttered her eyelashes and smiled. 'Oh, I think I can live with that.'

He drew her in for another kiss but then stopped himself. 'Come on, if we start that again I won't be able to keep my hands off you. And then we'll never get out.'

Would that be such a bad thing?

But she told herself that she didn't want Jamie to think of her as the kind of girlfriend who just came round for sex; she wanted him to see her as a partner in every sense of the word.

And if we go out for a drink, there'll be plenty of time for that kind of thing afterwards . . .

Jamie took her to a pub on the corner of the street called The Contented Pig. It was a traditional English pub, with a polished wooden bar, frosted windows, a snug, a pool table and even a dartboard. It was busy, with a mainly older crowd Nicole assumed to be locals, but the two of them managed to find a table in the corner. Jamie drank a pint of lager while Nicole had a vodka, lime and soda, and they picked at a bag of mixed nuts they opened up between them. Nicole talked to Jamie about her friendship with Albert, and Jamie regaled Nicole with more stories about Toby's messiness and aversion to personal hygiene.

When they started on their second drink, Jamie took hold of Nicole's hand and smiled at her with his eyes. He was wearing a blue jumper that accentuated their blue but when he tilted his head she could also make out the green. She felt a balloon of happiness swelling inside her. But she reminded herself that she'd suspected him of pulling back and had come to Leeds to find out why.

Come on, girl. If something's going on, you need to know what it is.

'Baby,' she began, 'you've been a bit quiet lately. Have you been busy with work?'

'Yeah, I have actually.' He took a swig of his lager. 'But now you've brought it up, I should probably tell you my parents have been giving me grief again.'

'Oh no, are you serious?'

'I'm afraid so.'

Nicole let her hand slip out of his and began picking at the nuts. 'OK, so what have they been saying now?'

Jamie explained that his worst fear had come true and they'd threatened to cut off his allowance unless he broke up with her. 'Obviously, there's no chance of me doing that,' he added quickly, 'but at the same time I don't know how I'll survive financially without their help.'

She remembered how, the last time they'd talked about this, she'd lost her temper. *This time, stay calm.*

'Have you tried standing up to them?' she asked.

'Yeah, of course I have.'

'Really? How hard?'

He rocked back on his stool. 'Nic, I don't want to piss them off – I've told you that. But they can be hard work. Honestly, you don't know what they're like . . .'

Nicole pushed away the nuts and folded her arms.

'So come on, what's their objection?' she asked, managing to keep her delivery free of emotion. 'Can they still not get past the fact I'm a single mum?'

Jamie ran his hand through his hair, leaving a tuft sticking up. 'Now you mention it, they're not keen on that, no. They keep saying they don't want me to be so young and saddled with a stepchild – their words, not mine. They keep saying they only want what's best for me.'

Nicole gave a pinched smile. 'Well, in that case, I guess you've got to work out what *you* think is best for you. I guess you've got to work out what it is you want—'

She stopped herself with a reminder that she didn't want to issue him with an ultimatum. *If I lure him away from his parents and they cut him off, he'll only end up resenting me and we'll break up anyway.*

She took a sip of her drink. 'Look, I know this is hard for you, Jamie, but it's hard for me, too – knowing you're backing away from me to keep them happy.'

He frowned and took another pull on his pint. In the background, Nicole could hear the sound of a pool cue tapping a ball.

'I know, and I'm sorry about that,' he said. 'But I don't know what to do. I just keep hoping they'll come around.'

'But why would they suddenly come around? Come on, baby, it's not going to happen.'

'Maybe not, but I graduate in July. And then I won't be dependent on them any more.'

'Yeah but that's not good enough, Jamie. I don't want you to kick this into the long grass until the summer. What am I supposed to do until then? And alright, maybe you won't need their money in July – that's assuming you get a job straight away. But they'll still be your mum and dad. They'll *always* be your mum and dad.'

He drained his glass and set it down on the table. 'So what

are you saying? Are you saying I have to choose between them and you?'

'No, I'm not saying that – I'm absolutely *not* saying that. What I *am* saying is I need you to fight for this rather than just trying to fob us all off. Because I don't know about your parents but I deserve more than that. So either you stand up to them and stand up for me or I'm not doing this any more.'

Girl, did you just say that?

It had just come out naturally. As it had, Nicole realised she might still be holding on to some of her old insecurities, but that didn't mean she couldn't also be strong.

Jamie picked up his glass and gazed into the bottom of it. In the distance, Nicole heard the sound of a pool ball dropping into a pocket.

He pushed back his stool and stood up. 'Let me get us another drink. And when I come back, let's talk about something else.'

She shook her head. 'No offence, Jamie, but I don't want another drink. I want to go home.'

'But Nic, you've come all this way.'

'I know, and I'm glad I did – because we needed to have this conversation.' She checked her watch. 'But if I go now, I can catch the last train.'

He looked at her pleadingly. 'But Nic, I don't want you to go.'

She let out a sigh. 'Yeah, but Jamie, we've been seeing each other for nearly six months now and if you're not one hundred per cent committed, I don't want to stay.'

She asked if he'd call her a cab, and he nodded reluctantly.

As she stood up and began pulling on her coat, a thought occurred to her. *If I get on that last train, I can text Albert and tell him to wait up for me.*

She kissed Jamie goodbye and felt a twinge of regret that she wouldn't be spending the night with him. But it was easy to dismiss. Because after the conversation they'd just had, that wasn't what she wanted.

What she wanted was a cup of tea and a chat with Albert.

Chapter Thirty

'Come on, kid,' Albert said to Nicole, 'let's do this.'

It was Saturday night and the two of them were standing at the top of Canal Street. Albert drew in a slow breath and let it out loudly.

It had felt like a long week building up to this point. On Monday there'd been a blizzard so heavy he hadn't been able to get into work and had spent the following two days battling through the snow just to complete his regular routine. For a while the weather had been all anyone had been able to talk about. Then the rain had come and washed away the snow and people had started to slowly grapple their way back to normality. For Albert, as well as re-engaging with work, this had meant refocusing on his search for George – and preparing himself for tonight. He was still nervous; he had no idea whether he was minutes away from finding George or he'd simply be uncovering the next clue in a longer trail. Either way, he just wanted to get on with it.

As they took their first step on to the famous street, he

was immediately surprised to see that it wasn't cobbled as people said but actually paved with red bricks. As it was still cold, there weren't as many people milling around outside as there had been in some of the photographs he'd seen. On his left was a row of trees with fairy lights hanging from their branches, lining a waist-high concrete wall that separated the street from the canal. On his right was the start of a long row of bars, each of which had rainbow flags hanging from its walls and equally colourful banners advertising themed parties, drag shows and offers of discount drinks. As Nicole had assured him, the bars along Canal Street weren't all full of young people; some more mature men were funnelling into the first few they passed. But there was no doubt that the ones that set the atmosphere of the area were the rowdier bars catering to a young crowd.

They walked past a glass-fronted venue that had condensation running down the windows and was so packed with people all Albert could make out was a tangle of bodies – most of them half-naked – pressed up against the glass. A queue of excitable teenagers and twentysomethings was waiting outside and every time the bouncers opened the door, a blast of Hi-NRG pop escaped. A drunk of indeterminate gender came staggering out, held up on either side by two friends, and within seconds another three people shot in to take their place, whooping in excitement. Through the open door Albert could just about make out the sight of a shirtless male dancer writhing around on a podium as another man wearing nothing but a pair of silver hotpants wiggled his bum up, down and all around him. It was nothing like anything he'd seen on

Coronation Street. It was nothing like anything he'd ever seen in his whole life.

'Thank God we're not going in there,' he said to Nicole.

'Oh, I don't know,' she replied, mischievously, 'I quite fancy it.'

'Yeah, well, don't go getting any ideas,' Albert said. 'We know where we're going – I don't want you getting side-tracked.'

The New Union was situated at the bottom of Canal Street, at the opposite end to Piccadilly Station. As they headed in that direction, it was so cold it shook Albert's heart. He pulled his coat around him and clapped his gloved hands together to keep warm. But not everyone seemed bothered by the cold; barrelling towards him was a group of women wearing just mini-skirts and bra tops. As they roared past, Albert saw that one of them had been plastered in L plates and was wearing a wedding veil, while the others were draped in sashes advertising her hen night and were dragging along an enormous inflatable penis. Suddenly it was as if the last month had never happened; he could feel himself blushing, despite the cold.

When they came to the first bridge over the waterway, Albert and Nicole crossed the road that intersected Canal Street. On reaching the next block, the first thing that greeted them was the sight of two boys leaning against the wall, kissing tenderly. When Albert looked closer he saw that they were only teen-agers – not much older than he and George had been when they'd spent their spring and summer together.

Is this what boys our age do now? Can they just come out here and kiss in public?

He noticed that the straight couples walking across the bridge didn't bat an eyelid, and cars were drifting past as if the sight were nothing out of the ordinary. But he couldn't divert his eyes. Just then, one of the boys pulled a scarf around his boyfriend's neck, made sure his hat was covering his ears, and kissed him on the forehead. As he watched the show of affection, Albert was hit by an emotion he couldn't identify.

Is it joy? Sadness? Pride? Or a bit of all three mixed together?

It reminded him of something Daniel had said to him when he'd delivered a package to his house earlier that week. Although Albert was going to the Village to find George, Daniel had told him to be aware that the trip also marked his first night out on the gay scene – and this was an important ritual in the life of any gay man. He'd warned that entering a world populated by men of all different ages and from all different backgrounds, all coming together to celebrate the one thing they had in common – a thing that may in the past have provoked in them feelings of horror, shame or even disgust – could be emotionally affecting. He'd said that, while some people found it exciting and thrilling, others couldn't help finding it frightening and unsettling. And for Albert, the experience reminded him of what George had said to him on the moors, that August evening when he'd shared his dream about getting together with other men like them for a big party. *And I poured cold water on his idea – I said he was being daft because we had nothing to celebrate.*

Suddenly – just as Daniel had predicted – Albert felt overwhelmed by his emotions. He drew in another long, steadying breath.

I won't let this put me off. I won't let my emotions hijack the night.
He walked on purposefully.

They crossed another bridge and passed a sign that said 'Welcome to Manchester's Gay Village' and a mural adorned with an image of Batman and Robin locked in a passionate kiss. Their attention was drawn to another noisy bar, outside which a gaggle of smokers was cackling with laughter, while a girl wearing a blue wig, a tutu and fairy wings held up her phone and filmed her male friend dancing along to the music of a deep-voiced diva that came pumping out from inside.

When the boy spotted Albert, his eyes sparkled. 'Hello, daddy!' he called out.

Albert put his head down and scurried past. 'What's he on about?' he asked Nicole, once they were at a safe distance. 'Does he think I'm someone else?'

'Albert, you do crack me up,' she said. 'He *fancies* you! He thinks you're hot!'

Albert couldn't help giving a little gasp. *Bloomin' 'eck, what is this place?*

As they carried on walking, one or two people looked at them curiously and it struck Albert that the two of them must make an odd sight strolling down Canal Street. Just as he was about to remark on this to Nicole, they rounded a corner and narrowly avoided a collision with an unfeasibly tall drag queen in unfeasibly high heels with an unfeasibly high beehive perched on the top of her head. She was closely followed by a pair of men who were covered from head to toe in leather with dog masks over their faces and enormous padlocks hanging on chunky silver chains around their necks. As Albert stood back to let them past, he reflected that he'd been expecting to encounter a splash of colour on Canal Street but this was like a whole riotous, explosion of colour.

He looked ahead and saw a pretty little brick building, the bottom half of which had been rendered and painted white. There were baskets of plants hanging on either side of the entrance and awnings over the windows advertising a hotel upstairs. Lit up at the top of the side wall were a series of golden letters that spelled out the pub's name – The New Union.

Albert felt his stomach perform some kind of somersault.

'What do you reckon?' said Nicole. 'Are you all set?'

He drew in another breath and could feel the cold air hitting his lungs. 'I am that. Let's get in there and crack on.'

When they reached the entrance, they were stopped by a bouncer. He gave them a grave look.

'I'm sorry,' he said, 'but you do realise this is a gay bar?'

Albert answered without a moment's hesitation. 'Yeah, that's alright, I'm gay.'

It was only the second time he'd said the words out loud but it struck him how easily they skipped out of his mouth.

The bouncer gave him a smile. 'In you go then. Have a good night.'

When Albert entered The New Union, he discovered that it was very different to the other venues on Canal Street; it had the decor and atmosphere of a traditional pub rather than a modern or cool bar. But it was just as busy – and there was so much going on that for a second he almost forgot he was there to find George.

Just as he was taking off his coat, he felt Nicole's hand slip into his.

'Come on,' she said, 'let's check the place out.'

She led him into the centre of a large dance floor that was rammed with mainly middle-aged men accompanied by a sprinkling of female friends. Many of them were already drunk, but there was nothing threatening or aggressive about their behaviour; they seemed much more interested in dancing, which they did with a remarkable lack of what some might call dignity but Albert decided to see as inhibition.

And I know a thing or two about that.

The DJ was playing music old enough for Albert to recognise, mixing from a Donna Summer song out of the seventies straight into something by Bananarama in the eighties. An enthusiastic man with ginger hair and a pot belly launched himself on to a pole, gripped it between his thighs, and began whipping his hair around wildly. A drop of sweat landed on Albert's cheek but he wiped it off with a laugh. *I'm getting used to this now.*

Next to the dance floor was a stage area. Although it wasn't currently being used, it was decorated with posters advertising a karaoke night and shows by drag queens called Anna Phylactic, Cheddar Gorgeous and Narcissa Nightshade. As Albert studied them, a huge, hairy-chested man draped in a rainbow flag and with a fireman's helmet sliding off his head began pogoing around him. Without thinking about it, Albert gave a little shimmy in return.

Nicole tugged on his hand and led him through to a seating area, where the music was quieter and the atmosphere calmer.

It was dotted with comfortable leather sofas on which a group of chubby men wearing the shirts of a gay rugby team were discussing the day's game. In the corner were a group of lesbians in wheelchairs who were chatting about what sounded like a dramatic relationship break-up.

As he took it all in, Albert concluded that the venue was welcoming and friendly rather than stiflingly fashionable or judgemental. And it was camp in a distinctly northern way; it wouldn't have surprised him if Bet Lynch had walked in off the set of *Coronation Street*. He could feel a smile lifting the corners of his mouth. When he'd set off on his search for George, he'd had no idea where it would take him – but it made sense that it would bring him here.

He reasoned that, if George did still work here, the most likely place to spot him would be behind the bar.

'Right,' he said to Nicole, 'what do you want to drink?'

'I'll have a vodka, lime and soda please.'

He handed her his coat and nudged his way over to the bar, where he examined the staff while he waited to be served. But they were all at least thirty years younger than George and when one of them did serve him, he was a lithe Latino with a buzzcut, tattoos and jeans so tight that for a moment Albert wondered whether he wasn't actually wearing any and had just coated his legs in body paint. Once he'd handed over their drinks, the man thrust a pair of free shots at Albert, which he said everyone received with their first drink. Nicole suddenly appeared from behind him and took hold of one of the glasses.

'Come on,' she said, 'we need to get in the mood.'

Before Albert could argue, she raised the glass to her lips. He did the same and they downed a shot of sickly flavoured liqueur, screwing their eyes shut as it slipped down their throats.

'What was that?' he asked the barman.

The man shrugged. 'Does it matter?'

Albert paid him and they took their drinks through to the seating area. As the sound of the Pet Shop Boys blasted through from the DJ desk, a trio of men dashed to the dance floor, vacating a sofa that Nicole swiftly claimed. She proposed a toast to Albert's debut on the scene and they took a swig of their drinks.

'So what do you think?' she asked.

'I like it,' he said. 'But it's weird, because part of me feels like a fraud who doesn't deserve to be here, and the other part feels like I've finally found my people.'

She knitted her brow. 'Well, there's no rush. Why don't we sit here and you can slowly ease yourself into it?'

In that moment Albert realised how pleased he was that Nicole was here with him.

For the next half an hour they sat and chatted. Nicole told Albert the story of her first night out in the Village; she'd come with a boy she knew from her course in Huddlesden, but within an hour he'd disappeared with a slick-haired Italian he met on Grindr, leaving her to spend the rest of the night with a group of lesbians who were visiting Manchester on a hockey tour from Bratislava. Albert told her about his first nights out as a teenager, when he'd had the distinct feeling of not fitting in and had found himself pretending to be attracted to the same girls as the other boys. But then he'd met George and found himself drawn into something in which he not only fitted, but fitted perfectly.

As they spoke, his eyes flitted around for signs of George. By the time they'd finished their second drink, he was itching to resume his search – and this time to do it properly.

Nicole said she'd save their spot on the sofa. 'And I know it's a long shot, but if you do find him I don't want to gate-crash your reunion.'

Albert thanked her and set off to scour the venue. He lapped the perimeter of the main room and then broke off to wind his way through the crowd. He found a raised step on which he stood to examine the sea of heads bobbing around on the dance floor. And he visited the toilets, taking a long time to wash his hands so he could scan who else was in there. But after half an hour he'd had no success. The worst thing was, the second Albert spotted anyone of vaguely the right age, he peered at them so intently they either thought he was deranged, rude, or an overly intense flirt.

'Are you going to spend all night gawping at me?' said a man with white hair and a pork-pie hat. 'Or are you coming over to chat me up?'

'Oh, n-n-no, sorry,' Albert stammered, 'I was looking for someone else.'

The man gasped in outrage. 'Well, in that case, bugger off!'

Albert bought another round of drinks and returned to the seating area, where Nicole was flicking through social media on her phone.

'Any joy?' she asked as he sat down next to her.

'No, I don't think he's here.'

'Oh, I'm sorry. But let's not give up. Have you seen anyone who's roughly the same age? Anybody you think might know him?'

Albert thought of the man with the pork-pie hat but decided not to mention him. Suddenly, what he was doing seemed futile.

Oh, what's the point? Maybe we should go home and come up with another way of finding George.

'You know this place is nowt like it used to be,' came a voice from behind.

Albert whipped around to see who was speaking. 'You what?'

'I said, this place i'n't as good as it used to be. It used to be dead easy to cop off in here but now everyone cops off online. If you ask me, Grindr's killing the scene.'

Perched on the arm of the sofa was a bald man wearing jeans and a lumberjack shirt who Albert judged to be in his sixties. He also judged him to be extremely drunk; the man's forehead was dripping in sweat, running along his nose were the purple veins of a heavy drinker, and as he spoke, he slurred his words and took regular pauses to stifle burps.

'So have you been coming here long?' Albert asked.

'I have, yeah. But it's nowt like it used to be . . . I used to like it when it were men only, when we had to hide away from the rest of the world. But now they all want to come in and join us. It's all hen parties now – honestly, you can practically smell the oestrogen.'

Albert looked at Nicole and hoped she didn't feel uncomfortable.

'I'm actually looking for someone who worked here a while ago,' he said. 'I wonder if you knew him?'

The man almost slid off the arm of the sofa but righted his balance just in time. 'Oh yeah, who's that?'

'George. George Atkinson.'

The man took a sip of his drink but realised his glass was empty.

'He worked here in the 1970s,' Albert clarified. 'Although I've no idea what's happened to him since.'

The man tightened his mouth. 'I don't remember anyone called George. Your best bet is to speak to the landlord. He's been here donkey's years.'

Albert shot Nicole a look of excitement.

'Really? Where can I find him?'

'Oh, in the same place he always is – on a stool behind the bar. Sitting there like a queen on a throne.'

Albert sprang to his feet. 'Thanks, thanks a lot. Oh, and what's his name, this landlord?'

The man let out a painful-sounding burp and rubbed his stomach. 'God knows what his real name is but everyone calls him Phoebe.'

Albert nodded. 'Phoebe. Terrific, ta.'

'You know, this place i'n't what it used to be . . .' the man carried on. But by now he'd turned away and was talking to someone else.

Albert told Nicole he was going to find Phoebe. She gave him a smile and squeezed his hand.

He edged his way through to the bar.

'What can I get you?' asked the same barman who'd served him before.

'Actually, I don't want a drink,' he replied. 'I was hoping to speak to Phoebe.'

The man turned to his right. 'Phoebe!' he shouted. 'You're wanted!'

Albert spotted a man tucked away in a corner, almost hidden from view. The man slid off the stool and stepped out of his hiding place. As he approached, Albert saw that he was wearing a purple suit and a pink shirt, with a fresh white flower poking out of his buttonhole. He was skinny rather than slim, with grey hair and wrinkles but a kindly face.

'Hello, hello,' he said in a broad Mancunian accent. 'What can I do for you?'

Albert was so desperate to find out if he knew George that he dispensed with any preamble. 'I'm looking for someone,' he said, 'someone who used to work here.'

Phoebe fingered his collar. 'Oh yeah? And what's this someone's name?'

'George Atkinson. I don't suppose you knew him?'

But Albert could tell straight away from his expression that he did. At the sound of George's name, Phoebe's smile grew bigger.

'Of course I knew him!' he burst out.

Albert's stomach began flipping over. 'Really?'

Phoebe gestured to a speaker on the wall. 'Look, it's too loud in here. Come through to the back.'

Albert followed Phoebe into what looked like a disabled toilet but noticed that it also had a shower cubicle in which stood a mop and bucket and a stack of boxes of crisps. On a wall hung a full-length mirror, across which someone had draped a black feather boa and written the word 'SLAY!' in bright red lipstick.

Phoebe shut the door and leaned against the wall for support. 'Sorry,' he said, 'I can't get around as quickly as I used to. I'm going to be seventy-six next birthday.'

Albert smiled. 'Well, I'm not that far behind you.'

Phoebe waved his arm at a rail of garishly coloured women's clothes. 'This is where the girls get ready to go onstage,' he explained. 'We do drag shows a couple of nights a week.'

Albert nodded but didn't want the conversation to veer off course. 'So you knew George?' he asked rather abruptly.

Phoebe moved over to lean on the sink. 'I did, yeah. I used to know him very well. He worked here for ten years but he moved to London in the eighties. We kind of lost touch.'

Albert felt such a flood of disappointment he couldn't stop himself from letting out a little moan.

'Oh, don't worry,' said Phoebe. 'That was in the years before social media so people lost touch all the time. But we've looked each other up again since. I quite enjoy reading his posts and finding out what he's up to.'

In an instant, Albert's disappointment was wiped out by relief. This was the first time anyone had spoken to him about George in the present tense.

So he really is alive. And this man knows where to find him.

'But hang on a minute,' Albert protested, 'I've looked for George on social media and I can't find him anywhere.'

Phoebe lifted an eyebrow. 'Yeah, but what name were you looking for?'

'George Atkinson. What other name would I look for?'

Phoebe paused, and his eyes twinkled. 'His drag name.'

'His *drag* name?'

'Yeah, George is a drag queen. Didn't you know?'

Albert staggered backwards, shocked. 'No, I had no idea.'

'When was the last time you saw him?'

'Oh . . . well, it was a while back.'

Phoebe took out a cigarette. He opened the window and lit up. 'This is one of the perks of being the landlord, not to mention an old bag who's been around longer than God; there might be a smoking ban but nobody's going to complain if I come in here and have a sneaky fag.'

As he watched him breathe out a long plume of smoke, Albert tried to digest the news that George was a drag queen. He tried to picture what the boy he knew would look like in a dress, wig and make-up. But he found it difficult. At the same time, he thought it was perfectly logical that George would end up doing drag. Memories flickered back to life of the shows he used to perform for him on the moors. And when he played the female characters this ignited some kind of spark within him.

'Yes, George worked here as a drag queen,' Phoebe went on. 'I was the drag mother, of course – Phoebe Fortune – and George was one of my girls. He was a fabulous queen, one of the best.'

'And what happened?' Albert asked. 'Why did he move to London?'

'Oh, he just kept getting more and more bookings down south and then he was offered a residency in one of the

London venues. It was a big step up for him. It was fine, I totally understood. But I was gutted when he left.'

'So how can I find him? What *is* his drag name?'

Phoebe drew on his cigarette, inhaled deeply and tapped his ash into the plughole. 'Georgina. Georgina St James.'

Albert felt like his legs were going to buckle. He held on to the wall. 'Sorry, did you say *Georgina*?'

'Yeah, Georgina St James. I always thought it was one of the better drag names.'

'Yeah, but . . .' Albert was about to explain that Georgina had been the name the other boys at school had used to insult George, but he stopped himself.

'But what?' asked Phoebe. 'What were you going to say?'

'Oh, nothing,' said Albert. 'I was just remembering the George I used to know.'

One evening in the middle of August, Albert is sitting outside the bunker waiting for George. It's starting to go dark and George is late.

When he finally arrives, Albert sees that something bad has happened; George has a split lip, there's dried blood on his chin, and the area around his left eye is maroon. With a jolt, the anger surges through him. Before he can open his mouth, George beats him to it.

'Yeah, I know,' he says, forcing out a smile, 'I'm going to have a massive shiner tomorrow.'

'But what happened?' Albert asks, moistening his finger with his tongue and wiping George's chin. 'Who did this?'

George shrugs. 'Oh it doesn't matter. It were just some lads who jumped me in the street. I legged it before they could do any proper damage.'

Albert can feel the anger burning right down to his finger-tips. 'But which lads? Come on, tell me, George.'

He lets out a sigh and sits down. 'If you must know, it were Tom Horrocks and Colin Broadbent.'

Albert sinks to the ground next to him. 'But they're my mates. Or they're supposed to be my mates. They're certainly not anymore!'

George stamps the heel of his shoe into the ground. 'Yeah, well, I wouldn't get too het up about it. If it weren't them it'd only be someone else. We know what the world thinks about the likes of us.'

Albert can only tug in short, shallow breaths. 'Why do you say that? What did they say?'

'Oh, you know, just the usual stuff. Queer. Poof. Georgina.'

Albert has to stop himself from letting out a growl. 'I swear I'm going to go down there and give them a good battering.'

A vision of what he wants to do to the boys flashes through his mind and the violence of it scares him. *Would I really be capable of that?*

George is shaking his head. 'Violence won't achieve owt, Albert. That's not how we're going to win this battle.'

'Well, how *are* we going to win it?'

George stamps his heel again and dislodges a lump of earth. He kicks it away.

'I don't know, I'm still trying to work that out. But in the meantime, I'm not going to let them bastards grind me down. And I'm not going to start covering up the way I am. I'm not going to try and act like a proper lad for anyone. If anything, when people like that go for me, it only makes me want to be *more* outrageous.'

In the distance, an owl hoots.

Albert heaves out a sigh. 'George, are you sure that's wise?'

But George doesn't answer. Instead, he leaps on to the roof of the bunker.

'Come on,' he chirps, 'I'm going to put on a show.'

Trust George. Trust George to try to sing and dance his way through this.

'Really?' asks Albert. 'Are you sure now's the time?'

'Yeah, I am,' George fires back, smiling brightly. 'Truth be told, I couldn't think of a better time.'

Despite the anger still raging inside him, Albert can feel himself giving in to a smirk. 'Alright, fair do's.'

'Now what do you think?' George asks. 'Tonight, am I going to be a boy or am I going to be a girl?'

And he wiggles his bottom at Albert.

'Am I going to be George – or Georgina?'

In the disabled toilet of the New Union, Albert tried to digest the news that George was a drag queen called Georgina.

It struck him that he'd taken a word that had been used against him and twisted it around to make it work *for* him – so not only could it no longer hurt him but it was his way of getting his own back on the world. And not only that, if the other boys had mocked what they saw as George's feminine traits, then dressing up as a woman and being applauded for it was surely another way of doing the same thing. He felt a fluttering of pride.

Phoebe breathed out another curl of smoke. 'So how *did* you know George?'

Albert explained.

'Aha.' Phoebe tightened his eyes. 'So you're Albert?'

The shock of it stopped Albert's breath. As Phoebe said his name, it was as if George himself were reaching out and communicating with him.

'Yes, I'm Albert,' he said. 'Why, did he tell you about me?'

Phoebe smiled. 'Not much – he was always very cagey about whatever had happened between you two. But he said enough for me to know there'd been a big tragedy in his life. Something that had left him feeling very sad and let down.'

Albert looked at the floor. 'Yeah, that sounds about right. I did let him down. But I'm trying to make up for it now. And I know it's nearly fifty years too late, but I'll do anything I can.'

'Good man,' said Phoebe. And then he stubbed out his cigarette and tossed it in the bin. 'I'm pleased to hear it.'

'I just need to find him,' Albert said, his voice cracking. 'So if there's anything else you can tell me . . .'

Phoebe pulled the window shut. 'Oh, you don't need anything else from me. Georgina St James – that's all you need to know. That queen is all over the internet. You can't miss her!'

*

An hour later, Albert was standing with Nicole on the platform at Piccadilly Station, waiting for the last train home. All around them, drunks were releasing their boozy fumes into the cold night air. Albert glanced up and down the platform and saw a group of teenage boys devouring a McDonald's, a straight couple indulging in what could only be described as foreplay, and various bleary-eyed single men desperately firing off text messages to try and rustle up a late-night sexual rendezvous. He nodded towards a bench where he and Nicole could sit down.

On the walk up from Canal Street, he'd filled her in on everything Phoebe had told him. Once he was sitting down, he typed into Facebook the name Georgina St James.

His finger hovered over the Search key. 'Now let's have a look at him.'

Nicole put her hand on his arm. 'Just a minute, you do know you're supposed to say "her" if you're talking about a drag queen?'

Albert looked up from his phone. 'Really? But I thought a drag queen was just a bloke dressed up as a woman?'

She rolled her eyes. 'I think you'll find it's a bit more than that. The whole point of drag is about taking on a female alter-ego and becoming a different character, usually one that's very extra. Don't you watch *RuPaul's Drag Race*?'

'I can't say I do,' said Albert.

They were interrupted by an announcement informing them that their train was delayed by five minutes.

'Hell fire,' said Albert, 'it's freezing out here.'

But despite the cold, he didn't want to put his gloves on; he was too eager to resume his Facebook search for George.

He hit the Search key and was offered a link. When he clicked on it, he was taken through to the Facebook page of Georgina St James. Filling the screen were images of a heavily made-up drag queen wearing a succession of sequinned dresses and blonde wigs. But in every photo the transformation from male to female was so complete, it was difficult to make out the George he knew. He tilted his phone towards Nicole.

'So I guess this is him,' he said. 'Or her.'

Nicole nodded her approval. 'Her drag's on point, I'm impressed. But what does it say? Does she have any shows coming up?'

He scrolled down and found out that Georgina made regular appearances at various bars and clubs in London, including one called the Royal Vauxhall Tavern, where she was scheduled to perform in two weeks' time.

'There you are,' said Nicole. 'There's your chance to go and watch her. And if you hang around after the show, you'll get to meet George.'

This was it. This was what he'd wanted. But Albert was suddenly assailed by insecurities.

Can I really do that?

Can I really go to London?

'Oh I don't know . . .' he said.

Nicole edged forward on the bench. 'What do you mean? This is what you've been waiting for, Albert. You can't back out now!'

In an instant, Albert was once again hit by every emotion he'd felt over the course of the night – and once again he found it overwhelming.

He looked at the picture and scrolled down to see that listed underneath was a link to Georgina's own website. He clicked on it and saw that it contained some video footage shot just a few weeks ago. He clicked on it and pressed Play.

As Georgina St James began parading up and down the stage and performing some kind of stand-up routine, the George Albert knew suddenly burst back into life. Suddenly, he was back on the moors, sitting on his rock and laughing away as George larked around and performed just for him.

The shock of it made Albert feel like he was going to throw up. He concentrated on swallowing until the sensation passed.

'What's the matter?' said Nicole. 'Are you alright?'

Albert shut down his phone and dropped it in his pocket. 'I don't think I can watch that, at least not here. I might have to wait till I'm home, if you don't mind.'

'That's OK,' said Nicole. 'I get it, don't worry.'

Their train began approaching and they stood up. A guard appeared and barked out the name of the stations it would be serving. Albert listened out for Toddington. But when it came, in his head it was replaced by the name of another destination.

London.

If Albert went there in two weeks' time, there was a chance he'd finally be reunited with George. And it may have come as something of a shock to see glimpses of the man he'd loved in the video footage, but now that he had, there was no doubt in his mind about what he had to do.

Chapter Thirty-One

Georgina St James strutted up and down the stage, twirling the curls of her peroxide blonde wig, flaunting her outrageously padded boobs and hips, and showing off an outfit that was a riot of clashing animal prints, including leopard, tiger, snake and even zebra. Her appearance formed the perfect complement to her polished onstage persona, which was built around the character of a comically common northern housewife who had aspirations of leading a much more glamorous life. In the clip Albert was watching, she was letting loose her naughty streak in a spirited rendition of 'Big Spender'.

It was late Sunday morning, the day after his trip to Manchester. He was lying back on a sea of pillows and working his way through all the clips of Georgina he could find. And he was engrossed.

Most of the clips contained performances of classic musical theatre numbers but others centred on the gags or short stand-up sequences she delivered in between, which drew on a very northern tradition of humour. When Albert watched

Georgina chat to the audience he was reminded again of *Coronation Street*'s Bet Lynch but also music hall comedian Hylda Baker, Gracie Fields – his mam's favourite performer – and all those male comedians who used to drag up as gossiping housewives, such as Norman Evans and Les Dawson.

And the more I see of it the more it makes sense. Of course this is what George would be doing. How could he ever have done anything else?

Once he'd run out of videos to watch, Albert scrolled down the menu on Georgina's website and clicked on a link that led to her biography. This explained that she'd learned her craft on the drag scene in Manchester before moving to London in 1985. And it said that she'd recently turned sixty, something that was a manipulation of the truth as George was just a few weeks younger than Albert, so must also be coming up to sixty-five. But it was the next line that jumped out at him and made him sit up.

'Georgina may be a woman of a certain age but she'd like all eligible bachelors to know that she's single and looking for love.'

Albert read it again to make sure he hadn't made a mistake. But there it was in print on her own website. He could feel the excitement build inside him. If George was single then what he wanted more than anything was now within his grasp.

Oh I wish I could go to London straight away.

As he got out of bed and went downstairs, he tried consoling himself that he had plenty of things to be getting on with in the meantime, things that wouldn't just distract him but might even help prepare him for the radical change he was hoping to bring about in his life. As he worked through them, he'd mark off the days on his kitchen calendar. He started by taking out a pen and drawing a cross over today, Sunday 3rd February.

Thirteen days to go . . .

'And how are you feeling about your retirement?' Marjorie asked.

Albert had been putting off having this conversation with Marjorie. But on Wednesday afternoon – with ten days to go until his trip to London – he finally felt ready to face it.

'I'm actually looking forward to it,' he answered, sitting opposite her in her office. 'I mean, obviously my life's gone through a lot of changes lately. But I suppose because of that I'm feeling less scared and more optimistic.'

She nodded and smiled. 'And have you thought about how you're going to fill your time?'

Albert wanted to say that he was hoping to spend his time with George but didn't want to come across as naïve or deluded, not when he still had no idea how George would greet him when he arrived in London.

'I thought I might go on a cookery course,' he answered, 'so I can start being more adventurous in the kitchen. Oh and I might join a walking club. I've found one online that's just for gay men.'

Marjorie grinned. 'That's great, love. Good on you.'

She moved on to talk about his pension and handed him an information pack he promised to read later.

'Now I don't know what your finances are like,' she said,

'but don't forget, if you need a top-up you can always do the odd shift for us through one of the agencies.'

Albert wrinkled his nose. 'I think I'd rather make a clean break if you don't mind.'

'Oh yeah? You want to get shut of us, do you?'

'No, it's not that. It's just that my life has revolved around work for a long time now. I think I owe it to myself to see what else is out there.'

'Well, for what it's worth,' said Marjorie, 'I think you're doing the right thing.'

She turned her attention to a form she'd given him to complete in advance of the meeting; it was similar to the one he had to fill out every year as part of his Performance and Development Review. It consisted of a series of questions probing his feelings about work, what he'd learned during the period of employment, and how he felt he'd grown as a person. Albert usually ignored these kinds of questions, but this time around he'd found himself writing long paragraphs and had actually enjoyed the process. It had prompted him to reflect on the last fifty years of his life.

'I have to say,' said Marjorie, 'you put a lot into this. I really enjoyed reading it.'

'Thanks,' he said, 'there was a lot to think about.'

'You've worked for us for so long, it must have been like writing the story of your life.'

Albert nodded but, as Marjorie began chatting through each of his answers, it dawned on him that what he'd written didn't actually tell the story of his life; it told the story of how he'd used work to *stop* living, how he'd used it to fill in the gap left by the one thing that had made him feel alive. He'd applied for the job when he'd been seeing George, and the night before he'd started work had taken his new uniform up to the war bunker to show him. The following morning he'd put his hand in the pocket to find George had slipped in a big block of his favourite cinder toffee wrapped in a good-luck note. Every day since George had disappeared from his life, he'd eaten some cinder toffee. And when the shops had stopped selling it, he'd switched to Crunchie bars – as a reminder of George. As a reminder of what was missing in his life.

And now that my job's ending, I'm hoping it won't be missing any longer.

The following afternoon – with nine days before his trip to London – Albert arrived at Has Bean, a coffee shop near the Corn Exchange in the centre of Leeds. He'd taken a day off work to help out a friend. But he was worried that what he was about to attempt could go awfully wrong.

As he walked in, he saw that the walls were covered with the same standard-issue white tiles as the walls in the public toilets in Toddington, and it had mismatching tables and chairs that looked like they'd been sourced from a junkyard. Albert could immediately tell he was the oldest person in there – and he also noticed that he was the only man without a beard or tattoos. He felt terribly out of place but told himself that it didn't matter; he was only there for one thing.

He'd looked up Jamie in Nicole's list of friends on Facebook and had sent him a message asking if he might be free to meet up for a chat. Jamie had seemed pleased at the suggestion and said he'd meet him in this coffee shop. *And now here I am, hoping to talk some sense into him.*

He approached the counter and perused the menu but was bewildered by all the choice. *What's pour-over coffee, cold brew or single-origin espresso? And how can you get milk out of an almond?*

He quickly placed his order – a regular tea with regular milk – and found himself a table. Thankfully, he didn't have to wait long.

After a few minutes, the door was opened by a young man with a boyish face and a robust frame. He came to a stop in front of Albert and held out his hand.

'Hello,' he said, 'you must be Albert.'

'Yeah,' said Albert, shaking his hand. 'Is it that obvious?'

Jamie pulled a face. 'Sorry, I've never been in here before. I only picked it because it was central. I didn't realise it was so hipster.'

Albert had no idea what that meant but smiled.

Jamie excused himself to go and buy a coffee and returned with a dark liquid that was in some kind of jam jar. He sat down opposite Albert.

'So how's Nic?' he asked.

On Jamie's face Albert saw a look of concern he found encouraging. *Maybe he doesn't need bringing to his senses after all.*

'Yeah, she's alright, thanks,' he reassured him. 'Although I didn't tell her I was meeting you.'

'No, I thought you wouldn't.' Jamie ran his hands through his hair and a little tuft of it was left sticking up. 'You know, it's all so unfair. You match with someone online and you start a relationship and it's all great. But then suddenly all this aggravation happens with my parents.'

'I agree,' said Albert, 'but you're not the only one to face that kind of thing. I don't know if she's told you my story.'

Jamie's hair flopped down again. 'She has, yeah.'

'Well, I know what it's like when bad stuff happens – really bad stuff. But the thing is, when it comes down to it, it's not the bad stuff that's important. What's important is how you deal with it.'

Jamie took a sip of his coffee in silence.

'That is, if you deal with it.'

Jamie remained silent.

'You know, I've spent fifty years separated from the man I wanted to be with,' Albert went on. 'And I regret that every day – which is why I'm now trying to find him. But the truth is, I've no idea whether he'll even want me when I do. Because I let him down. I let him down badly.'

'So is that why you wanted to meet up?' Jamie asked. 'To make sure I don't let Nic down?'

'Not really, because if you're not committed to her then I can't force you. Besides, I can't imagine you'd suddenly change your mind to please an old gay postman.'

Jamie laughed. 'No offence but I don't think I would, no.'

Albert took a sip of his tea. 'And that's exactly as it should be. But I did want to share with you what I've learned since I started looking for George, in case there's anything you can learn from it. And one of the biggest lessons I've learned is that people can only really like you if you show them the real you and give them the chance to.'

At the next table, a man with a French bulldog stood up to leave.

'Since I've been looking for George,' Albert went on, 'I've had to open up to all kinds of people, all kinds of people I didn't think would respond very well to an old postman coming out as gay. But I've been surprised. Really surprised.'

'That's great,' said Jamie, 'and I'm really happy for you. But I don't understand what that's got to do with me and Nic.'

Albert took a big swig of his tea and began cradling the mug in his hands. 'Well, at the moment your mum and dad don't know Nicole, do they? So they're judging her according to all kinds of prejudices that might disappear if they met her.'

'Do you think so?'

'I don't know. But surely it's worth finding out?'

Jamie finished his coffee and set the empty container down. 'You know, the funny thing is, I've always thought my mum and dad would get on with Nic. In some ways they've got a lot in common.'

'So what's the problem? Why not give them the chance to change their minds?'

Jamie clapped out a beat on the table. 'Albert, thanks so much.'

'What for?'

'For giving me the answer. I *do* want to be with Nic, despite all the aggravation. I've always known that, of course I have. I just couldn't see a way out of this situation with my parents. But now I can. And, thanks to you, I know just what to do.'

★

The following morning – with just eight days to go until he could get on a train to London – Albert delivered a scented candle to Edith, together with another anonymous note. Once again, she was delighted with both and invited him in for what had become their regular end-of-the-week chat. They sat in their usual positions – she on the armchair and he on the sofa – and she placed the candle on the coffee table between them. Even though it was daylight, she took out a match and lit it.

'Now isn't that lovely?' she said. 'And it smells beautiful.'

'I don't suppose you've any more idea who might have sent it?' he asked.

Edith gazed at the candle and shook her head. 'No, not really. Although to be honest, I'm not sure it matters any more.'

'Oh no, why do you say that?'

'Well, he'll make himself known if he wants to. But for now, whoever he is, he's shown me that I'm still worth caring about. And if he wanted to make me feel less lonely, he's succeeded.' Edith looked up from the candle. 'Anyway, how are you getting on finding George?'

He updated her on his trip to Manchester and his discovery that George worked as a drag queen. Then he perched next to her and showed her a clip on his phone.

She nodded in approval. 'He's very good. And I've seen quite a few drag queens in my time.'

Albert went back to sit on the sofa. 'Why does that not surprise me?'

'I was actually quite friendly with one or two for a while.

Now that I think about it, I wish I still was. But I was never very good at holding on to friendships.'

'Oh, really? Why do you think that was?'

She rested her head on her hand. 'I suppose in theatre and fashion I got used to people coming and going all the time. I took them for granted while I spent all my energy chasing love and romance. I never imagined that one day I'd be lonely.'

'I was lonely,' Albert found himself saying. 'I spent years and years feeling lonely. But I didn't really know what it was at the time – or at least I pretended not to know. And when I did face up to it, I was too ashamed to tell anyone.'

He began telling Edith about his upcoming retirement and how hearing about it was what had first made him step back and look at his life.

'You might think you got the balance wrong but I definitely did,' he said. 'I focused way too much on work and let everything else fall away.'

'Yes but now you're changing. Now you're putting the balance right. That's the important thing.'

His eyes were drawn to the flame of the candle. The heady scent of fig tree was spreading around the room.

'You know, what you're doing has inspired me to look at my life, too,' Edith continued. 'It's inspired me to start a little search of my own.'

Albert sat up straight. 'Really? What's that?'

She gave a coy smile. 'Let's just say I've decided to look up one of my old flames.'

'Bloomin' 'eck, are you serious?'

'Perfectly serious.'

'Well, that's terrific. Who is he?'

'William.'

'The one that got away?'

'Yes, the one *I let get away*. The solicitor from Preston. The one who was always sucking Uncle Joe's Mint Balls. Although why I let that bother me I've no idea. I suppose I thought he was a bit of an old fuddy-duddy and didn't think he was handsome or exciting enough. But those things don't matter any more.'

She explained that earlier that week she'd caught a taxi to the local library, where a member of staff had helped her search for William on one of the computers. She'd managed to track him down to an assisted living facility not too far away – and they'd arranged to meet up one day next week.

'I only hope he forgives me,' she said, with a tremble in her voice.

'Forgives you? For what?'

'Oh, I didn't treat him very well. I didn't do the right thing by him. And for a while I think he was angry at me – and quite rightly.'

Into Albert's head flashed the image of George's face the last time he'd seen him. And the bitter, sickening memory of what he did to him – what he did to make George so angry – came rushing back.

One evening in September, Albert and George are hiding in their secret place on the moors. It's a meeting that's been arranged at the last minute, after George's mam was called back to Yorkshire to visit a sick friend. When George sent him a note to tell him he was free, Albert jumped at the chance to see him; his dad's working late and his mam hasn't left her bed for days.

Earlier that week, Albert started his new job at the Post Office – and he's excited to tell George all about it. But no sooner has he started to do this than he becomes aware of an unusual noise coming from outside.

'Hang on a minute, what's that?'

He stands up to peer out of one of the openings in the concrete wall. Something's moving towards them through the woodland. The fear cuts through him.

'What the hell—?'

With a jolt, Albert realises he must have been followed. Within seconds he sees that the noise is coming from two figures battling their way through the overgrowth with canes and electric torches. When the light falls on one of them, he sees they're policemen.

George's face goes ashen grey. 'Shit,' he whispers, 'what do we do?'

Albert has never known fear like it. A bolt of panic runs down his spine and it's as if his bones sharpen. Into his mind rush images of what will happen to the two of them if they're caught – the public disgrace, the disgust hurled at them in the street, the shame that will rage inside him, more intensely than ever.

'We can't let them catch us,' he splutters, 'we absolutely can't let them catch us.'

At that moment, a flash of light passes over the second policeman. It reveals, to Albert's horror, that it's his dad. His entire body is seized by panic.

'Leg it,' he hisses to George. 'We've got to make a run for it.'

As the boys haven't been in the bunker for long, they're still dressed. But they don't have their boots on and Albert knows he won't get far without them. He quickly pulls his on and gestures for George to do the same.

'Come on, follow me!'

He claws his way to the exit and races out of the bunker and on to the moors. The blood is pumping in his head so loudly it makes him feel dizzy and disconnected from his senses. He thinks George is directly behind him until he hears him cry out in terror. He looks over his shoulder and sees he's struggling to put his boots on and has been apprehended by one of the policemen.

'No!' he hears him bleat. 'Let me go!'

A flash of torchlight reveals the man gripping George's arm is Albert's dad.

Hell fire. My own dad.

Albert's breath fails and anger rips at his heart. He wants to intervene and turns back.

'Get off me!' he hears George pleading. 'Leave me alone!'

But Albert sees the silhouette of the second policeman coming for him and he feels another surge of fear. Some kind of survival instinct kicks in and before he knows it he's sprinting away. As rivers of adrenaline course through him, he sprints away, abandoning George to his fate. Abandoning him to be marched down to the police station alone. Abandoning him to be treated like some kind of loathsome criminal.

Even as he's running, he can feel the guilt flooding into him. So much cloying, nauseating, suffocating guilt that even in that moment he's not sure he'll ever be able to get rid of it.

And how am I ever going to forgive myself? How's George ever going to forgive me?

'So you're not the only one who needs to ask for forgiveness,' Albert said to Edith.

She tried to reassure him, but already he was awash with fear. And it suddenly struck him that, although he'd been counting down the days until his trip to London, he still wasn't prepared. Because he had no idea of how he was going to apologise to George, of how he was going to ask for his forgiveness.

Chapter Thirty-Two

Fighting the instinct to turn around and head for the safety of home, Albert approached the front door. When he reached it, he stopped and gave himself a little pep talk.

Come on, it's Saturday . . . you've only got a week till London now. Just try and relax and enjoy yourself.

He knocked on the door and, as soon as his knuckles made contact, he noticed it was open.

'Hello?' he called inside.

There was no answer.

He wondered what the etiquette was about letting himself into his boss's house but imagined he and Marjorie had gone past the point of worrying about that kind of thing.

He stepped into the entrance hall, the floor of which was covered with abandoned shoes and boots. He added his to the pile and dropped his coat on to a mound in the corner. From further inside the house he could hear a cacophony of voices talking over a soundtrack of Kool & the Gang's 'Celebration'. He followed the noise down the hall and into the front room, which was so full of people he could hardly see the walls. It was the kind of sight that just a few months ago would have sent him bolting for the door. Now he could feel himself stiffening, but only slightly.

'Hiya, love!'

Straight away he was greeted by Marjorie, who swept over and gave him a hug. Before he could say anything, she'd taken the bottle he was carrying out of his hand and was whisking it away.

'I'll just put this in the kitchen,' she shouted. 'Wait there and I'll bring you a drink!'

He was at a party to celebrate the departure of Marjorie's grandson for Disney World, which had been arranged quickly because his health was deteriorating. Marjorie wanted to say thank you to everyone who'd contributed to the campaign, which meant she'd pretty much invited the entire office. She'd also explained that a photographer from the local newspaper was coming to take pictures of Bradley leaving for the airport and she wanted it to look like they were 'giving him a good send-off'.

'So what do you think?' she asked as she swept back in and plonked a plastic glass in Albert's hand. 'It's a decent turnout, i'n't it?'

'It is, yeah,' he said, 'it's terrific.'

'Now, the rest of your booze is in the fridge,' she went on, 'and there's a buffet in the kitchen. But before you do anything, let me introduce you to our Brad.'

Just as she was about to lead Albert into the back room, another guest arrived and she swivelled around to greet him. Albert was left standing on his own.

He looked around and to his left saw a group of men holding their pint glasses as if they were a natural extension of their arms, discussing the dream cars they wished they could own if they hadn't been forced to settle for a family-friendly option. To his right was a group of women picking at paper plates of food, joking about their husbands' interest in cars rather than romance. Unfortunately, Albert had nothing to contribute to either conversation. He started to worry he was going to feel like he had at the Christmas party.

'Albert!'

Calling his name from the other side of the room was Tsunami. She was standing with a man who was in the process of manoeuvring an entire slice of quiche into his mouth.

'Albert, get over here!'

He could feel his shoulders loosening with relief. He nudged his way through the mass of people and reached Sue just as the man swallowed his quiche.

'This is our John,' Sue said. 'I've been dying to introduce you.'

Albert shook the hand of a man who was so tall he had to stoop so his head didn't touch the ceiling.

'I know we've spoken on the phone,' John said, 'but it's good to meet you in person.'

'Yeah,' said Albert, 'it's good to meet you too.'

They discussed the decorating job Albert had recently asked John to do, stripping the old Anaglypta wallpaper from his mam's bedroom and redecorating it entirely. Albert handed John the spare set of keys so he could let himself in and start that week.

Before long, Smiler came over to join them. 'Alright, guys?'

He bounced from one foot to the other as he gnawed his way around a chicken drumstick. He was wearing a black felt hat with an image of Mickey Mouse on the front and two round ears sticking up at the back, which he explained he'd bought when he'd taken his own children to Disney World.

'Our Olivia's with me now,' he said. 'Let me introduce you.'

He called over a teenaged girl who was fresh-faced and pretty and holding on to the hand of a gangly mixed-race boy of around the same age, who she introduced as her boyfriend, Josh.

''Ere, Olivia,' said Smiler, 'tell my friends from work about that time we went to Disney World.'

'Oh yeah,' she said, 'it was epic.'

As she recounted their trip, Albert couldn't pick up on any surliness from her – and once or twice she even drew her dad into the conversation. He could only conclude that she and Smiler had weathered the worst of the difficulties they'd been experiencing.

Conversations continued to come at Albert from all directions and very soon he was relaxed and enjoying himself. He'd often seen gatherings like this taking place through people's windows and had wondered why being part of them seemed to give the guests such pleasure. At last he was starting to understand.

Before long, Marjorie appeared and took hold of his arm. She began steering him through to the back room. 'Come on,' she said, 'it's time to introduce you to our Bradley.'

'Oi, Albert!' called out a voice behind him. 'Come over 'ere a minute!'

He turned around to see Jack, who was working his way through a plate piled high with food. He stopped and listened as Jack told him that last night he and Doreen had stayed in for their regular movie night and had watched *Brokeback Mountain*, a film he described in such detail Marjorie gave up waiting and slipped away to see some other guests.

'It were a beltin' picture,' Jack said, 'although it had a right sad ending. It made me realise how tough things used to be for gays, like.'

Albert couldn't help thinking Jack was over-compensating for his earlier homophobia, but appreciated his effort.

'Any road,' Jack added, 'I hope you have a happier ending with your George.'

Next to come over and chat to him was Marjorie's sister-in-law and Nicole's tutor, Joyce. She introduced herself and told Albert she'd heard all about his search for George. Albert made a point of mentioning how much help and advice Nicole had given him.

'And she gave me a terrific makeover,' he added. 'It was so good I had a young lad chatting me up on Canal Street.'

Joyce laughed. 'Well, that's good to know. I always say that part of the job of any health and beauty professional is making their client feel special – and giving them a safe space to talk about whatever they want.'

'Well, she certainly did both of those things,' said Albert. 'Honestly, I'd give her top marks.'

'Right, I'm taking Albert back now,' Marjorie intervened. 'Come on, love, let's get you to meet our Bradley.'

Albert excused himself and allowed Marjorie to lead him

through an archway to the back room, where he spotted Nicole and Reenie. But Marjorie steered him past them and into a corner in which a boy of eleven or twelve was sitting on an armchair. He was thin and pale, but otherwise didn't look ill; there were no tubes running out of his nose and no catheter hanging out of his arm. In fact, Albert couldn't help thinking that he looked strangely calm and relaxed. Suddenly Albert felt humbled and embarrassed that so many people had remarked on how brave he was since he'd started telling them about his search for George.

How can I be brave compared to this lad?

'How do,' he said. 'Are you enjoying the party?'

Bradley gave a shrug. 'Yeah, it's alright.'

Albert remembered how daunting it had been as a child to be drawn into an adult conversation. 'And are you looking forward to Disney World?'

'Yeah, I can't wait.'

'Which ride are you most excited about?'

Bradley's face suddenly became more animated. 'Pirates of the Caribbean! And Tower of Terror! Oh, and I want to see the alligators!'

At this, a blonde woman in her thirties turned around. 'Yeah, alright, love, we've already spoken about the alligators. I said we'd have to see.'

She looked at Albert and tutted.

'This is our Jackie,' said Marjorie, 'Brad's mum.'

Albert nodded and smiled but the mere mention of Jackie's role as the boy's mother made him feel an ache of sadness. *What must it be like for her to know she's going to lose her son?*

'I won't know how dangerous it is till we get there,' she told Bradley. 'But I promise we'll see them if it's safe.'

She smiled at him and ruffled his hair and Albert was struck by the simple, uncomplicated love in her action. *That's exactly as it should be, that's exactly how a mother should feel about her son.*

'Come on, everybody, grab your coats,' shouted Marjorie, standing up to address the room, 'we need to get outside!'

She explained that it was time for them to have their photograph taken, and introduced everyone to Gary, a middle-aged man from the local newspaper. He asked the guests to follow him into the street and Albert stepped back so that Marjorie and Jackie could lead Bradley out first.

On the pavement outside the house was a black taxi that had been decorated with balloons, ribbons and a banner saying, 'GOOD LUCK BRAD!' The photographer positioned Bradley in front of it and arranged his family around him, then invited the other guests to fan out from the sides. Albert took his position on the back row and was pleased when Nicole and Reenie came over to join him.

'Alright, kid?' he asked Nicole.

'Yeah, I just had a long conversation with my tutor from college. She was telling me about a business course I might be able to do when I've finished this one.'

'Get out of it! That sounds terrific.'

Nicole was so excited her words were coming out much faster than usual. 'She also says she knows the woman who owns my favourite salon. She's looking for maternity cover from June, and Joyce is going to fix me up with an interview! Isn't that unreal?'

Albert decided not to mention the conversation he'd had with Joyce. 'Bloomin' 'eck, that's great news!'

'OK, I want to see happy faces from everyone!' shouted Gary.

As he raised his camera, Albert picked Reenie up and gave her a little bounce in his arms.

'That's grand!' Gary shouted. 'And now if you could all give a loud cheer.'

Albert waved his free arm and Reenie joined in.

'And now Mum and Nan,' Gary said, 'if you could give Brad a kiss on each cheek.'

Jackie and Marjorie leaned in and planted their lips on each side of Bradley's face.

'That's it!' said Gary. 'Perfect!'

As Albert posed alongside Marjorie's family and friends, he was hit by a warm feeling he hadn't experienced before. *Is this what it feels like to be a member of a community?*

He remembered how his job as a postman used to make him feel like part of the community, albeit a community he chose only to observe. He could see now that he'd been fooling himself. *But now I finally am a member of my community. Now I finally know what it feels like.*

'And could everyone in the background give Brad a big wave goodbye!' said Gary.

As Albert did as he was directed, it struck him how lucky he was. For a long time he'd brooded on the bad luck he'd been dealt in life, the bad luck that had forced him and George to grow up gay in a world that didn't accept them. But he could see now that they'd had much better luck in life than Bradley. They still had the chance to be together. They still had the chance of happiness.

And I owe it to Bradley and his family to make the most of that.

Chapter Thirty-Three

Albert opened the oven and stepped back to avoid the escaping heat. He lifted a large fish pie off the worktop and slid it inside.

It was Sunday evening and he was cooking a meal for Daniel and Danny. Now the date they'd arranged had finally arrived, he was feeling nervous. It was the first time he'd hosted a meal at his home and there were so many things he was unsure of.

Should I wear my slippers or put on a pair of outdoor shoes?

What happens if they ring the doorbell while I'm busy in the kitchen?

How can I serve them drinks in the front room while I'm making the meal in here?

The logistics of it were so much more complicated than he'd imagined. At least he was feeling confident about the meal itself. Earlier in the week he'd searched online and found recipes for tomato soup and a fish pie with mashed potato and had done a practice run of both. He'd made so much food he'd been eating it for the rest of the week so wasn't particularly looking forward to eating the same thing again. But at least he could make the meal without any problems.

But what will Daniel and Danny think of it? Will they think it's dull and boring?

Now that he considered this, he realised just how much more sophisticated they were than him. They'd lived in London for years so were bound to have eaten in all the best restaurants. He suddenly pictured the two men awkwardly forking his food around their plates and making a brave attempt to pretend they liked it.

Bloomin' 'eck, I hope this isn't a disaster.

He opened the fridge to check the temperature of the white wine he'd selected purely because it was one of the most expensive in the supermarket. He logged into the music streaming service Nicole had downloaded on to his phone and tested the connection with a pair of speakers he'd bought. He'd already picked out a playlist called 'Classical Dinner Party' and, once it was piping through the speakers, he rearranged the daffodils he'd placed in a vase in the centre of the table. They were a reminder that spring was finally on its way – and a reminder that he'd promised himself he'd find George before he saw the first bluebells. Now it looked like he'd succeed; the calendar hanging on the wall showed there were just six days until he went to London. But he still had no idea how George would react when he found him. *Or if he can ever bring himself to forgive me.*

He checked his watch again; there were ten minutes until his guests arrived. He decided to set the table.

As he spread out the mats and arranged the cutlery, he

remembered why he didn't usually like eating at the old family dining table; it was around this table that he'd been forced to endure the confrontation that had brought about the end of his relationship with George. It was a confrontation he'd tried not to think about for a long time but one he'd probably have to discuss if he was eating at the table and talking about his search for George.

He suddenly felt much more nervous.

'So how are you settling in?'

Before they could answer, Albert handed his guests a glass of wine. He'd decided to keep things simple and serve drinks in the kitchen, and Daniel and Danny seemed to like the informality. They held up their glasses and said, 'Cheers!'

'Cheers!' echoed Albert.

Once Danny had taken his first sip, he returned to the question. 'Yeah, we've settled in well, I think. It's more chill now but at first everyone was literally falling over themselves to hang out with us.'

'I should just point out that it was lovely everyone was so friendly,' said Daniel. 'But lots of them seemed to think we'd be able to give them advice about their sex lives. And if one more person tells me they've met John Barrowman!'

The three of them laughed.

'I wouldn't care,' said Daniel, 'but I don't really know who John Barrowman is.'

'Although I do like giving sex advice,' said Danny, with a wicked glint in his eye. 'And darling, I am *seriously* good at it.'

Albert couldn't help laughing again. He tipped back a swig

of his wine; the three of them hadn't even sat down yet and already he was enjoying himself. He realised he'd forgotten to take off his slippers and replace them with smart shoes but it didn't matter any more. He topped up his guests' glasses and invited them to sit down for the starter.

Once he'd dished out the soup, he asked about their backgrounds. They told him they'd met in London ten years ago at an event held in a bookshop called Gay's the Word, a shop that only sold LGBT-themed books. Daniel had been working full-time as an academic and had just signed a publishing deal to write his first book about his specialist subject, gay history, and Danny had been a graphic designer with a high-profile job in a big agency. Since then, Danny had been made redundant but had seized the opportunity to go freelance – and he'd used his payout to allow the two of them to move out of London.

'We realised that now we've got each other we don't really want to be in the hustle and bustle of the big city,' said Daniel.

'Now that I'm a one-man woman,' added Danny, 'I'm legit happy to slow things down.'

They continued chatting as Albert cleared away their bowls and served the main course. By now he was starting to feel the effects of the wine and relaxing even more. And he was delighted when his guests complimented him on the food.

'It's delicious,' said Daniel, 'the best meal we've had in a long time.'

Albert grinned. 'That's great to hear. I really wanted to impress you.'

Danny put down his cutlery. 'You don't need to do that, darling. There's no need to impress us.'

Daniel nodded in agreement. 'We're all on the same side, aren't we?'

Albert felt another flush of that warm feeling he'd experienced at Marjorie's party.

Once everyone had finished eating, he cleared away their dishes and began telling them about his trip to Manchester. He said that he liked The New Union but Daniel had been right when he'd predicted his first night out on the gay scene would be emotionally overwhelming.

'It'll be much easier the next time,' Daniel promised. 'Although you must remember that just because you're gay doesn't mean you'll be into wild nightlife. It's never been my thing, if I'm honest.'

'I was legit wild when I was single,' chipped in Danny, his lip gloss shimmering in the light, 'if I didn't go out every night I'd get serious FOMO. But Daniel's right; not every gay man can be a scene queen.'

Albert looked down at his slippers and gave them a wiggle. 'Well, I don't think there's much chance of that with me.'

They asked if he'd found any more clues in his search for George and he told them what he'd learned from Phoebe. When he mentioned that George performed regularly in the Royal Vauxhall Tavern they told him they knew the venue well and, like The New Union, it was a long-established, old-fashioned gay pub that wasn't remotely pretentious.

'But I'm frightened,' Albert found himself blurting out. 'I'm frightened I'll meet George and he won't forgive me.'

Daniel took off his glasses and began to massage the little indentations they'd left on his nose. 'What makes you say that?'

Albert drew in a long breath and let it out. 'Because of the way our relationship ended. Because of what I did to him. Because of what happened around this table.'

On the night George is arrested, Albert runs over the moors for what feels like hours. As he isn't following his usual route, he loses his way several times and ends up with his trousers and boots covered in mud. When he finally arrives home, he sneaks in through the back door and begins pulling off his boots. But when he switches on the light, his dad is sitting at the dining table.

Oh no, is he waiting for me? Does he know?

'Where've you been?' he asks. He's still wearing his uniform but he isn't fiddling with his moustache the way he usually does; he's sitting bolt upright with his hands clasped tightly in front of him. And he's holding himself perfectly, chillingly still.

Albert looks down to avoid his gaze. 'Oh, just out.'

'I know that. But where?' his dad presses. 'And why are you covered in mud?'

Albert pulls off his second boot and sets it down by the door. He moves over to the table but doesn't dare sit down. He stands behind a chair and holds on to the back of it. 'Oh, you know what it's like,' he says, trying his best to sound blasé, 'me and the lads were just messing about.'

His dad lets out a sharp breath. 'Messing about? Is that what you call it now?'

Hell fire, he knows.

His dad's eyes flick up to the master bedroom, where Albert's mam is sleeping, and he lowers his voice. But Albert finds the quietness of it much more frightening than if he were shouting. 'I know where you've been, Albert,' he says. 'You've been with that dirty little queer, George Atkinson. You've been in that pillbox up on t' moors.'

Albert doesn't say anything. He stands there listening to the sound of his own short, frantic breathing overlaid with his dad's long, heavy breaths.

What can I say? What can I possibly say to make this better?

His dad looks at him with an expression of revulsion. 'I let you get away because I didn't want the shame of having a queer son in t' family. I didn't want people looking at me like I had owt to do with it. Like I were the shit on their shoe.'

Albert clings on to the back of the chair. He tries not to feel rotten and despicable and wrong.

'You, Albert, are the shit on *my* shoe,' his dad adds.

In his eyes, Albert can see the hatred burning. He tries to swallow but his throat has gone dry.

'Anyway, you needn't worry,' his dad goes on, 'your filthy secret's safe.'

'Safe? What do you mean?'

'We questioned George but he refused to let on who he were with. Truth be told, I rushed through the whole thing so I could be done with it and chuck him in a cell. But I'm pretty sure he won't say owt. He were a plucky little thing.'

Albert feels the guilt thump into him.

So George is plucky while I just ran away and left him.

He pictures George sitting in a cell down at the station.

He knows how much he'll hate it. He knows how much he'll be suffering. Just imagining this makes his guilt morph into anger. To his surprise, it flares up to the surface.

'Dad, how could you?' he says. 'How could you do that to him?'

His dad looks stunned.

'Why couldn't you have just left him alone?' Albert goes on, his nostrils flaring. 'We weren't doing anyone any harm. Why couldn't you have just left us both alone?'

Without any warning, his dad springs up and hits him across the face. The impact of it makes Albert stagger back from the chair.

'Leave you alone?' his dad hisses. 'Leave you alone like a pair of perverts?'

Albert's hand rushes to his cheek. His dad has hit him with such force it's left him feeling dizzy.

His dad leans in closely, so closely that Albert can smell the cigarettes on his breath. 'You disgust me, Albert,' he whispers. 'You well and truly disgust me.'

For a moment Albert feels almost paralysed by pain and shock and shame. But he can feel himself rallying. He tells himself that he isn't going to feel the way his dad wants him to feel. He isn't going to give in.

No, I'm going to fight. I'm going to fight for what I know is right, for the way I feel when I'm with George.

'Dad, it's not like that,' he argues. 'There's nowt disgusting about it. Me and George are in love.'

His dad's face flushes a deep shade of burgundy. Albert's never seen him so angry.

'What are you on about?' he splutters. 'Queers can't love, everybody knows that. Whoever heard of owt more ridiculous?' And he repeats, much more emphatically, 'Queers can't love.'

'Why not?' Albert argues, the defiance ringing in his voice. 'Why can't they?'

But rather than replying, his dad spits at him. He spits in his face.

As he wipes it off with his sleeve, Albert knows that whatever he says, his dad won't listen. This is a fight he can't win.

'I'm not talking about this any more,' his dad announces. 'Unless you promise me you'll break off with George and never see him again, first thing in t' morning I'll slap him with a charge and he'll be chucked in prison. And I won't hold t' lads off him, either. They'll give him a good battering, just like he deserves.'

Hell fire, is this really happening?

'But if you agree to stop seeing him,' his dad goes on, 'I'll make sure t' lads don't touch him. And I'll let him off with a caution. He won't have a criminal record so he'll be able to leave town and start a new life somewhere else.'

Albert feels his body sag in defeat. He can't bear to think of George being hurt. And he knows what life will be like for him if the news of what happened comes out and spreads around town. However much he loves him – and however much he wants to be with him – he can't put him through that.

He tries not to think about how much his dad's plan will hurt both of them. He tries not to think of the unhappiness he's about to unleash into both of their lives. He tries not to think of what his own life will be like without George.

He screws up his eyes.

He says yes.

Danny reached over and rubbed Albert's arm. 'Darling, that's a terrible thing to be carrying around with you all this time. But did you explain any of this to George?'

Albert picked up his empty glass and began twisting the stem between his fingers. 'No.'

'But surely if you told him now, he'd totally get it,' Danny argued.

'They were brutal times back then,' said Daniel. 'I know from the research I did for my book that lots of gay people had to live through that kind of thing. Even though decriminalisation happened in 1967 it only applied to people over the age of twenty-one and they still weren't allowed to meet in public places – so the police carried on raiding bars and cruising grounds for years. In fact, there were more prosecutions carried out against gay men in the seventies than there were in the sixties. And those who were convicted would end up on the sex offenders' register, alongside rapists and paedophiles. They'd often lose their jobs; the law offered gay people no protection from discrimination in the workplace.'

'At the time me and George didn't know all that detail,' Albert pointed out, 'but we did know we'd be in serious trouble if we got caught. That's why we never wrote anything down – not at first, anyway. But then I guess we must have got carried away.'

'Is that how you got found out?' asked Danny. 'Is that how your dad knew where you were going to be?'

Albert said his dad had told him he'd received an anonymous tip-off. 'But now I know that's not true.'

He stood up and pulled another bottle of wine out of the fridge. 'Over Christmas I went through my mam's things. And I found the notes George sent me in her box of souvenirs. She'd kept them all.'

He began drilling the corkscrew into the bottle.

'That last night we met, George sent me a note telling me he was free and I should meet him in the old war bunker. That's all it said – that and "I love you" – but it was only signed with an initial. He put it in the usual place, between two loose bricks in our back wall. But my mam must have found it and it must have made her suspicious. She must have wondered why I was being so secretive. Either that or she knew me better than I thought.'

He pulled out the cork and began topping up the glasses.

'But how do you know it was your mother who found the note and not your father?' asked Daniel. 'How do you know he wasn't lying about the tip-off?'

Albert sat back down. 'It's possible, I suppose, but why wouldn't he have just said that? It's not as if he held back on any other front.'

'And what about the rest of the notes?' asked Danny. 'Where did you keep them? And when did you notice they were gone?'

'Later that night,' said Albert, 'I looked for them in their hiding place under my bedside cabinet but they'd disappeared.

I always assumed my dad must have searched my room for any incriminating evidence. But if he did find them, there's no question he'd have destroyed them; don't forget he was a policeman trying to keep me out of it. So my mam must have been rummaging around and found them. That must have been how she worked it all out. And she must have been the one who tipped off my dad.'

Danny swilled the wine around his glass. 'Darling, that is seriously shady. Your own mum did the dirty on you.'

Albert nodded. 'She did, yeah. And when I found out, it changed everything I'd thought since then. When we were sitting around this table, my dad warned me never to mention anything about what had happened to my mam because the stress would kill her. She was always ill and quite fragile by then.'

Daniel began rubbing his beard. 'So he used emotional blackmail on you, effectively.'

'I suppose you could call it that, yeah. And that's why I stayed in the closet for so long – because I was afraid of upsetting my mam. But it turns out she knew all along. And it turns out she didn't deserve the sacrifice I made.'

'Well, it sounds like you've lived through a trauma,' said Daniel, 'especially if you've stayed in this same house with all those unhappy memories. It must have had a profound effect on you.'

Albert took a sip of his wine. 'Funnily enough, I was thinking about that before you came; I was worried about sitting at this same table and going over all the memories.'

'And how do you feel now you have?' asked Daniel.

Albert shrugged. 'I don't know. Relieved, I suppose.'

'Good,' said Daniel. 'Maybe it's helped exorcise some of the pain. Maybe this was the perfect way to do it – sitting here and talking it over with your gay friends.'

As soon as he'd said the word 'friends', Albert knew he was right.

Danny sat up straight. 'Do you have any pics of George?'

Albert nodded. 'I do have one photo, yeah. I used to keep it in the same hiding place as the notes. My mam must have found it when she searched my room.'

'Do you mind if we see it, darling?' asked Danny. 'I'd love to know what he looked like.'

Albert stood up and went to retrieve the photo. When he came back, he handed it to his guests and for a long time they sat gazing at it. After a while, Albert noticed a tear forming in Danny's eye.

'You both look so sweet,' he said.

Out of nowhere, Albert could feel himself becoming tearful too.

'You both look so young and innocent,' Danny went on, knuckling the tear out of his eye. 'It's so upsetting to think people could be so horrible to you, that they could want to hurt you, to just hack away at your happiness – and your own parents too. They're supposed to be the ones who look after you and love you just the way you are. They're supposed to want you to be happy.'

For the first time Albert realised that he hadn't ever allowed himself to be upset. He'd been so terrified of the consequences of his secret being exposed that he'd switched into survival mode. When he'd first found the notes, all these years later, he'd let the tears flow – but he'd been crying for what he'd lost, crying for George. It had never occurred to him to cry for himself, to cry for what he'd been through, to allow himself to feel upset in the way he should have felt upset all those years ago. That feeling only descended on him now.

As his face crumpled, Daniel and Danny stood up and put their arms around him. Albert had no idea whose shoulder his tears were wetting but he couldn't stop them flowing. And he didn't want to.

'Come on, Albert, let it all out,' urged Daniel.

And he did – for some time. His face shuddered and his voice moaned. And he cried until his face was raw.

When the tears were finally subsiding, Albert drew back and wiped his eyes. 'Bloomin' 'eck,' he said, blowing his nose, 'I think I needed that.'

Danny picked up his glass. 'Come on, darling, let's have a toast. Let's have a toast to George.'

'To *Albert* and George,' corrected Daniel.

And they brought their glasses together with a clink.

As they sat back down, Danny asked when Albert was going to London. He explained that he was catching the train down next Saturday but still hadn't worked out where he was staying.

'Why don't you stay in our place?' offered Daniel. 'It's in Stockwell so you could walk it to the RVT in fifteen minutes.'

Albert said he didn't want to impose, but they insisted. And they spent the rest of the evening helping him make the arrangements. It felt good to have their support and, as they were getting ready to leave, he thanked them.

'You don't need to thank us,' said Danny.

'It's like I said,' added Daniel, 'we're on the same side.'

And that was when Albert understood why, earlier in the evening, he'd experienced the same warm feeling as he had at Marjorie's party. Because he didn't just belong to one community, he also belonged to a second. It was one he'd often read or heard about but had always dismissed – and certainly had never really understood – until now.

But now I really am part of it. And I couldn't think of a better place to join it than around my kitchen table.

Once Daniel and Danny had left, Albert made himself a Horlicks. He switched off the dinner party playlist and began playing clips of Georgina's show. To the sound of a naughty number she introduced as 'Don't Tell Mama' from the musical *Cabaret*, he began jigging around the room as he cleared the table and washed the dishes. This time he turned the music up loud and didn't worry about the neighbours hearing.

When the song finished and Albert heard Georgina unleashing her signature northern humour on the audience, he thought again that it was just the kind of humour his mam had liked when she was younger – and this time he allowed himself to wonder what she would have made of Georgina's show. He found himself imagining his mam sitting down to chat with Georgina – and then meeting George. He pictured a different outcome to his secret relationship than the one that had been forged around his dining table. And he reflected on something that had been bothering him since he found the notes and photo in his mam's room.

Yes, I'm angry with her for betraying me. But why did she keep the notes? Why did she keep the photo in her box of treasures? She must have understood that one day I'd find them.

What if there was a part of her that had wanted to save them for him? He wondered if that was why she'd kept the notes neatly bundled in the order in which George had sent them.

His memory rewound to that night in 1975 when he and his parents had been watching *The Naked Civil Servant*. His dad had launched into his usual homophobic rant and his mam had insisted on switching off the TV. At the time Albert had interpreted this as agreement with his dad. *But did she do that because she could see how I was feeling? Was she trying to make things easier for me?*

He remembered the last thing she'd said to him, moments before she'd died: 'Sorry.' That was all it was, one word. At the time Albert hadn't understood what she'd meant; he'd assumed she was saying sorry for being sour and bad-tempered and so relentlessly critical of him.

But was she apologising for betraying me and George? Did she see how unhappy it made me and come to regret it?

He stacked the final plate on the draining rack. As he dried his hands on a tea towel, he thought about what he'd said to Jamie in Leeds. He'd advised him to give his parents the chance to change their views, to give them the chance to come round. Had he said that because that's what he would have wanted of his parents?

He dismissed outright any idea that his dad might have let

go of his prejudices. He wrote him off as a lost cause; he'd died so long ago that he didn't really have any choice but to leave him suspended in a time when most people around him shared his prejudice against gay people.

But would Mam have come round if I'd told her about George, if I'd told her what he meant to me? Could she have loved me the way I was?

He sat down and took a sip of his Horlicks. As Georgina launched into a heartfelt rendition of 'I Dreamed A Dream' from *Les Mis*, he told himself that he had no way of knowing, but the very possibility allowed him to move on from his resentment.

It's time to let it go.

When the song stopped, he turned off the music. This time next Saturday, he'd be standing in the audience watching Georgina sing. And as soon as the show was over, he was going to find a way to speak to George.

By the end of the night he'd have the chance to finally face his past.

And to know much more about his future.

Chapter Thirty-Four

Nicole handed over the menu and the waiter left her and Jamie alone.

They were sitting in an Italian restaurant called Ciccone's, which was situated just outside Toddington. It was housed in an old pub that had been converted, although the stones on the walls had been left bare and the original fireplace had been restored, so there was no doubt they were in Lancashire rather than Italy. Nicole glanced around at the other couples enjoying the romantic, candlelit, Valentine's Day atmosphere, and judged that this was just the kind of place she'd always wanted to come with Jamie.

Earlier that week, Jamie had texted and asked her to keep Saturday afternoon free. He said he'd reveal why on Valentine's night; he'd arranged for Albert to babysit so he could take her out for a meal.

'So, come on,' she ventured, 'what's going on?'

He gave a cheery smile. 'Oh, well, it's quite simple really. I absolutely do want to be with you and I'm one hundred per cent committed. I'm sorry if I haven't always given that impression.'

Nicole couldn't help breaking into a smile. 'That's a good start . . .'

'And I told my parents quite categorically that whatever they've been imagining about you must be wrong. I told them as much as I could about what you're really like. And now I'm going to introduce you so they can see for themselves.'

'Oh, shit, right.' Nicole hadn't expected this and felt thrown. 'Sorry, I mean, that's great. But when?'

'Saturday.'

'*Saturday?* As in, the day after tomorrow?'

'Yeah. Is that OK?'

She drew in a shaky breath. 'Yeah, yeah, it's fine,' she managed. 'I just wasn't expecting everything to happen so quickly . . .'

'Well, I wanted you to know I've listened to what you said and I'm serious about us.'

She felt a flutter of nerves. 'Just a minute, I don't have to try and act all fancy, do I?'

The waiter reappeared and poured Prosecco into their glasses.

'Of course not,' said Jamie, once he'd gone, 'I just want you to be yourself.'

'But what makes you so sure they're going to like me? From what you've said, they're dead set against me.' Nicole picked up a breadstick and rammed it into her mouth.

Jamie reached across the table and took her hand. 'In case

you're worried, I should probably let you know they haven't said anything racist. And I really don't think that's the problem. My mum's sister is married to an Indian guy and their kids are mixed-race. My mum adores them. Oh and her partner at work is black.'

'Your mum's partner is black? You never mentioned that.'

Jamie nodded. 'Yeah, they've run a GP practice together since before I was born. And I know that doesn't necessarily mean anything and I know these things are complicated. But if I had the slightest suspicion my parents were being racist then I promise I wouldn't be doing this. I wouldn't subject you to that.'

He stroked her hand reassuringly.

'And what about the single mum thing?' Nicole popped the rest of the breadstick into her mouth.

Jamie let out a long sigh. 'Well, at the moment they're only seeing that on paper. They can only see it as an obstacle to me being happy. They haven't met Reenie or seen how much I love being with her. Just like they haven't seen how much I love being with you. That's why I want to show them.'

Nicole stopped chewing and swallowed.

'I want to show them how much I love you, Nic.'

She could feel a lump of breadstick lodge in her throat and reached for her glass of Prosecco to swill it down. 'Sorry, what did you say?'

'I said I want to show my parents how much I love you.'

There they were, those three little words she'd wanted him to say so badly for such a long time. Those three little words she'd been afraid to say to him first, in case he didn't feel the same way and she scared him off. Those three little words she'd been preparing to say to him on Boxing Day but had backed out of saying when he'd told her he was going to leave. And now he'd said them.

'I love you.'

Hearing them made Nicole feel so happy it was like nothing could hurt her any more. All the hurt she'd felt when Dalton had left her, when her mum had let her down and her grandma had died, suddenly all of it vanished. And suddenly she couldn't care less what Jamie's parents thought about her. Suddenly she knew she could win them round.

'Oh, baby,' she said, 'I love you too.'

Jamie lifted up her hand and kissed it. 'Good. And I'm sorry it took me so long to say it. I guess I just needed a bit of help to see things clearly.'

Just then, the waiter interrupted to bring their food. As soon as he'd left, Jamie picked up his fork and attacked his Parma ham.

'Right,' he said, 'no more talk about my parents. Let's eat!'

The next morning, Nicole was so nervous she couldn't eat. As she walked down the High Street towards her interview, her stomach rumbled. She wanted this job so badly and couldn't stop thinking about how many of her problems it would solve. But she was tormented by the idea that she'd never been good at making first impressions and people often mistook her shyness for rudeness. Then a voice crept into her head.

Remember, Jamie loves you.

Almost like magic, this knowledge made her feel stronger

373

and more confident. She took a deep breath and straightened her spine. She even managed to block out her hunger.

When she arrived at Top to Toe, she paused for a moment to look through the window. It was a busy day and the salon was buzzing with activity. Nicole remembered coming to look at it when she was making her New Year's resolutions just six weeks ago. All she'd wanted then was to move one step closer to achieving her ambition. She'd had no idea she'd be given the chance to take that step quite so soon.

She imagined Albert speaking to her. *'Come on, kid, you can do it.'*

She tugged in another breath and pushed open the door.

Standing behind the reception desk was a plump brunette girl who greeted her with a cheery hello. When Nicole explained why she was there, the girl told her that the manager, Janet, was doing a treatment and running a little late. She invited Nicole to take a seat.

While she waited, Nicole looked around the salon. A few of the girls she recognised were doing treatments, chatting to their clients about Valentine's Day and upcoming holidays. An album of ballads by Celine Dion was playing and in the air hung a smell Nicole recognised – it was a mix of various delicately fragranced beauty products and the kind of industrial-strength spirits, potions, glues and bleaches that were used in a salon. It was a smell Nicole loved.

God, I want this job. I want this job so badly.

She wondered how Janet would respond if she suggested adding treatments for Afro hair to the salon's menu – then remembered how her first tutor in Huddlesden had reacted to a similar suggestion. Just when she was feeling her nerves beginning to stir again, a voice called out to her.

'Nicole? Is that you?'

It came from a blonde girl who was having a manicure at the front of the main treatment room. As she peered closer, Nicole recognised her as Scorpia, the sales assistant from Klobber.

'Oh, hi,' she said, 'how are you?'

Scorpia beckoned her over and asked what she was doing. When Nicole explained, Scorpia let out a squeak.

'Oh, you'll love it here, it's my favourite salon! Honestly, the staff are incred!'

She said she was bursting to know how Nicole had got on when she'd taken Albert to the Gay Village. As Nicole told the story, the beautician who was doing Scorpia's nails broke away to listen. Then a flamboyant male beautician sidled over to tell them he'd once seen Georgina St James perform in a gay bar in London.

'And what was she like?' asked Nicole, her eyes owlishly wide.

'She slayed,' said the man. 'I swear to God, she's one of the best queens I've ever seen.'

As the group continued chatting, Nicole could feel her nervousness being replaced by a warm, comforting feeling. The edges of her worries were softening and the world around her suddenly seemed more cosy and welcoming. She wondered if this was because she was ceasing to see herself as an outsider and was gradually starting to feel like she belonged in her new hometown.

Before she could work it out, she was approached by a

woman in her thirties who had a beauty spot above her top lip. 'Excuse me,' she asked, 'are you the new girl?'

'Oh, I'm not sure about that,' Nicole replied, modestly. 'But I'm here for the interview, yeah.'

The woman smiled. 'I'm the one who's going to be dropping a sprog – the one you'll be covering for.'

'Oh, congratulations – and it's nice to meet you.'

'I'm only four months gone,' the woman continued, 'so I'm not going for ages yet. But I think Janet wants to snap you up while she can. Joyce has given you a brilliant recommendation.'

Nicole felt touched but there wasn't time for her to get emotional; the woman explained that Janet was waiting for her in the office. She said goodbye to Scorpia and the rest of the staff.

'Good luck, babe!' chirped Scorpia.

'See you in June!' shouted the gay man.

As she strode through the salon, Nicole caught sight of herself in the mirror. She was walking tall and her face was ablaze with confidence.

I'm going to nail this interview.

It was an unseasonably bright February day and, as they looked out at the blue sky, Nicole and Jamie had to shelter their eyes from the sun.

They were waiting for Jamie's parents in the car park of a local beauty spot – the reservoir around which they'd gone for a walk on their very first date the previous summer. Jamie had said he'd chosen it because it had special significance for them but also because he thought if they could keep moving and not have to sit facing his parents, this would relieve some of the tension.

Reenie had fallen asleep in the car and Nicole had managed to lift her out and fasten her into the buggy without waking her. She looked at her head slumped against the side and thought it might not actually be a bad thing for her to sleep through the introductions.

'Here they come.'

Jamie pointed out a silver vehicle driving down the lane towards them. Nicole didn't know anything about cars but this one was raised high off the ground so she thought it might be what they called an SUV. It looked to her less like a car and more like a tank.

When the vehicle crunched to a stop on the gravel, the doors opened and a pair of legs swung out of each side. Nicole felt a stab of fear but this receded when Jamie reached out and took her hand.

He loves me. He actually loves me.

The first to step out of the car was Jamie's dad, who was called David. He was grey-haired and slightly ruddy-faced and wearing a green Barbour jacket and a flat cap. A few steps behind him came Jamie's mum, who was called Christine. She was dressed in a thick woollen coat, with black leather gloves that Nicole couldn't help finding vaguely menacing, and a headscarf that reminded her of the ones the Queen wore when she went riding horses. The hair poking out underneath it was dyed a shade of brunette that made her look severe but which Nicole made a mental note she could help soften. Not that Christine looked like she'd welcome that kind of suggestion today. As she approached, Nicole saw that she was wearing a stony expression.

Jamie introduced everyone and they exchanged rather stiff handshakes and immediately began walking, with Nicole pushing the buggy.

'Well, isn't it a lovely day?' said David.

'Yeah,' jumped in Nicole, 'we've been very lucky.'

Christine smiled thinly. 'Of course, it's all down to climate change. It's terrifying what's happening – the seasons are all skew-whiff. I'm not sure we should be feeling lucky.'

'No, but it'll be spring soon,' chipped in Jamie, brightly. 'And then we'll be able to feel happy about the sunshine.'

David kicked a stone to the side of the path. 'So Jamie says you're studying to be a beautician?'

Nicole told them about her course and said she was particularly interested in nail care. But as she couldn't see Christine's nails underneath the gloves, she had no idea whether or not she shared this interest – and the hint of a sneer that twisted briefly across her face suggested otherwise. When a jogger ran past and they all had to edge out of the way, Nicole was glad of the distraction.

'Nic's decided to do a business course after this,' Jamie offered. 'Her ambition is to run her own salon.'

Christine shot her a frigid look. Nicole tried to ignore it.

'Oh, and she's just got her first job,' Jamie added proudly.

Nicole explained that she'd been offered a job covering someone's maternity leave in her favourite salon – and that the owner had responded positively to her suggestion that they add treatments for Afro hair to the menu. She'd be starting in June and could fit her hours around the new course. 'After that, I thought I'd set up as a mobile beautician so I can get some experience of running my own business.'

'I know how driven she is,' Jamie said. 'I think she'll do a great job.'

'Thanks, baby,' said Nicole.

She noticed Christine roll her eyes. *OK, so she's obviously the one causing problems.*

'Of course, running a business is very difficult with a family,' quipped Christine.

Nicole wanted to tell her that she should try being a single mum with no money. But snapping at her would be the worst thing she could do. She smiled sweetly. 'Funnily enough, I was going to ask you about that. I was wondering if you had any tips. Jamie says you managed really well when he was little.'

She hoped her flattery didn't sound desperate but it did at least prompt Christine to chat more freely. As they crossed a bridge, she told them about the GP surgery she'd run for nearly twenty-five years; she'd decided to cut back to part-time hours while her sons were young.

'My partner didn't mind filling in for me,' she explained. 'He's gay so never had a family.'

Black and gay? She's starting to sound woke.

Nicole smiled to herself. 'And what were your boys like when they were little?'

'Oh, they were a real handful,' said Christine. 'They both had so much energy to burn off.'

'You're not wrong there,' David chipped in, 'I always said this one had ants in his pants. He wouldn't sit still.'

Nicole smiled. 'I can imagine. I don't know much about boys but from what I can tell they tend to be more boisterous than girls. And Reenie has her moments.'

'I always wanted a girl,' said Christine, suddenly sounding much gentler.

'I didn't know that, Mum,' said Jamie.

'Yes,' Christine went on, 'I wasn't fixated on dressing her up in pink or playing dolls, I was never one of those mothers. But what's that saying? A son's a son until he finds a wife but a daughter's a daughter for life.'

Nicole tried not to let the fear register on her face. *Is she accusing me of trying to steal her son?*

Jamie moved closer to her and glared at his mum.

'I'm sorry,' said Christine, 'that wasn't meant to sound combative. It's just we do have experience of that kind of thing in my family. My brother married a woman who turned him against the rest of us. It was all very upsetting, especially for my mother. I suppose it's just left me wary of the same thing happening again.'

Jamie widened his eyes. 'OK, Mum, but maybe let's not chat about that now. The whole point of today is to try and make sure that kind of thing *doesn't* happen. Remember?'

She nodded sombrely. As they continued to walk, they hit a clumsy silence.

Eager to lighten the mood, Nicole realised the time was right for her to release her secret weapon. As she pushed the buggy forwards, she pressed her knee into the back of it until Reenie stirred.

Within a few seconds, she gave a little mewl. Nicole stopped the buggy and feigned surprise. She squatted down and stroked Reenie's cheek.

'Hello, big girl. Did you have a nice sleep?'

Reenie sat up and opened her eyes but started crying – and very soon her crying turned into a howl.

'Sorry,' Nicole said, 'she's always a bit grouchy when she wakes up.'

Surprisingly, Christine gave her a smile. 'That's OK, Jamie was always crabby when he woke up after a sleep.'

David stifled a giggle. 'He still is a bit.'

'Yeah,' said Jamie, 'thanks, guys.'

At the sound of Jamie's voice, Reenie held out her arms. 'Jamie!' she shouted. 'Carry!'

Nicole unfastened the buggy and Jamie leaned down to lift her out. As soon as he pulled her to his chest, her crying subsided. As he introduced her to his mum and dad, Nicole couldn't help noticing that both of them angled their bodies towards her to get a better look – and they were both smiling.

OK, this is good. We just need to keep it going.

She swept around Jamie's back and eased George Pig into Reenie's hand. 'If I don't give her this now she'll only start crying for it,' she explained.

They resumed walking.

'Jamie used to have a blanket,' said Christine. 'He took that everywhere. Even when I put it in the washing machine, he'd sit on the kitchen floor watching it go round and round.'

'Aw, how cute,' said Nicole.

'Yeah, I'm not sure I want my girlfriend to be hearing this,' joked Jamie.

David paid him no attention. 'You should have seen the state of it towards the end – it was like a scrappy old rag. And he wanted to take it with him when he started school.'

'So what did you do?' asked Nicole. 'How did you coax it off him?'

'The summer before he started in reception,' said Christine, 'on the day we set off on holiday, I just left it at home and didn't tell him. He was really excited about going away so he hardly noticed. And by the time we got home he was over it. Although I do remember him wanting lots of cuddles.'

'He was a right cuddle monster, this one,' said David, giving his son a playful elbow in the ribs.

'Oh, I bet he was adorable,' said Nicole. 'I'd love to see some photos.'

'We've got plenty,' said David. 'We'll show you them some-time.'

Nicole looked warily to Christine for a sign of disapproval, but there was none.

As they approached the children's playground, the sound of the other children stirred Reenie. She began wriggling in Jamie's arms and tossed George Pig towards her mum.

'Play!' she squealed.

Jamie lowered her on to the floor and she toddled off towards the swings. Nicole quickly parked the buggy and ran after her. She lifted her into one of the seats suitable for younger children and, as she began pushing, the others gathered around.

'Look at that smile,' said David. 'You can tell she's going to be a heartbreaker.'

'Yes, she's gorgeous,' agreed Christine.

Nicole pushed Reenie higher and higher until she began giggling. Within minutes, Jamie and his parents were beaming at her. Harmony reigned – until Reenie spotted a café.

'Treat!' she shouted. 'Treat!'

As she began wriggling in her swing, Nicole grabbed the seat and brought it to a stop.

'I'll take her,' offered Jamie.

'I'll come with you,' said David.

Before Nicole could argue, the two men were bouncing off in the direction of the café, carrying Reenie with them and leaving her alone with Christine.

Shit, what happens now?

Nicole could feel herself stiffen. She pushed her hands into her pockets and lowered herself on to a bench. To her surprise, Christine sat down next to her. They looked out at the reservoir in silence.

After a while, Christine spoke. 'I'm glad we've come out today. It's been good to meet you.'

'Thanks,' said Nicole. 'It's been good to meet you too.'

Christine turned to look at her. 'I don't mind admitting I tried to get out of it. But Jamie was very insistent. He's obviously very taken with you.'

Nicole smiled. 'And I'm very taken with him. He's a great guy.'

'Yes, we think so too.'

In her pocket, Nicole's hand found a funny-shaped pebble Reenie had picked up the other day and she began turning it around in her fingers. 'You seem like a close family, which is nice.'

'Yes, we are.' Christine looked down at her hands. 'I suppose after what happened with my brother I've always wanted to keep my boys close. I've never wanted anything – or anyone – to drive us apart. But I'm sorry for what I said earlier. I didn't mean to sound like a bitch.'

'That's OK, I totally understand.'

The words just slipped off Nicole's tongue – something she was expected to say – but as she heard herself speak, she realised she *did* understand. Because she couldn't bear the thought of ever losing Reenie – and she wouldn't like to think of what she'd be capable of doing if she was ever faced with a threat to her family.

'Without going into the messy details,' Christine said, 'what we went through with my brother was very distressing. Let's just say he married a woman who was from a very different background to us and basically she exploited that. We've hardly spoken to him for years now.'

Nicole stopped turning the pebble in her hand and let it fall to the bottom of her pocket. 'I'm sorry,' she said. 'That's very sad.'

'Well, yes.' Christine gazed out at the reservoir again. 'I suppose that's why I've been so mistrustful of you. I know it might sound harsh, but I just wanted to protect my family from the same thing happening again. I just want Jamie to be happy.'

Nicole thought of her vow to turn herself into a lioness and to do anything she could to protect Reenie. 'Don't worry, I totally get that,' she said.

Christine turned back to her. 'Anyway, you're obviously a

nice girl. And it's obvious you make Jamie happy. So you have my word that from now on I won't put up any more barriers.'

'Thanks, Christine. And you have my word that I won't do anything to hurt Jamie – or take him away from his family.'

'Thank you, I appreciate that.'

Nicole couldn't resist giving a wry grin. 'Besides, there's more than enough of him to go round.'

Christine grinned back at her. 'Absolutely. I don't want him all the time.'

'Me neither!'

They gave a little laugh.

'What are you two cracking up at?'

They looked up and saw Jamie and David walking towards them, with Reenie toddling in between. She was triumphantly eating an ice cream, despite the fact it was February.

'Oh, nothing!' Nicole and Christine said at the same time.

As they drew closer, Nicole could see that Reenie had ice cream smeared around her mouth. From its bright green colour she deduced that the flavour was mint choc chip, the one she used to eat with her grandma.

Are you sending me another sign, Grandma? Are you trying to tell me everything will be alright?

Jamie sat down next to her and slipped his hand through hers. 'I love you,' he whispered in her ear.

In that moment, Nicole saw a vision of their future together and could see exactly how this would work, how she and Reenie would fit into Jamie's family. And she knew that everything *was* going to be alright.

'Come on,' said David, 'let's keep going or we'll get cold.'

'Especially those of us eating ice cream,' joked Nicole. She gave Jamie and David a smirk. 'I can see you two are going to be soft touches. It'll be down to me to be the hard one.'

Christine shot her a look of cautious solidarity. 'Welcome to my world, Nicole.'

And they laughed again, a little louder this time.

Chapter Thirty-Five

Albert arrived at Toddington Station and looked at the departures board; there were still twenty minutes till his train left for London. He'd arrived early because he hadn't wanted to be stressed – but he was so early his train still wasn't ready for boarding.

He sloped over to a bench and lowered himself on to it. A pair of pigeons were picking at some crumbs that had been left on a table outside Burger King.

'The train now arriving at Platform 3 is the 11.53 for Carlisle,' announced a voice over the tannoy.

Albert pulled out his phone and checked his digital ticket.

For the first time in his life, he was going to London. And the trip was going to take him much further out of his comfort zone than his recent visits to Bradford, Blackpool and Manchester. London was bound to be much louder and much busier than anywhere he'd visited in his life. Suddenly, it felt like he was about to embark on a journey to another world.

The enormity of what he was doing hit him and panic raced through him like an electric charge.

Do I really want to do this? Do I really want to put myself through it?

And then he was hit by another thought.

What if I go all that way and George still hasn't forgiven me?

It's mid-September and Albert has been working as a postman for nearly two weeks, long enough for him to be settling into the route of what everyone in the office calls his 'walk'. But on this particular day there's something different – and he gradually becomes aware that he's being followed. After glancing over his shoulder, he spots someone hovering in the distance. It's George.

The two boys haven't spoken since the night of George's arrest. Since the night Albert abandoned him to run away over the moors. Since the night Albert made a deal with his dad to break off the relationship and never see him again.

In that time, Albert has worried constantly and slept terribly, gripped by an awful dread of what he knows he has to do – and unsure of how he's going to do it.

Well, it looks like there's no avoiding it any more.

Albert ducks down a backstreet and signals for George to follow. As he waits, he leans against a brick wall and tries to steady his breathing.

When George does appear, for the first time Albert doesn't

feel his heart leap. As he approaches, it's as if an invisible barrier has sprung up between them. They stand a few metres apart and shuffle awkwardly around on the spot. Albert isn't sure what to do with his hands so holds on to the strap of his bag. He still has no idea how he's going to say what he has to say.

In the end, he settles for a banal, 'Are you alright?'

What a stupid question. Of course he's not alright!

But George answers stiffly, 'Yeah, I'm alright, thanks.'

Albert runs his hand up and down the strap of his bag. 'I'm sorry,' he says. 'I'm sorry I ran off and left you.'

George swallows. 'Don't worry about it. There wouldn't have been much point both of us getting arrested.'

Trust George to want to make me feel better. Trust George not to be angry.

'No, but I shouldn't have left you,' Albert insists.

George smiles. 'Yeah, well, maybe I should have been a better runner. Maybe I should have made more of an effort in PE.'

Trust George to try and make a joke out of it.

Albert's heart heaves.

How could I possibly love him any more?

There's a pause, and somewhere in the distance, he hears the sound of an ambulance siren.

'Albert, my mam and dad have decided we're moving,' George states, abruptly. 'We're leaving town tomorrow.'

Albert lets out a little breath, as if he's been punched in the stomach. 'No.'

At this, all George's emotions come tumbling out. He

explains that over the last few days, his mam and dad have been attacking him constantly, blaming him for getting the family into trouble and all the upheaval and money the move is going to cost them. 'It's been hell, Albert,' he bleats. 'I don't want to go with them. I know what they're like; there'll be no end to it.'

More than anything, Albert wants to wrap his arms around George. He wants to squeeze him tightly and kiss him and make him feel safe. He wants to make it feel like it did when it was just the two of them on the moors, when the world couldn't hurt them and nobody could tell them they were wrong. When they knew, without any doubt, that they *weren't* wrong.

He stops himself.

'But how can you get out of it?' he asks. 'If you don't go with them, where are you going to live?'

George moves closer and takes Albert's hand. 'Let's run away, Albert. I don't know where to but let's look for that special somewhere in our song. Let's go and find it together.'

Albert draws in a wobbly breath. This is exactly what he wants to do. He wants it so badly he feels like roaring out loud.

But he's made a promise.

What if Dad arrests George and ruins his life? What if he gives him a criminal record and he can't get a job? How on earth could the two of us possibly be happy then?

'Oh, I don't know . . .' he struggles.

George tugs on his hand, raises it to his lips. 'Come on, we only get one chance at life. This isn't a dress rehearsal.'

Albert pulls his hand back. He looks at the ground and kicks a stone.

He doesn't want to tell George about the deal he's made because he's worried George will fight against it and make the situation worse. He knows how passionate George is and he wouldn't put it past him to march down to the police station and demand he's prosecuted, as if to take some kind of stand. *And then he really would be in a mess.*

So instead he says, 'I can't, George. I just don't think I'm built for that kind of life. Always being looked down on, always being hated, always having to move on.'

'Yeah, but it wouldn't always be like that,' George insists. 'And we'd be together, so what would it matter?'

There's something about the smile George gives him, there's something about the hope in his voice, that brings tears to Albert's eyes.

'The world's changing, Albert,' he goes on. 'I told you, *I'm* going to change it. And if our special somewhere doesn't exist now, I know it will one day.'

Albert begins picking at a weed that's growing out of the gap between two bricks in the wall. His entire body feels like a dead weight, loaded down with guilt.

'Come on,' George pleads, 'let's go off and have an adventure. Let's have an adventure together.'

'I can't, George,' Albert repeats, tossing the weed on to the floor. 'I just can't.'

'You *can*, Albert. You *can*.'

Albert remembers the anger on his dad's face as he forced him to make the deal. He's witnessed the consequences of his anger on many occasions – the smashed crockery, the fists through walls, the smacks he gave him as a child. *If I go back on the deal now, who knows what he'll do? He might come after us, he might turn the police on us . . .*

I've got to let George go.

The only way he can think of doing this is by lying.

'George,' he says, firmly, 'I'm not coming with you because I don't *want* to. I don't *want* to go with you.'

George steps back and lets out a whimper as if he's been wounded. It's the most distressing sound Albert has ever heard. Even in that moment, he knows it will return to torment him for a long time. He knows it will stay with him for ever.

George recovers his composure. He draws himself up to his full height and looks Albert in the eye. 'I never want to see you again,' he says, resolutely. 'Do you hear that? Ever.'

As he turns and walks away, a shutter comes down in Albert's soul. And he knows that nothing – and no one – else will ever make him remotely happy.

He stands in silence, clinging on to his bag of mail as he watches George walk away and out of his life. The September sun shines down on him and creates a halo effect around his fair hair. That silhouette is the last Albert sees of him.

Sitting in Toddington Station, Albert cradled his head in his hands. After all these years, he was about to board a train that would take him to George. He was about to see him again for the first time since that dreadful conversation.

But how can he ever forgive me for telling him I didn't want him?

Suddenly his nerve endings felt raw and what he was doing seemed hopeless.

I can't do it. I just can't do it.

He let out a mournful sigh.

Just as he was standing up to go home, his phone pinged to tell him he had a text. He opened it up to find a message from Marjorie.

'Hi, everyone,' it read, 'I have some very sad news. I'm sorry to tell you our Brad died last night. He had a great time at Disney World but got home and took a turn for the worse. He passed away in hospital surrounded by his family. We're all terribly sad. Will let you know when the funeral is. Love Marjorie xx'

Albert sank back on to the bench. Although he'd only met Brad once, he felt hollowed out by the news.

He began to compose a reply.

'Hi, Marjorie, I'm very sorry to hear that. I'm thinking of you and sending my love. Albert xx'

He pressed Send and let out another sigh.

He looked up at the Departures board. There were ten minutes to go till his train left for London. It was now ready for boarding.

He sat back and closed his eyes. When he pictured Brad's face, he could feel the sadness bloating inside him.

Then, to his surprise, another emotion took hold. It sprang almost out of nowhere and began to revive his spirits.

Come on, lad, you can do this. You've got to do it.

Do it for Brad.

His phone pinged again and he snapped his eyes open. He had a new message from Marjorie.

'Thanks, luv,' it read. 'We're gutted beyond belief but it's nice to know our Brad touched so many people. At least his life was full of love. Marjorie xx'

Albert breathed in and out slowly as he thought over her words. Brad's life may have been short but it was worth something because it was full of love.

He looked at the clock and saw there were just over five minutes till his train departed. He stretched out his feet and pointed his toes.

George may still hate me. He may still refuse to forgive me. But at least I'll have the chance to explain.

And there's still a chance he won't feel like that. There's still a chance he'll be happy to see me.

Albert realised that this was his chance to fill his own life with love – and he had to take it.

Albert examined the map and counted the stations until he arrived at Stockwell. He'd be getting off the train in about fifteen minutes.

He was on the London Underground, on his way from Euston Station to the area where Daniel and Danny had a flat. Once he'd arrived, he'd have a few hours to find somewhere to eat, change his clothes and freshen up, before setting off for the Royal Vauxhall Tavern – or the RVT, as Daniel and Danny called it. He'd allowed himself enough time to relax into his surroundings before the show started – and to prepare for his reunion with George.

On the train down from Toddington, he'd been so affected by the news of Bradley's death that he'd felt sombre and strangely calm about what he was going to do. But now he'd arrived in London, his nervousness had returned.

He looked around and saw people of all ages and ethnicities crammed into the carriage. Sitting opposite him, two Mediterranean-looking men were gesticulating at each other wildly, while next to him, a pregnant Indian woman was engrossed in something she was reading on her iPad. Hanging from a strap in front of him was a young black man wearing earphones and tapping his head to the music, while waiting by the doors was a wiry white man tapping his foot, anxious to alight at the next station. As it was raining above ground, the floor was slippery and there was a faint whiff of wet, unwashed wool filling the carriage. Albert remembered reading somewhere that you could pick up more germs during a short journey on the London Underground than you could from licking a toilet bowl. He tried not to think about it and looked down at his lap.

In his hands was a postcard of some of the best-known landmarks in London that he'd picked up in a souvenir shop in Euston Station. He was going to send it to Mina and Tariq in Bradford to thank them for helping him track George down. He turned it over and saw the back of it, blank, waiting to be filled in with the outcome of his trip. Once again, panic slammed into him.

He tried to distract himself by taking another look at the map. Although he'd never been to London before, the names of the Tube stops were so familiar he could pretty much picture what the streets would look like above ground. The train passed through Oxford Circus and then came to Green Park, where a recorded voice told passengers to exit for Buckingham Palace. He imagined how excited George would have been the first time he'd heard that announcement and remembered that, in just a few hours, he'd be seeing him for the first time in fifty years.

As the panic surged through him, his confidence fell away. He took several deep breaths and counted the remaining Tube stops.

One . . . two . . . three . . .

When he reached Stockwell Station, he caught the escalator to ground level and found a quiet spot by the exit. He took out his phone and called Nicole.

'I don't know if I can do this,' he blurted out as soon as she answered. 'It just feels like it's all too much.'

'I believe in you,' she reassured him. 'I know you can do it.'

'Do you really?'

'Yes! But it's perfectly natural for you to have the odd wobble. You've just got to stay focused on the end result. And remember, we're all rooting for you. Your friends are rooting for you, Albert.'

He thought back over the last few months and all the kind things his friends had done for him – and he also thought about how good it had felt to do kind things for them. All that had only started when he'd embarked on his search for George. He remembered how lonely he'd been before that, how it was his loneliness that had spurred him to set out on his search in the first place. *Well, I owe it to all the friends I've made along the way to see this through.*

He gripped the postcard in his hand and cleared his throat.

'Ta, kid,' he said. 'I'll be alright. I'll just have a minute to myself and I'll be alright.'

He thanked her again and tucked his phone into his pocket. He stepped back and watched the crowds streaming through the ticket barriers and out of the station. He wondered if George had ever passed through this station and tried to imagine him rushing through on his way to a show.

Then he remembered that he didn't have to try and imagine George any more. Because very soon he'd be seeing him for himself.

He picked up his bag, stepped out of the station, and – for the first time in his life – on to the streets of London.

Chapter Thirty-Six

Albert walked into the Royal Vauxhall Tavern and paid his entrance fee to a shaven-headed lesbian wearing a black bomber jacket. He noticed that she had a Liverpudlian accent and overheard somebody calling her Tricky. She held out a stamp and asked for his hand, explaining that he needed a stamp if he wanted to leave the venue and re-enter. The mark she imprinted reminded Albert of the postmark on a letter, albeit one that was a little smudged.

He stashed his coat in the cloakroom and went inside. Although it was still early, the venue was already filling up. On his right was a long wooden bar, at which stood a huddle of mainly middle-aged men waiting to be served. Straight ahead of him was a dance floor broken up by several pillars, and this was overlooked by a slightly raised balcony fanning out on his left. The walls of the balcony were lined with red velvet banquettes and floor-to-ceiling mirrors in which a few younger men were making last-minute adjustments to their appearance, one of them rolling up the sleeves of his top to show off his biceps, another unbuttoning his shirt to reveal a heavily tattooed chest. Overhead hung several sets of coloured lights, two giant mirrorballs, and heavy speakers that pumped out crowd-pleasing, lightweight pop. And jutting out into the dance floor was a large stage that was currently covered by red velvet curtains. It was the stage on which Albert would soon be seeing George.

Before setting off, he'd spent a long time choosing his outfit for the evening. He was wearing the casual jeans and boots he'd bought on his first visit to Klobber, together with a plain green fitted shirt he'd picked out because he remembered George saying he liked him in green.

Let's hope he still does.

He'd also called into Boots to buy an electric body groomer and had made his first, rather inept, attempt at manscaping. Just remembering it made his cheeks prickle with embarrassment. He hoped nobody could tell he was blushing – and he hoped that by doing it he wasn't being presumptuous.

He bought a pint of cider and found himself a spot by a pillar on the dance floor, next to a tubby man with a garland of flowers around his neck who was chatting to a man with a bushy beard and a diamante tiara plonked on his head.

Albert took a swig of his drink and checked his watch. The show began at eleven o'clock and it had just turned ten.

One more hour to go.

At eleven o'clock sharp, the DJ announced it was show time. To the sound of a recorded fanfare, the red velvet curtains were drawn back.

And there she was.

Georgina St James.

She was wearing a platinum blonde wig, bronze stilettos, gold chains strewn across her cleavage, and a reflective silver dress that occasionally caught the lights and made the audience squint. As the opening bars of a song began playing, she introduced her first number as 'One Night Only' from *Dreamgirls*. It was clear from the roar of approval that it was a favourite of the audience. Albert couldn't help thinking that none of them could have any idea why he was there – or how much emotion he had invested in the evening. *None of them can have any idea that this is one of the most important nights of my life.*

Although he was struggling to contain his emotion, because George was playing a character, he could just about detach enough to enjoy the performance. He'd watched so many clips online that he knew exactly what to expect. And, as Georgina blasted her way through the opening number, he couldn't resist mouthing along.

'Do you like my dress?' she asked, as soon as it was over. 'It's not too chip shop, is it?'

'No!' everyone chimed back.

She nudged a pair of rather lumpy fake breasts that looked like they'd been created by stuffing a bra full of tissue paper. 'And how do the girls look tonight? Are they perky enough for you?'

'Yes!' everyone bellowed.

Albert found himself joining in.

''Ere,' she went on, 'what do you call a drag queen with breast implants?'

Albert knew the answer already.

'A booby trap,' she said.

Albert laughed along with the audience.

'OK, it's time to ramp up the camp,' Georgina announced. And she introduced the next song – 'Hello, Dolly!'

She performed her regular mix of show tunes interspersed with bawdy chat and the audience lapped up every minute. Albert was spellbound. But he was careful to keep himself tucked away behind the pillar, just in case Georgina caught his eye and recognised him; he didn't think it would be fair to put her through that while she was in the middle of a show.

Then, all of a sudden, Georgina announced that she was going to do something different, something she'd never done before. 'I want to sing a song for someone I used to know,' she said. 'Someone I knew a long time ago.'

As the audience fell silent, Albert recognised the introduction to 'Somewhere' from *West Side Story*.

Georgina launched into a heartfelt rendition that represented a marked change of gear to the rest of the show. Straight away, Albert was overcome by the full force of his emotion. Suddenly it wasn't Georgina he was watching onstage but his George. Suddenly the two of them were teenagers again, dancing on the hillside.

He held on to the pillar and felt his knees give way.

I can't do this. I need to get outside.

He staggered to the door and almost collided with Tricky. 'Are you alright, mate?' she shouted after him.

But he was already outside. A gust of cold air hit him as he lurched on to the street. His head was spinning with adrenaline and his heartbeat was thudding in his ears. He drew in deep lungfuls of air.

Once he'd composed himself, he dipped into his pocket and pulled out one of the letters George had sent him fifty years ago. It was his favourite, the one that repeated the words George used to express his feelings for Albert, the words he'd first used when they'd been together on the moors.

'I love you a little bit more than yesterday,' George repeats, 'and a little bit less than tomorrow.'

Albert holds open his arms and George snuggles in to find a comfortable position.

'Yeah, that really is perfect,' says Albert, tugging his coat on to the pile of blankets and spreading it over them. 'But if you're going to love me a little bit more every day, can you imagine how much you'll love me by the time we're really old?'

He feels George chuckling against his chest. 'What, like, in our sixties?'

'Yeah,' says Albert, 'when we're *ancient*.'

George begins singing a few lines from the Beatles' 'When I'm Sixty-Four' and they both laugh.

'Anyway, I stand by it,' George says, 'I do love you a bit more every day – which means by the time we're sixty-four I'll love you a hell of a load more than I do now.'

'Terrific,' says Albert, 'I'll look forward to it.'

'Me too,' says George. 'Me too.'

Outside the RVT, Albert let the letter fall to his side and looked up at the inky sky. A white van zoomed past and he stood back from the kerb.

Come on, lad, you're going to do this. You're going to see it through.

He leaned against the wall of the pub and could hear the final round of applause for Georgina and then the DJ introducing a song by Britney Spears. With a jolt, he realised how cold it was and that he was standing in the street without a coat. He went over to Tricky, told her he was feeling better and flashed his stamp to gain re-entry. But within seconds of being back inside he was caught up in a scrum for the bar. The venue was now packed and lots of people were starting to become rowdy and drunk. He retreated to the cloakroom and picked up his coat.

'Excuse me,' he said to Tricky. 'But is there a Stage Door?'

'You must be kidding, mate,' she replied. 'It's not the Palladium.'

'Oh, right,' he said. 'Well, what should I do if I want to see Georgina?'

She raised an eyebrow. 'Are you a friend of hers?'

He nodded. 'Yeah. Yeah, I am.'

At least I think I am.

'Well, your best bet's to wait by the back entrance in the smoking area. She usually slips out that way once she's changed.'

Albert thanked her and walked round to the smoking area. But it was crowded with men laughing and joking as they puffed away on their cigarettes. Leaning against a wall, two men dressed almost entirely in PVC were engaged in a passionate kiss that was accompanied by some clumsy groping. And one young man and his female friend were performing a dance move they called 'slut dropping', which as far as Albert could make out involved seeing which of them could lower their bum the closest to the ground. He couldn't possibly stage his reunion against a backdrop like this.

He took up position just across a little street, in the shadows of some railway arches.

To the side of the smoking area he noticed some kind of outdoor urinal into which several men were popping to relieve themselves, presumably to avoid the queues inside. It reminded Albert of the public toilets back in Toddington, and how he'd conquered his fear of them by realising that he wasn't so different to the men who'd met in there after all, that in fact he was just the same.

And then it hit him that, in waiting to be reunited with George, he wasn't just seeing through his search on behalf of all the friends who'd supported him. He wasn't just doing it for Bradley. He was also doing it for all those gay men who hadn't been as fortunate as him. All those gay men who'd been arrested and fined or sent to prison. All those gay men who'd lost the men they loved to AIDS. All those gay men who'd been torn apart from the men they loved.

'I'm doing it for *you*,' he said out loud.

And he felt a surge of strength.

He directed his eyes at the door and waited for George.

At just after 1 a.m., George finally emerged.

Although he was still standing across the street, Albert recognised him immediately. His hair was completely white and he was wearing trousers and a trench coat and wheeling a little suitcase along behind him. A few of the people in the smoking area accosted him to congratulate him on the show, one of them speaking so loudly that every word he said could be heard across the street.

'Darling, you were sensational!' the man drawled. 'Absolutely sensational!'

Albert couldn't go over while George was surrounded by so many people, so he decided to hang back and follow him until he came to somewhere quiet.

As George set off down the street, Albert followed him along a passageway that ran underneath the railway arches. But it was full of teenagers smoking some kind of drug and thundering around on skateboards, their cries echoing off the walls.

He followed him through to a main road but the pavement was lined with queues of people waiting to get into a row of nightclubs. A drunken straight couple were having a heated argument, shouting loud obscenities that made Albert shy away. He felt threatened by their aggression but George glided past as if it were nothing.

Albert tracked him across the main road and over to a bridge that led across the river. He looked around and saw that the crowds were thinning out.

This is it. This is where I'll speak to him.

But just then, he was approached by a homeless woman who asked him for money. She had no coat and was shivering in the cold. Albert felt sorry for her and stopped to give her his change. As he dropped it into her hand, he glanced over in the direction of George.

Come on, lad, don't lose sight of him now.

By the time he resumed his pace, George had nearly reached the end of the bridge and Albert had to rush to catch him up.

Before he could, George crossed another main road on the opposite side of the river. But by the time Albert had reached the same point, the traffic lights had changed and the cars were whizzing past.

Hell fire.

He kept George within his sights and watched him turn off the main road and into a side street. It suddenly hit him that, as he had a case and was walking home, he couldn't live far – and might be turning into his own street. When the lights changed, Albert crossed the road and broke into a run. As he rounded the corner, he saw that he was right; George was standing just a few metres away from him, outside the entrance to a block of flats. He had his back to him and was keying a number into some kind of security panel.

Albert stopped to catch his breath.

It's now or never.

He opened his mouth and shouted, 'George!'

A loud beeping sound signalled that the door was unlocked. But George ignored it.

There was a silence.

George stood still but didn't say anything.

Then he turned around.

He turned around and looked at him.

'Albert?'

Their eyes met.

Albert's heart felt like it was going to burst.

It's him.

My George.

For what felt like a long time the two men stood staring at each other. Albert was struck once more by the intense blue of George's eyes – so blue they were almost violet. Just like the bluebells he used to pick for him when they met as teenagers on the moors.

I can't believe I'm looking into them now.

I can't believe George is standing here right in front of me.

Albert tried to read the emotion on his face but couldn't. He attempted a smile but could only manage a weak one.

It provoked no response.

'Albert?' George repeated. 'Is it really you?'

'Hello, George.'

Albert thought about all the things he'd planned to say but suddenly his mind was empty and he couldn't remember any of them. All he could say was, 'Yes, it's me.'

George nodded slowly. 'I thought you'd come. Phoebe told me you were looking for me. But it's still a bit of a shock.'

Albert frowned. 'Sorry about that.'

Then George drew in a shaky breath. 'Do you want to come in?'

Chapter Thirty-Seven

Albert followed George through to an entrance hall, the walls of which were painted a shade of white he imagined had once been bright but had since become dull and dirty, scuffed by the countless bags and cases that had been dragged through. Albert could tell from the notices pinned on to a board that the block was owned by the council and home to hundreds of people. George didn't say anything and sauntered through.

'You know, I loved the show,' Albert began blabbering as he kept pace behind him. 'It was terrific. And the audience loved it too.'

George assumed a rather serene silence and pushed open the door to a stairwell. Albert was starting to feel awkward and tried to drown this out with chatter.

'I've seen some of the videos on your website,' he went on, 'but you're much better live.'

George picked up his suitcase and began climbing the stairs, the sound of his shoes squeaking on the steps.

Albert followed. 'Oh, and I liked that outfit you were wearing – with the bronze, silver and gold. Very clever.'

He became aware of his Lancashire accent booming around the stairwell. For some reason it seemed much more pronounced now that he was in London.

When they reached the first landing, George stopped. 'This is me,' he said. His accent was softer than the one he used onstage but it hadn't disappeared completely.

He led Albert on to a balcony that overlooked a courtyard. They walked along for a few metres, then George stopped outside an emerald green front door.

'Here we are,' he said. 'Home sweet home.'

Albert tried to read George's expression but still had no idea how he felt about seeing him again. As George took out a key and slotted it into the door, he resumed his babbling.

'You know, you look beautiful as Georgina. I mean, she's beautiful. Or sorry, should I say *you're* beautiful?'

George didn't answer but opened the door and stepped into the hallway. Albert followed him, all the time continuing to spout compliments. George shut the door behind them and switched on a rather harsh overhead light. It shocked Albert into silence and the two men just stood there, looking at each other.

'Right,' said George, 'now you can get a proper look at me without any make-up. I'm not so beautiful now, am I?'

Although his eyes were still the same, Albert could see that his face was heavily lined. But that didn't do anything to change his opinion.

'You *are* beautiful, George. You might not think so, but *I* think you are.'

George smiled. It was the same gentle smile he'd had when they were teenagers but now it was overlaid with something else. *Is it sadness?*

'Anyway,' Albert added, 'I've aged just as much as you have. So I hope you don't think I look old.'

George tucked his suitcase into a corner and hung his coat on a stand. He held out his hand and Albert gave him his coat.

'I think you've aged well,' George said. Then he noticed Albert's shirt. 'And I always liked you in green.'

So he remembers. Albert started to feel more hopeful.

'Thanks,' he managed. 'I can't believe I'll be sixty-five soon. It's my birthday next month.'

'I know,' said George, 'the seventeenth of March.'

There was another silence. But Albert could feel the hope swell inside him.

'Of course, I can't expect you to know how it feels to be that old when you're only sixty,' he joked. 'Or at least, you are according to your website.'

George chuckled. 'Oh, so you noticed that, did you? I guess that's me rumbled. Promise you won't tell anyone?'

'Don't worry,' said Albert, 'your secret's safe with me.'

George looked at him and his smile grew into a grin. In that moment Albert could tell that he was pleased to see him – and he could feel a rush of confidence.

'Come on,' said George, 'come through to the living room.'

Albert followed him down the hallway and into a much more softly lit room that was painted a soothing, chalky shade of green. Along the main wall was a grey suede sofa on which were scattered several pale green cushions, and the room was dotted with numerous pot plants, including an enormous yucca and what Albert was pretty sure was a bonsai tree. On a side table stood a few framed photos of George posing with friends and a cluster of candles he began to light. Contrary to what Albert had expected, there were no signs of his life as a drag queen.

'I keep all Georgina's paraphernalia in the spare bedroom,' George said. 'This is where I come to switch off from all that.'

'It's nice,' said Albert. 'You've got much better taste than Georgina.'

George chuckled. 'Thanks. Do you want a drink?'

'No, ta, I'm alright. I had plenty to drink in the pub.'

George slumped on to the sofa. 'Yeah, me too. And I'm always shattered after a show. The last thing I want to do is hit the booze.'

Albert lowered himself down next to him. While he was feeling confident, he decided to approach the subject he really wanted to talk about.

'You know, I loved it when you sang "Somewhere",' he said. 'Although it came as a big surprise. I got a bit het up and had to go outside.'

George sucked in a deep breath and let it out slowly. 'Yeah, well, when Phoebe got in touch I started to think about you and it brought back lots of memories. But what happened, Albert? Why did you suddenly start looking for me?'

Albert began to tell the story of his search and the events leading up to it. He told George about his crisis at Christmas, the death of little Gracie, his trips to Bradford, Blackpool and Manchester, the new friends he'd made along the way, coming out to everyone, the death of Bradley, and, finally, his journey to London. But instead of telling the story in chronological order, he was so eager to get it all out that he couldn't help jumping around the timeline and jumbling up the details. He decided to come straight to the point.

'Look, George, I'm sorry I didn't leave Toddington with you all those years ago. Of course I should have done and of course I wanted to. I only said I didn't because I thought it would be better for you to get away and make a new start. But I lied to you that night. I wanted to go with you more than you could imagine. But I let you down. And I came here tonight, because . . . because, I was wondering if you could forgive me.'

Albert realised in his rush to come to the point he'd forgotten to tell him about the deal his dad had forced him to make, a deal he'd thought he was making for George's own good. But the words and emotions were tripping out too fast for him to keep track of them.

George let out another long breath. 'Albert, you've no idea how much I wanted to hear you say this – for so long. But all that happened nearly fifty years ago now. And so much has happened since.'

He began to sketch out some of the details of his own life and some of the history he'd lived through. He told Albert that, when he'd started performing in drag in the 1970s, the police still routinely carried out raids on gay bars. Then, during the hysteria around the AIDS crisis of the 1980s, they began to raid bars wearing rubber gloves. By the 1990s the raids had stopped, but by this time George had lost countless friends to a disease that had ignited terror amongst the gay community. The trauma of living through it made him more and more political; once he moved to London he dedicated much of his time to campaigning for equal rights such as a lowering of the age of consent for gay men, while spending his evenings performing as Georgina in bars and clubs like the RVT. Then, as equality gradually inched closer, acceptance grew with it. Drag went mainstream, first with Lily Savage and then RuPaul, and he was rewarded with more and better bookings. For the first time in his life, he was finally able to stop worrying about money. And that was when he'd bought this flat from the council – a place he could call home, at last.

'That's pretty much it,' he said. 'Well, the headlines anyway.'

'It's very impressive,' said Albert. He wanted to say he was proud of him but wasn't sure he could claim that privilege.

'Oh, and if you want to know about men,' George continued, 'they've come and gone, I'm not going to deny that. But I've spent most of my life on my own. And I'm still on my own now.'

Albert nodded thoughtfully. 'You shouldn't be on your own, George, you never should have been. *I* should have been there to do all that with you. *I* should have been there to live through it all. I'm sorry I wasn't. But I want to make up for it now.'

George shifted in his seat. 'What do you mean? What are you saying, Albert?'

He decided to come straight out with it. 'I want us to be together again, George. I want us to spend the rest of our lives together. I want us to go on that adventure you invited me on fifty years ago.'

There was a silence. Albert was suddenly aware of the magnitude of what he'd just asked George. He hoped it didn't sound ridiculous.

George blinked, slowly. 'But Albert, you've only just met me again. I might have changed in fifty years. You might not even like me any more.'

'Well, yeah, I can tell you've changed, obviously. But at the same time, I can tell you're still the same. You're still the same boy I fell in love with.'

And I've never stopped loving you, he wanted to say. But he was worried about how those words would sound out loud.

George brought his palms together and moved them up to touch his nose. 'But Albert, isn't it too late? What happened between you and me happened in another world. Yes, it's good to see you. And yes, I did our song onstage tonight. I'm not saying there aren't still feelings there. But don't they belong in the past?'

Albert inched closer to him. 'They don't have to, George. Who says just because we were together fifty years ago it couldn't also work now?'

'But Albert, you can't just turn up after all this time and expect us to pick up where we left off. It doesn't work like that.'

'Why not? Couldn't we give it a try? Couldn't we start slowly and see what happens?'

George stood up and moved over to the window. 'Never look back – that's my motto. I've used it about all kinds of things that have happened in the past. When I've been upset by things, the only way I've been able to survive is by putting them behind me.'

'Yeah, but one thing I've learned is that if you try to do that, you never do put the past behind you – it just tags along in the present. And it burrows into you like some kind of poison. It's only by facing up to it and dealing with all the feelings it brings up that we can learn from it and move on.'

Until he'd expressed this out loud, Albert hadn't realised he *had* learned it. He hadn't realised he'd become so wise.

There was a long pause. From the courtyard below, Albert could hear the sound of two people laughing.

George turned back to face him. 'I need time to think about this, Albert. I'm sorry, but it's a lot to take in.'

'I understand.'

George took out his phone and sat next to him so they could exchange numbers. 'Look at us,' he said, 'swapping numbers on our mobiles. If our teenage selves could see us now.'

'They wouldn't believe it,' said Albert.

And then he thought of something else he wanted to say. *Go on, say it.*

'But it's for those teenage boys that I've done this,' he began. 'It's for those boys that I've been trying to track you down. And the funny thing is, a couple of times today I nearly gave up, but I thought about all the people who wanted me to do this, all the people who've helped me or people I don't even know who weren't as lucky as me. But the truth is, I haven't done this for any of them. I've done it for us – I've done it for the boys we used to be. And I think we owe it to them to see it through. Or at least try to.'

He stopped and raised his eyebrows. He'd no idea where his speech had come from.

'OK,' said George, 'let me have a think.'

Albert nodded. There was nothing else he could say. He stood up and went to get his coat.

'Oh, and Albert?' George called after him.

He turned around. 'Yeah?'

'I do forgive you. Of course I forgive you. You don't even need to explain what happened. They were hard times for all of us. We were all innocent. We were all victims.'

Albert nodded. 'Thanks, George. I appreciate that.'

George gave him one last smile.

'Goodbye,' Albert said. 'I hope I'll see you again soon.'

He realised that during their whole meeting he hadn't once touched George. Albert wanted to reach out and hug him but had no idea whether this would be welcomed. So he stepped outside and closed the door softly behind him.

Chapter Thirty-Eight

ONE MONTH LATER

Albert crossed the railway bridge behind Toddington Hall and accessed the gravel footpath that led up on to the hilltops. He was setting off on his usual Sunday walk, although this was the first walk of the year during which he'd felt the presence of spring. It was much warmer than it had been over the last few months and the sun peeped out in breaks between the fluffy clouds that drifted across the sky. When he reached the moors, they were losing the sepia tone they'd adopted over the winter and beginning to turn green again. And on the edges of woodland, he spotted the first bluebells of the season.

He remembered his vow to find George by the time he saw his first bluebells and couldn't help feeling downcast. Because yes, he'd found him – but since then he hadn't heard a word.

Four long weeks had passed since Albert had arrived home from London, four long weeks during which he'd hoped and hoped to hear from him. And now it was coming up to his birthday, a birthday George had made a point of telling him he remembered. This year it would be accompanied by his retirement, the news of which had prompted Albert to set out on his search for George in the first place.

But after all that, I'll be retiring on my own.

Rather than heading to revisit the war bunker, Albert decided instead to stop at the boundary stone. He turned around to look back over the town, and picked out the familiar landmarks of the parish church and the clock tower of the town hall.

As he leaned against the stone, he reflected that even if he hadn't heard from George, he was still glad he'd found him. He'd been able to apologise for letting him down all those years ago and had been given George's forgiveness. This had finally allowed Albert to forgive himself.

He could also see how much his search had enhanced him as a person. It had led him to conquer his shyness and make some lasting friendships, become a member of both his local community and the gay community, and learn to love his true self for the first time in his life. He had no reason to feel downcast.

I might have set off to look for George but along the way I've had an unexpected awakening – and grown in ways I could never have imagined.

As the sun crept out from behind a cloud, Albert could hear the sound of birds tweeting in the distance. There was no question that spring was well under way. And, just as the scene around him would continue to change with every season, so too would he. He remembered comparing himself to one of Reenie's pictures that was still being coloured in; he could see now that he'd always be colouring himself in, just as everyone else was. But that was fine. Because the picture he was working on was much richer and much more colourful than it used to be.

The following Friday, it was Albert's sixty-fifth birthday – and his final day at work.

It began like a typical working day. He rolled into the delivery centre at 5.45 a.m. and stopped to say hello to Ste, who showed him the latest video he was posting of his bicep curls. He made his way through to the main office, where he chatted to his colleagues about their plans for the weekend, sorted his mail and ate his breakfast. Then, just as he was arranging his mail into sacks, Marjorie came over to his sorting frame with a home-made Victoria sponge and everyone gathered around to sing Happy Birthday. They presented him with a card they'd all signed and each of them helped themselves to a slice of cake. Then, one by one, they drifted back to their workstations, leaving him with a rather lacklustre smattering of best wishes for the future.

Well, that's that, then.

After the emotional intensity of the last three months, Albert couldn't help thinking that his retirement felt like a bit of an anti-climax. But he reminded himself that everyone was busy steering a course through their own dramas, that everyone was grappling with their own challenges in life. *They're all busy colouring themselves in.*

Determined to enjoy his last day, he jumped into a van and

set off down the high street, passing the shops, library and the statue of the nobleman. He drove up the main road of stone terraces, the moors winking at him through the gaps made by the side streets. And he parked the van outside Cod Almighty, where he unloaded his trolley and began what would be his last ever walk as a postman.

He tried not to think back to his first walk, when he'd still been seeing George and had no idea of the disaster that awaited them. Instead, he thought about how much the town had changed since then, how the boundaries of his walk had been reset when shops and businesses had opened and closed, when the old school had been turned into flats and the new one had been built and then rebuilt, when fresh streets had been laid down and lined with houses, and the decaying factories and mills that had been so important in shaping the town's identity had been demolished with little commemoration or even interest.

And the town will continue to change long after I've stopped plodding along these streets with my mailbag.

Over the next few hours, Albert delved into his bag to deliver letters, postcards and packages through low letter boxes, high letter boxes, narrow letter boxes, and letter boxes lined with the hard brush that scratched his fingers. He dodged his way through the familiar obstacle course posed by dogs, retrieving his stick from its usual hiding place to wave it at the aggressive Border collie but then tossing it into a bin afterwards with an acknowledgement that he wouldn't be needing it again. And he encountered the usual evidence of births, deaths, marriages and other major life events. Today this prompted him to reflect on all the life changes he'd witnessed over the last fifty years: the babies that had been born and grown into children and young adults, left for university or to travel, and then returned to start their own families, their comings and goings as regular and reliable as the cycle of the seasons. And, even though he was losing his privileged perspective on these comings and goings, he knew they'd carry on without him. And he was happy with that.

The only thing he did find troubling was that he didn't see any of his friends. There was no sign of Daniel and Danny, or even Edith, who rarely left her house. He imagined she must have gone out with William, who she'd been seeing regularly since their reunion – when she'd been delighted to discover that he had indeed forgiven her. As she didn't have a mobile phone, he couldn't call to check but resolved to visit her at home tomorrow.

I'll have plenty of time for that kind of thing from now on.

He ate his lunch of a tongue and piccalilli sandwich and sipped his flask of tea as he sat in his van and listened to the news on local radio. Today's stories were mainly animal-themed, with reports on a Labrador puppy that had been born with green fur and the death of a 25-year-old rabbit whose owners claimed it had been the longest-living bunny in Lancashire. He treated himself to his regular Crunchie with a sad smile and then set off in the direction of the Flowers Estate. Along Tulip Drive and Buttercup Avenue he said hello to the track-suited youths and gave a cheery wave to the drunk mumbling to himself in the bus stop. But he was disappointed to find that Nicole and Reenie weren't home.

Not to worry, I'll have plenty of time to see them in the future.

When he made it back to the office, he found that it was much quieter than usual. Most of the postmen and women had finished their rounds early and rushed off to start the weekend, and Marjorie had left him a note to say she'd had to go to a doctor's appointment but would catch him soon. He didn't feel offended as she'd only been back at work for a couple of weeks, after taking a fortnight off following Bradley's death – and he expected she was still grieving and didn't feel like putting on her usual chirpy front. But he was a bit miffed that so few of his other colleagues came to say goodbye.

Once he'd filled out his final batch of paperwork, he put all his personal belongings into a spare sack and cleared his frame so that the young agency worker Tyger could move in when he started Albert's job permanently the following week. He tipped what was left of his cake into the bin, scraping the crumbs and cream from the plate. Then he said goodbye to the few staff who were there and quietly sloped away.

As he left the building for the last time, Albert told himself that his retirement felt like such a non-event he wished he'd planned a leaving party. But he'd been so caught up in willing George to make contact, it had slipped his mind. He decided not to worry but to focus on the positive and how much he was going to enjoy his life without work. A life that may not be blessed with George but he reminded himself was much richer than it had been just a few short months ago.

★

'*SURPRISE!*'

'But I don't understand,' Albert spluttered as he opened his front door, 'what's going on?'

'We're throwing you a retirement party!' said Nicole, blowing on a brightly coloured plastic horn.

'But how did you get in?'

She explained that she'd liaised with Marjorie to get hold of the spare key from John, who hadn't returned it since decorating the back bedroom. 'Anyway, never mind that, the important thing is we're having a party. Now let's celebrate!'

Still struggling to take it in, Albert allowed himself to be led into the kitchen, where rows and rows of empty glasses were lined up on the worktop next to bottles of all kinds of wine and spirits. In the corner, someone had set up a barrel of beer that was being pumped into pints. And he turned around to see that spread out on his mam and dad's old dining table was a buffet that included sandwiches, mini pasties and sausage rolls.

When he walked through to the front room, he discovered that it had been decorated with balloons and a big banner that read, 'Happy Retirement!' Pumping out of a set of speakers was a playlist of songs that dated back to 1970, the year he'd started work for Royal Mail. Currently playing was 'Band of Gold' by Freda Payne, to which some of the older guests were singing along.

Albert was stunned at the effort everyone had made – and touched to see how much they all cared. He began weaving his way through the party, keen to thank them all.

Nicole was accompanied not just by Reenie but also by

Jamie, with whom she'd spent the last couple of Friday nights while Albert babysat. She told him that, as she was getting on so well with Jamie's parents, they'd been invited to spend the upcoming Easter weekend with them at their villa in Tuscany.

'It's going to be our first family holiday,' she said. 'I don't know who's more excited – Reenie or me!'

Edith was there with William, who Albert hadn't met before but found charming; he called her his 'duchess' and sucked on an Uncle Joe's Mint Ball, which Albert hadn't realised they still made but William told him he managed to source online. He also explained that he no longer drove so had hired a chauffeur to pick up Edith and take them out on day trips like the ones they used to enjoy when they were younger.

'We're going to Manchester next week,' she chipped in, 'to the theatre!'

Attracting a lot of attention were Daniel and Danny, who pulled Albert to one side to tell him that they weren't going to make an announcement yet but Daniel had just proposed and they were planning to get married the following year.

'You'd better get yourself a hat, darling,' said Danny. 'You're going to your first gay wedding!'

Albert gave them a congratulatory hug and continued to circulate.

As well as his close friends, he was delighted to see some other, less expected guests. Ted Hardacre was there and explained that he wanted to help celebrate a major event in the life of his longest-standing customer. Albert also saw the couple who lived next-door, who'd started popping in on him regularly since he'd been round to chat to their kids during their school's LGBT Week. And Jean Carter and Beverley Liptrot had somehow managed to secure themselves an invite. They were in the kitchen mixing cocktails, declaring enthusiastically that their latest concoction was called the Backdoor Buster and thrusting it into the hand of anyone who passed.

'Bottoms up!' they said with a mischievous wink.

But the majority of the guests were Albert's friends from work, which explained why he'd seen so few of them in the office that afternoon. He made time to chat to Ste and Delphine, who were now a couple and planning their first holiday at some kind of fitness resort that focused on mental wellbeing as well as just physical appearance. Smiler and his daughter Olivia were excited to tell him they'd just been accepted on to a TV quiz show that pitted members of the same family against each other and was called *Beat the Parent*; they were travelling to London to record their appearance next month. And Tsunami and John had two pieces of news they were eager to share: his business was taking off, with a new contract to decorate a block of flats, while she'd just won a competition for a week's holiday near Valencia in Spain.

'I can't wait,' she said. 'I'm so happy we can finally have a holiday!'

Hovering in the hallway, Albert noticed Jack. He had his arm around a woman who was petite but somehow had a commanding presence.

'Albert, meet the boss,' he said proudly. 'This is our Doreen.'

Albert shook Doreen's hand and told her it was an honour to meet her.

'Likewise,' she said, 'I've heard so much about you. Although I don't know how you put up with this one at work for so long.'

'Well, I won't have to any more,' Albert joked. And then he gave Jack a pat on the shoulder. 'Seriously, there was a time when I didn't think I'd say it, but it's been a pleasure.'

'Same here, mate,' said Jack. 'And don't worry, if I step out of line, I'm sure Doreen'll put me right.'

'Too right I will,' Doreen quipped. 'If *I* don't have a go at you, who else are you going to call a nag?'

Albert laughed and continued to work his way around the party.

After a while, he became aware that several people were calling for him to make a speech. Before long he accepted that he'd have to give in and asked Nicole to pause the music. Everyone gathered round and looked at him expectantly.

'As you know,' he began, 'I'm not the type to make speeches. And I might have gone through a big transformation over the last few months but there's only so much change even I can handle.'

A chuckle spread its way among the guests.

'What I will say, though, is that when I first found out I'd have to retire I was dreading it – absolutely dreading it. Because I thought I'd be lonely and I wouldn't have anyone in my life. But I can see now that I was wrong. Because all I had to do was be brave enough to show you who I really am and you'd all want to be my friends. It's been a privilege to get to know you all properly. And I'm really looking forward to getting to know you more in the future.'

Someone gave a whoop and there was a general buzz of encouragement.

'So thanks for being there, thanks for coming to the party – and see you in my retirement.'

Everyone cheered and raised their glasses for a toast.

'To Albert!'

Albert joined in with a big smile on his face. But as he did, he experienced a flicker of sadness that the one person he wanted to be there more than any other wasn't.

George.

Although he'd given up hope that George might contact him, he was able to quell his sadness with the recognition that, in a roundabout way, George *was* actually there at the party. *Because indirectly it's George who's brought all these people into my life.*

He decided to throw himself into the celebrations. But before he did, there was something he wanted to do.

As Elvis Presley began singing 'The Wonder of You', he approached Marjorie. She was much quieter than usual and, although he couldn't ease her grief, he could at least make sure she wasn't having a miserable time at the party. He tapped her on the shoulder.

'Alright, Marjorie? Fancy that dance I owe you?'

She turned around, her eyes swollen and lacking their usual sparkle. 'What are you on about, love?'

'You asked me for a dance at the Christmas do but I was too shy, remember? I was hoping I could take you up on it now.'

He held out his hand and she smiled and gave him hers.

As he began to steer her from side to side, he asked how she was feeling.

'Oh, you know,' she said, 'I'm bearing up.'

Albert nodded.

'I mean, I still miss our Brad every hour of every day. I don't think my life will ever be the same again. But I did find it a comfort to know that his last week was such a happy one – and he got to go on his trip. I want to thank you for making that happen.'

Albert feigned ignorance. 'What do you mean? You don't need to thank me.'

She rolled her eyes. 'Come on, love, I know it was you who donated that money.'

Albert was about to deny it but saw from her expression that she wouldn't believe him.

'It didn't require much detective work,' she joked. 'I told you how much we were short and an hour later the exact same amount appeared in our account.'

Albert tried to divert the conversation but she put her finger to his lips.

'It's OK,' she said, 'we don't have to talk about it. I just want you to know how much it was appreciated – and how much our Brad enjoyed himself. I'm glad our Jackie will always have those memories.'

Albert smiled. 'In that case, I'm glad I was able to help.'

And he continued to steer her from side to side.

His next dance was with Edith. As he gently guided her around his living room, she told him that she also knew he was the one who'd sent her the anonymous gifts.

'But I don't understand,' he protested, 'how could you know? I put all the presents in the proper packaging and wrote your address on the labels and everything.'

'You daft apeth,' she said, 'you forgot to put the stamps on them. Who else was I supposed to think they were from?'

Albert couldn't believe he'd made such a basic error.

'Anyway, it doesn't matter,' Edith insisted, 'because what you did made me start living again. It's thanks to you I found William – and I haven't been so happy in years.'

Albert smiled and danced on.

When the song was over, Nicole asked if she could have a word. She suggested they go upstairs so they could speak in private.

They sat on the edge of the brand new pine double bed in the freshly re-decorated back bedroom, its walls painted a cheery turquoise.

'Don't panic,' she said, 'I'm not going to tell you I know about you going to Leeds to talk some sense into Jamie.'

'Bloomin' 'eck,' he said. 'Who told you that?'

She roofed her eyes. 'When he suddenly got his arse into gear, it didn't take much for me to work out you'd had a hand in it. But it's fine, that's not what I wanted to talk to you about.'

'Thank God for that.'

'Although I do want you to know I appreciate it.'

'Alright, alright. But while we're on the subject, I really appreciate everything you've done with this party. I can't believe you organised the whole thing on your own.'

Now it was Nicole's turn to feel uncomfortable. 'Yeah, yeah, never mind that. What I wanted to tell you is you've got one more surprise.'

Albert hoisted an eyebrow. 'Oh yeah? What's that?'

'Go down to the ginnel and you'll see.'

'The ginnel? Why the ginnel?'

'Come on, I'll show you. But you might want to sneak out so you're not followed.'

Albert crept down the stairs and waited until no one was looking so he could slip out of the front door, then slunk round to the back of the house. As soon as he reached the ginnel, his eyes were drawn to a piece of paper sticking out from the space in between the two loose bricks.

No, it can't be.

He darted over and yanked it out.

See you in our usual place. I'll be there whenever you can get away. G

The words began swirling around the page. Albert's heart began racing. Excitement clutched at his throat.

Can this really be happening?

He turned around and saw Nicole standing at the end of the ginnel. She was holding out his coat and walking boots. 'You might be needing these,' she said.

He shook his head. 'Hang on a minute, do you—? But what about—?'

'Never mind any of that,' she interrupted. 'Just go and find him.'

Albert ran up the main road and along the path at the back of Toddington Hall. He could feel hot tears pouring down his face and his heart was pounding so violently it felt like it had leaped into his throat. He struggled for breath, a stitch tearing through his stomach. But he didn't slow down.

Where is he? Where's my George?

He raced up the hill and past the boundary stone, not even thinking about stopping to look back over the town. He turned right and veered off the path to gallop through the woodland, almost poking his eye out on a low-hanging branch and twisting his ankle on a loose stone. But he didn't care – he just wanted to reach his destination. He only slowed down to pick some of the bluebells and gather them into a small bunch.

When he finally stepped out of the woodland, he drew himself up in front of the bunker and wiped his eyes on his sleeve.

'George?' he shouted. 'George, are you there?'

A figure slowly emerged from the entrance. The low spring sunshine created a halo effect around his white hair.

'Hello, Albert.'

As Albert picked his way up the hillside, he came face to face with the man he loved, the man he'd never stopped loving.

'George. You're here!'

George smiled. 'Happy Birthday.'

'Bloomin' 'eck, this is the best birthday present ever,' Albert babbled. 'I can't get over it, you're actually here!'

George held up a hand. 'Now let's take this one step at a time. I don't want us rushing into anything.'

Albert nodded. 'No, of course not, absolutely.'

George gestured to the bluebells. 'Are those for me?'

'They are, yeah.' Albert smiled bashfully.

George took them. 'They're lovely.'

Albert remembered how much he'd wanted to hug George the last time they'd met.

Can I hug him now?

Without having to voice the question, he received an answer.

'I came to say,' George began, 'that if you're still up for that adventure, then I am too.'

He held out his arms and Albert stepped into them.

As he pulled George close, Albert could feel his tears starting to run again. They came pouring out of him in such strong shudders that he could only gulp in short, ragged breaths.

'Oh, George,' he said, 'of course I'm still up for it.'

As he felt the warmth of George's cheek against his, the two of them began to gently sway from side to side. Before Albert knew it, they were dancing. As George started to sing their song, Albert felt his tears slowly subside. He closed his eyes and for a fleeting moment allowed himself to think they were teenagers again.

But he opened his eyes and looked at George as he was now.

I've done enough dwelling on the past. It's time to focus on the present.

He listened to the lyrics of the song and realised George had been right all those years ago when he'd predicted that, one day, they'd find a place where their love could be accepted.

But I never imagined for one second it'd be here.

He still hadn't told George that he loved him, but realised there was no urgency. What mattered for now was that the two of them were finally about to embark on their adventure – and Albert was excited to find out where it would take them.

As they danced on the hillside to the sound of 'Somewhere',

Albert wasn't sure he'd ever loved George as much as he did in this moment.

And if I love him a little bit more today, I'll love him a whole lot more tomorrow.

Acknowledgements

First of all, a great big thanks to YOU, the reader, for letting Albert and his story into your life! Writing a novel is a long and difficult process and there are times when it's easy to feel downhearted and lose momentum. If this happens to me, I try to think about how amazing it'll feel when real-life readers get to experience the fictional world I've created. I know there are thousands of wonderful books to choose from out there, so thanks for devoting your precious time to reading mine. It's a privilege to write for you.

A huge thank you to my editor, Eleanor Dryden, who put so much energy and enthusiasm into the book – not to mention sharp and sustained editorial judgment. Now I've got you on my side, Eli, I realise what I'd been missing all along. As a writer, it's so much easier to shine when you have a brilliant and committed editor cheering you on; although I think the two of us might each have met our match when it comes to attention to detail! Seriously, though, thanks for restoring my faith in the publishing industry – and I can't wait to see what we come up with next!

Thanks to everyone else at my new publishing family, Headline Review, including Rosanna Hildyard, who somehow managed to steer the text through an almost never-ending barrage of tweaking and fiddling, Jo Liddiard and Rosie Margesson, for turbo-charging its launch into the UK with a kick-ass publicity and marketing campaign, Nathaniel Alcaraz-Stapleton, for turbo-charging its launch into the rest of the world by selling the foreign language rights (something close to my heart, as I studied foreign languages at university), and everyone in the awesome Sales and Audio departments who are doing such a terrific job here in the UK. I feel so confident knowing there are so many talented people in what I call the A-TEAM!

Thanks to Katie Brown for providing me with the idea of writing a book about a postman reconnecting with his community. I'd always wanted to write a novel about an older gay man searching for a lost love, but you helped light the initial spark that brought Albert to life.

Thanks to my agents Sophie Lambert and Deborah Schneider for whipping the early drafts into shape. And Sophie, well done on finding exactly the right home for it, for sticking with me, and for handling my anxieties and impatience for so long – we got there in the end!

Thanks to all the friends who helped me research the book, including Rachel Mason, for explaining how a vet might put down a cat; Irshad Ashraf, for his help with the description of the Chaudhrys' living room; and Cassa Pancho, for helping me fill out Nicole's memories of her Trinidadian grandma. Special thanks to my nephew Freddy for the line about loving someone even if they turn into a zombie! For the record, Freddy, I'd still love you if you turned into a zombie.

Thanks also to all those friends who were my first readers; my cousin Emma Newton, for checking I didn't make any mistakes in the scenes set at Royal Mail (not the Post Office!); my mum and dad, for checking the period detail (Dad, thanks for advising on whether teenage boys in 1970 would have said tits or knockers); Matt Bates, for reading a very early draft and giving me the conviction to keep going; and Rosie Robinson, for reading the final draft, advising on the way young people speak, and spotting some mistakes even the copyeditor had missed!

To all the usual friends who cheered me on when my morale slipped – Chris Bollinghaus, Amy Rynehart, Bianca Sainty, Laetitia Clapton, Ed Watson and Ste Softley. Thanks for keeping my spirits up, as ever.

And a big thank-you to all those lovely people in the public eye who've provided the quotes that have helped market the book and whose names you'll find adorning the cover. These things make such a difference and I really appreciate the support.

Finally, an extra-special thanks to my dedicatee and the love of my life, Harry Glasstone. We met when I'd already started writing the book, but you had a huge impact on everything that followed, just as you've had a huge impact in every area of my life. You often joke that I'm only with you for your printer – and I did take the piss by getting you to print off countless drafts of this book – but the truth is that you've given me so much more than that, and I couldn't have done any of this without you. And now, I can't wait for our wedding day! I love you, my little schnitzel xx

Read on, for conversations inspired by Albert Entwistle . . .

Hi, this is Matt Cain. Once I'd finished writing this book and started to hear reactions from early readers, I was struck by how surprised many of them were by Albert and George's story: by how unacceptable their love was considered to be, and by how cruelly they were torn apart. I realised just how rarely stories like these appear in books, films, plays and on TV. But, at the same time, Albert and George's story isn't anything out of the ordinary. So many gay men living in the UK had similar experiences, at a time when their love was condemned. I found myself wanting to hear some of these real-life stories, so I contacted a handful of men of Albert's age and above. We've shared snippets of my conversations here, and have changed a few names to allow the men I interviewed to speak completely freely about other family members. I found what they told me fascinating, but also very moving . . .

Simon is 80 years old
and grew up in Yorkshire

Simon: At sixteen, I was at technical college in York. I'd discovered cottaging [*meeting men in public toilets*] at least a year beforehand, when I was fifteen. I'd met this really great guy who was nineteen at the time. He was an architectural student. Very foolishly, I'd written him a love letter and I'd hidden it in the pocket of a jacket. I hadn't posted it or anything. I think I was saving it, to give to him when I saw him. I put the jacket in my wardrobe. Anyway, a few days later my mother decided to go through my wardrobe, to see what needed to go to the cleaners. And she found the letter, and freaked out, and showed it to my father, and he freaked out. And I came home, and my dad beat me up.

I was seventeen by then. He didn't throw me out, but I thought: 'Right, I've got to get away from this. I can't live here anymore, with this kind of attitude and the atmosphere that it creates.' I was lucky, because my boyfriend had qualified and he got a job in another part of Yorkshire. I was able to get a job in the same town, and so we found a couple of bedsits in the same house together and carried on.

Matt: Did you have to pretend you were just friends?

Simon: Oh, yes, of course. We could only afford a bedsit anyway, each of us, because flats were a bit more expensive.

Matt: It's amazing to me, Simon, that your relationship survived your parents finding out and taking it out on you.

438

You didn't let what they were saying affect you. That's quite amazing.

Simon: I didn't think it was a dirty secret. Though I knew it had to be hidden. I wasn't stupid.

Matt: Did your relationship with your parents recover?

Simon: It recovered to a certain extent. You know, I just had my life and I got on with it. I had my life while I was living with them – I was still going out, and would still go to the gay bars. I think my father was just frightened. He was frightened for me. My mother was hugely disappointed, of course, and it was kind of, you know, awful; but they had to get on with their lives, and I got on with mine. I'd already determined that I was going to leave at the first opportunity, and the opportunity came along. So I left. I made excuses, and lied, and said I was being transferred by the company I was working for. And they kind of accepted it. It seemed sort of reasonable. It wasn't an outrageous lie or anything. I think that, as with most parents, once they've got over themselves, they accept you back, if you like. You know, they've made the adjustment.

I always remember a really beautiful black guy who picked me up in North Woolwich, in this wonderful gay bar that used to be there. And he lived on the other side, in Woolwich itself, in a little working-class two-up and two-down, and he invited me home. He'd told me he lived with his mother, and I said, 'What's your mother going to say?' He said, 'She doesn't mind at all.' I always remember that.

Matt: You mentioned a gay bar in York that you went to, in what must have been the late fifties. What kind of setup was that? Were you afraid of raids, or being caught?

Simon: No, no, no. You must understand that all this was controlled. The police knew what was going on in all those bars, and it was useful to the police to know where we were. That was part of the policing of the community. They knew perfectly well where the gay bars were and it was better that they weren't raided, because otherwise they'd have had to go to the trouble of finding where we'd gone to. It was just useful for the police to know.

Matt: You make it sound like there was a whole underground scene in Yorkshire.

Simon: Oh, there was an underground scene. Everywhere you went.

David is 66 years old and grew up in Wolverhampton

David: From about eight years old, I realised I wasn't like other boys at school . . . Fortunately, I was at school with two other people like me. One of them was older than me, the other was in my class. The three of us went round together because we all felt the same way.

Matt: How did you find out that they were the same way as you?

David: When I was about ten, we started experimenting sexually with one another, and with other boys in the class. And that was what it was like, all the way through school. We didn't really want to be gay. We wanted to be like everybody else. And so we went through a phase where we thought we could maybe get cured. We went to the Samaritans in the end, the three of us, and we told them that we were gay and we wanted to be cured. And this lady at the Samaritans sends us to the Accident and Emergency in Wolverhampton.

We went into three different cubicles. My other two friends were seen to first, and I heard them talking. We had to fill a form in, when we first entered the cubicle, to say what you were in there for. And, instead of putting homosexual thoughts et cetera, one of them put that he couldn't get on with people; and the other, that he was depressed. But I'd already filled in my form, saying that I was gay. Anyway, when it was my turn and the curtain opened in the cubicle, to my horror, there was my uncle! I didn't even know he worked at the hospital. He said, 'What's wrong with you then? What are you here for?'

And I said, 'Well, I can't tell you.' And I actually sat on the form, so he couldn't see it.

And then my two friends, they said, 'Let's go, let's go.' And they ran out of the hospital and I ran after them.

I left my form behind and I was terrified that my uncle would tell my father. But he never did. And I never spoke to my uncle about it, so I don't know . . . I think it was very good of him, really, not to say anything.

Matt: And what about your friends?

David: Well, I was annoyed that they had let me down. I felt let down by them, but they thought it was hysterically funny, you know?

Matt: A lot of men of your age I've spoken to say that they've felt lonely and alone, that they were the only one who had these feelings. It must've been a comfort to you that you didn't just have one friend, but that there were three of you.

David: Yes, it was a comfort. Definitely. And I'm grateful for that, really, because it would have been terrible if I'd been totally isolated. In a way, we felt part of a secret society. I actually felt proud that I was gay. Even at that young age. It felt a bit like being a wizard in Harry Potter, I suppose. We even had a kind of our own language, in Polari [*a form of slang, used by the UK's gay community in the twentieth century*]. The gay Polari – that's the gay banter. So I felt a bit special, really, I suppose.

Matt: Did you visit gay pubs in Wolverhampton?

David: Yes, I did. When I was about eighteen, I was going with this guy called Brian, and we visited a club called The Silver Web, which was owned by a gay brother and sister, Betty and Norman. You went up some very, very steep stairs, to get to the club at the top. It was a great disco club, but the position of it was right opposite a straight club, called the Club Lafayette.

When you went through the doorway into this club, you had to look left and right, and hope that no one saw you going in. If they did they would jeer at you, and you would get discriminatory remarks: 'You're a queer, a faggot, a poof' – everything, you know.

Anyway, we went to this club, one night. We had a good night, but Brian got a bit drunk. We came out of the club, and we had to go past the Club Lafayette across the road and past this hot-dog store which everybody used to stand outside, all the straights. And, as we walked past them, they started calling us 'queers' and 'poofs' and all that. Anyway, I said to Brian, 'Don't say anything, Brian, whatever you do.' And, as we got to the corner, he shouted back and told them where to go.

So then they came running after us. Our car was parked just around the corner. Brian managed to open the driver's side of the door. And in the meantime, this gang gathered around him and they said, 'What did you say?'

He said, 'I didn't say anything.'

And so, they gathered round me, and said, 'Well, it must've been you.' They attacked me, and I had to fight for my life. Basically, they were trying to get me on the floor. There was about five of them, and they were punching me like mad. Anyway, I had to punch them back. I remember I did rip the sleeve off the suit that one of them was wearing, but it was just out of pure terror and adrenaline.

Anyway, in the meantime, Brian had managed to open the passenger side of the car, and I managed to get in, and we locked the doors. As we were driving off, they were kicking the side of the car, making big dents. And I had lumps all over my head where I'd been punched by these people. But thankfully I got away with my life.

Matt: Did you report it to the police?

David: I didn't, no. The police weren't very sympathetic in them days. I think they would have maybe said, 'Well, it's your own fault for being queer.' We didn't trust the police like we do now. We were frightened of the police.

Matt: So you learnt to live with this fear.

David: Oh, yeah, I did, yeah.

Matt: Would you say that when you moved to Manchester, in 1978, you had a happy ending?

David: In a way, it was. Because I had an ever-growing circle of friends and I felt like I was part of a family, rather than being isolated. A family of gay people.

I went on the first Pride march in Manchester, which was through the Arndale Centre. It was just like a parade of people on a protest walk. And I remember holding my boyfriend's hand, walking down and thinking, 'Oh God, I'm amazed I'm doing this.' Another time, some people got arrested for being in a club in Manchester – I think it was called Rockies, in those days. It was what became Legends. The police raided the club, late at night, and they arrested about sixteen men. I ended up joining the protest against them being put on trial, in Winchester magistrates' court.

Anyway, I was at the front of this demonstration, standing underneath a banner that said: 'I was arrested for kissing my boyfriend'. I was on the front page of the [*Manchester*] *Evening News*.

Peter is 68 and grew up in the West Midlands

Peter: They all called me queer, even at school. I remember, one day, we were walking around the local reservoir and these lads started calling me a 'wench'. My dad went absolutely berserk because he thought they were talking about my mother and I just said to my dad, 'Oh no, Dad, they're just talking about me.'

I got a good kicking for that one, but I could see no wrong in it. And that was the irony of the whole thing. To me, it was me; it was who I was. I was inquisitive, I had an enquiring mind and I was clever. And that just didn't fit in with living in a small mining village.

Matt: Would you talk to us about the situation at home?

Peter: My mother was the worst. She would find any excuse to beat me. If I'd done nothing wrong, I'd get a beating. I used to wet the bed, right up until the day I left home. But she used to make me go to the laundrette and wash my own sheets and pyjamas; I just found the whole thing totally unjust, and it wasn't fair. It wasn't my fault. And yet, I'd be dragged out of bed during the night because I'd wet myself, and get beaten again. But it didn't matter. You could beat me as many times as you like: I'm not going to change.

Matt: The fact that you were wetting the bed suggests that there may have been psychological torment for you.

Peter: Oh, absolutely. The minute I left home, I stopped. I mean, I was called 'lazy', 'idle'; I was 'doing it on purpose'. Plus all the other sexual innuendos, as well. Everywhere I went, I'd be called 'queer'. But it was just one of the strangest situations – I knew exactly who and what I was, and where I was going with it. And I was quite comfortable with that, but it was just the injustice of the whole thing. It wasn't my fault. I wasn't doing it any of it deliberately. It was me.

You could meet men in toilets. And so that was what I pursued, oh God, for eight years: actively looking for men. I wasn't aware of the dangers I was putting myself in. I wasn't interested in that; I wanted sex with men – and that was through all my teens. Well, it carried on all through my life, basically. Looking back, anything could have happened to me. Absolutely anything.

Matt: Did you ever come out to your mum and dad?

Peter: Oh yeah. When I was seventeen, I went home and said, 'Look, Mum, I'm gay.' And, to this day, she's never accepted it. I even got married, for God's sake, to a bloke; and she couldn't accept it.

She still doesn't. I haven't seen her for God knows how many years. No birthday cards, no Christmas cards, no telephone calls, nothing. It doesn't bother me. I don't want to know. I haven't spoken to my brother for God knows how many years, either. To me, I have no family. I've made my own family, with all my friends and the people who actually touched my life, and influenced me, and educated me. And all the things I craved to learn about: like the arts, music. Each person that touched my life has given me something, and I've absorbed it like a sponge. They gave it freely and willingly. It's made me who I am now.

The only recognition I got was from my dad. He ended up with dementia, and I actually went back to the nursing home to see him, with my husband, and he hadn't got a clue who I was. And suddenly he said, 'Oh, hello, son, you're married now, aren't you?'

I said, 'Yeah.'

He goes, 'I'm really sorry for the way we treated you as a kid.' Then he said, 'I love you.'

I said, 'I love you too, Dad', and I gave him a cuddle.

And – he'd gone again. He didn't know who I was. It was almost like he'd had this on his mind for God knows how long, and he just wanted to get it off his chest.

Matt: How did it make you feel? It sounds like it's making you emotional still now.

Peter: I just fell to pieces. Absolutely. I mean, I was in my fifties. It's taken him fifty years. But at least he said it, and I sort of had closure with my dad. I never saw him alive again. He died twelve months later. All that I went through, it made it all worthwhile, because he was sorry. He meant it.

Matt: You've talked about the fear you experienced, as a gay man exploring your sexuality. How does it feel for you, when you look at young people now?

Peter: I don't think they've got an idea in the world of what we went through. The troubles, the strikes, the struggles, you know, the Gay Liberation Front's campaign for homosexuality, going on marches, et cetera. If it wasn't for us, back in the seventies and eighties, going on these marches, they'd have nothing. They'd still be where we were then, now.

I'm not looking for recognition or accolades. It needed to be done, but I think that there ought to be a far wider understanding, educationally, of what it was like back then. I think it's important for our gay history that stories like these are told and then listened to.

But me, personally – I carried on as normal. I wasn't in the closet. I was out, you know, screaming about it. Sitting around in silks and velvet trousers. It didn't bother me. And the strange thing is, I've never had any animosity or homophobia thrust against me through my adult life. People I've met, the straight people I've met, they've all been totally accepting of me. My sexuality didn't matter, it was who I was they liked.

Geoff is 71 and grew up
in Bishop's Stortford

Matt: When you were growing up in the fifties and becoming aware of your desires – what you would later discover to be your sexuality – did you have the tools to understand it?

Geoff: Well, basically, being a young child in the 1950s, there was just nothing to turn to. At first, I didn't realise other boys didn't find boys, as well as girls, attractive. That never occurred to me. Throughout the fifties, I don't remember reading anything or being taught anything – certainly it was never raised in school. Given that in the fifties there was a real clampdown going on around gay men – which, of course, I was unaware of – there was a silence because people couldn't be visible. They couldn't be visible because they could lose their jobs, their friends, their family, their neighbourhoods, their communities.

Matt: We should point out that it was also illegal – so they could end up in prison.

Geoff: Oh yes. And, you know, even though the law changed – to a very limited extent – in 1967, the number of arrests actually went up. Police activity went up. So it wasn't until . . . well, in fact, 2003 was the end of 'gross indecency'; and 1989 saw the highest number of arrests.

So, I'm growing up in a period when people, if discovered, would be at best shunned and have to move, or be ridiculed or be beaten up – or be arrested, at worst. Many people would have gone into marriages. You see, you grew up in those years with a sense that men and women were very, very separate in gender roles. Women were at home, largely. If they did go to work, they earned almost nothing. Men went to work. Men were butch and women were feminine – in theory. That's how it was meant to work. So, you were trying to fit this role – or, *I* was trying to fit this role and not succeeding terribly well, while not knowing what it was that I wasn't succeeding at.

I wasn't like the other boys at school. And that became more and more obvious. I think that it probably came to a head when I went to secondary school. I suppose I would have been around twelve when I started to hear words like 'queer', 'poof', 'pansy'. I started to hear stuff being said about finding other people of your own sex attractive. Not that it's all about sex, but identity.

Matt: From what I remember, growing up in the eighties, it always *was* about sex. Nobody ever talked about two men loving each other. There was this squeamishness and this hysteria around what we did sexually. Was it the same when you were growing up?

Geoff: Very much so. I can't talk about the fifties from my own experience, but certainly by the sixties I was aware that, because I suppose the law revolved around the sex we had, therefore we were identified by what we did in bed. I know ninety-eight per cent of the time what we do in bed is sleep.

But it all revolved around what we did rather than who we were.

Matt: If you didn't fit in, did your parents notice this, and did either of them raise the issue with you?

Geoff: No. Funnily enough, it was me who raised it with my father. We lived just outside Harlow New Town, and we were cycling along the bypass. I just remember, I asked him how he would feel if I grew up to be a man who liked other men, and his response was: 'I'd be terribly sad, because society wouldn't accept you.' Now, it's a great response in some ways, but I didn't hear it like that. What I heard was 'I won't accept you.'

Matt: At what point did you start to act on your attraction towards boys?

Geoff: You couldn't kiss or show affection, because that was 'queer'. We experimented with each other, but there was a distinction in boys' minds between what we were doing and the 'extra' element, which was stroking, cuddling, kissing. That, you did not do, because you weren't queer.

Because of talks with my father, growing up, and because of my upbringing, I never had any guilt complex around sex itself. But I couldn't see a future, because I didn't know anybody else who was openly gay, or who I could look at and go, 'Oh, you're like me.' There was one boy at school with whom I formed a closeness, but neither of us could carry on as fully as we'd have liked to.

Matt: So the emotional development of that relationship was suppressed, stamped out?

Geoff: Yeah. I wasn't able to explore it, if you like, and go down that road, because both of us were obviously fearful. In a way, you want it so much, but you're also fearful of it, because that's going to be a rubber stamp on who you are, and you're trying to avoid that.

I think the first time I actually remember voluntarily going into something and it being warm and beautiful, I would have been about eighteen. That was at a party. By that time, I had a girlfriend on the go and there was a party at her house. It was by Epping Forest, and this guy and I went off to look for some cigarettes or some tobacco.

We walked through the forest, on the way to where the pub was. And when we got back, Monty Python was on television, and they were doing the Silly Walk. We put our arms around each other's shoulders and we're doing the Silly Walk. Funnily enough, we tripped ourselves up and just found ourselves rolling and kissing and hugging. It was like, suddenly, 'Oh my God. Yeah, this is what it is!' And it was beautiful . . . But once the party was over, that was it.

Matt: There was no chance that the physical could progress to the emotional?

Geoff: Well, there was nothing around me, no context in which to put it, is how I would say it. There were no places we could go, as far as I was aware. I didn't know where gay people met. I didn't even know there *were* gay people. Obviously, I'd realised that there were people like me by the time I'd met that man, and a few others. But there was no context. There was nowhere in Harlow, Sawbridgeworth or Bishop's Stortford – that I knew of – where we could meet. We didn't have gay pubs. There probably were gay places, but I didn't know where they were, and if you didn't stumble on them, then you were on your own.

Matt: When did you first become aware that living a gay life was a possibility, and that it could be something you could embrace?

Geoff: I went to London to study at Goldsmiths College, which was part of the University of London, on a teacher-training course as a secondary school English teacher. I was staying in a hall of residence in Brixton. At the time, there was the under-ground press: *International Times*, *Friends* and then they became a newspaper called *Ink*. I was reading a copy of *Ink*. And I saw this – I can't remember if it was an article or an advert – 'Are you homosexual? The Gay Liberation Front is having meetings in Notting Hill Gate at All Saints Hall, Powis Square.'

I went along there by bicycle from Brixton. I parked my bike and my memory is that I walked around the hall one way, then walked around the other. Then somebody came up to me, saying, 'Are you wanting to go in?' So I went in, and, when I walked through that door, that would be the first time I can ever remember truly relaxing. I felt warm inside. It was like a melting. 'This is my tribe. This is my family,' I thought.

And there was a room full of people, I don't know how many, but to me it was like, 'Oh my God. They're all like me.' And they were smiling and laughing and I was crying. I remember being held. It was like coming home. It's like, I hadn't been home all my life, and I was twenty-one years old.

That was the first time that I heard the message: 'We have been taught to hide. We have been taught to remain invisible. We have been taught to be ashamed. It is time to get visible, stand up and be proud. Gay is good. Gay is proud. And gay is angry.'

I took that on board. I thought, 'Oh yeah, that makes total sense to me.' And then I linked it with other people's struggles, whether they're around gender, race, class. Whatever the struggle was, I understood I was oppressed, and then I wanted to link in and connect with other people.

Ted Ainsworth has always worked at his family's ice-cream business in the quiet Lancashire town of St Luke's-on-Sea.

He doesn't even *like* ice cream, though he's never told his parents that. When Ted's husband suddenly leaves him, the bottom falls out of his world.

But what if this could be an opportunity to put what he wants first? This could be the chance to finally follow his secret dream: something Ted has never told anyone . . .

BECOMING TED

A brand-new uplifting novel from Matt Cain.

Coming soon from

REVIEW